ADVANCE PRI

This Disaster

"This delightful novel is stuffed full of surprises, not least of which is how well it combines humor with a deeply moving account of a love lost and a future found."

—Liam Callanan, author of *Paris by the Book* and *When in Rome*

"A charming novel about the memory of a lost wife and her husband's quest to find her. I was drawn in, delighted, and surprised by this love story, which has both sweetness and depth. I highly recommend escaping to the story of *This Disaster Loves You.*"

—Miriam Parker, author of *The Shortest Way Home*

"There's warmth and wit on every page of *This Disaster Loves You*. But beyond Richard Roper's usual easygoing charm lies keen insight, an enthralling mystery, and an emotional ending that simply blew me away. I absolutely loved this book."

—Matthew Norman, author of *Charm City Rocks*

SELECT PRAISE FOR

Something to Live For

"[A] winning debut novel . . . Roper illuminates Andrew's interior life to reveal not what an odd duck he is, but what odd ducks we all are—lonely, confused, misguided, bumbling, and, as we learn in the book's powerhouse ending, profoundly bereft. Roper's unbridled compassion for his characters is the book's greatest strength." —*The New York Times Book Review*

"Offbeat and winning . . . *Something to Live For* gives resiliency and the triumph of the human spirit a good name."
—*The Wall Street Journal*

"Roper's delightful debut is as funny as it is touching. . . . This story of a neurotic, tenderhearted man struggling to learn how not to be alone is irresistible." —*Publishers Weekly*

"Quirky and heartfelt . . . Andrew's past traumas are revealed gradually, and the reasons behind his isolation are heartbreaking and poignant. A moving and funny look at grief, hope, and the power of human connections." —*Kirkus Reviews*

"[A] charming debut . . . *Something to Live For* tackles a painful subject with good-hearted characters it's easy to root for."
—*USA Today*

"The pleasure in Roper's winning, good-hearted tale is seeing this lonely sad sack cautiously rejoin the world." —*People*

"Dark, hopeful, humorous . . . For readers who like to root for a flawed but likable protagonist." —*Library Journal*

"Darkly humorous." —*Entertainment Weekly*

"Just the kind of book I wanted to read in these times. Charming, empathetic, witty, emotional, and hopeful, Roper's cast of quirky, vulnerable characters make for a truly warm and affecting debut."

—J. Ryan Stradal, author of *Kitchens of the Great Midwest*

"Wryly funny and quirkily charming—perfect for fans of *A Man Called Ove* and *Eleanor Oliphant Is Completely Fine*."

—Eleanor Brown, author of *The Weird Sisters*

"A magnificent read. Tender, funny, compelling—this wonderful book deserves to be huge!"

—Lucy Foley, author of *The Guest List*

SELECT PRAISE FOR
When We Were Young

"Richard Roper writes with wit, soul, and beautiful prose."

—*Good Morning America*

"A funny, tender British bromance." —*People*

"Need a feel-good book for your nightstand read? Roper's nostalgic, sweet, and funny story of two childhood friends is a wise choice." —CNN.com

"This delightful, endearing outing becomes a heartfelt meditation on male companionship, forgiveness, and navigating life's ups and downs. Roper's story shimmers." —*Publishers Weekly*

"Writing with both great humor and heart, Roper has a light touch that keeps the reader laughing even while he gently pulls on the heartstrings. . . . A funny and poignant portrait of friendship."

—*Kirkus Reviews*

"Bittersweet and full of heart, this book will appeal to fans of Jonathan Tropper and Matthew Norman." —*Booklist*

"Roper possesses a wry and formidable wit. But his real gift is the ability to infuse that humor with such immense heart that it becomes the path for an uplifting and redemptive journey."

—Steven Rowley, author of *The Guncle*

"*When We Were Young* is such a warm, uplifting read. It's a celebration of the bond we have with our oldest friends, and it's so funny, without ever losing its poignancy—Richard Roper writes humor brilliantly."

—Beth O'Leary, author of *The Flatshare* and *The Switch*

THIS DISASTER LOVES YOU

ALSO BY RICHARD ROPER

When We Were Young

Something to Live For

THIS DISASTER LOVES YOU

RICHARD ROPER

G. P. PUTNAM'S SONS
New York

PUTNAM
— EST. 1838 —

G. P. PUTNAM'S SONS
Publishers Since 1838
An imprint of Penguin Random House LLC
penguinrandomhouse.com

Library of Congress Cataloging-in-Publication Data

Names: Roper, Richard, author.
Title: This disaster loves you / Richard Roper.
Description: New York: G. P. Putnam's Sons, 2024.
Identifiers: LCCN 2023044445 (print) | LCCN 2023044446 (ebook) |
ISBN 9780593540701 (trade paperback) | ISBN 9780593540695 (ebook)
Subjects: LCGFT: Romance fiction. | Novels.
Classification: LCC PR6118.O643 T55 2024 (print) | LCC PR6118.O643 (ebook) |
DDC 823/.92—dc23/eng/20231003
LC record available at https://lccn.loc.gov/2023044445
LC ebook record available at https://lccn.loc.gov/2023044446

Printed in the United States of America
1st Printing

Book design by Ashley Tucker

For Eleanor

THIS DISASTER LOVES YOU

PART ONE

The County Arms (Thrupstone, UK)

★★★★★ (210)

MaryAtkinson5 wrote a review, May 9, 2007

Charming pub, wonderful owners!

My husband and I stayed here for our honeymoon and can't recommend it enough! It's such a charming pub, tucked away right on the coast, and the views are incredible. The food was absolutely amazing—lovely wine and local beers too. Really friendly atmosphere. The open fireplace must be incredible in winter. The best thing about the place is the owners, Brian and Lily, who are simply delightful. They've not been running the place long but they're clearly doing a fantastic job—what a good team they make! We'll be back one day for sure. Highly recommended.

The County Arms (Thrupstone, UK)

★★★☆☆ (1,156)

MaryAtkinson5 wrote a review, May 9, 2017

Such a shame!!

My husband and I came here ten years ago on our honeymoon and we remembered having such a good time that we decided to come back to celebrate our wedding anniversary. Such a shame to see how downhill the place has gone over the years! I'm afraid the owner, Brian, who we remembered as being so cheerful and welcoming when we were last here, seems like he's completely given up. What on earth went wrong?

1.

TODAY'S MEMORIES

How she'd shed her clothes where she stood, like she'd spontaneously combusted.

The mysterious way she'd select a mug for her tea, absorbed in the task as if it was of life-changing importance.

The dangerous flash in her eyes when she knew she was about to win an argument.

The birthmark on her hip that I thought looked like Mount Rushmore and she thought looked like a sparrow taking off. We compromised on Ringo's hair.

Her bitter contempt for the existence of glacé cherries.

The conversations she'd have with herself—me with front-row seats to the new hit one-woman show: *Should I Dye My Hair? No, Lily, Don't Do That.*

"I've got a headache," I said.

"Almost certainly terminal," she replied, cracking eggs into a pan.

How long it took me to wake her when she was having a nightmare.

A stray hair of hers, come loose, surfing down the banister, clinging on for dear life.

Her hand squeezing mine—once, twice. Our signal. *Time to go.*

2.

THE COUNTY ARMS

NOW

At some point during the night, I must have crossed over into the unfamiliar terrain of my wife's side of the bed. Lying there now, I'm trying to remember whether we ever had a conversation about who would take which side, or whether one of us just staked our claim with a bedside table—planting a flag with an alarm clock or a paperback.

I sit up in bed. It's bittersweet, to have come across a gap in my knowledge like this—a blank space in the vast collage of memories of my life with Lily. I'm aware that if I'm not careful I could spend the whole morning here, searching for that memory—seeking out the others that are missing too. It wouldn't be the first time I've sat here, lost to the past, unaware of how far the morning sunlight has crept across the wall.

Not today, I think. Digging deep, I swing my legs out of bed, hearing the now-familiar cracks and creaks as my body splutters into life. My right knee always seems to hurt first thing these days, I don't know why. I did Google it not too long ago while making my morning cup of tea, and I'd diagnosed myself with leprosy by the time the kettle had boiled. I should go to the doctor, I suppose, but the last time I went with a minor complaint like this she told me "these things just happen when we get older." That put a spring in my step, I can tell you.

I'm distracted by something lying on the floor between my feet. It's Lily's watch, face down on the carpet. That's odd, I must have knocked it off her bedside table during the night. Clearly, I'd been flailing around in my sleep, though I can't remember having a nightmare. I put the watch back in its rightful place, then I'm up and dressed in my carefully curated look of a forty-seven-year-old man who's just got off a long-haul flight, and brace myself for another day.

I wonder how many other people are waking up this morning in a pub. To be clear, I'm the landlord, so I've got an excuse. My pub is called the County Arms (*purveyors of fine ales & spirits since 1874*), and my—our—bedroom is up above the front bar. Even though it's been over a decade that I've been coming down the narrow stairs and through the door that brings me out behind the taps and pumps, it still feels peculiar to be in a pub at this time. The thousands of memories created in this place all seem to leave a little of themselves behind, like the ancient tobacco smoke that's colored parts of the ceiling a dull yellow. Despite the thick silence—the place as still as a painting—if I close my eyes and concentrate I can just about remember what a busy day felt like here: the convivial chatter, glasses being clinked, the distant chaos of the kitchen. Even if I sought two minutes of calm up in our bedroom, I'd still be aware of the constant symphony below of muffled voices, cutlery on porcelain, the swift crash of the cash register announcing another pint sold, and, most of all, Lily's laughter. Standing here now, it's so quiet that if it weren't for the distant cry of a seagull I'd feel like the only living thing around for miles.

I open the hatch and come through the bar. Ever since I can remember, I've liked to do a circuit of the downstairs first thing. Ostensibly this would be so I could clear up anything we'd missed the night before, but I also used to feel so in awe of how this place was actually ours, that we had managed to find our dream pub, that I just wanted to take in every inch of the place to remind me of that fact.

It's not quite the same, these days. There's nothing to clear away, and I haven't had to make up a room for a guest in months. When I glance around I see a rotten window frame that's stuck fast with an inch gap at the bottom, the booth with an unexplained slash through its fabric, the damp patch by the skirting board. I assume the latter is what's causing the musty smell that pervades the pub, though I'm no longer sure how bad it is, because I've got so used to it.

As I finish my circuit, it strikes me that I can't actually remember the last time I left the building. A week? Longer? Best not to think about it too much. I comfort myself with the thought that when we first opened, over eleven years ago now, we were so rushed off our feet that we barely had time to leave the place then either. I stoop to pick up a beer mat, the one thing that's out of place. As I turn it over in my hands I think, *Well, who's to say Lily and I won't be as busy as in our heyday once again?* I look back to the bar and picture us there, caught up in one of our furious ballets—Lily flicking the Guinness tap on while I dive for Twiglets, limbs looped through limbs, constantly in motion.

I toss the beer mat onto a table and come back around the bar, settling myself on my stool. It isn't the most comfortable place to sit, up here. I'm twisted at a funny angle, and my knees are cramped for room, but crucially it gives me the clearest view of the main entrance. There was so much riding on Lily and me making a success of the pub once we took it over that the fact we had any customers at all was an enormous relief. But it wasn't until I started to notice people's faces when they came through the door that I knew we were going to be OK, that it had all been worth it. It was a wonderfully addictive thing to see—people shedding whatever worries had been occupying them as they set foot inside. That sense that they had opened a door to a new and exciting world while simultaneously coming home after an arduous journey. I'd sit here and watch even the most seasoned pub-goer looking around in awe at the hearty fire, the gleaming taps, the dimpled glasses suspended above the bar catching the light. *Yes,* that look would say, *this will do us nicely.*

These days, I watch the door even more closely. I wish I could say it's because of some delightful new phenomenon where the sunlight coming through the frosted glass casts beautiful shapes in silhouette. But there's really nothing particularly noteworthy about the door. The flowery motif etched on its glass is charming, but it's fairly standard Victorian public house fare. Nor has the door played a part in some notorious historical incident, the kind you often see dubiously referenced in pubs on chalkboards proclaiming that Shakespeare "probably" drank a piña colada on this spot before he dashed off *Hamlet.*

What I *do* know is the time it takes from someone's form becoming visible through the frosted glass to them opening the door. That seven out of ten people will (correctly) guess that the door needs to be pushed, not pulled. That three out of five people who've incorrectly pulled first will give the door a reproachful look for misleading them. That a certain kind of man with a certain kind of beard will rub his hands together in anticipation as he approaches the bar. That women are more likely to whisper as they ask *where the loos are*.

This is all entirely useless knowledge, of course. Something Lily would be quick to point out. But it's the result of me sitting here every moment I can, staring at that door, wondering if today is the day, seven years after she disappeared, that Lily finally comes back home.

3.

NEW PEOPLE

THE BAKERLOO LINE
LONDON, JUNE 1995

Let me go back to the beginning. Or, at least, the beginning of the story of Lily and me, which in all honesty is the moment my life began in earnest. Leaving school, graduating university, getting my first job—these moments hadn't felt as significant to me as they seemed to for other people. I was waiting for the moment when something revelatory would happen—but my touchpaper had as yet remained unlit.

After graduating, I had kicked around at home, feeling a bit rudderless. By contrast, my friend Ed—who I'd met at university and who was far more outgoing—had moved straight to London, and had been badgering me to join him ever since. *There are so many new people to meet,* he'd tell me. As if this were a good thing. It often seemed like it was Ed's personal mission to rid me of my shyness and unleash what he very optimistically hoped was the charismatic raconteur hiding underneath. Eventually I caved and made the move to London, shortly after I'd turned twenty-four.

At first, I found the pace of it all completely overwhelming. When I went out with Ed and his revolving group of friends, I'd watch on enviously as people quickly forged connections with others they'd only just met. I was determined to get to this point myself—relying somewhat less on charm and more on homework and rigorous preparation. This led to one of the more mortifying moments in my life when I came home one evening to find a very drunk Ed leafing through the aide-mémoires I'd been keeping in my coat pockets, designed to make conversations with his friends easier.

"*Jenny. Doctor. Scared of birds*," Ed read, holding the card out of reach as I tried to snatch it back. When I finally relented and explained myself, Ed said, "So next time you see Jenny you'll say, 'Hi, Jen, how's things? Hope you've not had to give a heron CPR recently'?"

"If absolutely necessary, yes!"

Ed gave me a look he often did back then, like I was a spider drowning in the bath and he couldn't work out whether or not to save me.

"Look," he said eventually, "you're a bright, funny, lovable guy. You just need to show that side a bit more. I know it's been hard for you . . . with, well . . ."

Ed left it there, but I knew what he meant, and it made me uncomfortable. He was one of the few people who knew I'd had a slightly unusual upbringing, one that hadn't necessarily lent itself to me becoming the most easygoing person on the planet. But I was determined that I wouldn't let that define or hinder me, and so, gradually, by making myself show up to parties and pubs and blustering my way through, I began to emerge from my shell.

I'd got a job working for an insurance firm, and though I'd learned to tell people that it was deathly boring, and complain about my bosses—because that's what everyone else seemed to do when they were in the pub, cynicism being a strong currency—I secretly very much enjoyed it. The work itself didn't thrill me, but I was just rather proud of myself—not an emotion I was particularly familiar with—about the fact that here I was, in the big city, blending in with the great homogenous mass of suits and spreadsheets. I remember as a kid watching the news—where they'd use a shot of office workers walking down a busy London street on their lunch breaks as a backdrop to a report on the economy or something—and wondering about the lives of these busy, important-looking people, and now, lo and behold, I was one of them.

Having grown in confidence enough to make some friends, I found myself tentatively turning my intention to encounters with the opposite sex. (It was Ed who pointed out that using phrases like "encounters with the opposite sex" was why I wasn't having any.) My romantic history thus far had been limited to a brief, unhappy time at university with Morag Henderson, a girl in my accountancy course with a severe fringe and a personality to match. One of the many odd things about our relationship was that I couldn't actually remember it beginning. Morag had just seemed to decide one day, and frankly I was too scared of her to refuse. Our time together consisted mainly of sitting in cafés in strained silence, as if we'd been married for thirty years and had run out of things to say to each other. The physical side of the relationship had been even more baffling to me. We would occasionally kiss in the chaste manner of 1950s film stars, but I had only once built up the courage to take things further as we lay on the unforgiving single bed of her dorm room. Completely guessing at what I was supposed to do, I found myself pressing my hand to her bottom and then just . . . leaving it there, as if I were trying to guess the weight of a cake at a village fête. We broke up soon after, around the time we graduated. Much to my confusion, Morag wrote me a letter afterward in which she told me that I would always be the greatest love of her life. Since moving to London two years ago, there had been a couple of things that had seemed promising, but they'd all fizzled out fairly quickly.

"And that's why you're going to come to drinks on Friday," Ed said after my latest bad date, this one with a girl called Sophie *(flutist, shin splints, Dutch)* who had offered me a cigarette and caught me trying to surreptitiously drop it down the drain rather than tell her I didn't smoke.

"You need to get back on the horse," Ed continued. "Primrose Hill, Brian. Weather set fair. London in all its summer glory. Romance in the air . . ."

And so it was I found myself on the hottest day of the year on a packed Bakerloo line train, where romance was in very short supply. I was sorely tempted to get off and head home for a takeaway pizza and telly. But no, I told myself, I had to do this. I could be charming and charismatic. I pictured myself tossing an empty beer bottle over my shoulder into a bin, saying something like, "You should see what's for *dessert* . . . ," smiling self-effacingly as my new friends hoisted me onto their shoulders and paraded me around Primrose Hill chanting, "Bri-an! Bri-an! Bri-an!" . . . I was wrenched from this reverie when I realized I was about to miss my stop, ending up having to squeeze myself through the doors onto the platform like a sausage.

I arrived at the top of Primrose Hill, sweating and lamenting that I was wearing the new suit I had bought recently, which was two sizes too big for me and made me look like I was auditioning for *Bugsy Malone.* Ed spotted me and tossed me a beer, which I dropped, the can hitting a drain cover and exploding on impact. Ed looked at me despairingly and carefully passed me another, like an archaeologist handing someone a bit of recently unearthed pottery. Then he put his hands on my shoulders and pointed me toward the group of people sprawled on the grass behind him.

"Hey, everyone, this is Brian."

"Hi there!" I said, a bit too kids' TV presenter, and my new friends replied with halfhearted waves and hellos. I stood around with Ed, doing my best to join in—though this particular assortment of people wasn't the most welcoming. I watched and listened as they competed over who could be the most arch and unimpressed with life, not something I could ever pull off myself, because even though life could be hard at times there was still ice cream, for god's sake.

The first time anyone seemed to rouse themselves from their slumped form on the grass was when a new couple arrived. The boy was barefoot, wearing loose cotton trousers and a shirt that he'd unbuttoned to his waist, and there seemed to be great excitement that he had graced us with his presence.

"Oh my god, Daniel!" said a girl next to me. "I thought you were going traveling."

"Maybe next year," the boy replied enigmatically, flashing her a brilliant white smile. And then he said this actual phrase: "Gosh, where are my manners?" Followed by: "Everyone, this is Lily."

At first I was too busy trying to work out whether this guy

thought he was in a play to pay attention to the person he had introduced. But then—as Lily would never tire of reminding me in the years that followed—I performed such a cartoonish double take upon seeing her for the first time that I nearly gave myself whiplash.

4.

SOME THINGS I NOTICED

She was wearing a pale blue dress that exposed her shoulders, both of which were dusted with freckles. Her hair was light copper and seemed to have something of a life of its own—swishing and bouncing as she turned her head, always one step behind. Her chunky white trainers were bright enough to be brand-new but covered in quite a lot of fresh mud. While everyone else sprawled or sat cross-legged on the grass, she knelt. When somebody spoke, no matter who, she gave them her full attention. (Ironically, this meant that as I became increasingly keen to say something to her, the harder I found it to pluck up the courage to do so.) She told great anecdotes, although a good proportion of them ended up with her either forgetting what happened next in the story or going off on a tangent, so the phrase "Why I did I start telling that story?" became something of a recurring theme. This was accompanied by a smile that made me lose track of things—how to breathe, for example. She was tactile with those she'd just met, regardless of gender, usually when she was agreeing with something they'd said. She was fond of sounding scandalized—"*Stop* it!"—and she had a fantastic laugh, a great, unapologetically hearty honk of a thing, which she let loose generously and often, though noticeably not if someone made a joke that was cruel, which I thought was a devastatingly subtle way of her showing her disapproval without having to scold them.

5.

WEIGHTS AND MEASURES

NOW

It's just gone 12:58 p.m., which means for the next two minutes I'm able to take my eyes off the front door, because I know that the next person to come through it won't be Lily. I get down from my stool and reach for a dimpled pint glass, then hold it under the swan-neck nozzle of the Winchester Gold cask ale and draw back the pump handle, watching the autumnal liquid flow. I place the pint on a beer mat on the bar. A few bubbles dance on the sliver of foamy head before it settles completely, just in time for the clock to tick over to one p.m.

A faint silhouette appears against the frosted glass opposite. I can make out a flat cap and someone clearing their throat with the sound of a prospector panning for gold, and then the door opens. There's a short blast of salty sea air followed by Jeff Mackintosh. Jeff can't move too well these days—getting up onto a bar stool is a slow affair—but in the moment his eyes clock the pint on the bar it's briefly like the greyhound's seen the rabbit. Jeff summits the stool and takes a long, luxurious sip of beer. Only then does he speak.

"That's a proper pint, that is."

Jeff has been drinking Winchester Gold in here every day since Lily and I took over. He's the only person who likes it, and even though I make a colossal loss with the amount we waste, I haven't got the heart to stop serving it. It'd be like banning Popeye from spinach. The act of pouring Jeff his drink is both the one bit of structure to my day and one of the few things I take real pride in. I try not to dwell on this too much.

Jeff cut a lonely figure when I first used to serve him. He preferred to sit by the window, looking out to sea. It was Lily—in a decision she'd jokingly tell me later that she very much regretted—who brought him out of his shell. As busy as we were, she always made a point of going over to chat to him, and that meant he eventually swapped his window seat for a stool up at the bar—sacrificing comfort for company. They would talk there whenever Lily had a spare moment, and later, when we were so busy that she only had a few seconds free, she began what became an epic game of Consequences—scribbling the start of a story on a fresh roll of till receipt, then passing it on to Jeff, the two of them going back and forth until they had something that looked like a scroll bearing the decrees of a mad king.

I watch as Jeff takes his flat cap off, his ears springing out. They are enormous, battered things, mesmerizing to look at. Jeff opens his mouth to speak, and I brace myself. There are two important things you should know about Jeff. First, his ears are like that because of his days playing rugby for the England B team. Second, you shouldn't believe a word he says. There isn't a sport he hasn't supposedly triumphed at or a celebrity he's not hobnobbed with. Pop stars, Olympic athletes, politicians. You name it. Apparently, he's had careers in almost every industry you can imagine, including music—which leads me to my favorite tall tale of his, that he had a Christmas number one hit in Latvia. He told this to Lily and me with great relish one Christmas Eve, eyes twinkling, on a rare occasion when he'd overcooked it with the booze. He ended up taking a tumble, and after a bit of cajoling, he agreed to let us help him home.

"We need to make a pact," Lily said as we walked home, having deposited Jeff through his front door in the neighboring village.

"What kind of a pact?"

"To look after that man. He's such a sweetheart. But I think we might be the only people he talks to. We should remember that when he's off on one of those stories of his."

It's these words I think of now when Jeff's halfway through a tale I've heard a hundred times before about the day he climbed Ben Nevis for charity, dressed up in a badger costume. In Lily's absence, I've done my best to keep my side of the pact in place. What I try to ignore is whether there's a chance this was a loaded message on her part—that she knew even then that she might vanish one day, and she was trying to prepare me for life afterward.

As Jeff reaches the end of his story, I reach down to a shelf underneath the bar and retrieve my ancient laptop. I heave it onto the bar, open it up, and click on through to the pub's Tripadvisor page, feeling a familiar mix of dread and excitement. When Lily and I first took over this place, online reviews were a relatively new thing. We were still keeping a physical guestbook for people to write in, so if you wanted to be critical you had to do it with us smiling at you like fond relatives from a few yards away. The few complaints we did get in those days were, therefore, rather euphemistic:

"The room was a tad on the drafty side . . ."

"My beer was a wee bit murky . . ."

Cut to last week and our latest Tripadvisor review, the anonymous author of which described the failings of our Yorkshire puddings with the élan of a broadsheet critic and the violent invective of a football hooligan. Building to a startling crescendo via an unexpected detour to the nuances of the Weights and Measures Act of 1985, he concluded that the County Arms was, quite simply, "a shame."

It never used to be like this. By the time Tripadvisor had started to take off, Lily and I were running a well-oiled machine, and we'd reward ourselves every few mornings by reading the latest reviews, nearly always five stars—a tangible reminder that all our hard work was paying off. After she'd gone, I kept up the tradition, largely out of pride. But then, over time, the reviews began to reflect the pub's decline. At first, people just sounded disappointed, but then the feedback became increasingly angry—bewilderingly so. There was one review so disproportionately furious that I read it out loud to Jeff verbatim and we both hooted with laughter. How could anyone be *that* angry about curtains? From then on, after pouring Jeff's pint, I'd get out my laptop and look for anything similarly mad. There was gallows humor in this, I suppose. But the longer it's gone on, the more I've noticed that Jeff seems to have stopped finding it quite so entertaining. I still feel compelled to read them, but maybe the novelty's worn off for him. Sure enough, he gives me an apprehensive look as I tap my fingers on the bar, waiting for the page to load.

"That time already, is it?" he asks.

"It is indeed." I sort the reviews by newest. "Ha! Here we go."

Lo and behold, a new one-star effort has appeared, and the heading is one of the more striking I've seen recently:

Aviod At All Costs!!!

I read it out loud to Jeff, choosing not to correct the typo. The reviewer goes on to reel off a fairly standard list of complaints, concluding, "The whole place just seems so tired. Not sure how long it can last."

I look up at Jeff. "I think they might just be talking about me."

Jeff laughs, but only politely. That apprehensiveness is still there.

"OK, what's wrong?" I ask.

"No, nothing," Jeff says, fiddling with his beer mat. "It's just . . . you sure it's good for you, looking at these every day?"

"What do you mean?"

"Well, I know they're all nutters and everything, but, well, can't exactly be good for the soul, can it?"

I'm taken aback by this—since when did Jeff get so existential?—but I'm spared having to answer because there's an enormous crash from the kitchen, which means that my chef, Jacques, must have arrived.

"I better go and see what's happened," I tell Jeff, who nods in return but avoids my eye. I'm not sure I like the Jeff who's turned up today, asking me these sorts of questions. I much prefer the one who tells me about the time he had a fry-up at Mick Jagger's.

IT ALWAYS TAKES me a while to psych myself up before I go and see Jacques. I hired him five years ago after the previous chef quit, and he's never exactly warmed to me. On my way to the kitchen I stop off in the back bar and assess my reflection in the dusty mirror on the wall. I wish I hadn't. Up until my forties, I'd lived something of a charmed life with my appearance. I was never exactly the most handsome, but there was a pleasing symmetry to my features, and even when the first few silver flecks appeared in my hair, it seemed to suit me. The real aging happened without my noticing it, as if the universe had been reminded that my fifties were on the horizon and had decided to make up for lost time overnight. If Lily does come back, I sometimes wonder if she'll even recognize me.

Another great crash from the kitchen has me folding my arms and practicing the look of someone who's not easily intimidated. The effect is only slightly undermined by the yogurt pot lid stuck to my elbow. I've no idea where it came from. I peel it off and make for the kitchen. I'm just going past the open cellar door when I hear muffled giggles and then someone saying, "Shit, what was that?"

Ah, so that's where the rest of my workforce is. I make a big show of clearing my throat. There's a flurry of activity and whispering, and then Sophie and Oliver appear, looking disheveled.

"Hi, boss," Oliver says. Oliver is nineteen, though he can already grow a better beard than me.

"We were just getting a mop and bucket," Sophie adds. "There's a leak in the gents. *Again.*" Three years Oliver's senior, Sophie favors dungarees and sports a mass of curly hair resembling Christmas lights retrieved from the loft. I hired them both last year after something of a false dawn following a busy period, and now their services aren't really required, but I haven't got the heart to let them go. Oliver is on a gap year, and has presumably only stuck around because of Sophie, who's not long graduated from university, where she studied catering management. They'd been working together for about a week before I first caught them in the sort of romantic clinch you'd normally associate with lovers in the French resistance. Since then, their romance has only increased in its intensity—stolen moments in the cellar, whispered nothings by the Pringles.

I can't tell how aware they are of the dire situation the business is in. But then again I'm not sure how aware I am either, given that I can't bring myself to sit down and go through all the accounts and the paperwork. I'm fairly sure, though, that unless we have a good few months it's likely they'll have to find employment elsewhere. But looking at them now, with their innocent little faces, like a pair of puppies I've caught shredding a cushion, I can't bring myself to say anything to them just yet.

"Have you got it then?" I ask, to blank stares. "The mop and bucket?"

"Oh, no," Oliver mumbles. "Forgot it, actually."

We all look at each other.

"Why don't you have another try?" I say, and they scuttle away.

I've put off my visit to the kitchen for too long. When I open the door I'm met by a searingly hot blast of air. Jacques is attempting to kick the oven door closed while simultaneously stirring something on the hob opposite. I dash forward to try to help, but he flicks me away with a tea towel. As he does so I get a whiff of his aftershave. He smells like woodsmoke and pine. I wonder what I smell like. Yogurt, I suppose.

I tell Jacques that we're looking a little bit quiet this week, bookings-wise (which is quite the understatement), and he just shrugs. I'm assuming that he's looking to move on, but then again he seems just as apathetic on the rare days we're actually busy.

As he disappears off to the larder, swearing under his breath, I find myself closing my eyes, picturing the scene in here back when the kitchen would be in full swing.

The food side of things was very much Lily's domain. She had been the one to pull off the incredible coup of persuading a top chef she'd got to know in London to move down here. Part of me had been a little envious that I hadn't been able to join in with their animated chats about the menu and ingredients to be sourced, but as a man who'd only recently learned what fennel was, I knew I'd be more of a hindrance than a help. I didn't truly mind, though. What mattered was that Lily was happy. After what we'd gone through, to see her excited again as she threw herself into making this part of the pub's appeal so strong, it was such a huge relief. *We've made it*, I thought. *We've got through to the other side.* This often stands out as part of why it's so hard for me to accept that Lily would just simply walk away.

I'm lost in this thought, eyes still closed, when Jacques walks back from the larder, ushers me toward the door, and, with a practiced backward kick, slams it shut in my face.

6.

WHAT I'D CHANGE ABOUT THE WORLD

THEN

I was returning from the off-license and had lost my bearings when Lily's laugh guided me back to the group like a beacon. As I approached, I decided that I simply had to take the plunge and speak to her, but by the time I'd got there I realized that the makeup of people had changed. I'd noticed Ed had been getting on rather well with a pretty girl with short, bleached-blond hair, and they seemed to have disappeared. A few others had departed, and the circle had closed up, and so now there I was, hovering, waiting for someone to notice that I had nowhere to sit.

Time moves very slowly in moments like these. The longer nobody moved aside, the more agonizing it became. These days I'd almost instantly reach for my mobile phone, frowning at the screen as if reviewing an unexpected fall in the NASDAQ while actually refreshing my weather app. But without such a shield I was completely exposed, until Lily noticed me standing there and told everyone to "shove up" so that I could sit down.

I had just worked up the courage to ask her something when her boyfriend Daniel launched into a monologue that apparently demanded all our attention, and from then on he began to dominate proceedings. He had a truly frustrating habit of derailing interesting avenues of conversation with what he obviously regarded as daringly philosophical bon mots, quite often talking over Lily, which was absolutely unacceptable behavior to me. The latest of these interruptions—accompanied by his hand on her arm to stop her midsentence—was so he could get the conversation back to his grand traveling plans.

"When I do go," he said, "I just want to head somewhere completely unknown and bewildering to me"—and I thought about saying, "What, like Birmingham?" before just about managing to stop myself. But then he began tossing more names out into the ether, each accompanied by a swish of his hand: "Bali . . . Cambodia . . . Vietnam . . . ," and then I just couldn't help it.

"*Swindon* . . . ," I muttered, and thought nobody had heard, until I saw Lily turning her head toward me.

"Nepal . . . ," Daniel continued, his audience still rapt. "Bhutan . . ."

"*Haverfordwest* . . . ," Lily said quietly, and I saw that she was looking directly at me now. Conversation moved on before we could see how far we got with this game, but when Lily went to get another bottle of wine and came back to the circle, she inserted herself next to me. From then on, I became astonishingly aware of the tiniest shift in our proximity, to an almost unbearable degree. With our shoulders practically touching, it was like victory and defeat came with each breath, as her arm moved toward me and away, toward me and away. When she asked me to pass the corkscrew I nearly jumped out of my skin, and the smile she gave me when I presented it to her with quite some reverence was knowing, somehow, in a way that made me feel quite overwhelmed. As her hair swished over her shoulders, I caught the faint scent of something like cinnamon. Up until this point in my life I had not known what the phrase "Love makes you do crazy things" meant, but in that moment I was perilously close to asking Lily if she'd been baking that afternoon, or if she always smelled like delicious cookies.

I suppose what happened next was a direct result of whatever chemical reactions were currently impairing my brain. I'd been dimly aware that a conversation was in progress where each person in the group was being invited by Daniel to give their opinion on something. A rather prim boy next to me had just said his piece and it had elicited approving noises from everyone else.

"What about you?" Daniel said, looking at me like I was a half-forgotten curio in his study. "Brian, was it?"

"Sorry?"

"We're just going around the group. Saying what one thing we'd like to change about the world if we could."

"Oh, right," I said. I was aware of everyone's eyes on me, Lily's most of all. I had absolutely no idea how to answer this question. What *would* I change? And then, from nowhere, it occurred to me.

"Last summer I was in the park and I got bitten by a mosquito. And I was scratching away at it and I remember thinking how brilliant it would be if the cure for the itchiness of mosquito bites was actually to scratch them."

This was greeted by complete silence.

"Um, OK," Daniel said at last. "Mark, what about you?" A boy with a thin little mouth sitting opposite me—who was still clearly distracted by my contribution—said, "Well, like you were saying, Dan, I guess changing how materialistic we all are has to be up there?"

People murmured their agreement enthusiastically.

"And you, Debbie?" Daniel asked.

A tall girl with the voice of a Radio 4 newsreader simply said, "Banning blood sports."

As everyone else voiced their opinions, largely on similar lines, I wondered if I could possibly get away with flopping onto my side and rolling away, unnoticed, picking up momentum until I was tumbling all the way down Primrose Hill, through central London, down to the Embankment, and into the Thames, eventually out to sea.

It was only when someone asked Lily if she was OK that I looked around to see that she was crying silent tears of laughter.

"Yes," she sniffed. "Completely fine. Don't mind me."

Before anyone could follow up on this, a golden retriever, let loose from its lead, charged into the middle of us and knocked over a bottle of wine before going for an open packet of sausage rolls. In the ensuing chaos, I felt Lily clinging onto my arm, and when the dog went for the ice cream she was holding I instinctively put my hand up as a barrier, fending it off.

"Gosh, thank you," Lily said as the dog ran off in search of something else.

"That's OK," I replied.

"Very brave of you."

"He does seem quite vicious," I said as we watched the dog gleefully licking at someone's face a few feet away, who was helpless with laughter.

Before I could say anything else I felt the presence of Daniel, who was standing behind us, holding what I presumed was Lily's denim jacket over his arm.

"We should go, Lil. We've got Kate's party, remember?"

"Oh, OK. Do we need to go just now?"

"Well, you know what Kate's like . . ."

At that point a gust of wind took hold of a plastic bag next to me and carried it off. As the closest to it I had no choice but to give chase, making several humiliating failed attempts to snatch it up. By the time I'd finally succeeded and headed back to the group, it was to find that people were beginning to leave—and that Lily was already halfway down the hill, arm in arm with Daniel.

7.

LILY IN BLUE

NOW

It's a particularly quiet day, even for us, so I decide to leave Oliver and Sophie in charge for a bit. I collect my jacket from its hook on the wall and glance back at the bar. I remember standing on this very spot on the July evening before Lily disappeared. She was looking beautiful in blue, regaling the rapt regulars around the bar with a story while she poured their drinks. The low sun was shining through a pane of stained glass and casting beautiful patterns on the bar, and as Lily reached the end of her story and threw her arms wide, motes of dust spiraled up, caught in the light, as if she'd just finished a magic trick with a puff of smoke, and she was beaming, face lit up, completely in her element. The following day, she was gone.

I feel a tightness in my chest, and it's with some urgency that I stride toward the door and push it open, gratefully taking in a lungful of fresh air as I cross through the beer garden, then climb the stile into the neighboring field. It's all farmland around here, and the familiar sight of a herd of cows greets me at the far end of the field. Lily and I used to remark on how guilty they always seemed to look, as if ten seconds earlier we'd have caught them all balancing on each other's backs in a pyramid. I cut across the farm track and go past the two hulking barns that stand near the end of it. The farmer—Davis—is under the bonnet of his Land Rover. He acknowledges me with a nod as I pass. He's not the friendliest. Possibly because his equipment keeps getting stolen from these barns. He always seems to look at me as if I'm in on it, like I might secretly be hoarding a combine harvester behind the bar.

There's only a little further for me to go before I reach the cliff top and the messy jumble of rocks, the only surviving sign of the Iron Age fort that used to be here. There's an old tree stump in among them, rugged and sturdy. As I run my hands across its familiar grooves, I think of the times when Lily and I would stop to admire the view here on one of our evening walks. This stump is where Lily would often set her watch down if the strap was irritating her skin, as it invariably did when it was warm. There was something I always found curiously enjoyable about the sight of her watch lying there. It looked as if it had been somehow embedded within the trunk, and that we had been the ones to find it after the tree had fallen in a storm—like we'd stumbled across some magical timepiece bearing unknown secrets.

There's a warm breeze drifting off the sea, thick with salt. I close my eyes and breathe it in. I turn back to look at the pub for a second. It seems its finest in the afternoon light, I think. One of the many quirks that appealed to Lily and me about the place was the fact that as well as the traditional pub sign, the letters of "The County Arms" are also spelled out handsomely in brass, fixed to the walls at the front and back, and they gleam beautifully in the sunshine at this time of day.

I spend a lot of time imagining Lily coming back and seeing the pub again for the first time, standing right here. I can't imagine it would look any different to her. From the outside, I've no doubt it would still look as magnificent as the day she left. But then she'd step through the door and immediately feel the emptiness of the place, smell the decay. And I hate to admit this to myself, but there's a horribly triumphant part of me that would want to say: "Well, what did you expect?"

I think of Jeff just now as I opened Tripadvisor, that apprehension on his face. I think I know what's behind it. He's aware I'm not reciting those bad reviews as a way of laughing them off. But what he probably doesn't fully understand, because it's hard to reckon with it myself sometimes, is that I find myself increasingly fueled by them. Those impotent outpourings of rage collect inside me, thick and oozing like tar, and I think to myself: *Look, Lily, remember the place we built together? Well, here it is now. It might still look elegant from the outside, but the beams are creaking, the floorboards are rotting, because it turns out I can't do this on my own.*

This is a far cry from how I felt in the weeks—even the months—after she'd disappeared. I did all I possibly could to keep the place sparkling. I wanted Lily to come back through that door and for not a single thing to have changed. She'd be proud of me for how I'd managed to keep going—how I'd refused to fall to pieces in her absence and let our beloved pub suffer in any way. And when she *did* come back, I told myself, we'd carry on as if nothing had happened. It didn't matter why she'd left, as long as she came home. I wouldn't need any kind of explanation. But then another month passed. Then another. Then a year. And then it wasn't as simple as that anymore.

8.

PRETENDING

THEN

The light was fading on Primrose Hill, and it was a fair way home, but I couldn't face the journey just yet. Someone had left a bottle of wine behind, and I began to drink, looking on enviously at the couples dotted around me, feeling a bit sorry for myself. A little while later I heard someone approach. I wondered if it was Ed making his way sheepishly back to the party, but when I glanced around I saw that it was Lily.

"Oh, hi," she said. She seemed distracted. "Don't get up," she added as I scrambled to my feet. "I've managed to go and lose my watch and I was just looking for it. Don't suppose you've seen it?"

"Afraid not," I said.

"Shit," Lily muttered. "When will I ever learn?"

"Is it expensive?" I asked.

"No," Lily said quickly, a trace of defensiveness in her voice. "It was my granny's. I have to take it off sometimes, though, because of the strap—it irritates my skin."

I put the bottle of wine down and started to help her look, but with it getting darker I didn't have much faith that we'd find it. We both dropped to our knees, crawling around and patting the grass. After five minutes of searching I'd found several empty lager cans, two lighters, and a half-eaten sausage roll—but no watch. But just as I was making my way back to Lily I knocked something with my foot.

"Hey," I called, "is this it?"

Lily got to her feet and rushed over, grabbing the watch from my hand and then throwing her arms around me with such force that I nearly toppled over backward. After a moment she let go. When she pulled away I saw that her cheeks were faintly flushed.

"Sorry," she said.

"No need to apologize," I said. And there really wasn't. I hoped she might have lost her keys and purse so that I could find those for her too.

We walked over to where I'd been sitting and Lily plonked herself down on the grass. She put the watch back on and stretched out her arm to admire it, as if trying it on for the very first time. It struck me as a little odd that Daniel hadn't come back to help with her search. Then I remembered, with a jolt of self-loathing, my contribution to his "what would you change about the world" conversation.

"Can I just take a moment to acknowledge how stupid I must have sounded before?" I said, sitting down next to Lily. "Your boyfriend must think I'm a complete moron."

Lily was quiet, and for one awful moment I thought she was going to say, "Well, who can blame him?" but instead she said, "Daniel isn't my boyfriend."

"Oh, right!" I replied, far too gleefully, and I saw the corners of Lily's mouth twitch. But before the smile could fully form she frowned and said, almost idly, "Sometimes I think I should just get it over with and go out with him, though."

It was fair to say this dampened my spirits. Lily looked at her watch again, as if checking it was really there. She shivered as a ripple of breeze hit us. Without stopping to think about what I was doing, I took off my jacket, only to pause in horror with it held out, suddenly aware of how clichéd the gesture was. Lily looked at me quizzically.

"Are you doing a magic trick?" she asked.

"God no," I blustered. "I thought if you were chilly you might like . . . but never mind."

"That was a joke, actually," she said. "So if the offer's still there . . . ?"

Relieved, I quickly handed her my jacket.

"Awfully decent of you," she said. Then she draped it over her shoulders and took a swig of wine, managing to transform my cheap suit and a bottle of corner-shop Shiraz into something from a French New Wave film poster.

She turned to me then and asked me how long I'd been in London, and whom I'd known that evening, and I felt a sudden urge not only to answer these questions, but to tell her every single thing about myself, even if that included my myriad shortcomings—just so that it meant she stayed here with me. In the end I just about managed to limit it to how I knew Ed, that I'd been in London for two years, and that—as she could probably tell from my less than flawless showing that evening—I wasn't particularly good with new people.

"Oh, I don't know about that," Lily said. "I mean, just tonight you returned a girl her family heirloom shortly after introducing her to a groundbreaking thought experiment about mosquitos. That's not bad going."

She passed me the bottle. As much as I appreciated her gentle ribbing, I still felt the need to explain myself.

"I feel like I'm not quite on the same wavelength as everyone else, sometimes," I said. "It's like I've turned up to play a sport I'm supposed to understand but everyone else is there in their cricket whites and I'm dressed in a suit of armor and wearing oven gloves."

Lily laughed. "Yes, but here's the thing, though, Brian," she said, and there was a familiarity with which she said my name that made my heart swell. "If you were to ask most of those people what they *actually* wanted to change about the world, it would probably be something like abolishing inheritance tax. Take Daniel, for instance . . ." My ears pricked up at once. "I mean, I suppose we're all pretending to be people we're not to some extent, but he's something else, believe me. He makes out to everyone that he's this anti-capitalist, free spirit type. But we go way back, and let me tell you, it's all just a pretense. He'll be working at his father's hedge fund once he's shagged his way around as many of the world's youth hostels as he can, and then he'll have to stop it with all the 'everything happens for a reason' nonsense."

I wrinkled my nose. I'd not heard Daniel say this, but I could very much imagine him doing so.

"I really don't like that saying," I said. "It just doesn't make any sense, does it? What with, you know, plane crashes and terminal illness. I can't really imagine the victims of Chernobyl looking around at the skin melting off each other's faces and saying, 'Don't worry, lads, everything happens for a reason!'"

A silence followed this, as it tends to when someone's said the phrase "skin melting off each other's faces." But thankfully it was only because Lily was trying not to spit out the wine she'd just drunk, and then she laughed—a proper booming one. It was joyful. Once she'd composed herself, she fixed me with what felt like a deliberately sly look and said, "Do you usually bring up Chernobyl when you're talking to girls you've just met?"

I swallowed. "No," I said. "Well, not every time."

"Sure."

"I mean, sometimes it's Vesuvius . . ."

"Right. But it's always disaster based, then?"

"Exclusively."

"And does it ever work on them?"

"It's not for me to say."

Had I imagined it, or had she moved a little closer to me?

Despite the growing gloom, we carried on talking, the conversation moving on to our jobs. Lily told me she was an assistant on the features desk of a magazine.

"What kind of magazine?"

"You'll know the sort," she said with a yawn. "Lots of tips, mainly. What to do with a slow cooker. Or a willy."

"Presumably not at the same time?"

"You'd be surprised."

She lay back, and I did the same, her hand brushing mine. I'd been told that there was too much light pollution in London to see stars, but in that moment I was sure a few glittered above us.

"What about you?" Lily asked.

"I'm in insurance," I said. "All very dull and boring," I added automatically.

"Is it?" Lily said.

This threw me. Usually this was the point where people nodded knowingly and told me they hated their jobs too.

"Well, it has its moments, I suppose. I actually . . ." Here, I tailed off, about to commit the cardinal sin of being sincere.

"What?" Lily said, nudging my hand.

"I got promoted not too long ago. Not a big one or anything, but . . . that was nice."

"Ha! I thought you were about to tell me you'd been fired for nicking *pens* or something. You know it is fine to be proud of your achievements, Brian."

I tried to hide how much this made me glow. "I'll try," I said. "Though please can we move on before I start talking very earnestly about the finer points of loss adjustment?"

"Fine," Lily said. "But given that I'd still count that as a deflection, I insist on you telling me"—here, with great timing, she yawned again—"say, two of the most interesting things about yourself."

"What, now?"

"Yes, now, in this park that I have just realized is exclusively populated with drunk couples getting handsy under blankets."

I was distracted by this, wishing we had a blanket, and forgot I was supposed to be answering a question. It was only when Lily began to poke me in the ribs—a tactic she would go on to employ to great effect in the years to come when there was a kettle to put on, a phone to answer—that I found myself blurting out, "Well, I'm an orphan. Does that count as interesting?"

Abruptly, Lily stopped poking me. And I'm afraid I couldn't help myself.

“Happy now?”

“Don’t do that!” she said, elbowing me this time. “That’s so unfair.”

“You’re right,” I said, feeling my ribs. “I’m sorry. I deserved that.”

After a moment, she asked me what had happened. I told her about the car crash that my parents had died in, which occurred before I was old enough to form any real memories of them, and that I’d been brought up by my grandparents. Apart from Ed, I’d only told a couple of people about all this since moving to London. I’d regretted it each time, because it turns out people do tend to fancy themselves amateur psychologists after a few drinks. But Lily wasn’t like that. She listened, properly listened, and I might have opened up more if I weren’t very aware of how this wasn’t exactly the avenue I wanted our conversation to go down.

“Anyway,” I said. “The second of the two interesting things about me . . .”

I wondered if Lily might try to steer the conversation back to what we’d just been talking about, but instead she said, “Go on . . .”

“I’m dermographic.”

“Wait, you’re what?” Lily said. “Hang on. Please don’t tell me that’s some sort of weird sex thing, Brian, because you were doing so well.” I laughed. “It is, isn’t it! You’re into women dressing up as clowns or something.”

“I’m not. Although . . . how do you think you know if you are?”

“Let’s clear up one thing at a time, shall we,” Lily said. “Please tell me what ‘dermographic’ means.”

I finished the last dregs of wine. "Basically, it means if I scratch my skin the mark stays there without fading."

"Whoa, really? For how long?"

I shrugged. "Depends. But a fair while. You could scratch a whole sentence on my arm and it would still be there the next morning. As I learned to my cost at school."

I could sense Lily trying to restrain herself from grabbing my arm, but as soon as I rolled up my sleeve she pounced and gently scratched me with her index finger.

"Fascinating," she breathed as a welt slowly rose. "We should talk about something else before I'm too tempted to write a dirty limerick on you."

In that moment, with her cheek close to mine, her hand still on my arm, I would have happily let her write her memoirs. With an index. And appendices.

I was horribly aware of how much we'd been talking about me. There was so much I wanted to ask Lily, and not just what she'd meant about Daniel when she'd said she should just get it over with and go out with him.

But just then a man with a torch appeared and barked that the park was closing, and we had to get up. It had been a while since I'd felt these particular nerves, the ones that seem to ferment so potently when you're walking with someone away from the safe bubble of the present—the place where you've felt an attraction sparking into life—to the terrifying future and the point where you'll part. Conversation was impossible because with every step I was getting closer to the point where decisions would have to be made. Would I kiss her? Would I just ask to see her again? The only thing that made me feel any better was that, judging by how she was chewing her lip, Lily seemed to be grappling with these questions too, and so for twenty seconds we walked along in a silence so charged I'm surprised our feet weren't kicking up sparks.

When we reached the road running behind Primrose Hill, Lily asked which way I was going.

"West," I told her, gesturing vaguely in that direction, although I may well have been pointing at the moon, because she was standing very close to me and my synapses were in danger of shutting down.

"I see," she said.

"Ed and I live in a flat above a garden center called Get Forked," I added, in an odd sort of voice.

Lily blinked at me, twice, very slowly.

"Is that a lie?" she asked.

"No," I replied.

"Fair enough."

"Do you—do you need, you know, walking anywhere?" I asked. "I can't promise I'll fight off any muggers, but I've got a very loud scream."

"Very chivalrous of you," Lily said, "but I'm only over there." *There* seemed to be just behind her. We really were standing very close now. If I was going to kiss her it was now or never. But then someone screeched around the corner on a motorbike and we had to jump back onto the pavement.

"He won't get there any quicker," I said, "as my grandma used to say."

Note to self, don't bring up Grandma in moments like this.

Lily smiled. "Well, Brian," she said. "I don't want to be too presumptuous, but I'm having a party in a week's time. If you fancied coming along?"

It was at this point I briefly lost my cool and replied "Yes!"

at a volume you'd more normally associate with answering the question "Is there anyone still alive down there?"

"Super," Lily said, luckily not seeming too taken aback by my response. She was still wearing my jacket and had begun to rummage in my pockets. "Have you not got a pen in here somewhere, Mr. Insurance?"

"Hmm, don't think so."

Panic rose within me at the thought she might discover a long-forgotten aide-mémoire: *Terry, actuary, alopecia*. But then she stopped.

"Wait, hang on . . ." She bent down and picked up a twig. Then she dragged me over to a streetlight, taking hold of my arm and rolling up my sleeve. She paused, twig poised over my wrist. "You're sure it doesn't hurt?" she asked.

"Depends on how long your address is."

"Well, you're in luck there, sir."

As she began to pull the twig across my skin, I wasn't aware of any pain. I was too distracted by the scent of jasmine in the air and the sound of the streetlight buzzing overhead, and the fact that my heart was still beating so hard I thought it might crack my ribs.

"There," Lily said, smoothing a hand over my arm. She lifted it to the light, and we watched the welts slowly rise.

"Twelve Langley Street," I read. "I probably could have remembered that . . ."

"I spared you the postcode at least."

It was clear we were about to go our separate ways, but I couldn't resist saying one more thing to keep the night going for just a few seconds longer. "You said something earlier . . ."

She narrowed her eyes. "I'm not dressing up as a clown, Brian."

"Shame. But no. Not that."

"Go on then . . ."

"You said something like, 'We're all just pretending to be people we're not.'"

I didn't necessarily have a follow-up point to this. What I ended up saying was possibly a little blunter than I'd intended.

"So does that mean you are too?"

Lily held my gaze, and it was as if the planet had juddered to a halt, waiting for this to play out before it resumed rotation.

"You'll just have to find out, won't you?"

9.

THE POSTCARD

NOW

When I get back to the pub it's to find that Jeff has a rapt audience of Sophie and Oliver. I can't bring myself to listen to the Ben Nevis badger costume tale yet again, so I slip past into the back corridor and make my way upstairs.

We never really settled on a name for the room just along from our bedroom. Nominally, it was our office, although that felt laughable considering how little admin we managed to get done up here. I remember on one occasion coming upstairs to find Lily sporting a particularly natty top hat fashioned from gas bills. If anything, I've neglected the paperwork even more now. There's a small chest of drawers at the far end of the room, stuffed full of unread insurance documents and goodness knows what else, things that have snowballed to a point beyond my control. Above the chest of drawers there's a noticeboard pinned to the wall. This was once used by Lily to help her brainstorm new menus. Now there's only one thing pinned to it. The postcard.

THE DAY I woke to find Lily wasn't in bed next to me, I assumed it was because it was her turn to get up early to prep for the day ahead. Unable to get back to sleep, I got up and made my way downstairs. But Lily was nowhere to be found. She wasn't in the bar, nor the kitchen or the cellar. I looked out in the beer garden, but there was no sign of her there either. Had she gone into town? No, the car was still there. I called her phone, but it was turned off. When it got to lunchtime, I began ringing around in case anyone had heard from her, but that drew a blank. Increasingly confused, I began to scour the place in case she'd left me a note—perhaps one that had slipped behind a cupboard, or her dressing table—but there was nothing.

By the time the shadows were starting to lengthen, I could no longer pretend I wasn't seriously worried.

"She'll be fine," Jeff kept saying. But I could see in his eyes that he was concerned. I'd been putting off calling the police up until then, because I knew what they'd say, and sure enough, as soon as they heard how long Lily had been missing, they told me it was far too soon for them to do anything about it.

After Jeff left that night, I stayed up in the bar in one of the armchairs, listening out for Lily's footsteps. I must have fallen asleep some time before dawn, and woke shortly after, but she still wasn't there. I called the police again, and this time they asked me to search Lily's belongings to check what was missing. Other than her phone (still switched off) and her purse, nothing seemed to be gone. It was possible an overnight bag was missing, but I thought she might have taken that to a charity shop a few weeks earlier. Her passport was still here, and her granny's old watch. She'd never leave without that, I told them.

It was that which really worried me. I started asking them if they thought someone else might be involved in her disappearance. Wildly, I speculated that the farmer, Davis, should be questioned, as he always seemed suspicious. The police wouldn't be drawn into this conversation (it would later transpire that Davis was in Ireland at the time) and asked me to focus instead on speaking to anyone I knew who might be able to help. The phone call to Lily's parents that day was one of the hardest I've ever had to make. We hadn't been on the best terms for a while by that point, but I still felt wretched as I heard the blame in their voices. I did my utmost to stay calm, letting them get it all out of their system. Their daughter was missing and they needed someone to lash out at—I got that.

It was different when I spoke to Rebecca, Lily's older sister, who responded with a kind of forced pragmatism. She told me that it was almost certain that Lily had just gone to stay with a friend or something and had forgotten to tell us. Rebecca is a lawyer, forthright and no-nonsense, but I was sure I could detect the faintest trace of doubt in her voice. Before we could talk for much longer, though, the police arrived.

A detective called Fairbanks asked me to walk him through everything I could remember from the last few days. As we spoke, I could tell he was trying to get the measure of me. But I wasn't going to be like one of those people on TV who take umbrage at being questioned, no matter how informally. So, I listened carefully and answered him to the best of my knowledge. No, Lily hadn't done anything like this before. No, I couldn't think of any reason why she'd have gone without telling me. No, we hadn't fought or argued. When it came to the question of whether Lily had seemed upset, I pictured the night before she'd left as I answered—Lily dressed in blue, in her element with the regulars, dust in the air like smoke, her face lighting up as if she didn't have a care in the world.

When Fairbanks left, I expected him to tell me not to worry, or that I could count on them to do their utmost to find Lily. But he left without any such reassurances. As his car engine faded, I remember being aware of how very alone I was.

The rest of the day passed, then the night, and still Lily wasn't home. The worry started to take its toll. I was beset with stomach cramps. I slept so little that I failed to focus on the most basic task. When I heard the clatter of the letterbox, at first I barely registered it. In fact, the first time I saw the postcard lying on the mat, I didn't even bother picking it up. I assumed it was junk mail. But when I walked past it again and stooped to pick it up, I turned it over and recognized the handwriting as Lily's.

Brian,
I'm going away for a while. I'm not sure when I'll be back.
Lily

My legs gave way and I crumpled to the foot of the stairs, the relief overwhelming. I picked myself up and called the police, then left messages with Lily's family and friends. I was so exhausted afterward that I crawled up the stairs to bed, finally knowing that sleep would come. When I woke, there was the postcard on Lily's pillow, and I felt relief swaddle me all over again. But it was only on rereading what Lily had written that the true meaning of her words cut through.

I'm going away for a while. I'm not sure when I'll be back.

I had been so relieved to learn that she was OK that the message itself hadn't truly sunk in. When *was* she going to be back? Days? Weeks?

For the rest of the afternoon, I pictured her writing the postcard, trying to imagine her state of mind and where she might have sent it from. There was the faintest hint of a postmark, but it wasn't legible. Lily could have been half a mile away or in the Outer Hebrides for all I knew.

I clung desperately to a single word: "when." She wasn't sure *when* she'd be back. But then another day passed. And another. And then it was a week. The awful milestones kept arriving. A fortnight. A month. I was calling the police again regularly by this point, but they seemed all too ready to dismiss my concerns. The postcard was clear evidence that Lily had left of her own volition, and that she was alive and well. I gathered that Lily's parents had been calling even more frequently. It turned out that while they'd briefly been relieved that she had made contact with me, they wouldn't be truly satisfied that she was safe until they'd heard from her themselves.

Eventually, after another agonizing month passed, the police agreed to look into the situation again. What seemed to concern them at this point, more than a lack of any further communication from Lily, was that she hadn't used her credit cards since she'd left, nor had she taken out any money from the bank. I could hear in their voices that they were worried, and now the postcard and those few scribbled words seemed like such flimsy evidence that Lily hadn't come to any harm.

I began to find it harder to cope, day to day. The only person apart from Jeff that I had to talk to was my old friend Ed, but the distance between us seemed so vast on the phone. He didn't really know what to say to comfort me. After a while, when I saw his name come up on my mobile, I found myself ignoring the call. I wasn't sure I could bear another strained conversation where we went round in circles.

By that point, sleep was impossible. The only way I could force myself into unconsciousness was by drinking. I wasn't aware of how out of control things were getting until the morning I came to in a police cell. The duty sergeant informed me that I'd arrived at the station incoherent. When they'd tried to clear me out, I'd become aggressive, and they'd been forced to put me in a cell and relieve me of all my possessions, along with my belt and shoelaces. He let this particular detail hang in the air. Mortified, I apologized repeatedly and said that it would never happen again.

I avoided the sergeant's eye as he handed me a tray with my wallet and keys. As I shoved them into my pockets I realized there was something else there—Lily's watch.

"Did I bring this in?" I asked. For a moment I just held it in my hands, staring at it, until the sergeant's impatient cough had me turning on my heel.

After six months, the police told me that they had made the "difficult" decision to close their investigation. They had tried every avenue available to them, but without further information coming to light they were no longer able to keep putting resources into the search. I raged at them. But it didn't make a shred of difference. From that point on, I was on my own, and all I could do was wait.

ANOTHER MONTH PASSED. Then another. But I remained steadfast. If I gave up hope, I realized, it would be the end of me. If the moment came when I didn't feel my heart starting to pound when I saw someone through the frosted glass of the door, then I'd give up the right to deserve Lily's return. *When*, she had written in that postcard. Not if, but *when*. If she came through that door and saw in my eyes that my faith had wavered, then I'd have failed her test, and maybe she'd leave all over again.

When the day approached that would mark a year since her disappearance, I received a visit from Rebecca. We'd been speaking on the phone sporadically—brief exchanges where we confirmed that neither of us had heard anything new. Rebecca always seemed as stoic as I was trying to be, aside from the occasional long pause where I heard her breathing become a little uneven. When I heard a car arrive outside and saw her getting out, I thought that must mean she had news. Anticipating this, Rebecca greeted me immediately by saying she'd not heard anything.

"Oh, OK. So . . . do you want to come in for a drink?"

She hesitated, her car keys clutched in her hand, but then she shook her head, and so the conversation carried on with us standing by her car.

"It's coming up to a year," Rebecca said, and immediately my heart sank. "Mum and Dad, and some of Lily's friends. They're—we're—going to hold a service. In the church in the village, back home."

"A service?" I said. "What kind of a service?"

Rebecca's eye contact didn't waver as she answered. "To mark the date."

"To mark it?" It slowly dawned on me what this meant. "So you're giving her a memorial."

"No," Rebecca said. "It's just a service. Like I said."

"You can call it what you like," I replied, anger building,

"but that's what it is. I'm just glad I've got more faith in Lily than all of you."

I could see Rebecca clenching her keys harder in her hand.

"I presume you've not driven down here to invite me?" I said.

"No."

"I was going to say. I can't imagine your parents would have me there."

"Don't," Rebecca said sharply. "I didn't come here to listen to your self-pity."

"Then why *are* you here?"

I wanted this conversation to be over. I wanted to be back in my seat at the bar, waiting for Lily.

"I'm here to tell you what I told Mum and Dad," she said. And I was surprised to hear her voice cracking. At the sound of this, I immediately regretted losing my temper and took a step forward, but she put a hand out flat to stop me.

"We need to face facts," she said. "I don't know what's happened to Lily. None of us do. I don't know where she is, or . . . whether she's still . . . but either way, she's gone. We have to start coming to terms with that. Because I can't stand watching Mum and Dad like this."

"But this sounds like you're giving up on her," I said. I could tell from how Rebecca spoke next that she was trying her hardest to stay calm.

"If we don't reach some kind of acceptance," she said, "then it's going to completely destroy all of our lives, and do you really think that's what Lily would have wanted, whatever's happened?"

I didn't know what to say to this. I didn't even want to consider it. Of course Lily wouldn't want the people she loved to be in this much pain. But it didn't make sense that she would leave in the first place, either. When I looked at Rebecca, and realized how hard it must have been for her to make this journey and say these things to me, I decided not to argue with her. We didn't have to feel the same way.

"Are you sure you don't want to come in?" I said.

"No, I need to get back." She paused for a moment. "I don't mind if you want to call me, if you ever need to talk. But as I've said to Mum and Dad—if it's because you're wanting to go over all the details again, or you're entertaining some new, wild theory, then I'm not going to have that conversation. OK?"

She didn't wait for me to reply, and with that she climbed back into her car. I watched her drive off, feeling bruised by what she'd said. I might have thought of myself as a rational person, but I simply could not accept that if Lily was gone, in the truest sense, I wouldn't know. Something would have snapped inside me. A clean break, the sound of it like the crack of a gunshot. And while I still felt intact, unbroken and whole, I wasn't going to consider it a possibility.

10.

ORANGES AND LEMONS

THEN

In the week that followed meeting Lily for the first time, I began to get the sense that Ed, who had spent so much time trying to get me out of my shell and meeting new people, was now starting to regret not leaving me to become a hermit. If I wasn't brandishing my arm and the ugly welts on it under his nose, I was repeating the part of the story where I'd given Lily my jacket, though of course in my version of the story I'd done this with a suaveness that made James Bond look like Ronald McDonald.

Ed had taken to brewing his own beer in the bathroom around that time, stirring away solemnly at the questionable liquid like a druid. That was where I found him the day before Lily's party, by which point I was a bag of nerves.

"What time do you think I should get there?" I asked him yet again.

"I think you should get there at the time you think you should get there."

"Yes. Right. Good plan."

Solemn stirring.

"Do you think I should bring something?"

"Yes."

"Excellent. Thought so."

More solemn stirring.

"Like what, though?"

Deep sigh. "A block of rubble. A snake. What do you think? Wine, obviously."

"Right, yeah. Wine. And what do you think about clothes?"

"Definitely wear clothes."

"Ha, yeah. But should I buy new ones?"

Ed told me that I shouldn't, and that I should just be myself.

I decided to go in an ever-so-slightly different direction, by buying a whole new wardrobe and entirely changing my personality.

AS I PREPARED to leave the house on the evening of the party, I asked Ed to wish me luck. He duly did, and then, looking a bit concerned, he said, "You do know what kind of people are going to be there tonight, don't you, given Lily's circle?"

"What do you mean?"

He put his hand on my shoulder. "Just remember that you've got nothing to prove to anyone, OK?"

It was a strange pep talk. My small reserves of confidence were drained by the time I arrived at Lily's house as I worried about what he'd meant.

I was clutching a bottle of red wine, some chocolates, and an enormous, unwieldy bouquet of flowers picked out for me by an opportunistic florist who realized I didn't know what I was doing.

I rang the doorbell. After a lengthy delay, the door opened.

"Lil," someone whom I couldn't see called, "there's a bunch of flowers at your door holding a boy."

"Tell them to come in!" I heard Lily call back, laughing her glorious laugh. I forced my way through the door, shedding petals.

The kitchen was packed with people all drinking glasses of champagne and white wine. Everyone seemed to be dressed as if they'd just come from a job interview, particularly the men in their suits. I tried to ignore everyone's eyes on me and my towering bouquet, and scanned the room until I saw Lily—who was sitting on the countertop and swinging her legs as she talked animatedly with a friend. She looked so beautiful, so full of light—as if the moment she left the room all the color would drain away. I caught her eye and waved madly. She mouthed "Hi!," beaming at me, and went back to talking to her friend. I felt a pair of firm hands on my shoulders and I turned to find Daniel grinning at me.

"For me? You shouldn't have. Need a hand there?"

"I'm fine, thanks," I said, sliding out of his grip and plonking the flowers unceremoniously in the sink. Daniel too was in what looked like a very expensive suit. Maybe he'd given up on the hippie shtick already. He went to take a wineglass from the cupboard and I used the opportunity to head over to Lily, but before I could get to her she was mobbed by a couple of new arrivals.

I looked around for someone to talk to—anyone other than Daniel—but everyone was clustered in little groups. After approaching one such cluster, and trying and failing to insert myself into the conversation, I resorted to simply standing behind them, like a penguin taking his turn to shelter a colony huddled against the wind. There I listened to them talking about "the markets" and foreign holidays to places I'd never heard of, desperately hoping I'd find something to contribute. But I'd been so keen to work my way into this new group that I must have missed Lily leaving the kitchen. With the light fading outside, I felt the urge to find her and for us to step out for a moment, to recall the soft summer air and shimmering streetlight of Primrose Hill.

I was halfway down the hall in search of her when I heard some excitable shrieking coming from the living room, and I quickened my pace. As I opened the door I was confronted by eight or nine people all standing in a line, bobbing up and down and yelling. A game was evidently in progress—one that involved each person clamping an orange under their chin and passing it to the person next to them. My heart leaped as I saw Lily at the end of the line, but just then I felt Daniel brush past me and insert himself between her and the wall, timing it so that Lily had no choice upon receiving the orange but to pass it on to him. As she did so, Daniel quite deliberately angled his head so that their lips met. Instinctively, I took a stride forward, though I'd no idea what I was planning to do, but then I saw the way that Lily reached up and put her hands in Daniel's hair, pulling his mouth to hers, and that felt like my cue to leave.

11.

A SIGN

NOW

As the years went by, I couldn't pretend that my feelings about Lily's disappearance weren't growing more complicated. You hear those stories about a faithful dog, refusing to move from a single spot, waiting for someone to come home. I felt envious of the simplicity of an animal's unconditional love. I was being tempted down darker paths. *Why couldn't Lily have just sent another postcard?* I found myself thinking one day. Even if it was to tell me she wasn't coming home after all. Didn't I deserve at least that much?

Having that thought was like piercing a pencil-thin hole through a dam, my anger rampaging through. Without stopping to think, I was up and wrenching Lily's things from the bedroom. I worked feverishly, possessed by an angry desire to show Lily what she'd done to me. I worked until dawn, until almost every trace of her had been erased from our room. I carried the boxes and bags next door to our so-called office and shoved them into the corner. But as I pushed the last box into place, the book piled at the top fell to the floor. I realized it was the last thing Lily had been reading, a paperback of some thriller or other. I could see where the page was folded down. She never did use a bookmark, despite my protestations. *Books are there to enjoy*, she used to tell me, *not keep as beautiful objects*. I hadn't known how serious she was until I'd caught her using the title page of *Jane Eyre* to get a new pen going, and I'd threatened to divorce her.

I slumped down to the floor, holding the book in my lap. The idea of me throwing it away, without giving her the chance to come back and finish it . . . my anger dissolved immediately, replaced by guilt.

I'm so sorry, I told her. *I won't let that happen again*.

But of course I did. Anger would assail me when I least expected it, shocking and unstoppable. In the aftermath of one particular outburst, looking for any kind of advice to stop it from happening again, I went online and began to read about other people's experiences of missing loved ones. There's a term I read about—someone's best effort to condense this cauldron of conflicting emotions into a phrase: ambiguous hope, they call it. Reading this, I took the thinnest sliver of comfort from the fact that I wasn't alone.

As I stand in our office now staring at Lily's postcard, seven years since she disappeared, I still don't have the answers to all those questions. I scan Lily's handwriting for the thousandth time in case there's something, anything, I might have missed. All I know is, I'm no closer to coming to terms with what's happened, or finding a way to move on. Hope and hopelessness still twist and wrestle inside me. Sometimes there's an immediacy to my grief and anger—a storm raging just feet above my head, or some dreadful creature, birdlike, sitting on my shoulder, talons digging into my skin. Sometimes it's all quite distant—a gathering storm out to sea, lightning on the horizon, a murmuration of birds twisting this way and that, a faint thumbprint in flux against the sky.

I turn away from the postcard, taking a deep breath as I prepare to go back downstairs into the bar. It all seems like such a lot of effort, to keep going. At the top of the stairs, I stop, thinking about that Tripadvisor review from earlier today. *Tired, worn out, not long for this world.* I might have been joking with Jeff, but I think he knows as well as I do that if something doesn't change, and soon, the next storm that arrives may not be one I can find the strength to weather.

A WEEK LATER, I'm again staring at the postcard when I hear a loud cracking sound just outside the window, and I see what I think are tiles flashing past, followed by a distinctly ominous thud down below. I hurry downstairs, knees complaining, to find that Jeff—who is always at his sprightliest at any hint of intrigue—has beaten me to it outside.

"Well, this could be interesting," he says as I approach. I'm about to ask what he means when he points to the ground at the large, brass letter "O" that has come off the wall, and then at the space where it's just fallen from. The County Arms has just been given a new name, and it's fair to say it's not quite the one I would have gone for, given the choice.

It's a good thing it's a Tuesday. Even for our standards it's quiet today.

"Shit," is my first response. And indeed my second. Jeff has his hands on his hips, carefully assessing the situation, and then he asks me where my ladder is. But of course I haven't got a ladder. Just then I hear voices, and my heart sinks. A bunch of walkers, all clad in professional-looking hiking gear, have materialized out of nowhere. I see one of them nudge his companion and reach for his phone. Before long nearly all of them are taking photos of the sign.

"This is *hilarious*," hoots a man in a particularly vivid green anorak. I make a rather pathetic attempt to implore people not to take any more pictures, but no one listens. Inexplicably, Jeff has a twinkle in his eye.

"Brian, I'm not sure you're thinking about this in the right way."

And with that he hops up onto a bucket, which he's magicked out of nowhere, and stands atop it with his arms outstretched, like some sort of mad village preacher.

"That's right," he says, "keep taking photos, and tell all your friends!"

I'm about to drag him down when he adds loudly, "But *first* you better get those aching legs of yours inside for a pie and a pint."

The walkers all look to Mr. Anorak, who seems to be their leader. He simply nods, and they all begin to file inside. Jeff flashes me a grin. I have to hand it to him, the wily old sod. We're about to have more customers in than we've had all month. I go to prime Jacques. Sophie and Oliver are nowhere to be seen, so Jeff comes behind the bar and helps me pour people pints, topping up his own glass as he goes. I can't remember the last time I was this rushed off my feet. After an hour or so some friends of the ramblers appear, and at least a dozen who tell us they've seen the photos online and have decided to come down to take a picture and have a drink.

By early evening there is a committed gang of drinkers who've bedded in, and there's a genuine magic about the place. *How odd it would be if Lily chose this moment to come through that door*, I think. We're still busy at last orders, and it takes some gentle cajoling from Sophie and Oliver (who eventually appeared, looking very confused) to get the last stragglers to leave. They do so, rather unsteadily, all of them making unrepeatable toasts to the pub.

Oliver slumps into a seat.

"That was intense," he says, like he's just been choppered out of a war zone. Sophie rushes to his aid, starting to massage his shoulders, and I quickly suggest they go home before it can go any further. I see them out of the front door, thanking them for all their efforts, and turn to see Jeff brandishing a bottle of single malt he's pinched from behind the bar.

"Nightcap?" he asks. I'm knackered, but after all his hard work, I can't find it in me to refuse.

"Go on then."

I'm thinking about all the punters we've had in today. The thought strikes me that maybe we've had some positive reviews online as a result. I fetch my laptop and when I get back it's to find that, despite it being midsummer, Jeff has taken it upon himself to light the fire in the grate, "to complete the effect."

We pull armchairs up to the fireplace and clink glasses.

"Quite the day," Jeff says.

I open my laptop and navigate to the pub's Tripadvisor page.

"Any new ones yet?" Jeff asks eagerly.

"No," I say. I'm surprised to find that I'm disappointed.

"Wait, there is one actually. Oh, but it's from someone who was in last week."

"Not good?"

"Not good."

It's a real greatest-hits affair, in fact. Normally I'd be reading this out loud to Jeff, trying to get a laugh out of him, but instead I find myself getting furious. *Who actually* are *these people*, I think, *who choose to take time out of their days to write these reviews?* I pose this question to Jeff.

"And it's not just pubs and restaurants they're reviewing, is it?" I add, before he can reply. "It's, you know, fucking coat hangers and cat food and owl sanctuaries. I mean, what did these people do before the internet? Were they all standing in the streets, bellowing away like town criers? 'Hear ye! Hear ye! Do not go to the Little Chef on the A46 Services, for their chips are served *lukewarm*.'"

Jeff laughs nervously, but by now I'm warming to my theme, feeling a bit unleashed. I feel compelled to know whether the person who's just dismissed my livelihood—styling himself as Travelchapster_4—has eviscerated any other establishments recently. I didn't actually realize that you can go to someone's profile and see their history of reviews, and sure enough I click through to find that this man has written *hundreds* of them, many complete with accompanying pictures: mediocre omelets, dusty shelves, a particularly thrilling triptych of apparently inadequate tea- and coffee-making facilities in a hotel in Crewe. I've hit my stride now, clicking randomly on other users and telling Jeff in no uncertain terms that the world has gone mad. He's not laughing at all now, but so furious and frustrated am I—years of pent-up anger let loose—that I am undeterred, right up until I look back at the screen after clicking on another reviewer at random and stop midsentence, because I've just realized the username is PinkMoonLily1970.

"You, um . . . you all right?" Jeff asks. But I barely hear him, because I'm no longer sitting here next to him. I'm hurtling back twenty-two years, to a rainy Saturday evening in west London, and a flat above a garden center called Get Forked.

12.

SHEPHERD #9

THEN

In the days after the dismaying events of Lily's party, I'd entered into such a bleak world of despair that Ed was at the end of his tether. He'd taken to playing loud pop classics from every decade at all times of the day, as a way of trying to clear the gloom that descended every time I walked into the room. After one of my particularly mopey entrances he decided to take things a step further. Packing a suitcase, he told me that he was taking an impromptu holiday to see his family on the Isle of Wight, adding in no uncertain terms that if I didn't cheer up by the time he came back, he would be either moving out or taking me to a vet and asking them to put me down "like a sad old dog."

I didn't bother to remonstrate. In Ed's absence I only got worse, slouching around in my dressing gown like a poet in the grips of a laudanum binge. Meeting Lily had been like glimpsing a dazzling kaleidoscope, and now I was back to my old gray existence. *Well*, I thought, *you know where you are with gray, don't you?*

It was a Saturday evening and I was lying on the sofa, listening to the rain hammering against the bay windows and joylessly working my way through a tube of Pringles, when our buzzer went. I wasn't expecting anyone, and I was tempted to ignore it, but when it went again—more urgently this time, five little jabs—I plodded reluctantly down the stairs and opened the door to find Lily—bedraggled by the rain, makeup running down her cheeks in long dark streaks.

"You *do* actually live above a garden center called Get Forked!" she said. "You told me on Primrose Hill," she added, a little uncertainly—possibly because I was just staring at her.

"Oh," I said at last, my astonishing vocabulary coming to the fore. I couldn't quite fathom that she was here in front of me. It was like a trick of the light, a waking dream.

"Can I, um, come in?" she asked, shivering, and this was the starting pistol I needed. I jumped to attention and ushered her in, stepping aside so that she could go up the stairs first. I had a momentary thought that she might have dashed through the rain to see me, regretting the events of the party as much as I had, but that thought vanished when I realized from her chaotic swaying as she navigated the stairs that she was, in fact, hammered.

I moved up the stairs behind her—my arms outstretched like I was spotting someone on a trampoline. Lily staggered into the living room and launched herself onto the sofa, face down, and immediately went very still. I hovered nearby, wringing my hands like a panicked royal attendant. A moment later she began to sing—well, *wail*—and then quite suddenly she was up again, half a Pringle stuck to her cheek, making a series of wild gestures which I belatedly realized were the internationally recognized sign for: "It is imperative that you explain with some haste where your toilet facilities are, as I need to be violently ill into them."

I ushered her toward the bathroom. To spare her blushes from knowing I could hear her throwing up, I turned Ed's hi-fi on to drown out any noise, forgetting that the last song he'd played in order to get me off the sofa was Hot Chocolate's "You Sexy Thing." I practically broke my thumb trying to eject the CD to find something more suitable to play, settling on some generic indie, and then I spent the next few minutes haring around trying to tidy the place up as best I could. I'd just shoved a crushed lager can into the bin when the door opened and Lily appeared. Her complexion was pale, and she was still shivering.

"I fear I'm not at my best," she said, one hand on the door frame. I was so overwhelmed by wanting to make her feel better that it clouded the practical side of my brain that knew how. Thankfully the fog cleared and I jumped into action, fetching her a glass of water, and when she asked if she might have a shower to warm up, I achieved a new land speed record as I found her a towel. I was about to leave the bathroom when I became aware that she was punching and prodding at the taps like a mad scientist. I started to help her but she suddenly abandoned her efforts and began stripping her clothes off instead, so I stumbled hastily back out of the room, cracking my elbow on the door frame as I went, throwing the door closed.

Eventually I heard the water go on, and I was able to finish tidying up, before changing into jeans and a shirt, desperately trying to flatten my wayward hair. A little while later I heard the water go off and then a good deal of clunking as Lily navigated her exit from the shower. I sat on the sofa, hands clenched, and then jumped to my feet as she poked her head around the door. She looked at me rather bashfully and said, "Don't suppose you've got some pajamas or something I could wear, Bri?"

I fetched some for her, and my dressing gown. A few minutes later she appeared from the bathroom in a cloud of steam, like a mystery guest being revealed on a game show, before curling herself up on the sofa. I still didn't know how she'd come to be here, or why, and I decided it wasn't really my place to ask. The record we were listening to had come to an end, so instead I asked if there was something she'd like me to put on.

Lily waved vaguely in the direction of her bag, and I eventually worked out that she meant for me to take her Discman from it. The headphones were knotted in a way that made me feel very stressed, but I pushed past it and took the CD out. "Nick Drake" was written on it in marker pen. I hadn't heard of him. I put the CD in and pressed play, and for the next couple of minutes we sat and listened to the satisfying acoustic guitar and the soothing voice singing strange words about a pink moon.

I waited until the song had finished before asking Lily if she wanted something to eat. She groaned and shook her head.

"Just some Marmite on toast or something?" I asked. "My grandad swore by it for settling stomachs."

Lily buried her face in her arms, but then she mumbled, "Okay then." When I presented the toast to her she eyed it apprehensively and tore a tiny bit off the crust with her teeth. When this tentative bite passed the test, she took a larger one.

"Is there anything else I can do?" I said, still hovering. "Something to drink? Or should I call someone, or . . . or . . ."

Lily waved a hand at me to stop my questions, then patted the space on the sofa next to her. "Please can you just sit down here next to me and talk about something?"

"Oh, OK, yes," I said, sitting down. "Like what?"

"Just anything. Something to keep my mind off throwing up again."

I visualized a dictionary, pages flitting past as I thought of a suitable subject. *Aardvarks. Acupuncture. Nope. On to the B's. Oh, bees?*

"Brian!"

"Sorry. My mind's gone blank."

She prodded me with her feet. "Tell me more about you and, you know, your life and everything."

I don't know if you've ever been asked to give a general account of your life "*and everything*," but it's not the most straightforward of tasks—particularly when there's the imminent threat of vomit. I didn't really know where to start. For some reason a memory came to me of performing in the Nativity play under the proud gaze of my grandparents, so I started with my tragically overlooked role as Shepherd #9, and then described the unremarkable commuter-belt town I had grown up in, my terribly normal schooldays, life at university (which I'd also had to refrain from calling "normal," though this was still the most appropriate word for it). I avoided mentioning my parents. There weren't many scenarios where I felt comfortable talking about them, and this certainly wasn't one of them. All too quickly, I had run out of things to say. Lily's eyes were closed, but every time I stopped talking or went to grab the blanket on the floor to cover her with, she prodded me with her feet so that I'd carry on. Having exhausted the early years of my life, I was getting dangerously close to having to talk about how my life was going now. I no longer felt particularly proud of my little insurance job. I thought of Daniel and felt the sudden need to invent things about myself, to assemble a personality and prospects that were worthy of Lily's attention: that I spoke twelve languages and was a grandmaster of chess, how I could recite *King Lear* verbatim and was the first person to have had a blue plaque put up while they were still alive:

BRIAN TAPLOWE
–POET, ARCHITECT, SPY, LOVER–
LIVES HERE.

At that moment Lily stirred and began to rearrange herself, almost catlike as she tried to find the most comfortable position, until eventually she curled up with her head in my lap. Instinctively, I went to stroke her hair, but thought better of it.

"But what about you?" I asked. "I've just been rambling on about myself. Same as that night I met you."

Lily smiled. "I like your rambling," she said. "Most people I know ramble about how much money they're making or where they've been skiing. You've just told me in great detail about pretending to be a shepherd."

"Not that I'd want you to typecast me. I'm very versatile."

Lily smiled again, then she opened her eyes and looked up at me, making my heart beat a little faster. I wondered if she could feel it.

"Also," she said, "I was watching you that night on Primrose Hill when we were with everyone else. I remember thinking how you were the only one not to have crowbarred in a story about yourself doing something brilliant to try to impress people."

Well, I thought, *that's because I haven't got any stories like that.*

"You're thinking about something self-effacing to say, aren't you?" Lily said, hiccupping as she did so—the most perceptive drunk I had ever met.

"Oh, I'm dreadful at thinking self-effacing thoughts," I replied. Lily nodded in approval at this joke, in the way I'd noticed she would on occasion—with the subtlety of a practiced bidder at Sotheby's going up another ten thousand.

She rallied then, and I finally managed to turn the conversation onto her. I learned that she'd grown up on the English side of the Scottish border, where her parents still lived. She had an older sister called Rebecca. She'd studied journalism at Manchester University. She had written stories as a child about a rabbit who solved crimes, often harrowing ones (a badger bludgeoned to death by a fox carrying a metal pipe, for instance). She only drank red wine between September and March, white and rosé in the remaining months (though all bets were off at weddings). She spoke passable French. She knew four swear words in German. She was allergic to cats. She thought that buying avocados was a false economy. Like an emerging butterfly escaping the chrysalis of her drunkenness, she was suddenly gripped with a kind of furious articulacy, and there was no stopping her. Within the space of an hour I had learned her thoughts on Nietzsche, origami, the Crufts dog show, artichokes, racing pigeons, the *Carry On* films of the mid-to-late 1970s, brutalist architecture, PJ Harvey, Occam's razor, and at some length, cookies. It struck me then that I'd never really known anyone who talked about things with such passion, no matter the topic, and that I'd probably never tire of throwing out subjects to see whether she had as many thoughts on the collected works of T. S. Eliot as she did on tiramisu.

As much as I was reveling in all of this, I couldn't deny that there was an elephant in the room—one wearing a shirt undone to its navel—but before I could figure out a way of bringing up Daniel and what had happened at the party, I realized that Lily had fallen asleep. There was no way I could extricate myself without waking her up, and so I stayed where I was, awake, wondering what this all meant, and what the dawn would bring.

IN FACT, THE dawn brought a lorry that beeped and revved outside at quarter past six, and Lily woke with a start. I'd managed to sleep for a little bit, still sitting upright, like a piece of performance art. I could sense Lily was extremely confused and I moved to give her the information she needed to rectify this as quickly as possible.

"I'm Brian Taplowe and you're at my flat in Shepherd's Bush."

She looked at me and blinked.

"And you're Lily . . . sorry, I don't know your last name."

"It's McCallister," Lily said, sitting up. "And I feel like there's a cactus in my head and that I'll never know happiness again."

I took a moment to digest this information.

"I'll put the kettle on."

Lily drank her tea with both hands clasped around the mug, still squinting a little at the early morning light spilling into the room. "I'm sorry I turned up at your house out of the blue and made you listen to Nick Drake and slept on you," she said.

"All part of the service," I replied, quickly regretting it. I removed the CD from Ed's hi-fi and handed it to her. "I realize I didn't actually ask you what you'd been up to last night before you . . . dropped by."

Lily watched the steam curling up from her mug. "Just another night out with people I'm starting to realize aren't very good for me."

The surge of happiness I felt at how "people" might well include Daniel was quickly tempered by how sad Lily looked. I really wished I had something wise to say to her to make her feel better. Either that or some chocolate Hobnobs ("the greatest of all cookies by any sensible person's criteria").

"Thank you for being such a lifesaver last night," Lily said, putting her mug down. "I promise I won't just show up unannounced like that again."

She looked at me for a moment, then dropped her gaze, seeming a little embarrassed. I suspect she thought I was letting my silence speak volumes—that I hoped she would live up to that promise. In fact, I was digging deep, clutching at my thin reserves of courage.

The idea of never seeing Lily McCallister again, in whatever capacity, was completely unacceptable. The future was stretching out in front of me in two distinct paths, one where she was in my life, and one where she wasn't. And when I thought of it like that, it was a very simple choice. Up until that moment, I didn't think I had it in me to simply tell someone how I felt about them, to lay myself bare, when I knew how painful rejection could be. But in that moment, in the milky dawn above a garden center, I would learn for the first time that when you fall in love with someone, it's like finding something you didn't know you'd lost—and once you've grabbed hold of it you'll do anything to keep it safe.

I cleared my throat.

"I wonder if perhaps next time you might show up . . . announced?"

13.

A SECRET

NOW

In as calm a voice as I can muster, I explain to Jeff that "Pink Moon" by Nick Drake is Lily's favorite song, and that 1970 is the year of her birth. I'm never usually one for coincidences, I'm really not, and yet . . . PinkMoonLily1970? I click through to the user's profile, and my heart begins to beat even faster. All the places they've reviewed are in the UK. The Ashmolean Museum, Windermere, Broadway Tower. From what I can see, the reviews all seem to be positive. Five stars for each, with simple headers such as "Wonderful!" and "Highly Recommended." Each review is short and to the point, only a couple of sentences in each. *What a lovely place this is*, they write of the Bishop's Palace and Gardens in Wells. *A Treasure Trove* is how they describe Cambridge's Fitzwilliam Museum. They don't have a profile photograph. Nor any contact details. But I feel another shock of excitement when I sort the reviews by date and find that the first one they ever posted was six months after the day

Lily left. Not only that, but it's for something called a "wellness retreat" somewhere in North Yorkshire, and simply reads: "Came here for a few days earlier this year. Wonderfully restorative. A great escape." Was that where she went? "A great escape"—should I read something into that?

Jeff and I glance at each other. He's looking at me intently, and there's concern in his eyes. I feel a pain in the pit of my stomach at the thought he's about to tell me to be realistic. *I don't want to be realistic*, I think. *I want to hope.*

"So," Jeff says, clearing his throat. "What do you reckon? Do you think it's her?"

I'm about to reply, but as I click back onto PinkMoon-Lily1970's profile, I start. A new post has appeared, written just moments ago. It's of a B and B in Cumbria, written in glowing tones, explaining that it's the perfect place to "begin this little adventure." I'm not sure what that means, but all I know is I can see her—*really* see her—settling down and typing this, now—right this second!—perhaps in the corner of some characterful little pub, a brandy (her own choice of nightcap) half drunk.

"I think it could be her, yes," I say, my voice coming out as a whisper.

We're quiet for a moment, though the blood is pounding around my ears and I'm finding it almost impossible to sit still. Jeff takes a sip of whisky. Then he clears his throat, and looking straight ahead at the fire, he says, "I realize that we've still never really talked, you know—properly—about what you think happened."

"What do you mean?"

Jeff tilts his glass around, ice clinking.

"Seven years is a long time," he says.

As much as I really don't want to hear what he's driving at, it's still frustrating to hear him talk obliquely like this. Every considered sip of his whisky feels like a dent in my hope that this is Lily, that I might be able to find her.

"Look," I say, "if you want to speak your mind, then go for it. We've known each other long enough, haven't we?"

Jeff nods. "We have, yes. But . . . sometimes I try and, you know, ask you about it all, and sometimes I get the impression that there's things you wish you could tell me."

I'm genuinely confused by this, and I'm becoming distracted by wanting to look through more of these reviews. So I'm even more thrown when Jeff says, "We've never spoken about the night you ended up in that police cell, for example."

I turn and look at him. "What about it?"

Jeff clears his throat again and drinks from his glass, though there's barely anything left. "You were obviously very upset. And worried."

"Right. Your point being?"

Jeff seems to realize that we're on difficult ground, because he clams up, but not before he's mumbled something about how I'd got very upset about Lily's watch.

I really don't want to relive the shame of that night, and whatever Jeff thinks he's getting at isn't enough to temper the excitement that's building inside me with every word I read of these reviews. I'm desperate to find a turn of phrase that tells me it's her—*my* Lily.

Jeff grabs the whisky bottle then, topping up his glass. He's still looking at me with that same concern on his face, fidgeting now too.

"What now?" I ask.

Jeff goes to answer, then stops. Finally, he says, "Who's going to hold the fort for you then?"

I frown at him. "What do you mean?"

"Well," Jeff says, tilting his head at my screen. "If that's her, then you've obviously got to try and track her down."

It takes a while for Jeff's words to sink in.

"I'm not sure I . . . I mean . . ."

Jeff holds my gaze, looking oddly defiant. "If you think it's her," he says, "then why aren't you packing a bag as we speak?"

"What?"

"What do you mean, 'what'?"

"Well, I . . ."

Jeff widens his eyes at me.

"What are you trying to say?" I ask, and Jeff reaches over and grabs me by the arm.

"Brian," he says, his voice almost fatherly now. "Don't you think it's time you at least tried to accept—to come to terms with the fact that Lily . . . that the most likely outcome is that she's . . ."

"Don't say it," I say. "Just, don't."

The fire crackles and spits.

"I just can't keep seeing you like this, mate," Jeff says quietly. "It's been seven years." It's this that hurts the most. Jeff has never talked to me about how long it's been before. I feel defiance rising within me.

"Well, that doesn't matter," I say. "Because you're right. I should be packing a bag. I'm going to go and find her."

Jeff holds my gaze, then he takes his hand from my arm. "OK," he says. "You do that. But will you promise me one thing?"

After a moment, I nod.

"If you find this person, and it isn't Lily, you'll at least try to . . . to move on."

I can't answer him at first. There's part of me that wishes he weren't here today to pour cold water on my hope. But it's only just dawned on me how much I've taken him for granted these last few years. He's been the one constant companion in my life. He's a good man, and I know I get frustrated with his stories every now and then, but all he's ever tried to do is look out for me.

It takes me a while to try to form the words to thank him for this, and by the time I do, I look across to see that his head is lolling. I carefully prize the whisky glass from his hand and gently shake him awake. He blinks at me, looking a bit lost.

"Probably time to head off," he says, when he's worked out where he is.

We both get to our feet.

"You're welcome to kip here," I say. "All the rooms are free. Obviously." There's a second when Jeff looks like he might accept my offer, but then he says, "Nah, you're all right. Better get back."

"Oh. OK. Long as you're sure. Do you want a torch?"

"No need," he says. He waves his hand vaguely in the air. "The moon shall be my guide . . ." After quite the balletic performance finding the arms of his coat, he pauses by the front door.

"What do you think you're going to do then?" he says.

I run a hand through my hair. "I'm not sure."

"But you'll think about what I've said?"

After a moment, I nod. Jeff pats me on the chest.

"Good. Oh, and don't worry about the sign business. I've got a ladder at mine. I'll sort it all out. No trouble."

I feel suddenly overwhelmed with gratitude, and I move to give him a hug. But I'm a moment too late and he's already turning to go. I swerve at the last second and pretend I'm just reaching to open the door for him.

Jeff doffs his flat cap, ears springing forth.

"Until the next time, dear boy."

14.

THE LONELINESS OF THE PINT UNDRUNK

Something's wrong.

It's 1:05 p.m. the next day, and Jeff's pint of Winchester Gold is sitting untouched on the bar. I think back to our conversation last night. Did he mention he might be late, or that he had other plans? I don't think so. I woke up this morning feeling like last night might have been a dream. As soon as I opened my laptop again, though, all the hope—the pain of it—came flooding back. The idea of Jeff looking at me with even a trace of skepticism had me pouring his pint and retreating. But when it got to five past and I hadn't heard him arrive, I was instantly concerned.

Just then Sophie arrives and I ask her to look after the place for a while.

"Everything OK?" she yawns.

I grab my car keys and clutch them tight. "I hope so."

By the third time I ring Jeff's doorbell, I'm starting to panic. I make my way around to the back of the house. The curtains are all drawn, so there's no way of seeing in. I'm about to knock on the back door when out of the corner of my eye I spot something that makes me stop. It's a ladder, leaning at an odd angle against the side of a shed. I make my way toward it through the long grass and the overgrown bushes. There's a fat little rabbit busily demolishing grass, seemingly unbothered by my arrival. But I'm not the only one there. Because sitting against the side of the shed—hands in his lap, head slumped forward like a regretful schoolboy waiting to see the head teacher—is Jeff. *Please be asleep*, I think. But as I take a few steps closer, I see that atop one of Jeff's knees is a snail, gazing out at the garden like an explorer surveying the view from a mountaintop. I reach to feel for Jeff's pulse. There is none. His skin is cold. I gently remove the snail.

The weight of the realization that I will never again hear Jeff tell me one of his stories makes me sink to my knees. I need to call the emergency services, but my mobile has conked out. I'm reluctant to leave Jeff on his own, but I drag myself back through the bushes and find that when I try his back door it's open.

The emergency operator tells me the police and ambulance should be with me within twenty minutes. After I've put the phone down, I realize I have absolutely no idea if there's anyone else I should call. Jeff never talked about his family, and the thought that he didn't have any makes me want to get back to his side. As silly as it sounds, I can't bear the idea of him being uncomfortable, so I go to find a blanket. As I pass what looks like a study, my eye is drawn to a framed photo on the desk. The scene is of someone standing at the top of a mountain. They're dressed up in a badger costume.

The top of the mountain turns out to be the tip of the iceberg. There are framed photos and cuttings covering the walls: Jeff mock-sparring with a boxer I vaguely recognize who's wearing a title belt. Another shows him in rugby gear being carried on his teammates' shoulders, holding a trophy aloft. And there he is with the actual Mick Jagger. At first, I have no idea what to do with myself. I want to stay here and explore, but I need to get back to Jeff. I go back outside and place the blanket over his knees.

"There you go."

There's so much more I want to say. Mainly I want to tell him I'm sorry for every time I rolled my eyes at one of his stories. But just then I hear a car pull up, and shortly after there's a crackle of police radio. I'll have to wait for another day.

15.

LAST ORDERS

A lot's changed in the last week. I'm still struggling to process Jeff's death. It's not just that he's been telling the truth all along about these stories, either. I've been replaying our conversation by the fire over and over in my head. What was he trying to tell me about the night I ended up in the police cell? What had I said to him that night? And then there was the moment he told me to think about what he'd said—about finding a way to move on. It's with a painful sense of regret that I realize I'll never be able to thank him for caring about me enough to tell me something he knew I needed to hear, even if he hurt me in the process. How can I ignore that now?

I don't know if I can honestly say that moving on is something I'm capable of. But I've got to do *something*. Because what's the alternative? Sitting here alone for another seven years, without even Jeff's company, staring at that front door? It's not really a life, is it? The planet keeps on turning, and the fact it's taken the death of my friend to remember that means that I have no choice now but to find a way forward in the time I've got left.

Two days ago, PinkMoonLily1970 posted a new review, from

York. It ended with the phrase "Not long before I leave this beautiful city."

I don't know if it's her—my Lily. My mind changes by the hour. But I know I need to find an ending, no matter how painful it may be.

Sophie and Oliver look faintly terrified when I tell them I'm putting them in charge.

"But . . . us?" Oliver says, possessing more self-awareness than I'd given him credit for.

"We're not ready for this, are we?" Sophie adds, eyes wide.

"Of course you are," I reply.

With my hands behind my back, I don't think they can see I've got my fingers crossed.

I TAKE ONE final look at the room upstairs. I half considered taking the postcard, perhaps even Lily's watch too. But the thought of losing either of them gave me enough pause to reject the idea.

The other decision I've been faced with is whether to tell Lily's family about what I've discovered, and what I'm about to do. In the end, I decided not to call her parents, worried the sound of my voice may shatter any peace they've found, but I've tried ringing Rebecca a few times. She didn't pick up, so I left her a message asking her to get in touch. I'm not relishing the idea of that conversation, but I wouldn't feel right about keeping this to myself.

I hear a van pull up outside and make my way downstairs, dragging my suitcase behind me. A few days ago I called someone about fixing our sign, but as I was talking to Trevor (of

Trev's Quality Signs), I realized the money would actually be much better spent elsewhere.

As Trevor shows me his handiwork downstairs today, I have to hand it to him. It's perfect. And it's right on time—the last tap of his hammer sounding at 12:55. We both stand back and admire his efforts. The plaque is affixed to the beam above Jeff's usual seat. The engraving reads:

HERE DRANK JEFF MACKINTOSH.
SCHOLAR, RACONTEUR,
ADVENTURER, FRIEND.

Trevor folds his arms. "He sounds like he was good value."

"Priceless," I say. Thankfully, Trevor gets the hint that I need a moment and swiftly takes his leave. At 12:58, I draw back the Winchester Gold pump—three smooth pulls—and place the foaming pint on the beer mat by Jeff's seat, watching the liquid swirl and settle.

At one p.m., I grasp my suitcase by the handle. With one final look around, I pull the door open and step out into the milky afternoon light, and the unknown.

PART TWO

16.

HOT POTATOES

THEN

It had been a week since I'd asked Lily if she would consider turning up "announced." Her response—a smile that slowly grew, and a calm reply of "OK then"—became a piece of archive footage I'd replay in my mind everywhere I went. As much as I'd enjoyed the strange romance of her scouring her address into my skin on Primrose Hill, I was grateful for the more traditional exchange of phone numbers. She wrote hers on a Post-it note that I stuck on the wall by my bed, admiring every flick of her pen: the loopy zeroes, the dynamic sevens, the frankly breathtaking fours . . . it was probably a good thing Ed had taken an extended holiday, as I suspect he would have killed me for yet another violent gear change in my emotions.

Lily and I spoke on the phone a few days later, and I offered to make dinner for her that weekend. I had practiced so hard at saying this as suavely as possible that I'd rather overlooked the fact I didn't actually know how to cook. The only recipe book I possessed was one given to me by my grandmother to take to university. A firmly fifties tome, it consisted of recipes primarily in the category of beige, the implication being that cooking something colorful was at best racy and at worst foreign. The one exception was a restrained potatoes dauphinoise, which I decided I'd cook with roast chicken, because how hard could that be?

I was excited about Lily's coming, of course, but something had been nagging away at me. For all Lily's mocking of Daniel, the cold hard facts of it were that she had kissed *him* at her party. There was no doubting that he was smooth and confident and charismatic, not qualities I was blessed with, so I decided that in lieu of this I could at least look the part.

And so I found myself standing on Bond Street, plucking up the courage to go in and buy an expensive suit. This would mean going into my savings, most of which had come from Mum and Dad. I felt like if I was to even touch what they'd left me, I'd need a good reason, and after some debate I'd decided that this occasion justified it. I endured the skeptical eye of the salesman and the unflinching hands of the tailor, and came out with a brand-new suit, one befitting the man I was going to pretend to be.

Things were going relatively well in the kitchen when Lily rang the buzzer. I was holding two saucepans at the time, but so excited was I at her arrival that I carried them downstairs with me, struggling to open the door and then standing with both pans poised, as if I'd been woken by a burglar in the night and had grabbed the closest weapons to hand.

"It's Edward Saucepanhands," Lily said, and I laughed very hard at this despite having no idea what she meant. We hugged, my saucepans clashing behind her back. She looked incredibly stylish, in a way that I still don't have the sartorial vocabulary with which to explain. What I can tell you is that she looked beautiful in a way that rendered me briefly immobile, until at last I snapped out of it and clanged my way back upstairs, beckoning her to follow.

When Ed's mother had visited the flat a few months earlier she'd described the place as "a little dingy." Those words had stuck with me, so I'd made sure all the lights were on and undimmed.

"Wow, it's . . . bright in here," Lily said, sitting down on the sofa.

"Thanks!" I replied.

I had spent all day carefully chopping vegetables with the precision of a scientist, but had left an auxiliary carrot so that I could have something to casually slice while we talked. Not that this stopped me from nearly chopping off my fingers several times, given how nervous I was.

I kneed the oven door closed—the potatoes and chicken now in to roast—and opened a bottle of white wine. We clinked glasses—a little too enthusiastically on my part, the sound ringing out.

"I feel like I should apologize again," Lily said. "For being such a catastrophe when I came here last time."

"Please don't," I said. "We've all been there, haven't we?"

Lily raised her eyebrows. "Even you?"

I was oddly stung by this, the idea that I would never have been so out of control because I was clearly so buttoned up. "Even me."

"I feel like it's only fair if you tell me of your worst exploits then."

She shifted in her seat so that our knees were touching, and I began to tell her the story of a school trip to Brussels and how

I had drunk three strong Belgian beers and fallen asleep against a statue in the town square.

This elicited a "*Stop it!*" from Lily, which pleased me immeasurably.

We got through the bottle of wine rather quickly, moving on to another, and I started to relax into the conversation.

"Here's a question for you," Lily said.

"Go on."

"Talk to me about the suit."

"That's not strictly a question."

"Gosh, sorry," Lily said, faux apologetic. "Will you do me the greatest of honors and tell me about this suit you're wearing?"

I was suddenly aware of how fiercely straight the creases on my trouser legs were, and the perfect knot of my tie.

"Well, you know—I just thought . . . I wanted to . . . step things up a notch . . . look-wise."

"I see," Lily said. "And you're wearing it on a Saturday. For our date. In your house."

It was the way she laid out the facts so calmly that made me see how ridiculous my choice had been.

"Well," I said, grasping for a way to make this seem normal. "Hang on, wait—I seem to remember . . . people . . . at your party dressed up all smartly."

Lily took a sip of wine. There was a look on her face as if she'd just had something she'd been wondering about confirmed. "Yes, well, I expect *people* had just come straight from the office."

"Ah, yes, well, that's it!" I said, far too eagerly. "Yep, me too, burning the bloody midnight oil as per bloody usual. I mean the candle, the . . . both ends of the candle and . . . on to the oil later, I expect."

Lily let this catastrophic word salad fall around our feet. It was clear that I had made a fatal error in trying to compete with Daniel like this, and I spent the next few minutes trying to loosen my tie in tiny increments, like one of those street magicians doing a pickpocket routine but on himself.

We didn't have a dining table, so I'd decided to set our places at the coffee table by the sofa. I'd bought new napkins, however, which I folded and placed down with great ceremony, which Lily must have thought was for comic effect because it really made her laugh.

The conversation had moved on from clothes, but I'd had my confidence knocked. I must have been deep in thought, worrying about how I could rectify things, when I realized that Lily was looking at me expectantly.

"Sorry, what did you say?"

"I was asking about that photo on the mantelpiece."

The photo was of Grandma and Grandad dropping me off at university. I'm standing in between them, their old brown Ford Escort behind us, smiling like the intensely shy person I was, my fringe raked down over my eyes like a shield. Grandma and Grandad are looking at me proudly, but with a hint of melancholy in their eyes too, because all of us are aware that Mum and Dad should be there.

"Are they your grandparents?" Lily asked.

I nodded.

"What was it like—if you don't mind me asking—being brought up by them?"

I clutched the stem of my wineglass between thumb and forefinger. "Just sort of normal, I suppose. I didn't really know any different. It was only when I got a bit older that I noticed they were a generation older than my friends' parents. They were quite old-fashioned as it was, and they'd had Mum when they were older, so knowing what to do with me when I was a teenager . . . Yeah, that was tricky."

"How do you mean?"

"Well, there was the time they did all this research and bought me what they thought was an Atari 7800, but they'd only got a controller rather than the thing itself—and I couldn't bring myself to tell them, so I left it in the box, but then they couldn't understand why I wasn't using it . . ."

"Oh, my heart!" Lily said.

"Yeah. I know."

"And are they still around?"

"Grandma passed away a few years ago. Grandad's in a nursing home, but he's pretty frail these days. And then Dad's parents are this ever-so-slightly-dodgy couple who live in the Costa del Sol. I've only met them once."

"And did you ever really know your parents?" Lily asked. "Or were you too young?" She reached over and touched my arm. "Tell me to shut up, by the way, I won't be offended."

"No, it's OK," I said. "I don't mind talking about it. I just feel a bit guilty when people are sympathetic. I was too young to remember much about Mum and Dad, so it wasn't like I really consciously experienced losing them. It's a bit hard to explain."

"Of course," Lily said.

I scratched at my chin. "I've only got one real memory of them. On holiday. It wasn't long before they died. I can remember Dad holding me in the sea, and Mum waving from the beach, and I can smell the sun cream on Dad's shoulders." I found it hard to look at Lily then, but I kept going. "I read somewhere that every time you replay a memory, it's distorted—

because you're actually remembering the last time you thought about it . . . so sometimes I worry that it's not real."

Lily held my hand. "I don't think you should worry about that," she said. "Who cares if a detail or two is skewed. How it makes you feel isn't any less real, is it?" I hadn't really thought about it like that before, and very unexpectedly, I found that I was in danger of welling up. Lily seemed a little unsure as to whether I wanted to carry on talking or not, and I felt very keenly that I should change the subject to lift the atmosphere.

"Just like I don't always talk about natural disasters on dates," I said, "I also only very rarely bring up my dead parents . . ."

Thankfully, Lily laughed, and the conversation moved on. But not long enough that when I made her promise not to tell anyone that I'd never read a Dickens novel, and she said, "Mum's the word," it didn't make her blush furiously.

"Oh my god, Brian, I didn't think . . ."

I hadn't seen her lose her composure like this before, and I found it very endearing. "Honestly, don't worry about it," I said. But Lily's guilt was not to be that easily assuaged, and the next thing I knew, she had reached for a napkin and put it over her head so that it covered her face.

"Please," I said, laughing now, "there's no need for the napkin of shame."

"There's every need for the napkin of shame!"

At first she resisted my attempts to pull it away, until eventually she let me take it from her. A strand of her hair had fallen in front of her face, and she blew it away. She still couldn't seem to meet my eye. I was aware that our dinner was very nearly ready, but I didn't want to get up and have her think I was upset.

"OK, listen," I said, and this time I placed the napkin over my own head. "Far be it from me to use this as an opportunity to tell you something shameful and get away with it . . ."

"Go on . . . ," I heard Lily say.

"The suit. I only really bought it because, well, I saw certain other people wearing very smart ones at your party, and I felt like it might be something you'd think made me seem more sophisticated and put together than I actually am. Which I only realize now is ridiculous." Lily was silent, and so I barreled on—mainly because the napkin of shame was really helping me say things I might not normally have been able to. "And I hope that hasn't put you off too much, because I feel really very lucky that you've agreed to spend an evening here with me, rather than taking up one of the infinitely more exciting offers you've no doubt had."

I felt Lily moving closer toward me. When she spoke her face must have been right next to mine.

"Brian," she said, "I am not here out of some sort of obligation. I didn't 'agree' to come and spend this evening with you. I very much wanted to. I happen to have spent all this week thinking about it in fact. So there."

Slowly, she removed the napkin from my face and dropped it beside her. In that moment, the feeling of wanting to kiss her banished every other thought in my head. Every thought, that was, apart from the one that told me I was about to burn the house down. Our lips were only inches apart when I said, "I'm really sorry, but I'm a bit worried the potatoes are burning."

Lily put her hand to the side of my face and looked me in the eye. "I've got two lessons for you, Brian."

"OK?"

"The first is that there's a very real difference between making an effort for someone and changing who you are for them."

Our lips were practically touching now.

"And the second?"

"Sometimes in life, you just have to let the potatoes burn."

LATER, THE GREATEST kiss I'd ever had by far eclipsing any worries about my blackened oven, we sat on the living room floor opposite each other, eating pizzas on our laps. I'd abandoned any attempts to salvage the burned potatoes and had called for a takeaway while Lily dimmed the lights, lit candles, and put on one of Ed's jazz records—deftly transforming the previous ambience of a hospital waiting room into an underground Parisian jazz bar, the lingering smoke only adding to the effect. This would become a common theme as our relationship progressed, Lily's ability to transform the prosaic into the elegant, though happily this only occasionally involved nearly burning the house down.

Lily reached for the bottle of wine on the coffee table and swigged straight from it like some sort of beautiful pirate.

"Please can I ask you something that'll probably annoy you?" I said.

"Such a tempting offer. Go on then . . ."

"Talk to me about you and Daniel."

I had been weighing up whether to go down this route. Part of me thought I should just ignore the whole thing, not break the spell of the evening. But I suppose what had happened at her party was nagging at me too much, and we'd been dancing around it without saying his name.

Lily chewed her pizza. "Must we?"

I shrugged. "I'm just curious."

"Well," Lily said, "Daniel is who I am supposed to end up

with." She took another swig of wine, as if to fortify herself for what she was about to say next. "The problem with me is that there are certain people in my life who are very keen that I follow the path they think is right for me, and even though they have my best interests at heart, there is a difference between what would make me happy and what would make me part of some kind of club I have no wish to be a member of. But when you've spent your life desperately craving someone's approval, the temptation's always there to do what you know would make *them* happy, even if it goes against your instincts."

I chomped away thoughtfully, but this was my way of pretending I'd fully grasped what she was talking about. So when Lily asked me what I thought, I just swallowed, clapped the flour from my hands, and said, "I'm not sure about a lot in this world, but I do know this."

"What's that?"

I realized with a sharp jolt that what I'd been about to say was the unfiltered thought that had been bouncing around my brain for the last half an hour, one that very probably should stay there.

"Come on, what were you going to say?" Lily asked, wine bottle poised midair.

I felt my cheeks beginning to glow. Was I really going to say this? I thought on balance that I probably would. And I wasn't even going to get a napkin first.

"I was just going to say that I think you're rather lovely, that's all."

17.

YORK

YORK Minster! what a monument is this
Out of one meek and simple life uprist!
Within these walls what skeptic but needs kiss
Thy garment's hem, O Christ!
—ROBERT LEIGHTON, 1842

Imagine my shock and disappointment when I traveled so far to see this abomination, which looks like it had been built by a drunk Stevie Wonder!
—ONLINE REVIEW, YORK MINSTER, 2019

NOW

Nearly a quarter of a century later, as I stand on this bridge in York looking down at the river Ouse, the memory of that night is still fresh enough to make my cheeks burn. Such talk is the preserve of the young, I suppose. While my grandfather undoubtedly loved my grandmother, I can only recall him telling her that once, and it was followed by the sentence:

"But if you stack the dishwasher like that again I'm calling the police."

I rest my hands on the rough stone of the bridge, watching the gray water flowing underneath, trying to regulate my breathing. I'm still a little scarred from the train journey up here. It turns out it's half-term, so the train was packed with young kids eagerly mainlining Peppa Pig and Percy Pigs and any other anthropomorphic porcine stimulants they could get their hands on. Most of their weary parents all seemed to be reading the same book—something called *And Breathe . . .* —which I gather from the aggressive posters advertising it absolutely everywhere is some sort of self-help book.

I initially lucked out with a table seat to myself, but it was quickly filled by a young Spanish couple. The boy sported the unfortunate haircut of an eighties prog-rock drummer, but this didn't deter his girlfriend, who could not have seemed more besotted with him. I was quite fascinated by the entirely unselfconscious way they behaved around one another, as if nobody else was there. At one point they began talking with such intensity that I thought he was about to propose—though my Spanish is nonexistent, so it could well have been about the railway replacement bus service.

I would die for you, my darling.

And I you. But first we must change at Didcot Parkway.

At no point did they seem to be bothered by or even aware of the children having meltdowns all around us, and I felt the urge to lean forward and tell them that they must enjoy being young and in love, to appreciate just how free they were now before life got in the way. Thankfully I restrained myself.

The chaos of York station was enough to leave me rooted to the spot, immobile amidst the families and commuters all swerving around me. Eventually I managed to force myself to move, and I found a certain comfort in standing on this bridge, watching the water flowing underneath it. But when I start to make my way into the city, confronted by the noise and bustle of it all, it's a complete sensory overload. I've barely left the confines of the pub for the last half decade, and now I'm suddenly hundreds of miles away from home, gazing up at the York Minster, the imposing Gothic cathedral, which towers above me. It's a disconcerting feeling, as if I've just time-traveled, and I have to sit down on a bench for a moment.

I reach into my pocket and pull out the photo of Lily that I've brought with me. The picture was taken by Ed when he came to visit us at the pub, the summer Lily left. Always the trendy one, Ed had wanted to try out his new (but retro) Polaroid camera, and the resulting photo of Lily shows her with Ed's coat around her shoulders, a glass of rosé in one hand, saluting the camera with the other. I've found it hard enough to look at this photo since she disappeared—she looks so playful and happy—but the idea of actually presenting it to strangers, asking them if they've seen her . . . do I really have it in me to do that? Suddenly the idea seems terrifying.

But as the cathedral bell chimes, I think of Jeff, standing by the door, the imploring look in his eye. I take some deep breaths and feel a bit better. I put Lily's photo in my jacket pocket and get to my feet. I'm not going to turn back when I've barely started this, no matter how tempting it is. So, PinkMoonLily1970, where are you?

MY FIRST PORT of call is the pub she's just been staying in, which she described in her review enthusiastically, albeit with a caveat that it was "a bit cheap and cheerful." Like all the best pubs, the Three Horseshoes seems to *reveal* itself—popping up from its hidden spot down a side street as if by magic, exclusively for the weary traveler. (I have a very specific memory of explaining to Lily the importance of "the reveal" when it came to pubs on an early night out, and seeing her make the mental calculation in real time that this was the sort of thing she was going to have to accept in me, like some bizarre sexual predilection, or having an enormous big toe.) In a more comforting example of the feeling that I've time-traveled, the beams and the glinting sign and the old oak door make it feel like there might be a couple of friars within supping ale from pewter tankards, but instead I'm hit by a blast of loud techno, which I notice is being piped in through speakers that are—sacrilegiously—nailed to the old beams. There are faux blackboards pinned up with things like "Free beer tomorrow" written on them. PinkMoonLily1970's caveat now seems like something of an understatement.

As I approach the young man behind the bar, he looks at me suspiciously, like I might be from Health & Safety. He doesn't seem much happier when I announce rather stiffly that I want to check in.

As he's leading me up to my room, I try to think of how I might engage him in some casual conversation that will make what I actually need to ask him seem less out of the blue. On the train I ran through the sorts of questions I might ask: *I don't suppose you remember a "Lily" staying here recently? My friend Lily recommended this place. Said she'd just been staying here?*

I was quite pleased with them then. But it's all very well when it's in your head. To ask these questions now, and produce the photo too, seems like the act of someone whose intentions you'd immediately question. All of this is perhaps why I end up waiting in strained silence while the man gives me the unnecessary tour of the room, and then out of nowhere, because I know I'm losing my nerve, I blurt out: "Was Lily—I mean, I had, have, a friend, Lily, who was staying here. Do you remember her?"

He looks confused, as well he might, and then a little suspicious. "I only work the odd shift," he says with a shrug.

"Right," I say with a nervous laugh. I try to compensate by casually dropping down onto my bed, though it's a bit lower than I thought and hard enough to leave me a little winded. Then I go to pull Lily's photo out of my coat pocket, but it's not there. After some mad scrabbling I finally locate it in my trouser pocket, but by this point the man is telling me that breakfast is served between seven and nine and then, after looking me up and down a couple of times, as if working out if he's going to have to give a witness statement at a later date, he leaves. *Well*, I think, *that went about as badly as it could have done.*

I imagine the man's already downstairs telling everyone in the bar about the weirdo up in room four, and I briefly have my head in my hands. I'm snapped out of this when my stomach gives a complaining rumble, and without thinking I eat a bag of nuts from the minibar, forgetting that it'll set me back a small fortune. I really do need to be more careful when it comes to what I'm spending. Most of my money has gone into the pub over the last few years, trying to keep it going, but I always kept a small nest egg in reserve separately. In my head, I suppose this was for when Lily came back—perhaps we'd go away together or something. But I've realized I've just been clinging on to it, like my hope that she'll return, and that it's far better that I use it trying to find her.

I look over to the windowsill. A spider is making its way along it but stops at the sound of a siren outside, as if its long life on the run has finally come to an end.

Once I've had a shower and put on some fresh clothes, I open my ancient old laptop and start to go through all the places PinkMoonLily1970 has reviewed in York, trying to work out which one to visit next. As much as my first attempt to ask after her was fairly disastrous, I'm glad that I've at least got it out of the way. I'll have plenty more opportunities, and it's not as if it can go any worse.

It's funny, because even as I'm having that thought, I realize I'm almost certainly going to regret it. It's like the sitcom character saying, "For the last time, Enid, you'll never get me on that old bike!" Cut to . . .

18.

THE HORROR

My first port of call is a café near the Shambles, an outrageously quaint little street with beamed houses leaning toward each other from either side. I gather from the sight of lots of wand-wielding teenagers dressed in black robes taking photos that this is where they filmed some of *Harry Potter*. I hear an American voice asking what *Shambles* actually means, before a local's gruff reply of "Slaughterhouse," which shuts the conversation down rather quickly.

My conversations with the staff in the café don't go much better than in the pub. I don't help my cause by the way I'm unable to look anyone in the eye as I show them Lily's photo and mention the Tripadvisor review. The staff are more distracted than perturbed, as it's incredibly busy, so at least when they tell me they can't help, it comes with apologetic smiles rather than suspicious looks.

As I move on to a tourist information center, and then another pub, I find that the more people I speak to, the less nervous and self-conscious I become. So far, at least, everyone's responses have been polite, if occasionally wary, and someone in an antiques shop on the high street even asks me for my number so that they can call me if they recognize "the lady in the photo." This gives me a spring in my step as I approach the one place on the list that stuck out as something of an anomaly.

York Dungeon is one of those interactive experiences, the sort of place featuring grotesquely made-up actors who tell you about the history of the place and make fun of the audience while they do so. PinkMoonLily1970's review simply said "A bit of fun!" but a fair number of the other reviews I scanned through read a little like the testimonies of kidnap victims.

The man I speak to on the front desk is instantly aggressive when I attempt to ask him about Lily, particularly when I really push things by asking if perhaps he could have a look on his booking system for her—which I know is a mistake as soon as the words come out of my mouth. In the end our discussion gets so awkward that I'm forced to buy a ticket for the experience just to calm the situation down. I spend the next hour gritting my teeth at the back of the rooms we're led through by the innuendo-spouting actors. I honestly can't imagine this is something Lily would have enjoyed, but then a memory comes to me of a play we saw, not long into our relationship. Up until that point in my life, my rare forays to the theater had very much been West End, but this was *experimental* theater, which took place in a vast hangar in the Docklands. The performance involved three people dressed in black doing an awful lot of wailing and writhing and, at one point, pretending to be sick. Glancing at the program, I gathered that the piece was about the Industrial Revolution. I did my best to take the whole thing seriously, for the sake of Lily, but then at one point she grabbed my hand, and I started violently. I thought it was because she'd been desperately moved by the interpretation, but it soon became clear that she was in the grips of hysterical laughter, and that set me off too. This has always stuck in my mind as the moment when I realized how much I was falling for her. I'd always imagined that love was about stolen kisses under the stars, but that night I learned that sometimes it's about watching an Oxbridge-educated banker's son miming the invention of the internal-combustion engine with his willy.

As much as this was a joyful experience at the time, in later years we both avoided anything similar, particularly if it involved audience participation. Yet PinkMoonLily1970 called York Dungeon "fun." I feel the needle swinging back toward the likelihood that this person is a stranger. I'm so dismayed by the thought that I actually swear out loud. Even though it's under my breath, it's brought me to the attention of one of the actors playing a judge, who decides to make me a part of the performance, asking "the bailiff" to come out and "restrain me." And despite the actor playing the bailiff barely putting his hands on my arms, I'm in such a heightened state of anxiety that we end up having something of a genuine struggle.

I very rarely get into arguments, particularly ones that happen in the fourteenth century, and the mocking—if nervy—laughter of the audience as I finally break free and scurry away to the exit follows me all the way out of the building and into the gray afternoon. As I trudge on, head down, I'm so gripped by a sense of defeat, wondering if I should just get back on a train home, that I very nearly step into the path of a bus. The driver slams on the horn and shouts, "Look where you're fucking going!" As he drives off, still swearing, I'm confronted with the adverts plastered all over the bus: *And Breathe . . .*

19.

DINNER AND A SHOWDOWN

It's started to rain, and I end up ducking into a pub to avoid it. As I go up to the bar to buy a drink, I clock an elderly chap nursing a pint, and reflexively I imagine telling Jeff about what's just happened over his first Winchester Gold of the day, before reality kicks me hard in the stomach. The rain doesn't let up, and I end up having a few more drinks than I should before I visit the last place on my list—a restaurant called Daly's, which PinkMoonLily1970 reviewed with unqualified superlatives. "*Order the ravioli—it's amazing!*" she wrote, and so I will.

It's been a long time since I've eaten out on my own. I forgot how awkward it is. The staff aren't happy that I'm here alone, taking up a table, but they grudgingly let me sit in the corner by the toilets. I'm surprised they haven't cordoned me off. Or put a sheet over my head.

However, my waiter turns out to be friendly, and he spends a long time considering Lily's photo. He doesn't recognize her, but he says he'll ask around the other staff. I'm torn, because I'm a bit worried about letting the photo out of my sight, but in the end I agree, thanking him for his trouble. As soon as he's back through the swinging doors that lead to the kitchen, though, I'm absolutely terrified he's going to lose it.

My pasta arrives, delivered by a different waiter, and when I ask her about the photo, she apologizes but says she doesn't know what I'm talking about. It's at this point that into the restaurant stumbles what appears to be a hen and stag party that have become merged, like some awful mythical beast. With depressing inevitability they are seated at the one table that is big enough, right next to me. I try to remain very still, like a mouse hoping not to alert a cat to its presence. I eat quickly, head down, keen to get my photo and get out of there. I've just eaten my last bite when I look up to see that one of the boys—and he is just a boy, really, in the way that men only really look like men when they've got a nose hair or two—is looking at me while whispering something to his friend. I give him a curt nod and look away, but when I chance a glance back I see him waving at me.

"Oi, mate," I hear him call, but I pretend I don't know he's talking to me. "Mate!" he tries again, and then I hear his chair scraping back. As he makes his way over—presumably this is some sort of stag-do dare—I decide I'm going to put some cash on the table and leave, then come back for my photo a little later on.

I grab some notes from my wallet and throw them down, and then I make for the exit. I'm traveling at some speed, and in my haste to leave I accidentally bump into a woman who's trying to push the door open as I go through it. Mortified, I apologize, my eyes on the ground.

"That's OK," the woman says, in an accent I can't place. "By the way, I think that man's trying to give you something."

I turn around to see the boy looking at me.

"Your credit card, *mate*," he says, slapping it into my hand, stinging my palm. "It was under your chair."

I'm about to offer my second profuse apology in ten seconds when I see the waiter heading over, Lily's photo in his hand.

"No luck on the photo, sir, I'm afraid. But a colleague tells me they definitely had a booking last week, name of Lily. Table for one. If that's of any help?"

20.

LESSONS

THEN

After the night of the burned potatoes, Lily and I officially became "an item," although she told me in no uncertain terms that this was not an expression I was allowed to use. See too: *better half*.

"Even though it's true?"

"Yes, even though it's true."

Those first weeks of "us" taught me an awful lot. They taught me that falling for someone can make you feel weightless, that it can heighten the joy of every taste, every sound, every color. And that it can also feel like a panic attack on a submarine.

I really did try my best to play it cool. Waiting for Lily outside whatever restaurant or gallery we were meeting at that day, I'd adopt an air of detached mystique, as if I were lost in intensely deep thoughts about the complicated beauty of the world—only to bound over with enthusiasm a Labrador might think a bit much when I spotted her. Thankfully, I got the sense that Lily found this lack of coolness endearing, and after a while I understood that it didn't make sense to pretend not to be delighted to see her when that's exactly how I felt.

For the first time since I'd moved to London, I started to understand what the hype was all about. I never thought I'd get to do all those things that couples do, but how wonderful to find it was finally my turn to have someone at my side in museums and galleries, particularly someone who'd only half roll their eyes when I pretended I thought a painting of a ninth-century monk was supposed to be Annie Lennox.

If Lily and I weren't at a gallery or museum, we'd be walking by the Thames and sprawling in parks, reading zeitgeisty novels about dysfunctional families. In the evenings we'd seek out art house films, which we'd dissect afterward in the pub at a million miles an hour so that we could get on to the important business of kissing like someone had told us the world was about to end. Up until then, I hadn't been that bothered about eating out in London, something that Lily felt compelled to rectify. This meant trips to trendy Soho restaurants, often daringly and illicitly expensed thanks to Lily's magazine contacts. She was obsessed with my limited palate, and I'd happily let her order for me. Our food would arrive and I'd raise a forkful of curry or sweet and sour chicken to my mouth as Lily watched on like Frankenstein bringing his monster to life.

Whatever we were doing, there was always a thrilling sense that we should get it over with so that we could be in bed together. Sex was something I'd always been a bit underwhelmed by. Like champagne. Or Alton Towers. But with Lily it made me want to write a letter to my younger self that said: *One day you will be with the most beautiful woman in the world, naked, in bed. You will be almost overwhelmed with a tidal wave of chemical reactions and transcendent revelations about the universe. You will be in a Travelodge in Margate.*

As sad as it might sound, until I met Lily I hadn't quite realized that life was there waiting to be enjoyed. Perhaps this was the legacy of being brought up by my grandparents. Their approach to life suggested that it was a series of challenges to be overcome, punctuated by a brisk trip to the same patch of beach for a week each summer, and this had clearly rubbed off on me. I had always been far too focused on whether I was *getting things right* to think about enjoying myself. The concept of "living in the moment" had always felt foreign, because the moments I lived in tended to be ones when I was thinking about council tax. But now that I was in Lily's orbit, she taught me the value of enjoyment for enjoyment's sake. How thrilling it was, to stay in bed for the whole day, or to eat whenever you were hungry rather than three square meals at the same time regardless of appetite. To just get up and get on a train to the coast for the day—without even checking the weather!

The very first time we shared a bed, I remember being aware of how *right* it felt—the way she curled her body into mine, how her head rested so perfectly on my chest. Even when she lay on my arm and it screamed with pins and needles, it still seemed a perfect fit. It was as if up until then I'd been built with a massive design flaw—a wonky old chair balancing on three legs—and now finally I had that fourth leg and was completely fixed. It was a shame that in the time between me realizing this was how I felt and me being brave enough to tell her, I hadn't managed to come up with a more romantic analogy.

"Well, that's charming," Lily replied once the words had tumbled from my mouth. "Shall I compare thee to a wooden leg? Thou art more *sturdy* and more *thick*."

"That's not what I meant," I grumbled, pulling her into me tighter and nudging her repeatedly with my nose. Lily wriggled.

"No, not the remorseful-woodpecker act, I beg of you!"

She retaliated by putting her freezing feet on my legs. Further strikes and counterstrikes followed. We called a truce over tea and toast.

Unfortunately, there was still a part of the old me that didn't trust all this. It was like at any moment an envoy from the universe was about to tap me on the shoulder and tell me there'd been some kind of mistake, or that Lily had only agreed to be with me as part of some elaborate prank, soon to be aired on prime-time TV. These were the only times I really erred, in the fledgling days of our relationship—when I couldn't hide this concern. For the most part, Lily ignored my self-deprecating jokes about our being a mismatch, but then things came to a head one afternoon in the pub when she caught me staring at her, lost in a moment of panic where I'd pictured her breaking up with me.

"What?" she said, eyebrows raised. "Have I got hummus in my hair again? You know I can't control it."

"No. Not today."

"Well, that's a relief. What then?"

"Nothing, I just, you know . . . feel lucky, to be here with you, that's all."

I gulped at my drink while Lily narrowed her eyes and put her book down. "That's the second time recently you've made reference to feeling lucky to be with me. It makes you sound almost . . . guilty."

It was the worry that she thought I'd done something wrong that compelled me to try to explain myself, which I did in such a tortuous way, employing various analogies—at one point supporting my words with the use of salt and pepper sachets as visual aids—that Lily seemed even more baffled than before I'd started.

"Have you had a bump on the head?" she asked me when I'd stumbled to my conclusion.

"I don't *think* so."

"Then I suggest you be quiet and drink your lovely beer, there's a good boy."

She ruffled my hair, and I did as I was told, making sure to be the breeziest version of myself for the rest of the day. I'm not sure if Lily knew then what I'd been getting at, or whether it only became clear to her in bed that night after a lot of hard work untangling the knotted nonsense I'd spoken, but the next morning I woke up to find the following letter on my bedside table:

From the Desk of Lily McCallister

Dearest Brian,
I am with you for many reasons, not limited to the following: You are kind. You are funny. You think about others more than yourself. You eat all the worst Quality Street chocolates in the box so that I can have the good ones and you don't even know I've worked that out. When you've thought of a joke there's a split second before you say it where you look so excited it makes me want to hug you until you burst. You inexplicably have the talent of an award-winning masseuse. It feels as if you like me for who I am, not because I tick some sort of box. When you kiss me it makes my knees buckle. You

have been through more than anyone else I know, but you are never cynical. We've never had an awkward silence—even that time you beat me at Scrabble and I called you a four-letter word and you pointed out that if I'd used that on the triple-letter I would have won.

There are more things, but I can't quite put them into words yet. I'm still finding out about you. And that is half the fun of all this. You're just going to have to trust me on that. OK?

Lily McCallister
BA Hons, CBE, OBE, HSBC, HEEBEEJEEBIES
References available on request.

From then on, I did my best just to enjoy the ride, but for all the excitement of *new things* in those early days, I confess that I was equally thrilled when we first showed signs of comfy domesticity—what Ed would tell me wisely was the "coffee-and-Sunday-papers phase." I vividly recall the first time I went out to buy milk and Lily shouted after me to pick up some kitchen roll too. We'd been staying in her house in Chalk Farm, which she rented with a couple of friends who thankfully never seemed to be there, which meant I occasionally fantasized about its being our very own place. I felt so light on my feet as I walked to the corner shop that morning that it was all I could do not to break out in song. As the toilet paper and batteries and bleach beamed at me off the shelves, a thought struck me: *We're going to have a family one day*. Whoa, I thought, where had that come from? This wasn't something I'd spent much time thinking about up until then. It was true that I had been robbed of the family I was supposed to have had, and that my childhood had been quiet and, at times, lonely. But I hadn't really considered the idea that having a family of my own one day would be a way of redressing the balance.

As I walked back to Lily's, idle thoughts flickered of packed-up cars with kids bickering in the backseat; raucous birthday parties; school plays; Lily and I older and grayer, holding hands tightly as we tried not to burst with pride on graduation days . . . I exchanged cheery hellos with the next-door neighbor as I let myself back into the house, whistling a little ditty as I climbed the stairs.

"What's got into you?" Lily said as I bent down to kiss her on the top of the head.

"Oh, I was just thinking—" I broke off. "Fancy the pub later?" *Don't jinx things*, I told myself. *It's very early days, you madman.*

I often go back to that moment, wondering what would have happened if I'd told Lily what I'd really been thinking. It's funny, when you're getting to know the person you want to spend the rest of your life with, you put so much effort into pretending to be the varnished, idealized version of yourself that it means the only time they get to see the real you is in moments of complete vulnerability—when you're in pain, or afraid—and it goes on like that, a never-ending negotiation, until the years strip you of all the layers you've gathered around yourself, and you're right back where you started.

21.

PASTRY WARS

NOW

I didn't get much sleep last night, and it wasn't just because of the people below me in the Three Horseshoes bar—and then in the street outside—singing "Come On Eileen" at the tops of their voices. I'd been replaying the moment over and over again with the waiter telling me they'd had a booking from someone called Lily, and how I'd immediately been able to picture her—my Lily—sitting in the restaurant, maybe even at the same table as where I'd eaten. I'd felt light-headed as I walked back to the pub through the ancient city's streets, the pendulum now swinging back in the opposite direction, toward hope.

I must have finally dropped off to sleep in the early hours, but when I'm woken up by my aching knee, I'm wide awake again, and eventually when it gets to seven a.m., I give up and head downstairs.

I'm contemplating the pub's breakfast offering—translucent fried eggs cowering on a scorched hot plate—when my phone starts to ring. When I see that it's Rebecca calling, it takes several seconds before I can bring myself to answer.

"Hi, Rebecca, how are you?"

"Brian, I'm late for my train, so can we make this quick?"

I ignore how she's made it sound like I'm the one who's just called her. I can hear her high heels pounding along the pavement in the background. I do wish we could exchange a basic pleasantry or two, just to give me some time to think, because I haven't really thought through exactly what I'm going to tell her. In the end I simply come out and give her the facts about the Tripadvisor profile I've discovered, and how I'm trying to track the user down. I don't tell her about what I learned from the waiter last night, because I'm trying to sound levelheaded and I know I'll become far too animated if I get onto that.

There's a long silence after I stop speaking. The call is still connected, because I can hear cars rushing past in the background. But by the sound of it, Rebecca has stopped walking, despite supposedly being late for her train. When she does start to speak her voice is taut with repressed anger.

"What did I say to you when I came to see you that time, Brian? No theories, no speculation."

"I know," I say quickly. "This is different, though, right? It's evidence. Tangible proof."

"Brian—"

"The point is," I continue, pushing past what sounds horribly like pity in her voice, "that I thought you had a right to know. I'm not expecting you to come and help, or anything."

"Good," Rebecca says, firm again now. "Because there's absolutely no way you're dragging me into this. It may have been seven years, but I'm still trying to take each day at a time. I've been getting better—stronger—we all have. Please don't even think about bothering Mum and Dad with this nonsense, OK? Brian?"

"Yes, yes—I understand. I just—"

But she's hung up.

I wasn't aware that I'd been raising my voice, but people having breakfast are shooting me furtive glances from their tables. Defiantly, I begin piling food onto my plate, but I'm not hungry anymore. I'm not sure I was expecting a different response from Rebecca, but it still troubles me to hear her getting so angry. The last thing I want to do is upset her, or any of Lily's family for that matter. It wouldn't have felt right if I hadn't told her what I'm doing, but it's clear I can forget about the possibility of her coming to help me. I rescue a final piece of charred bacon and add it to my plate, aware now, more than ever, that I'm very much on my own.

I CHECK OUT of the pub and find a café. I'm eager to see if Lily's written any new reviews that'll tell me where she's going next, but the sluggish Wi-Fi has me jiggling my knee up and down in frustration. There's still a rational part of my brain that's trying to tell me not to get carried away, particularly after speaking to Rebecca. But the more I've been thinking about Lily and the early days of our relationship, those endless summer days, it's like I'm throwing a rope across the chasm between the past and the present.

"Come on, come on," I repeat under my beath, refreshing the page, picking up my laptop and angling it in case I'll find a pocket of Wi-Fi trapped by the wall. I'm aware I must look a bit mad, but luckily distraction is being provided by two small children who are running around in circles playing a game that seems to involve finding new and inventive ways to injure each other with pastries. Their parents, a couple in their late thirties, sitting on a deep sofa, look beleaguered with lack of sleep and are watching the chaos unfold with a sense of helplessness. After one particularly bloodcurdling scream, a man at a table opposite me catches my attention and rolls his eyes.

When one of the children accidentally knocks into my chair, her father finally hoists himself off the sofa and comes over to say sorry.

"Honestly, no problem at all," I tell him, and he smiles, looking relieved.

"Don't suppose you fancy swapping places for an hour," he says with a weary laugh. I start to reply, but the words come out in the wrong order, and the whole encounter is suddenly awkward. I find myself digging my thumbnail into the back of my hand as the man makes his excuses and goes back to his family. A dark crescent moon blossoms on my skin. It'll probably be there for days.

Finally, the Wi-Fi struggles into life, and I jab at my keyboard until Lily's Tripadvisor page refreshes. I breathe in sharply as I see a new review has appeared, posted early this morning. "*Beautiful Edinburgh brekkie*" is the heading. I sit back in my chair. Damn it, she must have left York yesterday at some point. How long is the train to Edinburgh, I wonder. A few hours, I'd say. I go back to the review, which is ostensibly about a restaurant just off the Royal Mile, but my eye is drawn to the very last sentence: "*Looking forward to the rest of my time here.*"

OK, I think, regaining a hold on my optimism—that sounds like she's going to be there for a couple of days at least. But I'd best get a move on. Every second really does seem to count now.

I get to my feet, nearly knocking my chair over in the process, and shove my laptop into my suitcase before bustling out of the café. It's wild, I realize, that before yesterday I'd barely left home in years, and now I'm about to hop on a train to the capital city of a country I've never even been to before. I think of Lily. Once again, I'm living in the moment, and it's all down to her.

Thankfully I'm only a short dash from York station, where a train is leaving for Edinburgh in four minutes. On another day, I'm not sure I'd make it, but as I'm hurrying along the concourse it's as if people have been told to step aside to let me through, and with a final sprint and a leap I'm through the doors with only seconds to spare.

22.

EDINBURGH

Coming back to Edinburgh is to me like coming home.

—CHARLES DICKENS, 1858

Long story short: I did not enjoy Arthur's Seat. It is not clearly signposted which will leave you questioning whether or not you even climbed the right hill.

—ONLINE REVIEW, ARTHUR'S SEAT, EDINBURGH, 2019

If York is an impressive city to arrive in by train, then Edinburgh is just showing off. Even with my knees complaining because of the endless steps, I'm still blown away by the sheer scale and majesty of the castle, and the beauty of the twisting streets glistening with morning rain. It's even busier than York here, but I feel much more at ease with each hour I spend in a city again, which means I'm actually able to raise my gaze from the pavement and properly appreciate my surroundings. The sensation is akin to coming out of the cinema into the brightness of the world, where every sound is sharp, every color heightened.

As I come around a corner near Canongate, I exchange a smile with a woman holding a purple umbrella, and the interaction gives me a warm glow. My positivity receives a slight dent when I take my clunky old laptop out of my bag in a café and a teenager sitting nearby actually gasps and looks at me with sheer pity, as if I've taken out a balloon with a face drawn on it and pretended it's a friend.

I feel a jolt of excitement when I find that Lily has already posted another review, although I'm thrown somewhat by the title.

> White Water Rafting at Aberfeldy—amazing!!!

Hmm. Odd. I read on.

> I've never done this before but wow, I really loved it. Graham, who took us out on the raft, was charming and funny and got even the most reluctant of us onto the boat. What a thrill! I'm barely back in dry clothes but felt compelled to write this straightaway. Graham also gave me some excellent tips for the rest of my stay. Such a star.

Is he now. I try to refrain from feeling jealous of a man I've never met. After all, if I can track *him* down, then that's one step up from the waiter in York—this guy's actually spoken to Lily. It's a bit of a risk, as she's likely on her way back to Edinburgh—but without any details of where she might be staying, I think Aberfeldy and Graham are my best shot at finding my next clue.

I'm very much not used to all this rushing around, but though my body is crying out for me to sit back and rest, I'm far too eager to get going. So before my legs can seize up, I spring to my feet, gather my laptop into my suitcase, and make for the exit, the teenager bowing her head respectfully as I pass.

23.

PEACE ON EARTH

THEN

It was December, and I was practically living at Lily's place now, much to the thinly disguised annoyance of her housemates, Sue and Beth, who had taken to labeling so many things in the kitchen that it had started to look like a crime scene. I suspect part of the problem was that Sue and Beth were both recently single, and though Lily and I tried to keep a lid on our burgeoning love when we were around them, I'm not sure we always succeeded. For these were the days of leaving little notes for each other about the place, of making each other laugh so hard we thought we might die, of being intertwined on the sofa at all times like one amorphous creature.

No wonder they hated us.

With Christmas around the corner they had both headed home, making pointed references to looking forward to seeing me "at some time in the new year." I think they were hoping for October, at the earliest.

With it now being just the two of us, I began to imagine

what life could be like if Lily and I were to have a place of our own. I was starting to see more and more glimpses "behind the scenes" of Lily's life, the things she'd do that would have a goofy smile appearing on my face when I was bored in meetings at work. Because while of course I felt absurdly lucky to get to go out to the cinema or a gig with Lily on my arm looking beautiful, as she always did, I think I loved her even more when we were back home and she was plunging her arm deep into a box of novelty cereal and eating handfuls of it dry, or having animated one-sided conversations with the kettle. Then there was the first time she took me out in her car—a white Renault Clio, troublingly corrugated with dents—when I had to spend ten minutes clearing the detritus from the passenger seat. Burger wrappers, takeaway coffee cups, magazines, two hairbrushes, Polo mints, and balled-up tissues were just the half of it. The eyes might be the window to the soul, but Lily's glove compartment was a portal to a much darker place. And yet in the flush of youthful love, there I was removing half a Twix from between the pages of an *A to Z* street map and feeling like the luckiest man in the world.

To look at things from Lily's perspective, I wasn't entirely sure I possessed as many hidden quirks that she'd become attached to, though she did seem quite taken with the occasional antiquated saying of mine, almost certainly my grandad's influence. I'll never forget the look on her face when I described a spider in the living room as a "knife-and-fork job," for instance. She also took a great deal of enjoyment at how I made a packed lunch for work each morning in a Tupperware box. "Look at your little apple!" she'd say. "Your neatly wrapped sandwiches. *Adorable.*"

By this point, we had introduced each other to our respective friendship groups. For my part, I'd been able to do this in a single evening, inviting Lily to some drinks with Ed and my friends from work. I'd felt a happiness I wasn't prepared for when I turned around at the bar, drinks in hand, and saw Ed and Lily immediately hitting it off.

Meeting Lily's friends had been a more drawn-out affair, because they numbered the population of a small market town. I got on with them well enough, but there was still a sense that they were keeping me at arm's length—that I might not be worth their time and investment given that I probably wouldn't be around for much longer. The boys in particular, who all seemed to do the same job in the same part of the City, and all had the same haircut, appeared to find me a bit of a novelty. Partly this was because I seemed to be on a different wavelength than them in almost every conversation. They didn't really understand self-deprecation, for instance. So when I told a particularly slick man called Alistair that the one time I'd played golf I'd been dreadful, he responded by boasting about his handicap and offered to give me lessons. Lily, who had watched this discussion play out with undisguised glee, told me she was looking forward to the sight of me in an Argyle sweater.

At a certain point on these nights, the boys would end up getting competitive and boorish, and generally it was Lily who'd pull me aside and suggest we get out of there.

"Are you sure you don't want me to have a flat in Knightsbridge and a Hugh Grant haircut?" I asked her one night on the tube on the way home.

"No," Lily said, "I really don't. I love that lot, but it is a little bit like hanging out with clones sometimes. I'd much rather spend my time listening to your mad rules about what makes a good pub." I felt immeasurably proud until she said, "Now, if you were to have Hugh Grant's eyes and charisma, then that'd be a different story . . ."

We really were having the best time of it that December. Christmas in London was the perfect backdrop to falling in love. I was particularly relishing it because I didn't usually look too fondly on this time of year. Christmases with my grandparents when I was little had always been lovely, but by the time I was a teenager I'd listen to my friends at school talking about their huge family gatherings and quirky traditions, and I'd think about how my festivities at home meant Grandad falling asleep in front of the gas fire while Grandma did the dishes, everyone in bed by ten. I'd felt guilty for feeling envious of other people, because my grandparents had shown me nothing but selflessness and love, so who was I to complain? But I couldn't pretend I didn't feel lonely. And now that I was older, things hadn't exactly improved. The last couple of Christmases had been strange experiences. I'd spent one with my uncle Mike, a man who lived in what he called his "bachelor pad," a damp flat on the outskirts of Dover. Then last year I'd been on my own in London. Ed—a man possessed of more goodness than I ever would be—stayed in our flat until Christmas morning so that I'd have someone to have breakfast with on the day itself. We opened presents, drank a glass of one of our more bowel-threatening home brew attempts, had an awkward hug, and then he was off. I spent the rest of the week without seeing a soul. There was certainly a sense of freedom to this. I found out that Christmas alone is a bit like being on a boat in international waters. All rules go out of the window, and if you want to eat pickled onions washed down with Cointreau for breakfast, then you absolutely can. It's fair to say, however, that I was glad when Ed came home. I'm not sure if you've ever seen one of those videos of a soldier coming back to see their dog for the first time in months, but I was very much the dog in that scenario.

Now that I had Lily in my life, I wondered if things might be different. I knew it was too soon to ask her to spend this Christmas with me, but that didn't stop me from thinking about the future—and whether it might not be too long before we'd be lying in bed on Christmas morning, both dreading and welcoming the stampede of little feet at six a.m. on the landing, hiding under the duvet as the door flew open.

I was lost in these thoughts as we decorated a tree I had manfully carried halfway home (before we'd had to get the bus the rest of the way). Distracted, I tossed a strand of tinsel onto a branch and watched it fall down onto the floor. Lily picked it up, giving me a patronizing little pat on the head, and calmly repositioned it.

"Are you sure you'll be OK at home on your own on Christmas Day?" she asked me, reaching for another strand.

"Absolutely," I said. "Don't you worry about me."

I hung an ornament. Lily looked at it, shook her head, and moved it a single branch over.

"You know you can always come to mine," she said. And maybe it was because I'd been lost in those thoughts about the future again, but if there was any politeness or hesitation in her voice, I didn't hear it.

"Are you sure?" I asked.

"Yeah, course," she replied, diving behind the tree to untangle a stretch of lights. "I can't promise it'll be entirely stress-free, but if it all gets a bit much you can sit in the car and eat pickled onions by yourself."

"Well, when you put it like that . . ."

AND SO, ON the morning of Christmas Eve, we prepared to set off in Lily's car to her family home. We had a long drive ahead of us up to the Scottish border. As we made it out of London and hit our stride on the motorway, joyfully murdering the melody of every Christmas song that came on the radio, I asked Lily to give me the lowdown on her family again. My aide-mémoires were long forgotten by now, thankfully—nothing like pulling a cracker and a bit of paper with *Bill, diabetic, divorced* flying out of your sleeve—but I was keen for a refresher so that I didn't commit any gross faux pas.

Lily seemed oddly unforthcoming, though, when it came to telling me any more than she already had about her family, or her home, or who was actually going to be present. Her mum and dad—Verity and Forbes—would be there, and possibly her sister, Rebecca, and Rebecca's husband, Rupert, although Lily said she wasn't sure.

"It's always a bit of a free-for-all."

"But they know *you're* coming?"

"Yes," Lily said, quickly reaching to change the radio station lest we suffer a single second of Cliff Richard.

"And me too?" I asked. I looked over, but Lily had her eyes set resolutely ahead. Just then a motorbike veered into our lane and she was forced to take evasive action. She unleashed an impressive tirade of swear words in the motorcyclist's direction, neatly timed to coincide with David Bowie wishing people peace on earth, and then she swiftly changed the subject.

24.

ABERFELDY

The little birdies blythely sing
While o'er their heads the hazels hing,
Or lightly flit on wanton wing,
In the birks of Aberfeldy.
—ROBERT BURNS, 1787

The sausage roll was cold!
—ONLINE REVIEW, ABERFELDY TEA ROOM, 2020

NOW

The lady at the tourist information desk is very happy to have someone to talk to. She explains with much enthusiasm that since "that book" came out, the numbers of people rafting at Aberfeldy have gone through the roof. I feel awful when I cut her short to thank her for her help, but I really need to get going if I'm to make it to the coach pickup point in time.

I make the coach by the skin of my teeth. After a similar experience with the train this morning, I'm feeling quite the action hero, though admittedly I can't recall the Bond film where he gets the zip of his windbreaker stuck and has to take it off over his head instead.

As the tourist information lady alluded to, this is obviously a popular outing, and the coach is so full I'm forced to take the one free seat, directly behind the driver—who isn't my biggest fan after having to help me bundle my suitcase into the coach's luggage hold.

I was hoping to relax and enjoy the scenery as we traveled north—it's not long before I see some spectacular hills—or perhaps close my eyes and seek out more memories of those early days spent with Lily, but the atmosphere quite quickly becomes as raucous as a school trip; there's even some spontaneous singing at one point. Sneaking a look behind me, I realize that I'm the only man on the coach. This throws me, as I assumed that white water rafting would appeal mainly to the kind of men who are convinced that they could survive solo on a desert island with only a Snickers and a rusty spoon.

When we arrive and are greeted by the famous Graham, he's much more what I expected. Squat, barrel chested, and with a speaking voice the volume of a town crier ordering a drink in a busy bar, he seems disappointed to see me getting off the coach. But then he clocks all the women about to file off behind me and immediately cheers up, mock-bellowing at them to "fall out." I wait patiently until he's greeted everyone else before I approach.

"Can I have a quick word?" I ask, reaching into my pocket for Lily's photo.

"Time for questions later, pal, OK?" he says, walking off again. I bite my tongue and resolve to remain polite and calm, remembering how wrong I got it with the man in York Dungeon.

A persistent drizzle has blown in, and the imposing, snow-topped mountains in the distance that everyone was cooing about as we arrived are quickly obscured. For a moment I wonder if the change in conditions might mean the rafting is off—ideal from my point of view—but Graham seems unbothered. He begins to rattle off rules and instructions, telling us just how cold the water is, and I do my best to pay attention. When he's finished, the coach sets off to meet us downriver and we're all dispatched to a wooden hut to change into wetsuits (which seems a bit over-the-top) and what Graham calls a "personal flotation vest" and what I will call a life jacket. I'm faced with the decision of whether to leave Lily's photo behind or carry it with me up the sleeve of my wetsuit so I can show it to Graham. In the end I decide it's too risky to take it. I'm determined to grab my moment with Graham, though, so as we all walk down to the water, I trot up to him and ask if now's a good time for a quick chat.

"No, buddy, you can't steer the boat," he says very loudly over his shoulder, so that everyone can hear. Then, to me, suddenly businesslike: "Yeah, go on, what is it?"

I clear my throat and summon up as casual a voice as I can. "It's just about someone you took out rafting earlier today. Lily."

He ignores this and instead reaches for one of the straps on my life jacket and yanks it tight, which makes me feel like a toddler having his duffle coat done up. Then he sniffs aggressively and says, "I see hundreds of people every day, pal."

"Yes, but—" I stop, realizing that there's a very different tack I should be taking. "She just wanted me to thank you," I continue. "She thought you were really brilliant."

He's immediately interested, stroking his chin. "Go on . . ."

"She's called Lily, and she's my age. Coppery red hair, at least I thi—"

"Yeah," Graham says. "Rings a bell."

It's like someone's plunged their hand into my chest and squeezed my heart in their fist. I try to speak but no words come. And then before I have the chance to ask him anything else, he's off chivvying people along, doing a comedy jog down to the water and peeping away at his whistle as he goes.

Heavy rain is falling now, and there's a squalling wind. I'm so distracted, still desperate to follow up with Graham, that it's only as I clamber clumsily into the raft with my paddle and look at the broiling black water we're heading into that I realize what we're actually about to do. The people opposite me are tightly clustered together, exchanging reassuring words, and it feels a bit like that moment in a war film when enemy bombers are about to come screaming overhead. Graham, standing behind us at the back of the boat, pushes off into the river and the current grabs hold of us. It's gentle at first, but then Graham's shouting "Let's go!" and we're suddenly wrenched down what feels like a flight of steps, and I'm instantly winded. As I struggle to get my breath back, I'm slapped hard in the face by freezing water.

"Paddle, mate!" shouts Graham, poking me in the back. "Remember the briefing—we have to stay balanced." With grim determination, I get to it. It feels like we're hurtling along—really flying—and for what feels like an hour I find that the only thing I'm aware of is the complete lack of control I have over where we're going. On we hurtle, until eventually we hit a calmer patch of water. Everyone's whooping and squeezing each other on the arm. Someone even taps me on the shoulder and says, "Good work!" But as strangely exhilarating as this all is—and I can't remember the last time I had this much adrenaline rushing through me—I'm desperate to hear more from Graham.

I wait until he's steered us right over to the water's edge and then, heart still pounding, I start to get to my feet.

"Whoa, whoa—sit back down there, mate."

He's angry, but alarmed too—possibly because the look in my eye must indicate I have no intention of doing what he says. I ignore everyone else's protestations and continue to clamber toward him.

"Did she say where she was going next?" I say, my foot sliding on the bottom of the boat and nearly sending me sprawling.

"What?" Graham says. "Just sit down, will you? Stop playing silly buggers so I can get us moored."

"Lily. Did she say where she was going next? What color were her eyes? Were they green?"

This time Graham tells me to "Sit. Down. *Now*," and people are actually trying to pull me back. Someone takes me by the shoulder, and in the effort to yank my arm away, I lose my balance. The more I try to stay upright, the more I seem to flail my way closer to the edge of the boat, and even though the thought flashes through my brain that I'm not actually going to fall in the water, because this isn't a cartoon, gravity has very different ideas.

25.

SMUDGE

THEN

Snow started to fall late on our Christmas Eve drive, which was all very festive, but when the radio signal died as we went through the gates to Lily's family home—Challington House, according to the sign on the driveway—I felt the nerves creeping up on me. They weren't helped as the house itself loomed up ahead, resolute and imposing against the snowy skies, and I saw as we crunched up the gravel drive that it backed onto some large, pristine gardens.

"I wish you'd told me," I said.

"About what?"

I looked down at my scuffed trainers, my frayed jeans, then found myself pulling at the seat belt, which suddenly felt too tight across my chest. "Just a bit more about the place. And your family."

Lily reached over and squeezed my hand, though this was a placating measure rather than a reassuring one. "This is why I didn't say anything, because I knew you'd freak out. Or wear that suit of yours. Just be yourself, OK?"

Was I imagining it, or had she not quite committed to that last part?

As she swung the car around the front of the house, I saw a jaunty animatronic Santa waving back and forth in a ground-floor window. This reassured me a little. Maybe I was worrying over nothing. Letting my preconceptions get in the way. That was when there was a smart rap at my window and I turned to see a man holding a shotgun.

The gun may have been lowered, but it was enough to make me jump in my seat. The man holding it was tall, his Barbour jacket stretched over broad shoulders. He had a neatly trimmed gray beard and close-cropped hair. Even in the dusk I could see that his eyes were the same green as Lily's.

I went to open the door, forgetting my seat belt was still done up. While I was still fumbling with it, Lily jumped out of the car, calling, "Daaad!" as she skittered around to throw her arms around him.

"Hello, darling," I heard the man reply in a deep, rasping voice. "And who do we have here?"

I finally managed to extricate myself from the car. Politeness at the forefront of my mind, I hastily thrust out my hand for Lily's dad to shake. He considered me for a moment, eyes piercing mine, before he took my hand in a crushing grip.

"Dad, this is Brian," Lily said when she realized I wasn't going to offer up my own name.

"Forbes McCallister," he said. "How do you do?"

It was a question I had never known the correct response to, and so I said, "Very well, thank you, and how do you do yourself?"

Forbes ignored this entirely, turning to Lily instead. "I didn't know you were bringing a friend, Smudge."

Lily shrugged, as if to say, *Well, sorry about that.* I felt compelled to offer an apology, or at least an explanation. It hadn't escaped me that her father had said "friend," nor that Lily hadn't corrected him.

"It's very generous of you to have me," I said. "And I'm pretty good at peeling spuds, if that could come in handy. Or sprouts, for that matter, or anything really!"

Lily shot me a look that told me I should calm down.

"A real polymath," Forbes said, continuing to address Lily rather than me. I jumped at the chance to make a self-effacing joke in response, but Forbes cut me off.

"I'd say it's about teatime, eh?" he said. Then he finally looked at me. "And I loathe sprouts, by the way."

UP UNTIL THAT point in my life, "teatime" had meant PG Tips and, if my grandparents were feeling particularly decadent, a slice of fruitcake. As the delicate bone china cup I was holding rattled audibly against the saucer, Lily's mother, Verity—who peered inquiringly over the top of her tortoiseshell glasses at whoever she was talking to, which made me feel like I was constantly on the verge of being given detention—said, "The place is in such a state, I *am* sorry, Brian."

I looked around the spotless kitchen, complete with immaculately groomed sheepdog snoozing at the foot of the Aga.

"Oh no, not at all! It's like a scene from a Christmas jigsaw puzzle."

This didn't elicit anything more from Verity than a nod, as if to say, *Yes, that is the acceptable answer.*

"And thanks so much for having me," I added, still desperate to ingratiate myself. "I really appreciate it. Would have been a solo Christmas otherwise."

"You don't see your family at Christmas?" Forbes asked.

"No," I said simply. Forbes raised an eyebrow but Lily came to my rescue, asking her parents about the latest gossip from the village, and I was able to listen politely as Verity told us of the recent "scandals"—most of which seemed to involve planning permission—with Forbes interrupting every now and then to correct her on trivial factual mistakes that made no difference to the story.

I was pleased that I didn't have to contribute to the conversation. Instead I simply listened attentively and tried to get a measure of these people and how I was supposed to behave. I could sense that Forbes was continuing to size me up too. He kept saying things that made me think I might be expected to drink whisky and smoke cigars with him after dinner while the womenfolk gathered around the harpsichord.

As Lily and I got a moment to ourselves in her old bedroom after tea, I found myself making lots of nervous jokes about how I wouldn't know what fork to use with my quail at dinner, and how we should have brought a bottle of the '52 with us rather than the '58.

Lily humored me at first, but later, as we got ready to come down for dinner, I was still rambling on when I saw her looking at me in her dressing table mirror unsmilingly. I went over and put my hands on her shoulders, but she stiffened a little.

"Are you going to spend the whole time here taking the piss out of my family, or . . . ?"

"Shit, sorry," I said, looking at my reflection and flattening my hair, which sprung up again immediately. "I'm just nervous. Feeling a bit out of my depth, you know."

I needed to forget about whether Forbes and Verity knew I was coming. It didn't matter, really. What was important was that I won them over and showed Lily how well I could fit in.

"You look lovely by the way," I told her, pulling her to her feet. "And I'm sorry for being rude. I just . . . this is all a bit new to me. I don't want your family to think I'm not good enough for you."

Lily put her arms around my neck and gave me a searching look. "I can't pretend I don't care what Mum and Dad think about the important things in my life. But I am my own person, you know. I'm the one who decides who is or isn't good enough for me. And as it happens," she added, emotion suddenly coming to the surface, her voice trembling a little, "I love you."

This had to be the best recorded usage of the phrase "as it happens," a thought that I couldn't help sharing with Lily—but only after I'd told her I loved her, too. It was the first time we'd said those words. I'd never thought it would mean so much to hear her say it, and to get to say it back. Lily kissed me, and I pulled her close.

"Maybe we don't go down there at all," I said.

"Pretend we're dead?"

"Never leave this room."

"Tempting."

"Very tempting."

"But that quail won't eat itself . . ."

She nipped me playfully on the ear, then pulled away.

While I was still elated at the words we'd just exchanged in her bedroom, I couldn't help but ask about something that had been slightly troubling me.

"Here's a question for you," I asked as we made our way down the staircase (I'd resisted the temptation to ask her why the dinner gong hadn't been sounded yet). "Why does your dad call you Smudge?"

"Oh god, that," Lily sighed. "It came from a summer holiday when I was a girl." Here she cleared her throat and launched into a perfect impersonation of her father: "'There I'd be, you see, watching a perfectly blue sky, finally getting a moment's peace with my book, and then this little face would hove into view—like a smudge of dirt on a binocular lens—and suddenly I'd be expected to traipse up and down the beach while she played some game or other.'"

I was trying to think of something noncommittal to say about this when I heard the doorbell go and then, five seconds later, Lily's mother exclaiming loudly, "Oh, wonderful—Daniel's here!"

26.

PLUMS

Dressed in an immaculate black overcoat with a holly-berry-red scarf, a dusting of snow on each shoulder, he looked like a Hollywood version of a young British prime minister, especially when he directed his dazzling smile around the room. It faltered a little when it got to me, and I felt a belligerent stab of pride. That's right, mate. *This* chump's here.

"We grew up together," Lily had muttered hastily by way of explanation as we reached the bottom of the stairs. "Same village. His dad's friends with mine. He sometimes comes Christmas Eve, but he said a while back he couldn't make it."

"You don't have to explain!" I said, trying unsuccessfully to be breezy about it.

Verity took Daniel's coat and scarf, deferentially retreating to hang them up. Daniel thanked her and handed Forbes a bottle of scotch, which Forbes studied appreciatively while he shook Daniel's hand.

"Another belter. We'll have to sample her later."

Urgh, I thought, *her.* Evidently I hadn't quite managed to hide my disgust, as Daniel chuckled and said, "Not your drink then, Ben?"

"No, not really," I said. Lily looked at me, puzzled.

"It's Brian, not Ben," she said. It was hard to tell whether she was more annoyed by Daniel getting it wrong or confused by why I hadn't corrected him. I was rescued from the immediate awkwardness of this by the doorbell going again.

"Rebecca?" Lily asked her mother.

"I expect so," Verity said.

"And the mop," Lily whispered to me.

Rebecca was Lily's sister, older by a decade. Lily had told me she barely saw her as she was such a workaholic, a big cheese at some law firm or other. The mop turned out to be her husband, Rupert. Floppy-haired and plummy-voiced, he was a man who I soon learned had a habit of laughing about things that weren't intended to be funny:

"Mince pie, Rupert?"

"Ooh, yes please—ha ha ha!"

As Forbes ordered us all into the living room, I heard Rebecca say to Lily, "I see you've got yourself a bit of rough, Lil." I didn't know *what* to think of this. Was it a good thing?

The layout of furniture in the living room meant that we couldn't all sit in the same group, so inevitably I got stuck with Rupert on a chaise longue on the outskirts of the others, like minor wedding guests in a Shakespeare play. Though we clearly had absolutely nothing in common, I found that by just asking Rupert polite questions I could set him off on jolly stories in which people and places were invariably described as "rarely super" (which confused me until I worked out that this was just his accent, and that "rarely" was actually "*really*"). While he talked at me I tried to listen in on the other conversations in the room. From what I could tell, Daniel was holding court. Forbes's booming laugh and Verity's simpering titter rang out regularly in response to his jokes, and when I heard Lily laugh too I felt my shoulders tense.

At dinner, Forbes—who seemed to be putting away a good deal of wine—began to tell family stories. With each one, he got more animated, his voice growing louder and louder. Everyone joined in with the laughter, but I got the sense after a while that people were forcing it—dutifully rewarding his anecdotes and making sure he heard that they were enjoying them. The stories were mainly designed to embarrass "the girls," as he called them—the time teenage Rebecca accidentally fired a shotgun and blew a hole in his shed; when "little Smudge" had drawn all over the living room walls with crayons. "And then," he continued, banging his hand loudly on the table so that his cutlery rattled, "there was the day we found her downstairs on Christmas morning, ripping into chocolate! She was chomping away like a little truffle pig, completely oblivious to me standing there. You'd think she'd never eaten before."

"Dad!" Lily said with a laugh—one that I recognized as false, a note of pleading in it.

"Well, it's true!" he bellowed. He was about to carry on when, mercifully, and possibly deliberately, Verity chose that moment to clear his plate, and he was distracted enough to lose his thread.

In the slightly awkward pause that followed, Daniel said, "You done something new to your hair, Lil? Looks great."

Everyone looked at her, and she blushed.

"Nope," she said. "Same old, same old."

Daniel swirled some wine around his glass, a practiced gesture, and smirked to himself. I felt a deep desire then to stand up, proffer my hand to Lily, walk her to the car, and get us the hell out of there—back to London and our happy little bubble away from all of this.

IT WAS AFTER dessert when Rebecca, whom I'd noticed excusing herself with a meaningful look at Rupert, came back from the loo and stood away from the dining room table, hands behind her back.

"Ahem," she said, and then again, louder, to get Forbes's attention.

"Don't tell me, you want some money," he barked, winking at Daniel. Rebecca's face fell, and suddenly she looked like a little girl about to perform a dance she'd been rehearsing for the grown-ups.

"So," she began, rallying, "I can't imagine you've *not* noticed that I've been on the sparkling water all evening . . ."

Verity and Lily immediately shrieked and jumped to their feet to go over and hug her. Forbes didn't get up, but banged the table loudly and shouted, "Didn't know you had it in you, Rupert old boy!" Daniel glided around the table and shook Rupert's hand while I hovered on the edge of the huddle, never quite finding the moment to offer my congratulations.

Forbes broke out some champagne, which he got through most of himself, slumping back in his throne at the head of the table. Verity, Rebecca, and Lily were drawn into an animated conversation about boys' and girls' names and how the baby was currently the size of a plum, while Rupert and I listened and made the occasional dutiful interjection. Pleasingly, Daniel was stranded with Forbes, who was rambling on fairly incoherently now, grabbing hold of Daniel's arm every time it looked like he might turn to join in with us. Finally, Forbes went to the loo and I heard Daniel pull up the chair behind me, though I made no effort to move aside to include him.

"You'll be godmother, obviously," Rebecca said to Lily.

"Gosh," Lily laughed, "doesn't that mean I'm supposed to look after the thing if you and Rupert cark it?" She leaned down to Rebecca's stomach. "Good luck with that, Plum!"

"Oh, what tosh," Verity said, letting loose a little hiccup. "You'll make a wonderful mother."

Lily went to say something but Verity cut across her.

"And don't *you* leave it so long. I want more babies and more weddings, please. I'm very bored these days."

"That's a thought," Rupert piped up. "You two up next, surely? Wedding bells and whatnot!"

Lily and I glanced at each other and smiled. We started saying things like, "Who, us?" and "Crikey, look at the time . . ."

I went to smile reassuringly at Rebecca and Verity, suddenly worried that they thought I was being too flippant about the prospect of marrying Lily. But then I realized that they weren't even looking at me, after what Rufus had said. They were looking just past my left shoulder, to the person sitting behind me.

27.

A WET BLANKET

NOW

Someone is repeating the phrase "He's having a picnic" over and over again, which is confusing. Partly because I'm definitely not having a picnic. In fact, given that I'm shivering on all fours in a patch of mud, coughing up water, I'd say I'm doing the opposite of having a picnic, if that's even possible. But also because I'm sure I recognize that voice.

"He's OK, he's just having a picnic."

"I'm . . . not . . . having . . . a picnic," I manage to respond, perhaps the first time such a denial has had to be made, and as the same person tells me calmly to just breathe, and take my time, they are also having to stifle a laugh. It's that which finally distracts me enough to recover my breathing. I'm aware of someone's face quite close to mine, their hand on my shoulder. I turn my head to see a woman around my age, with striking gray-blue eyes and dark hair with what I think is a faint streak of purple in it. She repeats what she's just been saying to someone else, and this time I hear her properly.

"Oh," I say, "*panic attack.*"

She holds my gaze for a moment, then says, "Normally I'd hold no truck with someone making fun of my accent, but I'll let you off given the circumstances. I don't think I've ever seen someone fall so dramatically into such shallow water."

She's from Australia, or possibly New Zealand; at least I think she is.

"Have"—I start, before breaking off to cough one final time—"we met before?"

"Kind of," she says, without further explanation. She's smiling as if she's trying very hard not to let slip a secret. Or maybe that's just how she smiles. But before I can say anything else Graham stomps over and looms above us.

"Is he all right?"

"He's fine," the woman says. "But even with the wetsuit he's cold. We should get him warmed up pretty fast—don't want him going into shock. Can you get us back to the huts fairly sharpish?"

There's a calm authority to her voice. I'm grateful for this, as the way Graham is scowling at me suggests that if it weren't for her, he would leave me on the riverbank, or shove me coughing off down the river on a dinghy like an asthmatic Huckleberry Finn. He steers a little way downriver and the woman helps me off the boat.

"Not much further now," she says. I think I've narrowed her accent down to Kiwi.

Graham moors the raft and the woman helps me off. There's another hut here for people to change in, but it's currently occupied by a different group, so the woman ushers me onto the coach. As we board it, she asks the bus driver what his name is, and when he tells her it's Frank she says, "Great stuff, Frank, I'm Tess," and instructs him to hand over both the tartan towel on the dashboard and his flask of tea. He looks at me shivering away and complies, albeit reluctantly.

"Thanks, Frank," the woman says. Then she turns to me and says, "Right. Get yourself out of the wetsuit and get dry with the towel, please."

I look at the towel and then make eye contact with Frank in the rearview mirror. It's clear neither of us wants this to happen—particularly from my point of view, as who knows what this towel is there for—but the Kiwi tells me to get on with it before turning on the spot and folding her arms. There is something rather artful about the way she does this, as if she might know her way around the stage.

"I'm Tess, by the way," she says.

"I heard," I reply. "I'm Brian." With some difficulty I pull off the wetsuit and dry myself with the towel, which I wrap around myself. I realize it's the first time in a long while that I've been this naked in front of a person. (Two people, I suppose, if you count Frank.)

"Would you mind—my bag, it's on the seat next to you . . ."

Tess reaches for it and hands it back to me, still facing forward. I notice a small, delicate tattoo just below her left ear. I think it's a wave, or possibly the silhouette of a bird. With some difficulty, fingers still stiff from the cold, I pull my clothes on.

"OK, I'm, erm, decent," I say.

"What's that?"

"I'm, you know, clothed."

She turns around and looks at me quite intently. Despite now being dressed, I somehow feel even more exposed.

"Why don't you sit down," she says. "I'm sure you're fine but I better just give you the once-over."

"Ah," I say, things becoming a little more clear, "you're a doctor."

"Oh, nah, I'm actually a postwoman. But I've seen loads of *Grey's Anatomy*, so don't worry."

I stare at her. She frowns and puts her hands on her hips. "Hmm, ability to detect sarcasm clouded, maybe that's the hypothermia setting in already."

I smile weakly and take a seat by the window. Tess sits next to me.

"Show me your hands there, Brian."

I do so.

"Just hold 'em out and wiggle your fingers for me. OK, good stuff, you're doing great."

She reaches up and gently tilts my face around, watching where my eyes go. It's very strange, this contact. I don't really know what to do with myself.

"And can you just tell me where you are and what year it is."

I am well aware of the answers to these questions, but my brain is a bit scrambled and they seem to be eluding me just now.

"Brian?"

For the first time, concern appears on her face. Her eyes search mine with a little more urgency. Frank the bus driver is shuffling around, and his elbow bumps the horn.

"I'm fine," I say, the beep snapping me out of it. "Really."

She relaxes a little at this, but still insists on hearing me answer the questions so that she can listen to my voice—apparently slurring is a sign of hypothermia.

"So what do you do if a drunk person falls into that kind of cold water?"

"Oh, then I just flip a coin and hope for the best," Tess says.

I smile to show that this time I have correctly recognized humor. "I should clarify," Tess adds. "I'm actually just a physio."

"Well," I say, "you seem very proficient," which is so dreadfully and—unintentionally—patronizing that I'm close to running off and jumping back into the river. "Sorry, that's not quite how I meant that to sound."

"I'll let you off," Tess says.

Our fellow rafters have had the chance to change now, and they're getting onto the bus, glaring at me as they pass.

"Well, I better get back to my seat," Tess says. She lowers her voice: "Don't want them thinking I've been fraternizing with the enemy. Although personally your little swim was the highlight of the whole thing for me."

She gets up and I try to thank her, and to apologize for my clumsy backhanded compliment just now, but people keep pushing past us to get to their seats, and eventually Tess is swept up in the stream of people and carried off down the coach.

I'm disappointed not to have apologized properly, and I realize I never got to the bottom of whether we've actually met before, and then I remember with a massive, swooping jolt that this is all entirely inconsequential given what I learned from Graham before my unexpected bath.

28.

RESTING MY EYES

We seem to be back in Edinburgh, although I'm slightly concerned that I can't remember any of the drive. Did I fall asleep? I feel dizzy and disoriented. Maybe Tess the Kiwi was too hasty to pronounce me fine. I could go and ask her to check me over again, I suppose, but I'm wary of causing any more of a fuss than I have already.

We come to a stop outside a generic-looking chain hotel and the vast majority of the people—including Tess—start to funnel off. It's then that I realize I didn't get as far as picking accommodations for tonight, or even deciding on if I'm staying in the city at all. If there's an update from Lily I might need to head off again. Just then pain shoots through my temple. When I blink my eyes there are spots in front of them. Looking out of the window, I can make out Tess walking into the hotel, brow furrowed as she checks her phone. I decide that if I am going to collapse I'd best do it near a medical professional, and so I join the gaggle of people getting off the bus, grab my suitcase from the hold, and head inside. But when I get to reception Tess has disappeared already. The receptionist looks at me expectantly, and after another bout of dizziness hits I decide to be sensible and book a room. I just need to rest my eyes and regain my strength.

I haul myself and my suitcase into the lift and go up to my room, where I collapse onto the bed and close my eyes. I open them what feels like a moment later, but I'm lying on my front and have no sensation in either arm. By the time I've managed to shake some feeling back into them and got to my phone, it's to find out that I've managed to "rest my eyes" for five hours. *Shit.* Chastising myself, I drag my laptop onto the bed and connect to the Wi-Fi, then refresh Lily's reviews. There's nothing new, thankfully, so I have to assume she's stayed in Edinburgh.

I'm still not feeling my best. I've got a pounding headache and everything seems to ache. I swallow some paracetamol from my wash bag and turn on the shower. The water is either scalding hot and a dribble or as powerful as a riot control hose but freezing cold. I dry myself on a towel that appears to be made of uncooked kale and get dressed. I don't really feel like going anywhere, but my room—with its experimentally thin pillows and the nagging sense that someone has recently screamed into the bathroom mirror—is so miserable that I'm desperate to get out.

When I get down to the hotel bar, I feel like I should have stayed in my room. It's far too brightly lit and entirely empty apart from a man drinking a lager with a whisky chaser, staring out at the rainy street outside and muttering to himself. I decide to sit up at the bar so that there's no chance of him catching my eye, and order a pint of beer and some peanuts from a barman with lank, braided hair like damp linguini. As I wait for my drink I open my laptop and refresh Lily's page. Nothing new. For the next half an hour I shovel peanuts into my mouth with one hand and hit refresh with the other. I try to dismiss the realization that if I was at the County Arms I'd be in my usual seat, staring at the door—and that sitting here now refreshing Tripadvisor means I've just replaced one kind of vigil with another.

I hurl more peanuts into my mouth and manage to get some crumbs down my windpipe. I'm in the midst of a coughing fit when I feel a firm hand striking me on the back. It takes me a second to regain my breath, and when I turn to see who my savior is, I realize that it's Tess. She seems to have performed this potentially lifesaving operation without stopping—like the opposite of a drive-by shooting—because she's already halfway across the room, taking a table in the corner and pulling out a book. She gives me a friendly wave, which I reciprocate. I'm aware that not only is this the second time she's come to my rescue today, I've still barely thanked her for the first.

I refresh my laptop. Still nothing. I look around and see Tess well ensconced in her book, although I have a sneaking suspicion that she's just been looking at me. I drum my fingers on the bar. I don't want to interrupt her privacy, but at the same time the nagging guilt I feel is only going to get worse. I collect my laptop and drink and make my way over. As I get nearer, Tess looks up and smiles at me, and all at once this miserable bar feels a lot warmer.

"Hiya, Brian."

"Hi," I say. "Thanks for that just now. This isn't exactly top of my list of places where I'd choose to choke to death."

Oh god.

"Anytime."

"And of course earlier too, on the coach—thank you for checking on me. Not my finest moment."

"Ah well," she says with a shrug. She still has her finger on the page she's been reading. I feel like that's a fairly clear sign I shouldn't disturb her more, so I decide to complete my apology and leave her be.

"Well, I'm not sure it quite makes up for having my life saved twice, but just to say thank you, again. I promise I'll try and not die in your proximity again." I turn around, eyes screwed shut as I contemplate this gibberish, keen to get back to the bar.

"Three times, actually."

I turn back. "I'm sorry?"

"Although I suppose York's a bit of a stretch, in fairness."

I must be looking very confused because Tess laughs and says, "That restaurant? Daly's? That guy who picked up your credit card was pretty angry, but I managed to calm him down after you'd left. Luckily, I've watched enough *EastEnders* to know you're supposed to go, 'It's not worth it!'"

Stupidly, my first response to this piece of information is to say, "I didn't know they showed *EastEnders* in New Zealand."

"Oh, big-time," Tess says. "We import all sorts from the UK—*EastEnders*, Duran Duran, casual racism . . ."

Unbeknownst to me, the barman has appeared at my side, and I jump out of my skin as he speaks, much to Tess's obvious amusement, though she's good enough to hide it as much as she can.

"Can I get you something?" the barman asks her.

"Absolutely," she replies brightly, reciprocating a friendliness that wasn't there. Her eyes go to his name badge. "Please could I see a wine list, Callum?"

He looks at her as if she's asked him to fetch her the Galápagos Islands, or a rainbow, and without missing a beat Tess says, "Yeah, good point actually, I'll just have a large glass of house white."

"I'll get this," I say to the barman, realizing this is my way to make amends.

"You sure?" Tess asks.

"Least I could do."

"In that case, fancy joining me and we make it a bottle?"

I'm aware of the weight of the laptop in my hand, but I suppose, on balance, that a couple of drinks can't hurt. "Yes, that'd be nice. I promise I'll try not to swallow the cork or anything."

"Good-o."

Tess pokes the chair opposite her toward me with her foot, and I sit down.

Just a couple of drinks, I think. *That's all.*

29.

DRUNK ARCHITECTS

We've barely said a word before Callum's returned with our wine.

"Enjoy," he says, with a hint of an upward inflection, then shuffles off again. Tess fills our glasses and lifts hers up to clink mine.

"Enjoy?" she says.

"Enjoy?" I repeat.

There's a stylishness to the way she lifts the glass to her mouth. I can see her on one of those weekend chat shows where people cook and interview each other. As she puts the glass down, I notice the faint white band of skin around her otherwise tanned ring finger.

"I can see why he said 'enjoy' like that now," she says, wrinkling her nose. "Yikes."

I take a sip. She's very much right. "Yikes indeed."

She laughs at this, I assume because of my somewhat stuffy use of the word "indeed," and I feel warmth coming to my cheeks. In this light, it's harder to see the streak of purple in her hair. I wonder whether I might have imagined it. But just then she runs her hands through her hair, and I see it's definitely there. I'm obviously not being too subtle, because Tess sighs and says, "Oh, I know—I'm already regretting it."

"No, no—not at all. I mean you shouldn't. I just couldn't quite work out what color it was. But it looks good. Great, I mean."

"Hmm, thanks for that very convincing review. I'm still not sure. I was all for it until approximately four seconds after I'd walked out of the salon. I caught my reflection in a shop window and thought, *Oh great, Victoria and the girls have got a new member, it's Recently Single Spice.*"

At this point her phone starts to vibrate on the table. I wonder if the conversation she's about to have will last long enough for me to have a quick refresh of my laptop—but she just watches the phone as it creeps slowly across the table with every vibration, until eventually it stops.

"That makes it forty," Tess says. "No, wait, forty-one."

"Forty-one . . . ?"

She turns over the phone and shows me the screen. There are forty-one missed calls, all from someone called Mark.

A few immediate questions appear in my mind. I'm not sure it's my place to ask any of them, but after a moment Tess smiles and says, "I think I can actually see your thought bubbles appearing like a cartoon." She reaches over and pops the imaginary bubbles around my head, then lowers her hands, looking embarrassed. There is something rather endearing about this.

"Twenty-two years," she says, staring into the middle distance. "That's how long I was married for. *Twenty-two*, Brian. That's when pop stars are over the hill these days." She rolls her eyes. "Listen to me: 'pop stars.' Does anyone say that anymore? I'll be talking about the 'hit parade' next."

"If it's any consolation," I say, "the other day, I was speaking to a young person who works in my pub and I asked him whether he'd ever listened to Fleetwood Mac . . . and he'd never heard of them."

Tess gasps. I nod. We sip the horrible wine. Tess, I notice, manages to pull off the neat trick of looking attractive even when she wrinkles her nose.

"So you own a pub?" she says. "Is that as fun as it sounds?"

The image comes to me, jarringly fast and clear, of Lily behind the bar, smiling and in blue, in her element. It takes me a second or two to answer.

"It has its moments," I say. And then I wince, because I completely forgot about the letter O falling off the sign, and the pub's unfortunate new name. It's amusing watching Tess's shifting reaction as I tell her this, as she's clearly not sure whether she's allowed to find it funny. I go to get her off the hook by asking what *she* does for a living, but then I remember, of course, that she's a physiotherapist. I'm spared the embarrassment of the mistake when her phone rings again. This time she mimes dunking it in her wine, then slides it to the side of the table. But she doesn't actually switch it off.

The curiosity gets the better of me, and I ask if Mark is her husband.

"Was," she says.

"And do you mind me asking what the . . . state of play . . . is?"

"That's a very British way of asking," Tess says, smiling. "The *state of play* is that we've been separated six months. Divorce next, probably. Hence why I've flown halfway around the world on this trip to try to get away from it all."

"Well, I'm sorry to hear that," I say dutifully.

"Don't be," Tess says. "It had been on the cards for a very

long time. I thought we were going to push past it all but then—and this is so unlucky, actually—he accidentally had sex with our secretary several times."

"Ah. That *is* unlucky."

Tess nods. "*Isn't it?* The worst thing is she'd asked for access to both of our diaries, so she knew when he'd be free and I'd be busy. If only she'd been that efficient with my physio appointments!"

"Hmm. You could mention it at her annual review, perhaps?"

Thankfully, Tess smiles at this. I notice the laughter lines around her mouth, which very much suit her. I'm also rather taken with her eyebrows. She has a talent for raising each one individually, then at the same time, depending on which point she's making, to great effect.

"Is your husband a physio too?" I ask.

"No, he just managed the practice. I did think it was odd when he hired someone to help him. He spent enough time with his feet up." She sits back and folds her arms. "I think the worst thing about it all is how even when I try to comfort myself by looking back at the good times, they don't seem good anymore. Do you know what I mean?"

I nod but don't say anything.

"Take this, for instance," Tess says, reaching for her phone and turning the screen on. "Look, he's in there as Mark with a K, because that's how I thought he spelled it for the first month after we'd met, but he spells it with a C. And I never changed it, because the longer I left it the funnier it got, but now this and all those other little in-jokes, they're tainted, you know?"

I don't answer, because this is obviously rhetorical, but also because I get the sense that these thoughts have been percolating in Tess's mind for a while, and perhaps this is the first time she's had a chance to say them out loud. I hold back and top up her wine instead.

"And when you start pulling at that thread," she continues, "then you start thinking about all the rest of it. Do you know what I thought of the other day? I can't remember the last time he laughed at something I said. In a good way, I mean. In fact, the last time we were at a dinner party I was getting animated when I was telling some story or other, and maybe I was being a bit loud, I don't know—but I glanced over and saw his face and he just looked . . ." Here she has to break off for a second. "He just looked so embarrassed."

She breaks off again. I'm surprised at how cross this story has made me on her behalf.

Tess takes a sip of wine and smiles sadly.

"I very nearly said something. Bottled it, though. I overlooked quite a lot of stuff like that, I guess. Probably because it felt easier to pretend I was happy than the alternative."

She takes another, longer sip of wine.

"What I've realized, Brian, when I look back at it all, is that a relationship is like a house being designed by two drunk architects. It seems amazing at the time but then when you look at what you've built you realize it makes absolutely no fucking sense at all."

I smile at this. "I think that's the most profound thing that's ever been said in a Premier Inn."

Tess laughs, her eyes sparkling. "Oh god," she says, head in hands, "I bet you're glad you came over now, eh?"

For comic effect I make an exaggerated show of pretending I'm asking for the bill, which inevitably means Callum the barman comes over and I have to try to explain that I'm just joking. By the time he's finally got the message, Tess has got a full-blown case of the giggles, and I suppose it's been a very long day because it's not long before I capitulate too.

"Dearie me," Tess says, dabbing at her eyes. As I reach for the wine bottle I glance at my watch and realize it's later than I thought. *We'll just finish this bottle*, I think, *and then I'll get back to my laptop*.

"Thanks for letting me get all that off my chest," Tess says. "I feel much better for talking to you. Well, at you. It's either that or this weird wine."

"We're probably both an acquired taste," I say, though I'm not entirely sure why.

"I don't believe that about you for a second, Brian," Tess says, holding my gaze.

"So where have your travels taken you so far?" I ask, feeling the need to change the subject.

"Just York and Edinburgh so far," Tess says. "Fair old way up here, isn't it, once you've flown into Heathrow? I wasn't really sure where I was going but then obviously"—she taps her book—"spotted all the ladies carrying this and just followed them."

"Right," I say. Then, "Sorry, hang on, you've lost me . . ."

Tess turns the book over. I could have guessed what it is.

"*And Breathe* . . . Of course. What is that thing actually about? I keep seeing it everywhere but I'm still none the wiser."

Tess pushes it toward me. "Don't judge me," she says, "because it's pretty airy-fairy. But it's not completely woo-woo, you know?"

I do not.

"The author's this Canadian woman who had a horribly messy divorce blah blah blah, and then went on a *big journey of discovery* to the UK, where she learned that her husband had been holding her back, and now, delightfully, she's inspired a whole load of angry, bitter women to follow in her footsteps . . ."

"Her footsteps being . . . ?"

"Oh, it's a lot of 'experiences,' you see, everything from the quirky to the daredevilish, so one minute she's making cheese in Cheddar, then she's in the York dungeon, then she's white water rafting in Aber . . . but wait, hang on, this is what you've been doing, isn't it? Surely that's not a coincidence?"

She breaks off and looks at me, concern etched on her face.

"Um, you OK, Brian? Hey, you're not having another 'picnic,' are you?"

"No," I manage at last, taking a very large gulp of wine. I gesture toward her book. "Please could I just borrow that for a second?"

"Be my guest," Tess says. She's still watching me closely. "Are you sure everything's OK?"

I swallow. "Yes. I just . . . I'm fairly sure my wife is doing this journey too."

She pauses before she replies. "Oh, you're married?"

"Um."

"Separated?"

". . . Something like that."

30.

FREEZER SURPRISE

THEN

As the dust settled on that first Christmas with Lily's family, I didn't mention the business with Daniel and the wedding talk, but it took a fair bit of restraint not to propose to Lily there and then. I imagined sweeping her off to some remote island somewhere—us tying the knot in secret before having fifty kids and tilling the land, completely off-grid, outlaws and outcasts . . .

"What are you thinking about?" Lily would ask me when I was lost yet again in this peculiar fantasy.

"Oh, nothing," I'd reply, thinking how she'd still look great in a smock. "Nothing at all." Happily, this was just a small bump in the road.

Sue and Beth had come back to the flat in January and declared that they and their Post-it–noted lentils would soon be moving out. Much to my delight, it was Lily who suggested she and I move in together, and before long we had signed a lease on a rented flat in Archway. It was "modest yet characterful," as the estate agent put it, which meant it was small but the mice wore jazzy ties, but it was the best we could afford. I would stare enchantedly at the mold-flecked windowsill of the bathroom, on which reposed the mug with my toothbrush propping up Lily's, and feel immeasurably proud.

While moving in together might have seemed terribly grown-up, we still maintained a sense of silliness. We may have eaten our meals by candlelight, but those meals were usually anything-on-toast, or "freezer surprise"—the contents of unmarked Tupperware, which we'd reheat in the microwave while singing the *Countdown* theme tune, waiting to discover what we were about to eat.

Living with Lily meant I got to discover even more of what happened "behind the scenes." I remember waking up one morning and thinking that we were being burgled. It turned out that was just how Lily got dressed—yanking open drawers and rifling through them as if looking for keys to a safe. Then there was the night when I came upstairs to find her climbing into bed dressed in full running kit—everything apart from the shoes.

"Are you planning on having very energetic dreams?" I asked her.

"Har har, very funny," she replied. "No, I'm going for a run first thing tomorrow. This is the only way I know I'll definitely go through with it." She went on to explain that in the years before we met she had all too often been crippled by the curse of indecisiveness. Ordering from menus, for example, would be fraught affairs, often driving her friends and family to distraction, and even at work she'd often let problems pile up and go unanswered until they'd boil over. Things came to a head on a beach holiday to Brighton with some friends a few years before we'd met, when she spent forty-five minutes edging her way into the sea, inch by inch, never quite gathering the courage to dive in. From that moment on, she told me, she'd decided to change. She would do first, ask questions later.

The evidence for this war on indecisiveness often accumulated on our front porch.

"I wonder if I should be someone who knits," she mused out loud one morning, and then I saw the flash in her eyes and she was reaching for the phone and the yellow pages, searching for arts and crafts suppliers, and sure enough I came home from work a few days later to find that our house looked like the aftermath of an explosion in a wool factory.

"How's it all going then?" I asked, looking down at her on the floor, where most of the wool had accumulated.

"Well, it's not for me, but at least I tried it," she said.

I did think about gently pointing out that perhaps there was a middle ground that didn't involve turning our flat into a tripwire obstacle course, but I decided I'd be better off keeping schtum.

When Lily wasn't indulging her latest whim, she was guiding me through the choppy waters of an attempted lifestyle overhaul. Given that I'd had my clothes bought for me by my grandmother until the age of fifteen, I was never a natural when it came to style. With deliberate breeziness, Lily took me on shopping expeditions, framing them as fun outings, and gently explained what colors would suit me best—or that it was a false economy to thrift on a coat when spending money would pay off in the long term. Her expertise didn't stop there. One of the many practical skills that she had acquired—among the likes of carpentry, soldering, and how to use a spirit level, which did make me wonder if she might have been in prison at some point—was hairdressing. Every couple of months I'd be directed into "Lily's Salon" (the kitchen), where she trimmed and clippered my unruly hair, all the time pretending that she was going to make me look like Friar Tuck.

I'm aware that this sounds a bit clichéd—the stuff of useless, bored men being dragged around department stores, then being allowed to check the football results in Dixons' window—but it didn't feel like that. Lily wasn't trying to change me. She wasn't sanding down my edges, it was more of a case of coaxing a more confident person out of me. And it worked. For someone used to the shield of a straggly fringe and rounded shoulders—a posture that lent itself to going unnoticed—I began to stand a little taller and feel more self-assured. At work, I stopped doing stuff foisted on me by colleagues used to taking advantage. I began to speak up more in meetings. I even suggested a streamlining process to my boss, the indirect result of which led to our company being nominated for a prize at the National Insurance Awards.

At the black-tie reception (remarkably, there really was one), when it was announced that we'd won, I was persuaded to go up and collect the award. That night, with Lily on my arm, I might have been at some insurance awards that were sponsored by a (now defunct) kettle manufacturer, but for those few hours I felt like a movie star. It was even worth the calamitous hangover the next day, which left me prone on the sofa. Lily, who'd been more restrained, found great pleasure in mocking me, referring to me simply as *the disaster*.

"Now, does the disaster plan on spending all day lying here?" she asked, like she was reading a children's story. I groaned in response. "Or does the disaster want to see some daylight?" I groaned again. As Lily went to leave, I raised my head and said, "Hey, this disaster loves you, doesn't that count for anything?" and even though she simply raised an eyebrow at this, I'd like to think it did.

A LIGHT SPATTERING of rain during those otherwise fair-weather days came when I woke up to Lily asking me the following question: "Do you think it's a problem that we've never had an argument?"

My brain grasped for the correct response, like a panicked am-dram director arranging his cast—*Positions, everyone!*—and I eventually settled on the phrase "Isn't that a good thing?" Lily's expression told me it wasn't, although I couldn't quite work out why. I'd never understood why screaming matches and hurled ornaments supposedly made a relationship more serious or authentic. I made this case to Lily, but it continued to bother her, leading to the faintly surreal moment when we did have our first argument . . . about the fact we hadn't had an argument yet. In the heat of it all I remember being self-aware enough to think, *This should be the point where one of us storms out*, and so I did. I made it about eight minutes down the road before realizing how stupid it was. Even with the layer of artifice surrounding the fight, I felt wretched, and as soon as I came back through the door Lily flung her arms around me, evidently feeling the same way.

Later, lying in bed, Lily said, "Shall we agree to be a bit more open about things, though—about how we're feeling in general?" I agreed that we would, which meant for the next few weeks we practiced what we preached—Lily solemnly sitting me down to relay the devastating news that she got cross when I left wet towels on the bedroom floor, and I admitting that while I loved her cooking—and I really did—I did not care for her occasionally overzealous use of coriander.

On my part, that was as far as I ever went. In truth, my first experience of what an argument with Lily would be like had been upsetting enough to me that I was very much determined never to end up in that position ever again.

THE NEXT FEW years seemed to flash past. At twenty-eight, we were still carrying the puppy fat of youth (metaphorically in Lily's case, more literally in mine), but life was starting to feel a bit more serious. Lily got a new job as features editor at a recently launched food and lifestyle magazine, which meant even more trips to nice restaurants. I went up another rung at my insurance company, one that came with a salary increase that meant I didn't feel guilty for buying slightly fancy bread from time to time. Our salad days were becoming our ciabatta days, as I intoned loftily to Lily, who charitably waited until the third time I'd said it before she threw something at me.

An unwelcome consequence of time marching on came when my grandfather, who'd been slowing down a little but was still in good form whenever I went to visit him, passed away rather suddenly from a stroke. The funeral would have been a bleak affair if it weren't for Lily. I would never forget the reassuring look she gave me, the simplicity of her mouthing the words "It's OK" from her pew, when I was struggling to gather myself as I gave his eulogy. And then during the wake afterward, where she so effortlessly drew together the ragtag bunch of people in attendance, making introductions, finding common ground, speaking to them as if she'd known each of them for years, all of which gave me the freedom to compose myself by the mountain of egg-and-cress sandwiches in the kitchen.

I did all in my power to be there for Lily when she was going through her own tough times—ones that were often precipitated by phone calls with her mother, or dinner with her father when he came down to London. I gradually improved my sense of how best to go about making her feel better. Now I knew that sometimes she'd want to talk at a hundred miles an hour and get everything off her chest, pacing around the living room while I listened and surreptitiously sourced her snacks. On other occasions I knew it was silliness that would work: my impression of a giraffe chewing the leaves of one of our houseplants was a favorite around then.

Now that we'd weathered a few storms, I felt that we'd come out of the other side of them even stronger. That little rented flat of ours may have been gradually falling apart, but it was still our fortress. As long as we were curled up on the sofa, squabbling over whose turn it was to put the kettle on, going to great lengths to make each other laugh, I didn't think it was possible that we'd ever lose our grip on happiness.

31.

ON THE SPECIFICS OF CHEESEMAKING

NOW

Tess has been watching me in charitable silence ever since I grabbed her book without explanation and started flicking frantically through the pages. This new knowledge I have is an absolute game-changer. Before, I was flailing, desperately scrabbling for whatever new information I could unearth. But now—thanks to the unlikely intervention of a tipsy Kiwi thousands of miles from home—I'm finally on the front foot.

Tess clears her throat politely and says, "Brian, would it be ever so rude of me to ask what's happening?"

"Sorry," I say. "Of course. It's just quite a long story, that's all."

Tess gestures as if to say the floor is mine. I suspect she might not be prepared for what I'm about to tell her. When I end with the implications of finding out about the journey in this book, she sums up her feelings in a single word: "Wowzers."

Wowzers, I think, *is just about right*.

"So, wait, it's Cheddar next."

"Pardon?"

"The next place on the list," she clarifies, gesturing to the book. "That's where she'll be going tomorrow, right?"

"Oh, I see. I assume so, yes." I flick to the relevant page and read the introduction.

"What?" Tess asks, because I'm frowning.

"'Cheesemaking helped me lose myself, the timeless art a reminder of the way traditions can comfort and nourish us.'" I look up at Tess.

"It's not all like that," she protests. "OK, it is, bu—"

"Wait," I say, flicking the page over. "Sorry, but I've just realized something."

"What?" Tess asks.

"Well, I've been one step behind so far, haven't I? If I go to Cheddar tomorrow I'll probably just miss her again. But if I go to the place *after*—Bath—I'll be there when she arrives. That'll give me a much better chance."

"Good thinking," Tess says. She takes a sip of wine and there's a moment when she looks thoughtful before she says, "Do you think it's really her? Your wife?"

On hearing her say these words, it feels like I've just been pulled out of that freezing water all over again, sound rushing back to my ears, all the breath squeezed from my chest. There was no judgment in Tess's voice. Far from it. I think that's why it's stopped me in my tracks. If Tess had sounded incredulous, or even skeptical, I might have retreated into defensiveness. But she just sounded curious. Taking a step back, just for a second, I realize how much I've been letting myself get carried away when all I've really got as tangible evidence is Graham saying my description of Lily "rings a bell." I'm momentarily quiet and Tess starts to apologize—worried, I think, that her directness has upset me—but I tell her there's no need. I can't pretend some of my hope isn't swirling away down the plughole, but if I let myself get carried away, then won't that just lead to more pain in the end, if this isn't Lily?

"I'm, um, not sure really," I mumble. "But I suppose I'm trying to find some kind of . . . ending."

We're silent for a moment.

"I'm sorry," I say. "This is supposed to be me making things up to you for earlier."

"Oh, don't worry about that," Tess says.

"No, honestly. Let's change the subject."

I move to top up Tess's glass. I find myself wondering when was the last time I did that when it wasn't in my capacity as barman. Tess smiles at me as she swishes wine around her glass again, and I find myself sitting up a little straighter in my chair.

Thankfully, Tess is rather good at changing the subject. We seem to cover a lot of conversational ground after this, skipping from one topic to the next: musical instruments we learned as children (Tess too was forced to try violin, and it sounds like she was even more hopeless than me), jobs, and how everyone in city cafés seems to be just pretending to do one. The more we talk, the more I'm aware of how much I've missed this feeling. I find myself remembering stories I've not thought about for years, and experiencing that very particular buzz of realizing I'm spending time with someone I could talk to about anything—sincere or silly, important or trivial—and I'd never once get bored.

I'm aware that I'd like this evening to go on longer, but also that it's rather late. When Tess comes back from the loo, I say, "I suppose I should think about hitting the old hay"—not a phrase I'm sure I've ever used before. I can't help but notice that Tess seems a little disappointed. "But obviously I feel bad leaving you with the rest of this wine to work your way through," I bumble on.

"Don't worry," Tess says. "I mean, you've got a big day ahead of you tomorrow, right? Just spare a thought for the hungover me tomorrow, standing over a big vat of mold. At least I assume that's what's involved."

She's lost me here, and the confusion on my face makes her laugh.

"Cheesemaking," she says.

"Of course."

She raises a mock toast to herself.

I think about tomorrow. It's a long way down to Bath. I should go to bed, but I find myself lingering. The idea of saying good-bye to Tess now doesn't feel right—to get this new information from her and then immediately cast her aside. But, more than that, I realize that the idea of not seeing her again leaves me feeling rather sad.

"On second thought," I say, clearing my throat, "I did say I'd help you finish the bottle, didn't I? And I'm a man of my word."

"Well," Tess says, "if you insist."

And the smile she gives afterward makes me feel very strange indeed.

WE MAKE IT through the wine, the last (warm) glass providing a particular challenge. Tess makes us honor the moment by shaking hands. She insists we have to look solemn as we do so, while maintaining eye contact, and it takes us three attempts before we get through it without one of us cracking and smiling.

When Tess tells me a story about the last person she gave

physio to, I can't resist asking her for some advice off the clock on my troublesome knee, and why it hurts in the mornings. She looks concerned when I tell her this, and despite my protests she insists on coming around to my side of the table and stretching my leg out back and forth.

"How does that feel, me doing that?" she asks, looking up at me, and I'm slightly lost for words for a second or two.

"Yeah, fine," I say at last, though in truth it's hard to concentrate.

Tess also seems distracted, and as our eyes meet she quickly looks away, then retakes her seat, telling me she's sure it's nothing to worry about.

"Even though it crackles like someone popping bubble wrap?" I ask, feeling like I should get us back to solid ground.

"'Crepitus'—if you want to be technical about it." She's not quite meeting my gaze.

"Isn't that a small French pancake?"

Here Tess looks at me and raises a single eyebrow. I maintain my innocence until it gets too much and I start to laugh. Eventually, Tess can't help joining in.

Callum the barman begins stacking chairs around us. Tess stands up, and absurdly I rush to do the same, like I'm the Earl of Gloucester at dinner in his castle. We make our way to the lifts, and there's something about the silence that's amplified by the thick hotel carpet that makes me feel self-conscious about how I'm walking. Do I normally swing my arms at my sides like this?

We get into the lift and the doors close.

"I'm on four," I say, pressing the button. "How about you?"

"Three for me," Tess replies. She hums under her breath as we go up. When we reach her floor, the doors seem to take an age to open. Tess moves half out of the lift and says, "Well, Brian, it's been a pleasure. Thanks for such a fun evening. Who knew my favorite night of the trip so far would be spent in a Premier Inn bar . . ."

"All down to the ambience Callum created, I'm sure," I reply, which makes me annoyed at myself, because I've had such a nice time too, so why have I gone and undercut it?

"Well then," Tess says. "You ever need some physio advice from the other side of the world, you should look me up. I'll see you when I see you, Brian."

And with that she steps out of the lift, and the doors begin to close. I think it's Tess saying "the other side of the world" that makes me do it, because it brings home just how unlikely it is that I'll ever see her again. The next thing I know, I've stuck out a foot to stop the doors from closing and then I'm stepping into the corridor.

"Hi again," I say, before I quite know what I'm doing, and Tess turns around, looking surprised. "Far be it from me to ruin your schedule," I continue, "but if you'd rather *not* go to Cheddar, and fancied a bit of company instead, you could always come to Bath. You know, with me. Not that I can't see the temptation of stirring lots of buckets of fermented milk, obviously."

Tess looks confused. "Fermented milk?"

"Yes, you know. Cheesemaking? Fermented milk?"

"Oh yes. Fermented milk."

"I'm not actually sure if it is fermented milk, come to think of it."

Tess suggests that at least one of us should probably stop saying the words "fermented milk," and I agree that we should.

Tess runs her hand through her hair. It's only as she prepares to answer that I realize how much I want her to say that she'll come.

"Well, why the hell not?" she says at last.

"Great. That's, yes, great news. Shall we say downstairs at nine, then?"

"Downstairs at nine it is," Tess replies. "Night, Brian."

"Night," I reply. Tess turns and starts to walk down the corridor. As I return to the lift, I just about resist the temptation to turn and look back. But there's a window up at the end of the corridor, and when I see in its reflection Tess turning to sneak a glance at me, I feel very light on my feet indeed.

A hint of Tess's perfume lingers in the lift as I take it up to my floor. It's only when I step out into the corridor, and it's replaced by stale tobacco, and I'm walking past a hundred identical doors trying to find my room, that I find myself wondering if there's a chance, however small, that I might have just made a rather large mistake.

32.

US TWO NEXT

THEN

Two years after we moved in together, I proposed to Lily on a cold, soggy day on a beach in South Wales. This had not been the plan. In fact, I didn't even have the ring with me.

My intended proposal destination was Barcelona. I'd booked the holiday for that summer and planned the whole thing with the meticulousness of a bank robber doing one last job. But there was a moment as we gamely tramped along the stodgy Pembrokeshire sand, fighting back against a fierce wind, laughing at how ridiculous it all was as freezing rain pummeled us, when I just found myself overcome by how happy I was. To be the only two people on this quagmire, battered but unbowed by all the elements thrown at us, it meant too much to me to ignore it.

When I dropped to one knee, Lily looked at me—holding the hood of her parka over her ears, bracing herself against the wind—and shouted, "Have you lost something?"

"No," I shouted back. And then, in a rare flash of inspiration: "But I've found the person I want to spe—"

"WHAT?"

"I SAID, I'VE FOUND . . . never mind—WILL YOU MARRY ME?"

At first I thought she still couldn't hear me, because she was just standing there. But it must have been a delayed reaction, because shortly afterward she rugby-tackled me into the freezing sand. I took this to be a yes, but I made her confirm it as we sat in pajamas on the kitchen floor of the cottage we were staying in, clothes drying on the Aga.

We'd had a fair amount of practice with weddings over the last couple of summers. Even months before I proposed, I was using the receptions to take notes for my speech, which could be summarized as "keep it short and don't insult people." I couldn't quite tell whether Lily was spending as much time thinking about the day we'd be up there as I was. We were so happy together as it was that a part of me did wonder whether there was any need to change things. Would getting married and becoming husband and wife make everything a bit stiff and serious all of a sudden? Would we still be the sorts of people who'd dedicate whole evenings to imagining our dream pub, for instance?

(It was while we curled up in one particularly pleasing East End pub nook that we first set about this game—choosing everything from the drinks to the floorboards to the selection of board games we'd offer.

"Do you think I'd make a good landlord?" I'd asked her when we got home.

"Well, there's only one way to find out," Lily said. She pointed behind the kitchen counter. "You pretend to be behind the bar and I'll be a customer coming in."

We acted out this scenario several times, but I never quite managed to make a believable landlord.

"You need to find a balance between TV magician and troubled gamekeeper," Lily told me, a note that unfortunately I failed to file away.)

My concerns swiftly disappeared the moment we told friends our news. Their joy was infectious—Ed seemed genuinely delighted to be my best man—and it made me realize that getting married was about celebrating what Lily and I had, not changing it.

Forbes and Verity responded to the news less enthusiastically, it's fair to say. Forbes shook my hand like he was trying to squeeze the life out of a small animal. Verity hugged Lily and rocked her from side to side, her eyes closed, as if Lily had just told her she was gravely ill. Later, drinking champagne on the veranda, Forbes turned to Lily and said, "I presume you won't be giving up your job or anything as old-fashioned as that."

"No!" Lily laughed. "Why on earth would I do that?"

"Can't afford to, I expect. Remind me, darling, what is it you do these days?"

Lily looked a bit confused. "I'm at the new magazine, features editor. I told you, didn't I?"

Forbes rubbed his chin contemplatively. "Oh yes, of course. Of course. I just wonder if that's what you want to spend your life doing, being involved with all that tawdry tittle-tattle."

Lily blanched and looked at her feet. I was so stunned I felt my mouth actually fall open. But nothing came out of it.

"It's not tittle-tattle," Lily said.

"What?" Forbes barked.

"I said it's not tittle-tattle."

Lily gave him a fierce look, her eyes brimming with tears. But Forbes, I noticed, was more interested in me. "I think your husband-to-be rather shares my opinion."

My unchecked reaction to this was to laugh, purely out of shock at how ridiculous that was. Unfortunately, Lily took this to mean that I was agreeing with him.

"Well, I'm glad my career is such a source of amusement to everyone," she said, downing the rest of her champagne and walking off back to the house. I followed her, asking her to wait, but not before I'd seen Forbes watching us go with a triumphant smile on his face.

As the wedding approached, I found that while I was excited to celebrate the occasion with Lily in front of all our friends, I was also willing the day to arrive before Forbes had the chance to cause further upset. While I knew he disapproved of me—I was used to the remarks designed to undermine me by now—it felt like insulting Lily in my presence was a more targeted tactic to drive a wedge between us, and as much as I hated to admit it, I knew there was a chance it might work.

LILY AND I were married in August, both of us having turned twenty-nine the previous month. The wedding took place in a little church near Challington House. They didn't actually do weddings there, officially, but Forbes—as he reminded everyone on several occasions—had pulled some strings. When I saw Lily for the first time she looked so beautiful I thought I might have a heart attack. Rebecca, whom I'd not seen show the slightest flicker of emotion up until then, was quite weepy as she followed her sister inside. Her daughter, Edie, was on flower girl duties. Over the previous few days she and I had unexpectedly struck up our own little rapport. I was delighted to see her fix me with her best funny monster face when she spotted me at the end of the aisle. I duly reciprocated, pulling my cheeks apart with my fingers, much to the vicar's confusion.

Looking back at the congregation after Lily and I shared our first kiss as husband and wife, I couldn't help but notice the contrast between the pews on the left and right. Lily's side was packed—standing room only—and each person was immaculately turned out. Many of the men were in top hat and tails, the women with feathery fascinators set at the perfect angle—everyone with dazzling smiles, particularly Daniel of course. On my side, however, was a sparse collection of misfits spread comfortably across the pews—a couple of school friends whom, embarrassingly, I'd had to write letters to, hoping they'd reach the right place. Then some people from my accountancy course. That left Uncle Mike from Dover and a bunch from work who'd made the trip up and had obviously found a pub en route, judging by their enthusiastic hymn singing. I really missed Grandma and Grandad then. I wished they could have been there to see me get married. *But it's OK*, I thought, imagining the day, years from now, when Lily and I would be standing in a church like this again, watching our son or daughter get married. I'd get to be the one feeling proud, and that would make up for it.

Forbes seemed to have invited a lot of his friends and associates to the reception back at the house, unbeknownst to us. I got the impression he was using the occasion to curry favor with potential clients. Daniel was in the thick of it, laughing generously whenever Forbes made a joke. He seemed to know everyone there. At one point I actually heard him say, "Anyway, better circulate." I hoped he'd circulate into a pond.

Before the meal and the speeches I found myself sneaking upstairs to Lily's old bedroom, just to get a moment's peace.

When I walked in I found that Lily had had the same idea. She was sitting on the bed, peering out of the window. She looked so beautiful there, as poised as if she were posing for a portrait, that I half regretted interrupting her. That was until she looked around, beaming when she saw it was me, and said, "Well, if it isn't my husband! Quick, close the door."

I did so, then skipped over and dived onto the bed, taking her in my arms.

"Hello, my love," I said softly. "Is everything OK?"

"Yes, I just had to get away from Great-Aunt Miffy," Lily said.

"Is she the one who's brought her dog?"

"No, that's Barbara. Miffy's the one dressed as Mrs. Peacock from Clue."

Lily rolled onto her side, so we were facing each other.

"Dad's not been too much of a nightmare today?" she asked.

"Not really," I said. "He had a bit of a dig about my suit. He's taken to calling me 'captain,' I assume ironically."

"Sounds like you got off relatively lightly."

"Yep."

Lily leaned over and peered out of the window at the scene outside. "God, this is all absolutely mad, isn't it?" she said.

"I *do* feel a bit like I'm in a play."

"Ah, but not like one of those experimental ones I made you go to when we were first dating . . ."

"Do you mean the Industrial Revolution piece? Or the one about the crab?"

"The crab! I'd forgotten about that."

"How on earth could you forget about *this*?"

I got up from the bed and began moving from side to side, my hands as pincers. "What is the *state* of the cru*stace*an?" I whined.

Lily began to laugh, then flapped a hand at me to get me to stop. "Stop it, you idiot, my makeup!"

I got back onto the bed. "Sod your makeup," I said, and kissed her. Just then there was a loud rap at the door, and Forbes's unmistakable voice rasped, "Are you in there, Smudge?"

I made a rude gesture at the door, and Lily elbowed me.

"Just coming," she said in a singsong voice. We waited until we'd heard his footsteps fade away before we snuck out like a pair of guilty teenagers.

"LADIES AND GENTLEMEN," Forbes said for the second time as he tried to begin his speech. Visibly bristling at the fact he hadn't cut through the noise, he picked up an ice bucket and thumped it on the table, laughing as people jumped in their seats and finally paid attention.

The longer his speech went on, the harder it was for me to know what I would injure first: my toes, from curling them so hard in my dress shoes that I thought they might snap, or my teeth—set in a rictus grin that left them in danger of splintering. I'd been expecting some mild ribbing, but what I got was a full-on character assassination, with a real focus on how comically mismatched Lily and I were. There were some genuine gasps among the laughter. On and on it went, until I lost patience and my smile faded. At one point I picked up my spoon and dug around in my half-finished dessert, which got a nervous laugh from a few people. Unfortunately, this only seemed to spur Forbes on. And I probably could have taken it if it had been all about me, but then he moved on to Lily.

"Ah, but what is there to say about you, Smudge?" he said, winking at her.

"Hopefully nothing!" Lily said. People laughed, but like me they could clearly hear the strain in her voice and see that her smile hadn't reached her eyes. Verity, I noticed, was clutching the stem of her champagne flute tightly.

As Forbes tore into one inappropriate anecdote after another, most of which centered on Lily bringing boyfriends home ("We should have had a revolving door fitted!"), I found my anger building—partly at Forbes, but mainly at myself, for just sitting there, for letting him speak about Lily like this—until I reached breaking point.

But just as I tensed my feet to rise from my chair, the words "That's enough" forming in my mouth, Lily put her hand on my arm. She still had that fixed smile on her face, so that people wouldn't know something was amiss, but the look in her eyes told me a different story. *Don't make a scene.* And just like that, Forbes was done, finishing with a laughably sentimental line about how sad he was to be letting his "little girl go" and kissing her on the cheek. The next thing I knew, it was my turn to make a speech, and of course I was still so angry that I fluffed every line, forgot names, even messed up the "to absent friends" bit. In the moment when I said the words "my wife" for the first time, and paused for effect, as I had seen other grooms do with big goofy smiles on their faces, instead of applause there was a muted silence, as if people thought there might have been some sort of mistake.

Finally, my speech was over, and I made my escape, the whine of feedback trailing in my wake. In the cool sanctuary of the bathroom, I sat with my head in my hands. If I was going to get through the rest of the day, then I'd have to shake this off, paint on a smile like Lily had. I felt the spot on my arm where she'd held it. The last thing I wanted to do was ruin our wedding day by letting Forbes get to me.

Walking back down the hallway, preparing my best self-effacing shrug for when people asked about the speeches, I saw Forbes coming toward me. He was laughing over his shoulder as he exchanged a joke with someone, and then he turned his head and saw me. He straightened up as he got near me but didn't make eye contact as he passed. After a couple of strides past me I heard him chuckle to himself. If he hadn't, then maybe I wouldn't have said anything, but that little raspy laugh was the final straw.

"Forbes," I called after him.

He stopped and turned around.

"That was all pretty cheap, wasn't it?" I said.

"What's that?"

"I said that was all pretty cheap, the way you spoke about Lily."

Forbes's eyes narrowed. "I believe you'll find a few harmless jokes in a wedding speech is traditional."

I just looked at him.

"Now, if you'll excuse me—"

"*No*," I said, fists clenched now.

It was Forbes's turn to simply stand and look at me, and I started walking toward him as I spoke.

"I know you don't like me, but I don't care about that. I love Lily, and she loves me, and that's all that matters. So you can make all the jokes you want about me, but you need to stop being so hurtful to her."

Forbes, whose cheeks had acquired a ruddy glow, said, "You need to be very, very careful."

I shrugged. "Threaten me all you want. I don't care. We're going to go back out there in five minutes and it's all going to be rosy again, for Lily's sake, but as far as I'm concerned, we're done."

I heard a noise behind me and turned to see Lily coming into the corridor. She froze when she saw us and said, "What's going on?"

"Nothing," Forbes and I said in unison.

Lily looked at us both, then she turned on her heel and hurried away, hitching her dress up as she went. I went after her, calling her name, but when I reached the end of the hallway the only people I could see were eavesdropping waiters, who scattered like a flock of pigeons.

33.

FUNTIME

NOW

When I get up the next morning, there is only the dullest of pains in my knee. I wonder if just the bit of pulling and pushing Tess did yesterday has already had an effect.

I find myself taking longer than usual over what I'm going to wear today. As I take the lift downstairs, I'm wondering if there's a chance that Tess has simply left—waking up and realizing that actually she doesn't want to travel around with me after all. It would be easy to give me the slip. But when I come into the bar (which apparently doubles as the breakfast room), to my undeniable relief I see that Tess is already there. I grapple with this feeling as I approach her, trying to rationalize it. I'm not doing anything wrong, am I? I've offered Tess some company, and she's accepted. I haven't given up on Lily, and who knows, maybe Tess will prove a useful accomplice along the way.

The place is a little busier this morning—I'm guessing from the demographic of the other guests that there are a fair few *And Breathe . . .* adventurers among them. Tess has managed to bag the same table we were at last night. This, she explains, after we've said good morning, is a deliberate choice.

"I quite like the idea of being one of those incredibly rich women who live in fancy hotels," she says. "You know, the ones who have their 'usual table' and know all the staff by name—and they insist on talking to any new guests who they come across: 'George makes the most marvelous daiquiris, you simply have to try one.' That kind of thing. And I just go increasingly mad and sozzled and end up leaving all my money to my cats."

"I see."

This is quite a lot to take in before I've had coffee.

"I do tend to ramble first thing," Tess says. "Don't worry, I'll hit a wall in about an hour and then I'll probably fall asleep."

I somehow doubt this. She looks fresh and bright in a way I definitely do not, but I'm still pleased I made a bit of an effort this morning.

We discuss the day's logistics over toast and plan which train to get. I'm pleasantly surprised to find that Tess is as cautious about when to arrive at the station as me.

"It's the same with flying," she says. "I'd much rather—"

"Get through security early and sit with a book in departures for two hours?" I interrupt breathlessly.

"Yes!" Tess says. And we sit in the warm glow of our mutual travel anxiety for a few moments. It's at this point that a harassed-looking member of staff appears and tapes a sign to the wall by the buffet area, stepping away to reveal the words: *Sorry! Due to an unexpected issue there will be no sausages today!*

"Oh no!" Tess says. "Not an unexpected sausage issue!"

"The worst kind of sausage issue."

"Truly."

For the second time in twelve hours, we become mildly hysterical. When we've calmed down, a group of women come over and begin chatting to Tess, evidently remembering her from the rafting the previous day. I take the opportunity to head to the sausage-less buffet, keen not to be a blot on Tess's copybook with these people, given that I suspect I'm still persona non grata for curtailing their adventures yesterday.

Tess and I reconvene in the lobby. As we're checking out, Tess chats to the two members of staff on the desk as if they're old friends. The young lady who takes Tess's key card seems like it's made her day.

THE EARLY MORNING sun drapes Edinburgh in gold, and the castle sitting atop the ancient hill looks even more extraordinary than when I saw it on arrival here. It's strange that something can look so permanent and precarious at the same time. I'm sad to be leaving the city, but it's not as if I can't come back. The realization, as obvious as it might be, leaves me with a bit of a spring in my step.

We make it to the station with lots of time to spare, and Tess uses the opportunity to go and buy us some snacks for the train. When she returns I see she's carrying a bag crammed full of cakes and sweets, as if we might be off to a child's birthday party.

"I know what you're thinking," Tess says. "Yes, I *am* a medical professional. But that means I'm confronted with mortality more than most. Which means that quite a lot of the time I'll be telling someone to eat kale and do lunges when really I'm thinking that life's too short and sometimes your husband cheats on you and you should just have a"—she rummages in the bag—"Funtime Fizzy Straw."

"I can't really fault that logic," I reply, accepting one of the sweets, which I have to concede just about lives up to its name.

Our platform goes up on the board and we make our way to the train. Two Japanese tourists with enough gear for a North Pole trek are in our allocated seats. I begin to explain the situation, and when it's clear that they don't speak English I attempt a very complicated mime, which only baffles them further.

"May I?" Tess says, clearing her throat and calmly explaining the situation in halting but evidently understandable Japanese, given that the couple quickly stand up and vacate their seats.

"Possibly should have let you go first there, in retrospect," I say as we sit down. "When did you learn Japanese?"

Tess offers me another sweet. "Spent some time in Tokyo in my twenties."

"Ah. That sounds rather fun."

I must stop speaking like a benign uncle.

"Did you ever do that, the whole traveling thing?" Tess asks.

"Me? Yes—well, a bit. Spent some time in France in my youth."

This is unusually enigmatic of me, but when I turn my head to the window it's more to stop Tess from seeing that I'm blushing. I've made it sound as if I spent my formative years ambling around the Normandy countryside, squashing apples under stout oaks before heading to the city and breaking Parisian hearts in absinthe dens. The reality is that I had a week on a French exchange as a thirteen-year-old, seven days in which I failed to make eye contact with any of the family I was staying with, or speak a single word of French.

"What was Tokyo like?" I ask, keen to turn the spotlight back on Tess.

"Pretty wonderful. It's where I met my husband, actually."

She tells me they met at a bar in the Koenji district. Both on their own, both Kiwis, both partial to tequila. ("Stupid bloody fate.") They spent the next six months traveling around together, "which was fun, aside from the odd bump in the road—literally in one case." She shows me the scar on her elbow from where she came off her moped. I show her the one on my ankle from scraping it on a rock in Corfu. This exchange continues until we reach the possibility of removing clothes, at which point we give up, though I do end up telling Tess about my dermatographia.

"Fascinating," she says, and I have to refrain from asking her to repeat that word, because in her accent it sounds absolutely wonderful. But instead—after Tess reveals yet another string of missed calls from Marc—we return to her marriage.

"I was devastated when it ended, at first," Tess says. "I thought the affair was my fault. That I must have been doing something wrong. When I told him that, said I could change, I actually heard those words coming out of my mouth and I thought, *What on earth are you doing?*"

She bites into another sweet, tearing what I think is a frog's head off.

"I spoke to a friend about him, and she said she thought he'd always been a bit—well, she used the word 'controlling,' which I wasn't too sure about. I guess because he was so . . . nice. That was the word everyone used. 'Marco? Yeah, nice bloke.' My mum would say it constantly—how lucky I was to be with such a *nice* man."

Here another frog met its end.

"But the more I thought about it, the more I realized you can get away with stuff if you have a reputation for being a nice guy. It wasn't like he was this alpha bloke, telling me what I could or couldn't do, but—well, if I ever tried to change up our routine, that wouldn't fly. Especially if that meant I'd be doing something new—something for myself. I'd tell him I was thinking of joining a running club or something, and he'd just slowly list off the reasons why I shouldn't. It got to a point where—you know that feeling where you're lying on the beach, feeling the warmth of the sun on you, and then a cloud moves in front of it? That was like what it was like to be with him. If I ever suggested something he didn't like, I'd suddenly be in shadow."

Once again, I am struck by how angry I feel that anyone would make Tess feel like this. I want to tell her she is clearly better off without him, but I'm not sure if that's appropriate.

"I don't regret having my boys, obviously," she says, her face brightening instantly. "Well, I say 'boys,' they're both hulking great sods now. Time goes so fast, doesn't it? One minute they're screaming their heads off when you leave the room for five seconds, the next they're skulking around the place with their hoodies on like a couple of Dementors with protein shakes."

She takes her phone out and shows me photos of them—Sam and Dylan. One picture shows them lounging on opposing sofas playing video games, another has them standing back to back with their muscular arms folded, like they're on a film poster.

Tess puts her phone away and starts to ask me if I've got kids myself, but at that moment my mobile rings, and I have to perform a rather ungainly move to retrieve it from my trouser pocket. Tess reaches for *And Breathe . . .* from her bag. When I finally get my phone out it's to discover with a heavy heart that it's the pub calling. Surely whatever this is can wait until I'm back? When I answer, the signal's barely there, and I just catch the words "Everything's absolutely fine, but—" before I lose signal. I try them back, but I can't get through. I decide I'll call them later.

"So, Bath then," I say, turning back to Tess. "I've just realized I didn't actually read the chapter, so I've no idea what's waiting for us there." I have a horrible thought. "I hope it's not dancing."

"Hmm," Tess says, suddenly looking a bit troubled. She's running her finger back and forth across the page, as if making sure she's not made a mistake.

"What? What is it?"

"No, it's nothing bad," Tess says, clearing her throat. "Well, it's not dancing, anyway. I have to confess I kind of scrubbed Bath from my mind when I first read the book. But I remember now."

"Right. And . . . ?"

"OK, quick question for you. How good are you with heights?"

34.

BATH

Oh! Who can be tired of Bath?

—JANE AUSTEN, 1816

Literally £40 down the drain to look at a green puddle.

—ONLINE REVIEW, HISTORIC ROMAN BATHS, BATH, 2019

The answer to Tess's question is a resounding "Not good at all," which is a shame, because a little over twenty-four hours later I'm about to jump out of an airplane.

How in the name of god, I think, *have I managed to let this happen?*

When Tess told me that the *And Breathe . . .* activity in Bath was skydiving, I instantly relaxed—because I very obviously wasn't going to do that, so I needn't have worried.

It was a long slog down from Edinburgh, but Tess's easy company had made the time pass quickly. I was disappointed when she said she was going to meet a Kiwi friend who'd moved over a few years before. I ended up turning in early and ordering room service.

Now that I was on my own, my thoughts turned to tomorrow. Was I really about to see Lily again? I needed to sleep so that I could be truly ready for what the day would bring, but it was impossible to turn my brain off. I ended up pacing around my room and then getting the trouser press out just to give myself something to do. I finally managed to fall asleep, waking with shredded nerves and the smartest trousers in England.

I splashed some cold water on my face. *It's time to focus*, I told myself.

EXCEPT IT TURNS out it's quite hard to be focused when you're waiting in the foyer of a skydiving school surrounded by scores of people chattering and laughing and generally providing such a sensory overload that it's impossible to hear yourself think. Tess is an increasingly manic presence too, and not much help with scanning the crowd for Lily. I showed her the photo at breakfast, but she was already nervous, and I'm not convinced she took it in. I watch her bouncing on the balls of her feet, stretching her legs as if she's about to run a marathon, and then she's asking me a series of rhetorical questions about whether this is a mad thing to be doing, speculating over whether muesli was the correct breakfast before a skydive. When we're ushered into the room where we're having a safety briefing, she marches straight to the front row of seats, pulling me along with her by the hand. For the next forty-five minutes a man in fatigues explains how we're going to try to avoid breaking our necks, and all the while I'm unable to look around at who else is in the room. I half wonder if I might shout Lily's name and just see what happens, but I banish this thought when two people start whispering and the instructor gives them a filthy look.

I seem to be taking on board Tess's nervous energy as if by osmosis, and eventually I snap and spin around in my chair to see who's behind me. I am met by angry stares, as I've managed to interrupt the instructor at an apparently pivotal point. He waits for me to turn back before reprimanding me, and I'm forced to wait for him to finish so that I can get back out into the foyer and see if there's a new group of people.

Finally, the briefing's over. I'm expecting that we'll be able to go back out now and have a cup of tea or something, but the book's popularity evidently means they're trying to shunt through as many people as possible, so suddenly we're being asked to get up and form lines. Tess stands up, as do I.

"Right," I tell her. "Good luck. I'm going to head back out and—"

"Brian," she says, grabbing my hand in a very tight grip. "I don't think I can do this on my own."

"Right," I say. "Well, you'll be strapped to an instructor. So I think you'll—"

"No. I know that. I mean, I just know I'm going to get up there and refuse."

I'm turning my head as she speaks, because was it my imagination or did I just hear a voice that sounded familiar?

"I know I will," Tess continues, renewing her grip on my hand. "Because I've got my stupid husband's stupid disapproving voice in my ear telling me I shouldn't be doing it. And maybe he's right."

It's this that makes me look back at her. There is fear and defiance in her eyes. I feel like there's a good chance the former might win out, and before I realize what I'm doing, I'm taking her by the shoulders and saying, "Right, well, you've no need to worry, because . . . I'll be there. I'll come and do it too."

"Really?" Tess says, eyes widening.

"Well, yes," I say, which is very possibly my attempt to open the door to Tess's telling me that my words have been inspiration enough . . . but instead she grabs *both* of my hands in hers, and we walk like that, as if we're carrying something invisible, onto the tarmac, into the sickening drone of spinning propellers and a swirling wind.

SO HERE I am, lurching up into the sky, horribly aware that there's no backing out now. It's unbearably loud inside the plane, and every time the wings dip I can see them shaking out of the window. The whole thing feels so flimsy, like a toy. All of my fellow passengers are staring at the floor, looking sick with nerves. I feel a desperate urge to stand up and make an impassioned speech in praise of cowardice: *"We can always just give up! I'm* not *Spartacus!"* But it's too late. All too quickly, we're being instructed to stand, and then we're all clipped onto our respective instructors. Mine has seemed dreadfully bored about this whole prospect, even yawning at one point, but I suppose this is the equivalent of his commute.

I look around at Tess to find her breathing a little bit like someone in labor on TV.

"You OK?" I shout.

She shakes her head vigorously.

"You'll be absolutely fine. I'll buy you so many Funtime Fizzy Straws when you're back on the ground."

There's a moment when she seems to dig deep, summoning courage. When she looks back at me again she's smiling, and I feel overwhelmed in a way that's got nothing to do with jumping out of a plane.

It's Tess up next, and I give her one final reassuring squeeze on the arm before she's doing last checks with her instructor. I was expecting a bit more ceremony about the moment itself, but no, there they go, tumbling out of the plane into the sky. I hear a very polite Kiwi scream that is quickly swallowed up by the wind.

"You ready, Brian?" my instructor shouts.

"Not really," I shout back.

"That's the spirit. Right—here we go!"

We're hanging over the open door. Freezing-cold air is whipping around my legs. I'm just about to inquire exactly when we're going to jump, and how long it'll take to be back on the ground, when I'm rudely shoved out into the sky.

It's an ungodly sensation, falling without landing, and the only way to express what I'm feeling is with a low rumbling noise, which seems to start at the very base of my stomach and rise up and up, eventually erupting out my mouth. I have my eyes screwed shut so tightly it hurts. After a few seconds I try opening them, but no, it's not for me, thanks very much, so I close them again. I'm aware that my instructor is whooping, I assume for my benefit.

"How ya feeling, Brian?" he yells in my ear.

"Fine, thank you," I reply, like he's a waiter who's asked if everything's OK with my quiche.

"Chute going up on three," he says, and when it does it feels like someone's grabbed me by the scruff of my neck to stop me from falling out of a window, and I'm bracing and bracing, and then I'm just . . . dangling.

"Not a bad view, eh?" my instructor shouts.

"Yeah, wonderful," I lie, my eyes still closed. Maybe I'll be the first-ever skydiver not to see a single second of the experience. I'll have to lie to Tess. But what if I say I've seen something completely different than her? The thought is enough to embarrass me into slowly opening one eye, and then the other.

"Oh."

I'm looking down at a vast patchwork of fields, and the sprawling river that intersects it, coiled like a silver snake. There, hanging across it, is the Clifton Suspension Bridge. I saw this once up close on a school trip, cowed by the enormity of its steel, and now here I am looking at it as if it's part of a child's toy set. As we descend further I spot a white tent on a pristine lawn. A vintage red bus is parked nearby, a white ribbon across its front. Wedding guests have spilled out of it. The way they're positioned suggests they're having photos taken. Sure enough, at the front of them are the bride and groom, arm in arm. From up here they look like they could be wedding cake toppers.

I wonder if Tess is already on the ground. I'm looking out for her when my eye is caught by a field over to my left. It is pristinely carpeted, with bluebells I think. And then I'm back behind the bar, looking at Lily, dressed in blue, that smile of hers that always floored me, and I feel an intense urge to stop falling, to stay suspended above the ground, to struggle against gravity with all my might.

35.

HONEYMOON PERIOD

THEN

After the showdown between Forbes and me at the wedding, Lily was furious with both of us. She made us apologize to each other, but when we shook hands I gave as good as I got when it came to crushing Forbes's, his signet ring leaving an impression on my finger that would last for days. I looked him dead in the eye as he growled that he was sorry, and silently communicated to him that he had another think coming if he thought he'd take Lily from me without a fight.

I knew then that I'd almost certainly created a rift that would never be mended. And I felt guilty that Lily was stuck in the middle. I thought back to the night she told me that Daniel was who she was "supposed to end up with." She could have carried on down that path and avoided all this. But I was wary of getting tangled up in such thoughts. And, after all, we had a honeymoon to go on.

With the unexpected drama of the day rather taking its toll,

Lily and I needed our fortnight in Rome. Those evenings we spent in piazzas, sated by carafes of cheap chianti, were blissful to the point of dreamlike. Even when we headed back home to slate-gray England, the afterglow still burned bright for days afterward.

That's not to say there wasn't the odd sticky moment in the early days of our marriage. Money got in the way, as it tends to do. While we'd loved our little rental flat, we decided it was time to buy a place of our own. When Forbes got wind of this, having overheard a conversation between Lily and Rebecca, he immediately tried to step in and help. It might have been churlish to refuse his offer, but we needed a clean break. Luckily, Lily felt as strongly as I did that we had to show him we could stand on our own two feet. The fact she was choosing us over him made me feel like I'd happily live in a rusty wheelbarrow under a bridge.

And so we scrabbled together our savings and squeezed a joint mortgage out of the bank. A few months of utterly joyful and carefree dealings with estate agents and solicitors later ("I don't know who I'm going to murder first," Lily kept saying, angry at first, then chillingly calm), we had a two-bedroom flat of our own in Tufnell Park.

It was there we slid from newlyweds to recentlyweds, those first tentative steps turning into more confident strides.

The spare room was supposed to be Lily's office, as she worked at home more than me. But the morning light was better in the kitchen, and more often than not she stayed there for the rest of the day. That meant the spare room inevitably became more of a dumping ground for boxes of stuff that never seemed to fit anywhere else. I didn't dare ask Lily if she might want to jettison some of her impulse-acquired hobby equipment—the bread makers and seed trays and yet more wool, vast, never-ending balls of the stuff.

I suppose it had been a formality in my mind that at some point we would need the space for a crib more than we would for a five-thousand-piece jigsaw puzzle of the Sydney Opera House, but while Lily and I had talked over the years about having children, it had only ever been in the abstract. Then one evening about six months after we'd been married, we were at Lily's friend Cat's place for dinner. With our thirties on the horizon, six pints and chips in the pub was gradually being replaced by dinner parties featuring proper linen tablecloths. These evenings were enjoyable until people started talking about politics or property prices. Lily and I had developed a double-hand-squeeze signal for when one of us sensed such chat looming, so that we could make our excuses and leave.

Cat had just finished doling out lasagna onto our plates when she told us, in the same tone of voice she'd used when she'd asked us to pass the Parmesan around, that she was pregnant. There was a short pause while we all worked out if we'd heard her right, before everyone exploded into life, whooping and hollering so much the neighbors banged on the walls.

Later, when we'd all calmed down a bit, Cat's husband, Hugo, told us all very earnestly, "I feel an almost animalistic protectiveness toward Cat, now that we're pregnant. Every time we're separated I'm thinking, *I must get back to protect my mate*, you know?"

I'm afraid I didn't know. Conversation turned to the upcoming election, and Lily squeezed my hand twice—time for us to go.

"*My mate*," I said to Lily in the taxi on the way home. "Is that . . . normal?"

"It's very Hugo," Lily replied. "I imagine he's been waiting to say that kind of thing for ages." She yawned, and I shifted over so that she could use my shoulder as a pillow.

"You know what the worst thing about it is, though?" I said, grinning.

"Go on," Lily said.

"I can mock all I want, but I know I'll be the same."

Lily was quiet. As the silence stretched on, I wondered if she might have fallen asleep. But then she said, "We've never really talked about the whole babies thing properly, have we?"

"No," I said. "I suppose we haven't. You're still worried about me sullying your bloodline and giving them my wonky nose, though, aren't you?"

Lily lapsed into silence again. Perhaps it was because the taxi driver was now pretending very obviously not to listen to us.

"Shall we talk about it another time?" she said.

"Yeah, OK," I said, troubled by the change in atmosphere. For the next couple of weeks I kept wondering when this conversation would happen. I found that I pulled back from starting it myself, though I wasn't sure why. But then one Sunday evening we were having a takeaway in front of the TV when an advert came on—for nappies, complete with smiling, bouncing baby and parents grinning at each other like they were having the time of their lives clearing up poo—and that same strange silence arrived again.

It was Lily who broke it.

"So then," she said. "Babies and all that."

"Babies and all that," I repeated, snapping a poppadom in

half. We swapped takeaway cartons. Dhal for chicken. There was the sound of our chewing. Then Lily turned the TV off.

With great effort, as if each word she summoned she had to force out of her mouth, she said, "I . . . don't think I want to have children."

The look she gave me then was as if she'd just lit a fuse and had retreated to safe ground.

"That's . . . interesting," I said.

"'Interesting'?" she repeated.

"Yes."

"Is 'interesting' really the word you're going for?" She was smiling, but her voice didn't match it.

"I'm just processing," I said. "You know me, the old robot over here."

I had lost my appetite all of a sudden, but I kept eating, as if to show I hadn't been too thrown by what she'd said.

"Perhaps you could tell me why?"

Lily folded her arms, eyebrows knitted. "Does there have to be a 'why'?"

"No . . . but—"

"Why does it have to be the norm—to want to have kids? Why can't it just be an adult decision to choose not to bring someone into the world that you'll almost certainly mess up in exactly the same way as your parents did you. How on earth is *that* considered the most mature thing to do!"

She was up now, pacing, and I chose my next words carefully. "Is that what you're concerned about?" I asked. "Because that—well, I'm not sure that's something you'd need to worry about."

I hadn't chosen them carefully enough, though.

"That sounds quite patronizing," Lily said, and I got to my feet.

"No, listen, I didn't mean it like that. What I mean is . . . I know you have a difficult relationship with your dad, but it's not inevitable, that you put all of that stuff onto your own kids, is it? And isn't the whole point of having children to raise them and, you know, instill all the good stuff you've learned in them, leave behind the bad?"

Lily sighed resignedly at this, then sat down, back against the sofa. "That's what everybody thinks," she said. "But it doesn't work like that. They'd have all our hang-ups just as sure as they'd have your wonky nose and my weird hobbity feet."

"Well, the thing about that is . . . ," I started, but I didn't have anything to add to my argument. And the fact I was having to argue at all made me want to pull away from the conversation. There was a voice coming through a loudhailer at a distance, telling me to retreat.

"Yes?" Lily asked.

"Well, we'll be rich, won't we?" I said with a false kind of laugh. "With my nose and your feet, they're bound to get a lot of parts in sci-fi films. Job's a good'un."

Lily smiled and I sat down next to her and took her hand.

"I know," she said after a moment.

"You know what?"

"That you really want them."

"I've never said that."

"I can tell, though. The way you are with Edie, even Rebecca mentioned it. And then after your parents . . ." She trailed off, emotion getting the better of her, and I pulled her into me.

"That isn't something that comes into it at all," I said.

Lily sniffed but didn't say anything.

"We've still got time—lots of time—to figure things out," I continued, making it up as I went along.

“OK,” she said. I felt the warmth of her breath on my neck, and her body found its way into mine, curled into me with that magical sense of ease, of everything being right, and I felt a dangerous longing to turn the clock back to when our biggest decision to make was whether to eat on the floor or the sofa, when we weren’t yet bracing against the weight of the future.

36.

CONVERSATIONS WITH COATS ON

As the weeks and months went by, this weight only grew stronger. Turning thirty in the same year the new millennium arrived had the effect of making me properly aware of my own mortality—that life wasn't going to stay like this forever. This led to strange side effects. Having never been the most emotional person in the world, I found myself—to my horror—crying at films, and even songs. I couldn't really explain this, nor why I felt the need to hide my emotion from Lily. It was just stupid male pride, I told myself. But was it just that? I worried that it was actually because for the first time in my life I was yearning for some kind of meaning—wasn't there more to life than this?—and as time passed, it was clear the people we were close to had found their own answers to that question.

Lily's friend Cat may have been the first to announce that she was pregnant, but it was like dominos after that. We found ourselves crossing off things like "XMAS PUB CRAWL!" from the calendar on the kitchen wall and replacing it with "Roz's baby shower." Given my modest social circle, it was mostly Lily's friends having babies. It was slightly dutifully, then, that

I followed her around the city, laden with ready meals and muffins, as we visited these new parents. But then Ed had a baby, a boy called Jack.

Ed and I were still as close as ever, but in the way that men can say they are best friends but go three months and forget to see each other. We both blamed this on how we now lived on different sides of the river—that famously uncrossable vortex—but when we met up one afternoon and he told me his girlfriend Cynthia was pregnant, I felt horrendously guilty, as they had been together two years by that point and I'd only met her once.

"It's all been a bit of a whirlwind, right from the start," Ed explained. "I'd never met anyone like her, and I hesitate to say she felt the same, but . . . Anyway"—here, he took a long gulp of beer—"she did actually get pregnant once before, but things didn't, you know, work out. But we tried again, and she's four months now, so yeah, exciting—and fucking terrifying, obviously."

Things didn't work out. It took me an embarrassingly long time to work out what this meant. I felt bad on two fronts—that Ed hadn't been able to tell me, and that I didn't feel able to talk to him about it now. From then on, I tried to make up for this by taking the lead when it came to meeting up, making sure we didn't accidentally drift apart again.

When his son, Jack, was born, shortly after I turned thirty-one, Lily and I went to meet him, and I very nearly started crying as soon as we came through the door. As I held him in my arms, his hands raised up by his downy head as if in surrender, the lump in my throat rendered me speechless—which was a particular challenge when Ed put his hand on my shoulder and asked if I'd like to be Jack's godfather.

When Lily and I went out for dinner later that night, I

found myself making a lot of self-deprecating remarks about how emotional I'd been.

Lily tore some focaccia. "I think it's sweet. And you'll make a great godfather too."

For the first time I could remember, we spent the rest of the meal largely in silence, lost in our own thoughts. When we got home, it was as if both of us knew that we were about to have a hard conversation. We remained standing, coats on, in the kitchen, where the fridge seemed to hum expectantly.

"I really don't mind," I said, "that you don't want them."

Lily smiled sadly. "Funny," she said. "I was going to say I wouldn't be cross—I mean, I'd understand it, I really would—if you left me for someone who did."

I suppose it was that, really, which made things very clear for me. I was brought back to the moment in my flat in Shepherd's Bush, plucking up the courage to ask Lily out, and seeing those two possible paths ahead. I'd chosen the one where she was part of my life, and the other was now distant and dark, leading to nowhere, the exit miles and miles back. I loved her more than I ever thought it was possible to love someone, and I wasn't about to turn around now.

37.

IN THE MOMENT

NOW

It's fair to say that Tess and I are in rather different places after the skydive. Tess, shot through with adrenaline, can barely sit still.

"I can't believe we just did that! Can you? Did you get that sense of being completely in the moment? That sort of strange freedom of being completely powerless?"

I reply dutifully that I did feel like that too, yes, but though my heart is thumping, there's a lingering disappointment that we didn't see Lily. Why wasn't she there today?

After a while I get the sense that, though she's too polite to say anything, Tess is a bit frustrated that I'm not able to reciprocate her enthusiasm, and she turns to the people across the aisle, who are all too happy to include her in their conversation.

We pass a pub and I see a man heading inside, stooping slightly, and he reminds me of Jeff. As I hear Tess say, "Such a rush, wasn't it?" to her new friends, I remember sitting by the fire with Jeff—him asking me to think about what he'd said about moving on.

Is there a version of this story where I stop looking for Lily? Accept that she's gone? I picture myself taking down her postcard from the noticeboard. Reading her words one last time. Just then the bus has to brake sharply and there's a strange second of silence before the excited chatter of the skydivers swells up again.

We arrive at the hotel. As Tess and I get off the bus and make our way into reception, she's still talking at a million miles an hour, and by this point her enthusiasm is beginning to rub off on me.

"What are you thinking for the rest of the evening?" she says as we wait for the lift to come. I hadn't really considered it. I suppose I should get back to my laptop. Plan my next move.

"I, um, think I'll just get some room service or something," I say. "Work out what to do next."

"Right," Tess says. "Of course. Good plan."

There is evident disappointment in her voice. I wouldn't be as arrogant as to think this is because I'm denying her my sparkling company. I imagine it's more that after the adrenaline rush of earlier, she's now having to contemplate an evening of whatever film's on ITV4 and a slightly damp sandwich, and I realize then that I am definitely not going to allow that to happen.

"Unless you fancy heading out for a bite to eat?"

"Yeah, OK," Tess says, looking pleased. "That'd be nice."

"What do you fancy?"

"Oh, just pizza or something?"

"Pizza or something sounds good to me."

The lift arrives then, and we step inside. It's just the two of us, but for some reason it doesn't feel like there's much room. We certainly seem to be standing quite close to one another, anyway. It's an unfamiliar feeling to me, but I belatedly realize that this is one of the more charged silences I have felt for a very long time. It's broken by the sound of Tess's phone vibrating. She takes it out of her bag and lets out a little sigh. I can see from her screen that it's "Mark" calling. Tess lets it ring twice more, and then, with some ceremony, she turns her phone off and puts it back in her bag. The doors open a second later, and both of us try to let the other go first. We're so polite in fact that we risk the doors closing on us, and in the end Tess steps out but pulls me with her. "Downstairs in an hour?" she says.

"Perfect."

This is fine, I tell myself, back in my room. I'm not doing anything wrong. Just because I'm picking out the smartest shirt I've brought, and have spent an inordinate amount of time trying to flatten my hair, it doesn't necessarily mean anything. My laptop is lying closed on the coffee table, and I keep approaching but then finding reasons not to open it—socks to pair, a complimentary cookie wrapper to discard. Eventually I go online and go to Tripadvisor. There's no new post on Lily's page. I feel . . . I'm not sure what I feel.

I've got ten minutes before I need to be downstairs, and I realize that I should have probably found where we're going to eat. We decided on pizza, didn't we? I'm still on Tripadvisor, and for the first time in my life I use it as intended and look for the best-reviewed Italian restaurants in Bath. I feel a palpable sense of relief—and excitement—that the top-rated choice, Olivelli, is just around the corner from the hotel. As I go down in the lift, I decide I'm going to keep this information to myself and tell Tess that I thought I saw a nice place earlier that we could try. I'm wondering why I might feel the need to do this when the doors open, and I see Tess waiting for me, and I realize then I know exactly why. She looks lovely—in an elegant, understated way—and I suppose I should stop pretending to myself that when I offered her my companionship it was an entirely selfless act.

It's a gorgeous, warm summer's evening. I'd forgotten that England has about three of these days a year, where we feel almost Continental, with everyone sitting outside bars and cafés, giddy at the thought that they haven't even brought a coat out with them.

We're waiting to cross the road at some traffic lights. There's a little Mexican restaurant next to us with a couple in the window seat, both perusing menus.

"Do you ever play that game where you guess if people are on a date or not?" Tess asks. "Those two, for example. Date or no date?"

"Hmm, hard to say," I reply. As we turn the corner onto the road the restaurant's on, I wonder if there's a chance that Tess was floating that question because, like me, she's been wondering the same about this. I'm still thinking about it—that and how I've just noticed that Tess has linked her arm through mine—when I see the restaurant we're supposed to be going to: Olivelli. It looks charming and characterful, its outside painted blue. The same blue of Lily's dress, I realize, and I think of her turning to the regulars, the puff of dust like smoke, her face lit up, in her element . . .

"Where's this place then?" Tess asks.

"It's . . . just down this road," I reply, and we pass by Olivelli, hearing the soft music drifting out from inside.

38.

CAPTAIN BILL'S

Here we are," I say, doing my utmost to sound casual and as if I very much intended to bring us to this place, which I have belatedly observed is called Captain Bill's. Every Italian place we passed since Olivelli was clearly booked up, and we've been walking for a fair while now, so when I saw the flashing neon *Pizza!* sign at the end of the street and an empty table by the window, I decided to gamble.

But when I open the door, we are met not by the sound of soft music and the hum of refined chatter, but by children screaming. It takes a momentary scan to realize this is one of those family places with slides, ball pits, and climbing frames for the kids, that happens to serve food too.

I can't bear to look at Tess. I can only imagine the mental calculations she must be doing. There's a split second when I see a polite-looking family sitting down to eat that I think maybe it's going to be OK, but then we are greeted by a pirate who calls us "me hearties" and seats us in the Bluebeard zone.

"Just to be clear," I say, pausing briefly to let an earsplitting scream die away, "I didn't think it was going to be as . . . pirate-y . . . as this."

Tess, who is busy studying the menu, doesn't reply at first.

"Sorry," she says, looking up, "I was just checking to see if they were doing penne arrabiarrrrrrrta."

She looks at me. I look at her.

"Do you think they serve booze?" she says.

Thankfully, despite the occasional skirmish involving two gangs of eight-year-olds embroiled in a turf war for control of the ball pit, we're here just late enough that the place starts to quiet down by the time our pizzas arrive. I manage to keep my number of apologies in the single digits, though that doesn't feel like enough, and Tess is clearly canny enough to know that this isn't where we were heading originally. I can't help apologizing one final time and Tess tells me if I say sorry again she's going to make me walk the plank. We finish our pizzas fairly speedily, and after a few minutes when we speculate on whether the teenage chef on his cigarette break outside might actually be the eponymous Bill, Tess suggests we swing by somewhere for a drink. Well, what she actually says is, "Shall we go and find some alcohol now?"

"Somewhere a bit less . . . stressful than this?" I ask.

"Yes," Tess says. "North Korea, perhaps. Or an abattoir."

We find a pub around the corner, where Tess insists we both drink rum. By the time we're onto our second, I'm feeling slightly less mortified about where I took her, but then I'm thinking about the reason why.

"I'm going to spend a few days in London at the end of all this," Tess is saying. "Do you go much since you've moved away?"

"I've not been for a while," I say, distracted. *What if I'd spent more time looking for Lily today?* I think. *If I'd not been with Tess, might I have spotted her among all the people? What if she was even on the bus back from the skydive? Or could she be in the hotel even now?*

"I came once when we flew over to visit our cousins," Tess says. "We went to St. Paul's. I remember standing back, looking up at it, and thinking how unreal it looked, you know? Like someone had painted it against the sky. And then there's the whispering gallery inside."

"The what?"

"Oh, it's magic! If there's two of you, then one stands by the wall and whispers, and the other can hear what you've said, like, forty meters away. Me and Cath, my cousin, tried it, and I *swear*, Brian, I whispered, 'Cathy, can you hear me?' and she said, 'Yes!' and it came through clear as a bell. Then of course we tried out as many swear words as we could until our parents caught us."

I smile, but I'm not really listening. I'm starting to spiral now, flooded with anxiety. This feels wrong. Like I'm betraying Lily somehow.

Just then the door opens and the group of people Tess was talking to on the bus earlier comes in. Tess exchanges waves with them and they make their way over to a free table next to us. I shift positions on my stool and find my knee pressed against the soft edge of the bench. Except Tess then sits back and I realize it was her leg I was resting mine against. I wrench it away as if I've been stung, and in the process I knock into the table and spill my drink everywhere.

"Fuck it!"

Tess laughs at my disproportionate anger. "Hey, it's no biggie!"

I hurry up to the bar and grab a bunch of paper towels.

When I return I stand behind Tess and reach past her to dab at the table. Tess waits until I've practically scraped the varnish off it before she puts her hand on my arm and says, "OK, what's going on? Is this about the restaurant or something?"

I freeze, feeling tepid liquid soaking through the paper towel onto my hand. It's not her fault, I know it's not her fault, but I can't stop myself.

"You think I'm deluded, don't you?"

After a moment, Tess turns around and looks up at me. "What?"

"You think what I'm doing—looking for Lily—you think it's mad. You think . . . You think she's—"

"Whoa, whoa," Tess interrupts, "where's this come from?"

I feel woozy, suddenly, like I might pass out. I have to steady myself. Tess puts her hand on my arm again, but I pull away.

"I'm sorry," I say. "I can't do this."

And then I'm lurching toward the door, pushing through it and out into the street, taking in great lungfuls of warm summer air.

39.

A FAMILY OF TWO

THEN

Life with Lily over the next two years felt a little like we'd rewound the clock to the start of our relationship. There was no more getting home tired from work, reheating something for dinner, telly, then bed. Instead we were now filling our diaries with theater and the cinema, new restaurants and evening exhibitions. It had been an unspoken agreement, to throw ourselves back into London living like this. It was, I suppose, an attempt to go back to the most exciting days of our burgeoning relationship, when we were responsibility free and difficult conversations weren't yet on the horizon.

And, in truth, it worked. Having never been the most spontaneous person in the world, I now found myself going toe-to-toe with Lily on booking us last-minute gig tickets or finding any excuse to get out of the house on an excursion. One evening we were both climbing into bed when I received a text message from a friend at work that read: "THERE IS A PIG IN THE PUB I'M IN. REPEAT: THERE'S A PUB PIG!" I worked out that we could be there on the tube in twenty minutes, and so Lily and I got back into our clothes and managed to get to the pub for last orders, whisky mingling with toothpaste, and got a photo of us petting the pig.

Lily was still in the habit of launching herself into new hobbies, and I'd started to join in. This meant the spare room was now buried with stuff: a pasta maker, a table tennis table, and, the latest addition, easels and acrylic paints. It may only have been a single Sunday afternoon that we'd stood on Primrose Hill, inexpertly painting the view—but that felt like it was almost the point. We were free to get into something as seriously or as frivolously as we wanted, because, being responsibility free, our time was completely our own.

We'd been dutifully building up our savings over the last few years, and while it wasn't as if we'd ever sat down and talked about exactly what we were saving for, we reached a mutual understanding that it wouldn't hurt to dip into our pot now. Soon we began to head off on mini-breaks every couple of months—often at short notice—exploring parts of Europe neither of us had been to before. I never felt more in love with Lily than when we were off traveling to new places.

Life was hectic, but I felt fulfilled and full of purpose, and there was no sense that we were ever going to slow down. The more I thought about it, the more I began to think that the idea of having children really had been a kind of existential yearning—exacerbated by turning thirty. Had I told myself a story about needing to grow the family I'd never had in order to rationalize what I'd been feeling? I grabbed on tightly to this idea, trying to convince myself that it was true. It helped that when we met up with our friends who were new parents, they couldn't quite believe that Lily and I were still having so many adventures. It was like we were prophets bearing secrets of a mystical existence beyond their comprehension. They'd huddle around us, bleary-eyed, taking it in turns to ask questions about our latest fad or trip. I recall in particular speaking to Lily's friend Cat, who'd just had her second child, about how Lily and I had got back from a trip to Paris the previous week, having booked Eurostar tickets and hotels the evening before we'd left.

"What," she said, "so you just . . . went?"

"Well, yes," we replied, both a little sheepish.

Cat looked at us and said, "Please can we swap lives? Just for a bit? I want to remember what it's like not to have Spaghetti Hoops in my hair."

See, I'd think, *do you really want that life?* It helped too that I'd clearly been utterly naïve to the realities of parenthood. Up close, the whole thing seemed absolutely terrifying. Watching as our friends sank to their knees, desperately bargaining with their two-year-olds—"You can have a chip if you let me put your trousers back on"—was unnerving to say the least. These people were doctors and lawyers and business owners. If they were struggling, then how on earth would *I* cope? *Maybe*, I thought, *I'd have been a terrible dad anyway.*

Being a godfather was a different matter. There was one occasion when I was sitting across from Jack, making him laugh as I dipped my nose in my beer foam, that I had the profound realization that I might well be buying him his first proper pint in sixteen years or so. How great that would be, to get to do things like that! And maybe that was really enough. Lily now was godmother not only to Rebecca's daughter, but to the children of three of her friends. Was it not the best of both worlds, to have the responsibility without the day-to-day exhaustion of being a parent?

By this point, Lily had been promoted to editor at her magazine. While she'd always dreamed of doing that job eventually, the opportunity had been presented to her much earlier than expected after the incumbent had quit without warning. Lily was only given a few days to decide, and though she had some concerns, I told her she'd be mad not to go for it.

"I'll be so busy," she said. "Much more than now."

"That's OK—we'll still find time for painting, or interpretive dance—or whatever you're lining up next."

After one particularly full-on afternoon with our friends, I told Lily about how I'd been looking around at the surrounding chaos in that patch of the park with the prams and the wet wipes and the wailing kids and thinking, *Not for me, thanks!*

There were a few times when I'd said something to that effect, and Lily would smile, but she never joined in. I suppose it sounded performative on my part, or insincere, and so I stopped.

Though there were days when my angst about all of this threatened to overwhelm me, I would always find comfort at the end of the day when Lily and I moved into our usual position for sleep, my arm going numb as always. And even though sometimes I woke, just before dawn, to find that Lily wasn't next to me, sleep would pull me under once more, and any concern I'd have at why she wasn't there would be forgotten by the time my alarm went off.

40.

IF YOU'LL LOOK TO YOUR LEFT

NOW

I'm mid-skydive, but everything around me is dark and still. I can see the world turning, blue and distant. The sun is peeking around it—except it isn't the sun, it's Lily's watch, enormous and sparkling, hands no longer stuck but spinning wildly around, faster and faster.

I wake with a start. The cold blue light of my hotel room tells me it's early morning. My phone is clamped to my chest in my hand, like I've just been shot in the heart and I'm reaching for the wound. There's a missed call from the pub. The room seems to be both too hot and too cold all at once, and there are cleaners shouting to each other in the corridor. My head is pounding painfully, but it's nothing compared to the guilt I'm feeling about the way I spoke to Tess last night, and then how I abandoned her.

After ten minutes of listening to the cleaners talking about their bunions, I admit defeat and get showered and dressed. As I plod downstairs, I'm half hoping, half dreading that Tess might be down here already eating breakfast. But there's no sign of her. I take a croissant and eat it on the steps outside the hotel. The early morning sun has already burned through the clouds, and it's shaping up to be a beautiful day. Right now, I don't want to plan what I'm doing next or where I'm going, I just want to walk, and so I set off along the pavement, joining the groups of people strolling through the city, coffees and water bottles in hand. I catch the scent of sun cream in the air and think briefly of my father.

As I find my way down to the banks of the Avon, I watch the boats lining up to take people on river cruises. I've enjoyed my walk, and the idea of getting on one of these boats and being at the mercy of wherever I'm taken is suddenly very appealing, and so I queue up at one of the little huts to get a ticket. I'm one of the last to embark, and most of the seats on deck are filled up already. I'm scanning the rows for somewhere to sit when my eye is caught by a dash of yellow, a large sunhat, and as its owner tilts their head up I realize with a start that it's Tess. Seeing her sitting there, face raised to the sun, I feel the strongest urge to go and make amends, even though I'm probably the last person she wants to speak to.

I approach, hands in my pockets, and stop next to her. She has her eyes closed, and when I cough gently to get her attention, and she opens them, I feel my stomach turn over when her gaze meets mine.

"Morning," I say.

"Hello there," she replies, a politeness in her voice.

"Do you mind if I join you?"

She doesn't answer my question, but she takes the paper bag that was on the seat next to her, leaving it free. The bag is laden with bread and cheese and what looks like a bottle of farmhouse cider. I sit down just as the boat's engine splutters into life. I feel the vibrations resonating through my chest as I turn to Tess and say, "I'm truly very sorry about last night."

"Oh, don't be," Tess says, looking ahead. "Me, Glenda, and Jackie—the other skydiving ladies—had quite the night on the tiles. Those women can drink, let me tell you."

"Really?"

"Big-time. And, as it turns out, they're both basically in the same position as me—husband-wise—so we had what ended up being one of the more cathartic conversations in my life, fueled by"—she pauses to grimace—"tequila, and we ended up making something of a pact."

"Which was . . . ?"

Tess reaches for her water bottle and takes a long sip before screwing the top back on. "I may have lost some of the nuances here, but essentially that men are pigs, and that we were all definitely going to go through with our divorces."

"I see."

"Mm-hmm. By that point the pubs were all very busy, so guess where we ended up toasting the pact?"

I widen my eyes. "Surely not. But it was closed, wasn't it?"

"Glenda managed to charm Captain Bill into sneaking us in for a drink. Jackie and I ended up leaving them to it."

"Wow."

"Yes, I know."

"Well, I'm glad you had a good night in the end. But that doesn't excuse the way I spoke to you. Nor how I just left like that."

"It's OK," Tess says. She's studying me out of the corner of her eye, and I suppose it's the pained expression on my face—

the genuine regret—that softens her. "I've got some coffee in a flask if you fancy some?"

But I owe her more of an explanation, and this time I turn in my seat so that I'm facing her. "It may have escaped your attention," I begin, falteringly, "but I've been feeling really rather out of sorts, just now. Rather . . . thrown." Tess smiles. I suspect the phrase "no shit" isn't far from the tip of her tongue, but she's good enough to let me continue. "I started this journey because I was looking for some answers, of one kind or another. An ending, I suppose. I just wasn't expecting there to be a detour."

Tess readjusts her sunhat. Rather unhelpfully, our tour guide has chosen this moment to start telling us about things to look out for, his voice distorted and tinny over the speaker as he invites us to look to our left.

"The closer I get to finding these answers, the more I'm struggling to work out whether I even want them. There's an awful lot of stuff I've left dormant, for many years now, and it's even more painful than I imagined to bring it all up again."

At this point, perhaps because my voice has become rather strained, Tess puts her hand on my arm and gives it a little squeeze.

"It's been wonderful to meet you," I continue. "Really, it has. And I feel dreadful that you've been caught up in the middle of all of this. And so I really won't be offended in the slightest if you'd rather I let you be. As you say," I add, summoning a smile, "men are pigs."

Tess hands me her water, which I'm grateful for. My throat has gone rather dry. "As long as you don't mind," Tess says, "I think I'd like to tag along with you. You're pretty decent, as pigs go."

Relief washes over me. I've never been more delighted to get called a pig.

"It's been a strange old experience for me too," Tess says. "When I got on the plane at Wellington, Marc called me, trying to get me to change my mind and go back to him. And there was part of me that thought maybe I should—that I was naïve to think walking away from that life would be any better. Even when I arrived here, I still wasn't sure what I was doing. The *And Breathe . . .* thing seemed so great on—well, on paper—but when I got here I was jet-lagged, on the verge of tears half the time, and suddenly I'm about to go white water rafting in a storm. I was thinking I might pack it all in, after that. But then that evening we sat and talked over that terrible wine, and I finally started to relax and feel myself again."

She breaks off as our guide tells us things about a bridge we're about to go under, things that we'll forget as soon as we're out the other side.

"So you're saying me nearly drowning myself in two feet of water was actually quite helpful?"

"In a sense, yes." Tess smiles at me then, and puts her hand over mine.

"Well," I say. "I apologize again for my behavior last night."

"That's OK," Tess replies. "I think we're both still in pretty odd places, aren't we? A bit untethered, I guess. Maybe we just need to stick together, whatever happens next."

"That sounds like a pact I could be part of," I say. "I just wish we had some tequila to toast it with. Where's Bill when you need him?"

"Sailing the seven seas, I expect," Tess says. "Either that or cleaning out the pizza oven." She reaches down and picks up the paper bag. I get a whiff of fresh bread and cheese, and my stomach rumbles. "Hungry?"

"Starving."

She hands me the bag. I can feel the warmth of the bread. It must be freshly baked.

"Hey, guess what?" Tess says. "You're finally having a 'picnic.'"

She rummages in her handbag for a second, before bringing out what she's looking for—a little bottle of hand sanitizer. Applying some herself, she nudges me on the arm and hands me the bottle. And for the longest time, I just look at it. Because there is another version of my life, I realize, full of beautifully mundane little moments like this, with someone who's here, now, with me. As I reach out and take the bottle, Tess's hand brushes mine, and our eyes meet. To imagine this future, on this new path, where maybe I don't need to find answers, or an ending, makes me feel like I'm back in that airplane at ten thousand feet, about to hurl myself out into the unknown.

It's then, out of the corner of my eye, that I see a boat passing us in the opposite direction. I'm not sure what makes me turn my head, and it may only be a brief moment when I see her, but it's enough for me to know that it's her.

Lily.

PART THREE

41.

OUT OF SIGHT

NOW

I don't know what the nautical equivalent of "pull over" is, but that's what I keep shouting at the increasingly confused staff on board. At first they remonstrate, but I'm so insistent, and so loud, that they decide it's better to get me off the boat.

It takes an age for us to near the bank, during which time I'm bobbing up and down and craning my neck to see where the other boat has got to. I'm only vaguely aware of Tess standing next to me, asking what's going on.

As soon as we're near the path, I clamber over the side of the boat and jump down. I twist my ankle as I land, but the pain barely registers. From here I can see that the other boat—cutting a path in the opposite direction and now a good fifty feet away—is branded the same as the one I've just disembarked from: Pollock Cruises. I set up off the path, sending ducks scattering, and then dodge my way through ambling tourists. As I hit a clear stretch of path I'm aware of the low rumble of a crowd and realize I'm running parallel to the rugby ground, where a game is in full swing. A cyclist swerves around a bend and nearly collides with me, swearing at me as he goes. Up ahead there's a gap in the trees, and I can see a bridge coming into view. As long as I can get across it in time, I should be able to cut Lily's boat off on the other bank. The pain in my ankle is sharpening, but I urge myself on. The noise of the rugby crowd has been replaced by the rushing hiss of the weir that's sprawled across the river. If it comes to it maybe I could dash across—the water's probably not even that deep. My heart leaps as I see the boat slowing, its engines gurgling, becoming more tentative. But the next stretch of path has been blocked off by a temporary barrier and I'm forced up onto the road. With every second the river is out of sight it feels as if I'm losing Lily again. I stumble on, breathing heavily now, and finally I'm able to scramble over a low wall and go skidding down the grass bank and back to the path, and then I'm up the steps onto the bridge. I can still see the boat as I dash onward, feet pounding, people turning to look as I pass them. Then I'm down the steps at the other side. But as I come out onto the path, it's to find that there are several other Pollock Cruises boats nestled by the bank. Passengers are disembarking, but others are climbing aboard. I rush over, jostling people, calling Lily's name, but while a few people look around, none of them are her. I'm beginning to spiral. *She's not here. She's not here.* But then up ahead I get a glimpse of her. I stumble forward, and people move aside, the path opening up. Sweat is in my eyes, hampering my vision, and I wipe at them desperately, trying to stop Lily's form from blurring. I make the final few steps and stop. She's facing away from me, close enough for me to put a hand on her shoulder. I say her name, the sound escaping my mouth in a single low sob.

42.

MEMORIES, UNORDERED

A fleck of pastry on her right knee, the first time we ate breakfast in bed together.

"Why don't you mind *your* gap," she said on the platform at Green Park station.

Her crisp-packet origami.

A spot of red on the sofa, no bigger than a five-pence piece. Like a planet in miniature, fallen from the sky.

Lying side by side and serenading the leaf as it floated down on the breeze through the skylight above us, to the tune of *2001: A Space Odyssey*.

Holding her as she cried, the violence as she struggled against me—"I don't want to feel better."

A meadow. Soft, tall grass. She folded her arms to lift her dress over her shoulders.

Her watch. Cold from dew.

43.

CAN I HELP YOU?

NOW

Lily turns around, and she's the only thing in focus.

Except something's wrong. Where are the freckles on her shoulders? Why are her eyes that watery blue? I paw at my own, still trying to clear my vision. She's speaking now, but that isn't her voice either.

The chugging of the boats' engines and the voices of the people around us fade in and out like a car radio searching for reception. I try to speak, but I can't. As I go to take a step forward an arm blocks my path. A man with a firm but polite voice says, "Excuse me. Can I help you?"

His accent is European. Dutch, maybe. He has the neatest little beard I've ever seen. He's wearing round glasses with thin, almost invisible frames. I take a step back and this seems to placate him. He moves over to the woman, who is his wife, and not Lily, and I wonder in that moment whether these two confused tourists will think of me when they get home, or years from now when they're idling at traffic lights, or bored in meetings—

a nagging footnote in the story of their lives—or if they'll forget the encounter by the time they're asleep tonight.

I only just make it to a nearby bench, mumbling apologies as I go, before my legs give way. Some people come over and offer vague words of comfort. Am I OK? Is there something they can do? I can't summon the strength to explain, or even wave them away, and so I just sit there looking down at my feet until they drift off back into their clusters around the boats.

I'm not quite sure how much time has passed before I feel someone come and sit down next to me on the bench. Everyone else seems to have gone.

"I'm glad I found you," Tess says. When I don't say anything, she shifts over so that she's sitting closer to me. "What happened?" she asks. When I answer, my voice sounds thick.

"I thought it was Lily," I say. "But it wasn't. Just a very startled Dutch woman. Or maybe Swedish."

Tess puts her hand on my back, and our eyes meet.

"No," she says softly, "I mean, *what happened*?"

44.

CHANGING IDENTITIES

THEN

By the time the summer rolled around when Lily and I turned thirty-four, if you'd asked me to describe how I felt about life, I think I'd simply have said "content." In my twenties, despite enjoying those first hints at domesticity, the idea of this being something to celebrate would have troubled me, I think. Was that it? Was there not more to strive for? Now that we were creeping further into our thirties, I could confidently say that this was all I really wanted, and that I'd not felt this happy in a very long time.

By this point, Lily and I had slowed down when it came to traveling and finding the need to fill every free moment of our lives with new things. I didn't regret that we'd spent those few years living at such a dizzying pace, but now I found just as much pleasure spending a lazy Sunday morning in bed with Lily, reading our books, drinking tea, and eating croissants from the bakery on the corner. In those moments, both of us perfectly happy in our own little nest, I'd feel blissfully content. *You and me*, I'd think. *That's all we need.*

Life as godparents was still joyful. There was little better than the feeling of arriving at our friends' houses and hearing the genuine squeals of excitement from Jack, or Lily's godchildren, Edie, Flo, and Betty. And in the moments when my mind did wander, when I thought about a life where I was a dad, I felt content to sit with that feeling until it passed, and then go back home with Lily to whatever gloriously free evening awaited us.

It was one such evening when Lily received a text from Rebecca inviting us to go on holiday with her and Rupert. By this point Lily's sister was one of the most high-profile lawyers in the country and always spoke to me like I was on the witness stand, even if she was asking me to pass the salad dressing.

"I'm sure we'll have fun," I told Lily.

"I'll remind you of that when we're playing our ninth passive-aggressive game of Scrabble."

We arrived on the south coast in the middle of a heat wave that August, though an apparent microclimate by our rental cottage kept us on our toes, storms blowing in off the sea seeing us scrambling to get back indoors.

Finally we got a day that looked to be set fair, and we found a spot on the beach. Edie, a precocious eight-year-old by now, lay with her nose buried in the book Lily and I had bought for her. Her younger brother, Alexander (not Alex, on pain of death, as I had found out to my cost), had arrived two years earlier. Blond and tousle-haired, with a plump little belly, he barreled around on the sand as Rupert—carrying a little transistor radio so he could listen to the cricket—dutifully followed in his wake.

I was attempting to read the paper, but the calming waves tickling the shore and the gentle hum of the beach meant my eyelids were drooping. I must have finally dropped off to sleep, because the next thing I knew, Lily was poking me awake.

"Brian, wake up."

When I turned over I saw that she was sitting up, legs outstretched, and that Alexander was standing between them, pouring water out of a bucket onto her feet. I rubbed my eyes. The beach seemed packed all of a sudden, kids haring about while dads hammered windbreaks into the sand. I looked around but couldn't see the others.

"Where are Rupert and Rebecca?"

"That's the thing," Lily said in a strained voice. "Edie got stung by a jellyfish. Rebecca and Rupert have had to help her all the way back to the cottage to spray the sting with something and so . . ." She nodded at Alexander. "We're in charge."

I sat up, realizing the gravity of the situation.

"Want Mummy," Alexander said.

"Mummy will be back soon," Lily said in a new, singsong voice. "Shall we build a sandcastle while we wait for her?"

"No," Alexander said, like a despot dismissing the advice of his puppet mayor. Lily widened her eyes at me for help.

"I think a sandcastle sounds like lots of fun," I said stiffly, but Alexander didn't even bother to respond this time. Out of nowhere, it seemed, he began to bawl. Lily and I immediately panicked, trying to soothe him with no success. But just as soon as he'd started, he stopped. And then, looking at me dead in the eye, he said, "Need a poo."

I looked at Lily. She looked at me.

"Is he wearing a nappy?" I asked out of the corner of my mouth.

"I've no idea."

She peered around at his lower half, like she was inspecting a car.

"I don't think so."

"So . . . so what do we do?"

"I, um . . . I don't really . . ."

Eyes still fixed on mine, Alexander gave a warning grunt.

"Oh god," Lily said. "I don't know what the rules are!"

"Do we just . . . let it happen?"

"No! He's not a sheep."

"*Need a poo*," Alexander said with another grunt, and then, like a Formula 1 pit crew, we sprung into life. I lifted him while Lily yanked his swimming trunks off, and using our windbreak to hide him from view, we cradled him above the sand. With one final grunt, Alexander produced a sprawling, never-ending, unforgiving turd, while Lily and I watched, mesmerized, as it unfurled.

"Wet wipes," Lily said, like a surgeon. I reached around behind me and yanked a fistful out of Rebecca's bag. Lily got to work wiping while I did my best to hold Alexander still.

"OK," Lily breathed. "Think we're good." Alexander wriggled but Lily said, "Right, mister, let's get you trousered up, eh?" And this time there was a determined calmness to her voice that Alexander seemed to respect, and I let Lily take the reins and get him dressed. I found a *Spot the Dog* book in the bag and Alexander's eyes lit up. It had been a good choice. He took it from me and began manhandling the pages, ripping one clean out. We didn't stop him, though, because now we had a different problem.

"What the hell do we do with this?" Lily whispered, pointing at Alexander's efforts.

"God knows. I mean, we can't just leave it here . . . can we?"

"Absolutely not, no."

I glanced around, and then my eyes fell on Alexander's spade. I looked back at Lily, eyebrows raised.

"No," she said. "Absolutely not."

"Have you got a better idea?"

Lily opened her mouth but closed it. Evidently she hadn't. "Christ then, OK."

And so, while Alexander obliterated *Spot the Dog*, we set to work. I dug a hole while Lily pushed the sand I'd removed aside with her hands. We worked in silence at first, grimly determined, until I looked at Lily and said, "I feel like we're two murderers burying a body."

"Please don't make me laugh or we'll never get this done."

But I couldn't help myself. And then neither could Lily.

"Do you think we'll ever see each other again when this blows over?" she asked.

"I hope so. Now, here's forty quid. That should get you to the airport."

"Panama?"

"Precisely. Dye your hair. Change your name."

"But how will I ever find you?"

Our evidence finally buried, perhaps for confused archaeologists to discover somehow perfectly preserved in years to come, we collapsed back onto the picnic rug. We watched as Alexander picked up another book and began to turn the pages, but carefully this time. His little floppy sunhat had fallen off, and Lily and I reached for it. In the end we both lifted it at the same time and placed it reverently on Alexander's head, as if we were crowning a new king.

Alexander looked up at each of us in turn. Then he dropped

his book and waddled over to Lily, where he plonked himself down, curling up across her lap. His little round belly was moving up and down as if in sleep, but he was still looking around at what was happening elsewhere on the beach.

"I can't believe you're going to be a proper person one day," Lily whispered to him. She stroked his blond curls and he closed his eyes. It wasn't long before he'd drifted off to sleep. If you'd walked past us then, I thought, you'd have assumed we were a family of our own.

I picked up a fistful of sand and let it fall through my fingers.

"What do you think life holds in store for him then?" I asked.

Lily tilted her head to one side, considering Alexander. "Well," she murmured, "there are those things that are common to each of us, the inescapable aspects of life."

"Such as . . . ?"

"Hmm. Dancing badly at weddings?"

I shifted over to her. "And what else?"

"Well, pretending to laugh at your spouse's dreadful jokes, of course, and changing the Hoover bag, and watching while all your friends move to the stupid countryside."

"Uh-huh."

"And sometimes," she said, voice lowered now, "it'll all just seem like it's too much . . ."

Alexander opened his eyes for a moment, then closed them again.

"But then," Lily whispered, "something unexpected and wonderful usually happens, which makes it all worth it."

Her eyes had begun to brim with tears. I put my arm around her, and she rested her head on my shoulder.

"Hey, are you OK?"

"I don't really know," Lily whispered. When she turned her face to mine, she looked scared.

"What is it? You can tell me anything, you know that."

In the silence that followed, a wave crashed against the shore, and we both looked up. In all the drama with Alexander, the tide had sneaked in undetected, the water taking on an almost golden hue under the early evening sun.

"I need to ask you something," she said.

"Don't tell me *you* need a poo now too?" I replied.

Lily laughed, but it turned into a sob. And then I really was scared about what she was going to say next.

"Do you ever think we made a mistake?" she said.

"About . . . about what?"

She paused again.

"Deciding not to have children."

A wave crashed. Seagulls screeched. And I really didn't know what to say.

"I love you," I said at last. "And you're all I need. That's the only thing I'm sure about."

Lily chewed her lip. Had I said the wrong thing?

"Do you remember when I went to Greece two summers ago?" she said. "That girls' trip. What arrived afterward." I was thrown by this at first. And then I remembered how she'd been acting strange, rushing to the door ahead of me whenever the post came. But she'd told me what had happened, hadn't she?

"You mean when you were trying to hide Daniel's wedding invitation?"

I hadn't cared then about having to go to that. I'd been happy, if anything, to be there and see it happen with my own eyes.

But Lily shook her head. "That wasn't what I was waiting for."

I found myself going very still. "OK," I said. "So . . . what was it then?"

"It was a letter," Lily said. "A very badly written letter. I was drunk, in my hotel room. We'd been out. Cat and the other mums had been absolutely going for it because it was their first night off from the kids for ages. And at first I was all smug, because that was never something I had to worry about. And then we were all sitting around the dinner table talking, and they were showing photos of their kids around, and I was bracing myself for the whole 'You'll be next, Lily!' thing as usual, but then nobody said it. And when they didn't, it was like this great dull wave of something, I don't know what, just hit me. I thought of you then—pictured you holding our baby . . ."

She wiped quickly at her eyes, as if to hide her tears from me. That made me reach out to her and pull her close.

"But by then you would tell me how happy you were with our life as it was, and I kept thinking I'd say something but I just *couldn't*, and now look, it's all just such a mess."

I held her closer still, and she burrowed hard into me, as if pushing back against the words that she thought were pulling us apart.

"So are you saying . . . you'd . . . like us to have a family?"

She squeezed my hand then, hard. "I know that's not what you want anymore," she said.

We were quiet for a moment. I watched a wave crash, then fall back. The high-tide mark was twenty yards away. I wondered if the water might get past it today.

I was trying to let Lily's words sink in. It had been a journey, to arrive at this point. It was true that my mindset had shifted over the years. I really was happy with how things were. But in my heart of hearts, this felt right. I wanted it too. For us to be the ones dealing with grazed knees and science homework and all the rest of it. The thought that it could be real suddenly felt delicate, like a butterfly in my cupped palms. Unless I said something, now, I might lose it to the wind.

"I think I'd like that an awful lot," I said at last, struggling not to cry now myself.

"Are you sure?" Lily said, and the hope in her voice made me ache.

"Yes," I said. "Definitely."

"And you're not worried?"

"About what?"

"About if we're ready. If we'd be any good as parents. All of it, really."

I brushed some sand off Alexander's shoulder. "Is anyone?" I said. "I mean, the whole thing seems utterly terrifying, doesn't it? But then again, look at what we've just done now . . ." Alexander stirred, as if he knew I was talking about him, but then he laid his head back down. "We didn't know what we were doing, we just got on with it, and it was OK, wasn't it? I mean, maybe that's why people survive it. Not because they're better prepared to be parents, but because the whole thing happens so quickly you don't have time to think. It's all just love and chaos, isn't it?"

Lily laughed through a sob. "Love and chaos. I don't mind that."

"Matching tattoos?"

She turned her head and kissed me. "I think we've made enough big decisions for one day."

45.

DONUTS

NOW

It's late afternoon, and my mouth is dry from talking. I feel shattered. Tess has been so patient, listening to me as I tell her all this—things I've never spoken out loud to a soul, memories sparking tangents that have me off at a canter. It's only when I finally run out of gas that she gently suggests we find somewhere to have some food and a cup of tea. My leg has seized up from when I twisted my ankle earlier, and so rather embarrassingly Tess has to help me along until the blood flows back to it.

"I feel very old," I say.

"You should have seen yourself running along that riverbank earlier," Tess says. "You were like a greyhound."

"I'm sure I was more like a sausage dog."

We make it into town and find a café. Tess orders us donuts and tea. It's been years since I've had a jam donut. I've no idea why, they were always my favorite. I bite into it and jam squirts out everywhere. That's why. Tess politely ignores this calamity and sips her tea. I notice again the mark where her wedding ring was. I wonder how long it will take to fade.

I look at the clock on the wall. We must have been on that bench for hours. As much as it's hurt to dredge all this up, it felt like a necessary kind of pain—like I've been trapped and surrounded by burning-hot coals, and the only way to get out was by walking over them. But I'm horribly aware of how selfish I'm being, unburdening myself on Tess like this. I resolve to make it up to her when this is all over, though what "this" is anymore, I don't really know.

"I feel very grateful that you're here," I say. It's the least I can do, but I time my words poorly, and it coincides with the waitress calling out to everyone that they're about to close.

We get up to leave, brushing sugar from our clothes as we go. When we get outside, it's to find that it's turning into an even more glorious evening than yesterday, and Tess suggests we stroll along the riverbank. Sunlight is shimmering on the water. A swan glides by. As we pass a canalboat with people on board drinking champagne, Tess slips her arm into mine.

"You should keep talking," she says.

And so I do.

46.

TIME FOR THE WEATHER

THEN

I'd be lying if I said Lily and I approached trying for a baby with any kind of scientific strategy. We just stopped using the things we'd been using to stop from happening the thing that we now wanted to happen . . . Perhaps it was because of the roundabout way we'd arrived at our decision—particularly after the "business" with Alexander—but it was almost as if we felt a bit embarrassed about doing things with any sense of a rigorous approach. Even when we went to a doctor after four months of trying without success, we were concerned, of course, but we weren't close to catastrophizing. Our doctor, however, quickly put paid to that.

"Things won't be as straightforward as if you'd tried earlier," he said. "After all," he added, looking at Lily, "you *are* on the verge of a geriatric pregnancy at this point . . ."

He advised us, with an awkwardness that suggested he'd much rather one of us had come in with an unsightly boil or something, "to keep on with the intercourse as frequently as possible."

It was a race between us for who would use that expression first when we got home, and Lily beat me to it, doing her best Alan Bennett impression to boot, but our gallows humor could only last so long.

The months went by. We both turned thirty-five, and it felt like we'd spent a year of our lives doing nothing other than "keeping on with the intercourse." There were more than a few occasions when I couldn't rise to the challenge, the pressure getting to me. As it turned out, this was something of a warning for deeper problems that lay ahead, because it wasn't long before I was listening to another doctor, thankfully one with a bit more of a bedside manner, who told me that I was suffering from "low-quality sperm." With as much dignity as I could muster with Lily sitting by me, I asked the doctor to explain the difference between that and "low sperm count," which she duly did, and which didn't make me feel much better. I pictured a vast warehouse, filled to the rafters with fairground fish in plastic bags, all of them floating upside down.

When we got home, Lily tried to paint the diagnosis as a positive—"We know the problem, and that's half the battle." But it was a heavy burden for me to carry, and I didn't know how to handle it. I made lots of self-deprecating jokes that were designed to lighten the mood, but they came out with the bitterness that I actually felt, and then I'd overapologize, and I could tell the combination was driving Lily to distraction.

I found the practical steps I'd been advised to take more easy to deal with. Giving up alcohol, something that I wasn't sure was possible, turned out to be a cinch. I began exercising to the point where I actually started enjoying it—something I'd previously thought of as a myth. When the months continued to slide by without success, it was Lily who kept our spirits up—helping us find some playfulness again. We continued to discuss the idea of our dream pub while sipping orange juice on the battered sofas and creaky chairs of London's finest hostelries. While we weren't quite at the peak of our culture-vulturing, Lily did start getting us to the theater again—including a performance by a new, experimental troupe, like the ones we'd seen doing the crab routine all those years ago. It might have been a decade later, but sure enough, this was another case of fighting back the laughter as five very earnest drama students acted out the moon landings from the perspective of the moon. That night we rushed home, as giddy and in love as we'd ever been, and for the first night in a long while we made our way to bed without thinking of anything other than how much we wanted each other. As we rearranged ourselves before sleep, finding our position—my arm numb as ever—I think we were both trying not to say out loud what we felt: this time—*this time*.

A couple of weeks later, when I was woken up by the sound of Lily rushing into the bathroom, I lay rigid as a board in bed, wondering, hoping. But when she came back, suspiciously brightly for someone who'd been throwing up, she just said, "Must've been something I ate."

"Come here, poor thing," I said. But as she took my arm and clutched it to her chest, I could feel how hard her heart was beating.

A few days later I was having a rare work-from-home day when I heard Lily calling to me from the bathroom. I went upstairs and stood outside, asking her what she needed.

"Loo roll? The fire brigade? A priest?"

"Shut up and come in!"

I did—only to find her on the toilet.

"Whoa, whoa, whoa—I thought you said you never wanted to be one of those couples who were fine being in the same room while—"

"Just shut up for a moment."

I did as I was told, sitting down on the edge of the bath. Then Lily held up a stick, brandishing it like a conductor's baton. It took me a while to cotton on to what it was.

"Wait," I said, rushing over and going down on my knees. "Have you . . . are you . . . ?"

"I don't know yet," Lily said, lips pursed tight. "I think so. But I just can't quite bring myself to do it."

I was all set to give her a pep talk then, to tell her that even if she wasn't, then it was fine, it was OK, but the next thing I knew she was weeing and saying, "I'm doing it! It's happening!"

I shall never forget the madness that followed those two magical lines appearing, as we jumped around that tiny bathroom like lunatics. We'd sternly told ourselves that we wouldn't get excited or take things for granted if we got to this point, but after all the months we'd spent trying—all the doctor's appointments and the sense our life had been put on hold while we fought an increasingly uphill battle—dancing around seemed like the only reasonable response. Because, as Lily said, what was the alternative—shaking hands?

I knew that you weren't supposed to tell people at this early stage, but it was quite hard when I saw Ed for a drink and he asked me what was new. My two bits of news were that my wife was pregnant and that I'd discovered a new sandwich place near my office. That really did hammer home how much life was about to change.

Of course, as I'd once predicted all that time ago with Lily's friend Hugo and his talk of protecting his "mate," Lily could now barely reach for the remote control without me practically forward-rolling across the living room like her Secret Service agent to get it for her.

"My big silverback," she'd say in mock awe when I carried the *slightly* heavier of the two shopping bags home from the supermarket.

The spare room of our flat was still a monument to our discarded hobbies: Mountain bikes we'd ridden up precisely zero mountains on. That table tennis table, folded up. Felt and bags of flour and calligraphy sets. It would all need to go.

We hadn't planned on turning the space into "the baby's room" so soon, but it was a good excuse to rid ourselves of all the clutter, and once we'd done that we thought we might as well crack on with decorating the place—in an appropriately neutral style. We'd decided we weren't going to find out whether it was a boy or a girl, though Lily was convinced it was the latter. Secretly, I'd have been delighted if it was a girl. Maybe it was because of how much fun I'd had playing with Edie when she was little. Either way, I felt almost embarrassed about how excited I was to be a dad, how quickly I wanted life to speed up.

I found the decorating an unashamedly wholesome experience. Lily and I listened to records—I was a Nick Drake convert by then—while I decluttered and Lily painted. I have a particularly vivid memory of coming back in from a run to the rubbish dump to find Lily—hair tied up with a bandanna—standing back admiring her painting handiwork, hands on hips, basking in sunshine streaming in through the window. I crossed the room and put my arms around her, my hands instinctively drawn to her stomach.

“You look like the woman on that wartime poster,” I said. “The ‘we can do it’ one.”

Lily duly assumed the position, biceps flexed.

“That’s the one.”

Lily put her arms around me. “Would you go off to war while I slaved away in the factory? Would you *die* for me?”

“Absolutely I would. And it still counts if they put me in the marching band and I end up tripping over a tambourine and falling on a land mine, right?”

“Oh, absolutely.”

As we held each other, all I could think of then was that, for all my joking, I would really do absolutely anything for her—for my family. That word had taken on a brand-new meaning now. When we were younger, we used to joke about how funny it sounded to say “My wife” or “My husband”—these seemed like far too grown-up sorts of phrases for two people who ate Jaffa Cakes for breakfast. But now when I imagined saying “My daughter” or “My son” there was something truly wondrous about it, and though I was still desperate to tell people about our news, I enjoyed keeping this part secret, just for me.

47.

FALSE DAWNS

THEN

It was January, and we were on the long drive up to Scotland to attend Forbes and Verity's fortieth wedding anniversary. I would have been nervous as it was at attending such an event—relations hadn't exactly improved between Lily's parents and me—but I was even more so given that we'd decided to tell them our news.

It had been nearly a month since our twelve-week scan, and all was well, but we hadn't told a soul yet. I think both of us still felt like we would rather have kept it secret for the time being, but in the end we talked ourselves into it. As Lily pointed out, everyone was under such scrutiny at these parties anyway that it was no good her trying to make a thimble of watered-down white wine last all evening and expect it to go unnoticed.

"I guarantee that Rebecca will know as soon as she sees me anyway," she said.

"How?"

"She's got that kind of strange witch doctor–y thing about

her. She'll start speaking in tongues and make some grave prophecy, you wait."

We were greeted customarily by Forbes, who was patrolling the grounds. His hair was thinner now, and he moved a little more stiffly, but his mind was as sharp as ever. When he shook my hand he gave me a look as if we were two old foes meeting again, which at least hinted at respect. I wondered whether having a baby with Lily might change things further—whether it would soften him. It was hard to say.

The usual assortment of ruddy-cheeked golf friends and business associates and their long-suffering spouses was already at Challington when Lily and I arrived. Edie had hidden herself away in a big armchair, deep in a book as ever—though she did give me a wave—while Alexander tore up and down the hallway, golden curls flying, under the watchful eye of his parents. I looked on as Rebecca greeted Lily with the usual slightly formal air kisses, then she pulled away sharply and narrowed her eyes.

"Wait. Hang on. Something's different about you."

Lily laughed and said there definitely wasn't, and luckily Alexander chose that moment to trip over a cushion, his doleful cries summoning Rebecca. Lily came over to me, a big false smile on her face, and gave my hand the double-squeeze.

"We can't leave now," I laughed.

"Spoilsport."

We milled around for a little bit, Lily surreptitiously dumping champagne into a potted plant.

"No Daniel?" I asked, scanning the rest of the guests.

"He's away with Tabitha, I believe."

"Pity."

Lily rolled her eyes, then a twinkle came to them as she said, "Good name for a boy, though, Daniel . . ."

She skipped forward to chase a squealing Alexander before I had time to reply.

IT WAS LATER that evening and just the family was left, decamping to the living room, where Forbes began doling out the brandy. I was hoping this would be a quick drink, as I got the sense from Lily that she could really do with going up to bed.

"Darling?" Forbes inquired of Lily, decanter poised over her glass.

"Not for me, thanks," she said. I saw Verity and Rebecca exchange a look. It felt like if we didn't announce our news soon, then there was a good chance one of them might just come out and say something. I cleared my throat and looked around at Lily, but she stood up abruptly and excused herself. As I watched her go, I couldn't blame her for having second thoughts. It wasn't as if her family had reacted with unbridled joy when we'd told them we were engaged, or to any other vaguely significant announcements for that matter. There would be a barb or a funny look that would spoil things. But as I sipped some fortifying brandy, I still felt that we should do it. Perhaps this was a little selfish of me, but even though the response would almost certainly be confusingly complicated, it had dawned on me as the day went on that these were still the closest people to family that I had.

"Decent stuff, eh?" Forbes said, topping up my glass. He even patted me on the shoulder paternally as he did so. I looked around to see where Lily was. Goodness knows why I was suddenly in Forbes's good books, but if there was ever a time to do this it was very clearly now. It had been a while since Lily had disappeared, I realized. I was getting a bit tense, as Rupert kept yawning. It wouldn't be long before he said, "Up the stairs to Bedfordshire," a catchphrase of his that for some reason everyone always ignored. If I'd had to guess, I'd have said that Lily was up in her bedroom, hiding like we'd done on our wedding day. I was about to go and find her when I heard the old staircase creaking. As the living room door opened, Forbes grabbed me by the shoulder.

"Have I ever told you about my Australia trip, back in the day?"

He had, many times. The story ended with a punch line that hadn't been acceptable since about 1958. But given his vague show of affection just now, I couldn't bring myself to stop him. As he launched into the anecdote I felt Lily sit down next to me on the sofa. She took my hand in hers and squeezed it twice. I went to look at her but Forbes barked a question at me.

"Yes, so he was your accountant at the time?" I replied, like a willing chat show host teeing up his guest, and off he went again. I felt Lily squeeze my hand twice again. Normally I would have been up and ready to go in an instant, but I really did feel that we would regret it if we didn't use this opportunity when Forbes was in such a good mood, and so I tried to let her hand go. But as I did so she squeezed it again, the second time so hard I let out a little gasp of pain. I looked around. Lily was smiling, but her lips were thin and tight, her eyes wide and glistening.

"We should go," she said to me, her voice horribly strained, like a violin string strung so tight it might snap.

"Oh, OK," I said. "Right now?"

She nodded sharply, the smile still fixed desperately on her face. The others were looking at us. Even Forbes trailed off.

"What's going on?" he said.

"Nothing!" Lily said, manic and bright. Our eyes met again. And then I knew.

Before I could do anything, Lily had stood up.

"It's nothing, we just need to head off, don't we?" she said.

"At this hour? Don't be ridiculous," Forbes barked, draining his brandy. But he was the only one who didn't realize something was wrong. Rebecca and Verity were both on their feet.

"Lily," I said softly. "Do y—"

"Lovely to see you all," she said, cutting across me, still attempting a veneer of normality, but then her legs wobbled and her mother and sister rushed forward to help me lower her back to the sofa.

"Rupert, call an ambulance," Rebecca said. "Lily, listen to me, it's going to be OK."

Lily's face was white.

"An ambulance?" Verity said. "It'll take an age. We should drive to Berwick."

"No," Rebecca said. "Borders General."

Forbes stood up. "Is someone going to tell me what's going on?"

Everyone seemed to be talking then, voices raised. I could feel the helplessness descending on me. Rebecca and Verity pushed me out of the way, lifting Lily and starting to move her toward the door. I slumped backward and Forbes caught me. I looked down at Lily's fingernail marks on my wrist, like a bird's footprints in the snow, then at the sofa, where a tiny circle of blood had appeared.

"Brian," Verity said. "We need you. Now."

That was when clarity came to me, like lightning piercing the dark, illuminating everything around it. I dashed forward and helped support Lily as her legs went from beneath her. Rupert flung the door open and stood out of the way as we bundled past him.

Rebecca held her hand out. "Keys."

Rupert shoved his hands into his pockets until he'd found them, and Rebecca snatched them from him. We made our way across the gravel to Rebecca's Land Rover. As we got closer we triggered the security light. A blackbird was startled into action, confusing it for the dawn. I helped Lily into the backseat, dashing around to the other side and jumping in. As Rebecca hit the accelerator and the wheels spat out gravel, I looked back at the house and saw Forbes and Rupert, frozen against the living room window, looking like how I felt—like lost little boys.

48.

PINS AND NEEDLES

NOW

I can't remember the last time I cried like this. There have been moments when emotion has overwhelmed me and I've found my eyes glassy, a lump in my throat—but here I am, truly sobbing, gasping and gurgling in an unseemly mess. Tess, who is also crying, though in a much more dignified manner than I am, is rubbing my back.

I finally manage to get a grip on myself, regaining my breath. Someone cycles past us and quickly averts their gaze.

After a moment when we're both sniffing and clearing our throats, a strange little laugh escapes my mouth.

"What?" Tess says.

"I was just thinking how you might have ended up getting to know some twenty-two-year-old backpacker on this trip who'd show you the time of your life—take you clubbing and help you rediscover your lost youth. Instead you've spent most of your time on the benches of Bath, listening to someone having a breakdown."

"Oh, Brian," Tess sighs, "the chances of me discovering my lost youth are about as likely as me learning the lute, and, well—that's the thing with this trip and, you know, *life*. Sometimes things don't go the way you expect them to."

She hands me a tissue, and I blow my nose in the way only a middle-aged man like me can. The sound of a guitar is drifting over from a canal boat moored nearby. It's hard to tell if the music is coming from speakers or someone strumming an acoustic. This day feels like it's gone on forever.

"It must be late," I say. "We should head back."

I feel Tess shrug her shoulder against mine. "We don't have to. If this is helping, then you should keep going."

49.

THE WORST THING I EVER SAID

THEN

Lily wanted to go home to London rather than her parents' house, after she'd been let out of the hospital. She curled up on the backseat of the car, trying to sleep, and it took all my concentration to keep my eyes on the road rather than looking in the mirror to make sure that she was OK.

Lily couldn't face calling into work to tell them she would be off for a while, so I did, though I felt hopeless and wretched as I failed to simply articulate the reason why. I don't know why I was relying on euphemisms. What I hated most was that part of me didn't want to upset the person on the other end of the line. But why did that matter? Why did I care about not making something awkward for someone else when Lily and I were in so much pain?

I took all that fraught energy and put it into taking care of her. I was always ready to spring to my feet. I couldn't go ten minutes without asking her if I could get her anything—anything at all. I could go to the shops, if she needed something. Did she want to go for a walk, if she was up to it, or did she just want to rest?

"I don't know what I want right now," she said on repeat, lying curled on the sofa, eyes fixed on the wall opposite. This didn't deter me. *If I keep at it*, I thought, *she'll relent, and then I can do something that'll help—I'll chip away at her pain until it's gone.* But then Lily said, "Brian, please just let me be for a while, OK?" And rather than agreeing, I said, "But what can I do—to make you feel better?" and the rage in her voice when she said, "I don't want to feel better!" was like a kick in the chest.

Later that evening, we were standing by the kitchen sink, both drinking a glass of water. Lily was standing a foot away from me. I felt horribly aware of the distance between us—how much I craved her touch. I thought of the night we met on Primrose Hill, the nerves and excitement as I felt her shift toward me.

A TENTATIVENESS CREPT in between us over the next few days. It was like being with a stranger. We went to see the doctor, who told us in reassuring tones how common what had happened was. It was here, in front of another stranger, where the sadness I had been waiting for finally arrived, and the marks on my hand where I dug my fingernails in, trying not to cry, would still be there for a week afterward.

When we got back, I asked Lily if she wanted to go for a walk, but she said she was too tired. I went out on my own, hands thrust in my pockets, feeling like I was trudging through tar. It was late by the time I got back. When I did, it was to find that two of Lily's friends were there, sitting with her on the sofa. Their eyes were puffy and red from crying. I didn't know whether Lily had called them or whether they'd just come round.

I didn't get the sense I should be there, so I went to lie upstairs on the bed, listening to their murmured voices. It hurt when I heard Lily crying, but even more when, later, after the conversation had clearly moved on to something else, I heard her laugh.

I turned the lights out and got into bed. When Lily crawled in beside me, we found our usual position for sleep. After a while, Lily was breathing softly and my arm was growing numb, like it always did. Except this time I shifted her off me to free it.

"What is it?" she asked sleepily.

"Nothing," I said. "It just hurts my arm when you lie on it like that. It always has."

"Oh," Lily said. "I'm sorry."

It's a dangerous thing when you love someone, because it means you know how to hurt them too.

THE DAYS THAT followed were like mini endurance courses. Butter toast. Eat toast. Train to work. Produce spreadsheets. Home. Microwave leftovers. Try to sleep. It felt like we were clinging on to our lives by our fingernails. And still Lily and I hadn't really talked.

A week later I started to call Ed but hung up before the call went through. I didn't know what I'd actually say—or how I could expect that burdening him would be good for either of us.

Later, I came back from the shops to find that Lily wasn't in the living room, where she'd been when I'd left. Instead, I found her in the baby's room, sitting cross-legged on the floor. I went to go over to her but stopped myself.

"Shall I shut the door, or . . . ?"

She looked up at me and shook her head, then patted the floor next to her. I felt my heart contract with a painful kind of relief. When I sat down beside her she took my arm and rested her head on my shoulder, and I had to try very hard not to cry.

"I don't know what we should do," Lily said. This, I suppose, was partly to blame for the distance between us ever since we'd got home. The question that had remained unspoken. Would we try again?

"Me neither," I said.

Lily squeezed my arm and said, "I wish everyone would stop telling us how common it is."

"I know."

"So, is that . . . I mean, what do you think we should do?"

"What do *you* think we should do?"

Lily suppressed a sob, then composed herself, breathing deeply as she forced the words out. "I can't make that decision on my own."

I stiffened at this. "But I can?"

"That's not what I'm saying. It just feels like because I had to go through the physical pain of it all that that somehow means I have to decide whether we should try again, and I really don't want to have the weight of that on my shoulders."

"And I watched you in that pain," I said slowly. "I know that's not the same. But I don't want to ever see you that hurt again in my life."

Lily pulled me close to her, rested her forehead against mine. "So what do we do?"

I closed my eyes. Squeezed them shut so that pockets of light skipped and flashed. When I opened them I said, "Maybe we don't have to make a decision just yet. Maybe we take a breather. Be husband and wife for a bit."

Lily was quiet for the longest time. Then she kissed me.

"I think that's what I want," she said.

FOR THE NEXT six months, we found our way back to each other, until the final ice was thawed. When we went to bed and undressed each other, it was for us, and nothing more. As we went through that process, it was amazing how trivial everything else in my life seemed to become. Work, for example, just didn't really seem to matter anymore. Lily too had taken a step back. Normally she'd have been on the phone to people at the magazine at all hours, but now she'd ignore calls, or at most pick up and ask if someone else could deal with whatever "emergency" had arisen. For my part, it was hard to do anything other than turn up and do the minimum required. I'd clock-watch, just wanting to get home.

When the day came that I was called into a meeting with my boss, a ruddy-cheeked man firmly of the old school, and the head of HR was there, I was still too distracted to be worried by whatever this was. Even when my boss started using phrases such as "You know how much I like you personally," I didn't understand what was happening.

"The restructure was actually agreed a few months ago," he continued. "You would have been told sooner, but of course, ah, what with your wife and your . . . circumstances . . ." The head of HR cleared her throat quietly, and my boss clasped his hands together, as if to turn a lock to stop himself from talking.

I felt numb to it all on the way home that afternoon, explaining it to Lily in a monotone. When she got up and put her arms around me, I was surprised by the strength of her embrace. Later, while we were cooking dinner, she said, "You know what we've not had for a long time? A holiday."

It was true.

"I think it would be good for us to get out of London for a while," she added. "God knows I could do without having to think about the magazine for five minutes too. That place is driving me mad at the moment."

We found a last-minute deal for a holiday cottage on the Devon coast, not somewhere either of us had been to before. We drove down in the sunshine. Lily lowered the windows and put the radio on, and we sang at the tops of our voices all the way down there. It felt good to have left the confines of the house—like we had regained some kind of control over our lives. The good weather continued, and when we walked on the beach under an imperious blue sky, it felt like we were on a different planet than the gray, petrol-fumed existence we'd left back in London. As we sat with our books on the sand, I watched Lily raise her face to the sun, eyes closed, taking in deep lungfuls of sea air, and I knew then that I had her back.

ON THE FINAL day of the trip we took a cliff-top walk and had just passed some hulking barns when we saw a beautiful old pub reveal itself in the distance, its gold lettering glinting in the sun. It was a shame that the insides didn't quite match that initial sighting—it was tired and clearly needed renovation. But what potential it had! With a bit of elbow grease, Lily said—looking around admiringly—it's pretty much our dream pub, isn't it? Her words stayed with me as I was at the bar ordering our final one-for-the-road. I overheard the barman telling an old chap on a stool that the owners were thinking of selling up. I looked over at Lily, who was gazing out of the window, all the tension that had built in her shoulders now completely gone.

We were subdued on the drive home, both of us not relishing being back so soon. We stood on the threshold, suitcases in hand. The hallway ahead of us seemed so dark. And then there was the nursery upstairs, which we had left as it was. To change that room in any way would be to make a decision. A decision that we still had not returned to.

This is the moment I think back on more than any. About what I did next, and why. All I could think of, as we unpacked in silence, was how miserable we'd become there. What I'd give for us to be back under that enormous blue sky, breathing in that sea air. We had been free there, hearts filled with love, as carefree as we'd been when we'd first found each other.

That evening, while Lily was in the bath, I called the pub and registered my interest in buying it from the current owners. Then, after a slug of scotch straight from the bottle, I made a second phone call.

I MET FORBES quite literally on bended knee, tying my shoelaces, when he came into the café where we were meeting. I had cobbled together a business plan of sorts, although the stack of pages I'd scrawled it all on were out of order and crumpled. Forbes made me wait for a very long time before we even discussed it, instead regaling me with a few of his mainstay anecdotes about times he'd triumphed over weaker men in matters of business. *Yes*, I thought, *and you can add me to the list, if that's what it takes*.

When he'd finally read through my plan, having taken an

age to put on his reading glasses and then turning each dog-eared page with faux reverence, he said, "And what should give me the confidence that two thirty-six-year-olds without any prior experience will know how to make a success of this place, if I were to invest the capital?"

While I resented his talking about us like he didn't know who we were, I couldn't deny he had a point. Unless you counted spending the last decade and a half drinking in pubs and dreaming up what our ideal one would look like, it was true that we didn't have any experience. I rambled at Forbes, making it up as I went along, using the kind of phrases I'd heard him come out with when he was with his business chums. Eventually, when I began to repeat myself, he interrupted me with a single word.

"Fine."

"What, as in . . . really?"

"I think you mean 'thank you.'"

"Yes, of course, thank you."

"Better this than having you scrabble around trying to get back in the insurance game," he said. "That's if someone will take you on. And I gather from Verity that Lily's miserable at the magazine." He cleared his throat. "It'll be good for you both. After all that's happened."

Here, he dropped his gaze. I understood then that this was him showing us—or at least Lily—love, in really the only way he knew how.

"I won't let you down," I said. "Nor Lily. I promise."

He nodded at me, once, and then normal service was resumed. The afternoon dragged on. He insisted on taking me around his old wine bar haunts, regaling me with anecdotes forged in each. I let him have it. Did my best to pretend I was enjoying it all. I got home drunk, feeling like a teenager as I tried to overenunciate to pretend to Lily that I was sober. When I told her I'd been with her father she just laughed, then looked up when she realized I was being been serious.

"What on earth for?" she asked. "Why didn't you tell me?"

I rushed over then and dropped to my knees by the sofa, taking her by the hands. I explained about the pub and how I'd spoken to the owners. When I tried to talk about how it could be a fresh start for us, a new beginning, I couldn't articulate myself in the way that I wanted, and I made up for that with a kind of manic energy that I could tell was taking Lily aback.

"Let's talk about it in the morning," she said.

I barely slept. When we did sit down to discuss it, and I was able to explain myself a little better, Lily seemed able to take me more seriously. I wasn't sure what she was thinking. I suppose I'd been so electrified about the possibility of our new start that I'd got carried away thinking she would feel exactly the same. It was when she said, thoughtfully, "I suppose I am completely sick of the magazine at the moment . . . ," and I nodded vigorously, and she smiled, that I felt overwhelmed with relief.

"What if it all goes to shit?" she asked. "Could we just sell up and come home?"

This, I confess, wasn't something I'd actually considered. But I didn't want to derail the momentum.

"I'm sure we could," I said. "But it won't go to shit. I really believe that. The dream pub never goes to shit, that's why it's the dream pub."

Lily laughed. "There's the pragmatic businessman I married . . ."

I got to my feet and pulled her up by the hands, beginning a very uncoordinated slow dance around the kitchen.

"So shall I make the call then?" I asked. "Shall we do it?"

I twirled Lily away, then she spun herself back into my arms. She looked me deep in the eyes, and then she said, "OK," and in the space of two syllables our lives changed forever.

TWO WEEKS LATER, our offer was accepted. We drove down the following weekend, a muggy day in late September. I rolled down the windows so that we could sing again, but they were soon back up once we hit heavy rain as we joined the motorway. The closer we got, the more I found myself babbling away to Lily, the nerves getting the better of me.

The pub was still open, but there was barely a customer there when we came inside. We sat incognito in the corner. I was tapping my foot on the floor so much that Lily reached over gently and put her hand on my thigh to stop me.

I had planned to buy champagne but thought better of it. Taking two foaming pints of ale back to our table, I noticed Lily looking askance at the slot machine gently whirring away in the corner of the bar.

"What's up?" I asked. Lily took the drink from me and sipped at it.

"We'll be getting rid of that for starters," she said, nodding at the machine. "And we'll find some curtains that don't give off quite as much of a crematorium vibe. And now that we know we're doing food, I cannot wait to get rid of those laminated menus. That chef I was telling you about, the one we featured last month in the magazine, I wonder if he'd be tempted to come down here. In fact, I think he might be from Devon. I'll give him a call in a bit."

Just hearing Lily talk like this calmed me down. She could see the future for this place like I could. I had made the right decision. Even if it was going to take Lily a little while to come around to the idea as firmly as I had, that just made me all the more determined to keep going. It was my job now to make this new chapter in our lives a success, and to rip out all the pages that had come before it.

50.

A LETTER

NOW

Eventually, Tess and I take a taxi back to our hotel. She asks me if I want to go for a drink in the bar, but I'm exhausted and have to decline. We part ways in the lobby. I'm standing there trying to find the words to thank her, but my brain has just about given up, and so Tess comes to my rescue by putting her arms around me. We stand like that for a long time, listening to the hum of the hotel. It feels overwhelming to hold her. To be held by her. In those moments, something, I'm not sure what, seems to pass between us. With a final squeeze of my shoulders, Tess breaks off.

"Get some sleep," she says. "I'll see you in the morning."

I go to my room and kick my shoes off, lying back on the bed. I'm expecting to lie here awake with my thoughts, but the events of the day have taken their toll, and I end up falling asleep in my clothes.

I dream about Lily's watch again. This time it's tied to train tracks, like in one of those old silent films, and I can't free it in time. I jolt awake just as the train smashes into me.

It's very early morning, but the dream was so vivid that there's no chance of me falling back to sleep. I can see my laptop on the floor, and I drag it onto the bed. When I refresh Tripadvisor, I feel like I know there's going to be a new review, and sure enough there is. PinkMoonLily1970 spent an enjoyable day at the Roman baths and then a pasta-making class yesterday. My memory flickers back to Lily's pasta maker arriving. Her latest hobby. Is this her finally learning how to use one? Perhaps it's because I talked about things yesterday that I've not been able to for so long, but I suddenly feel close to her, and the thought that she is out there, nearby, is unbearable.

I sit up straight in my bed. It comes to me very clearly then that I have to end all of this. And I have to do it today.

I'm lost without *And Breathe* . . . but plenty of people online have put up blog posts about their journeys, and I see that the next place on the list is Stonehenge. That's where I'll go today. Now, in fact. I'll speak to every single person who approaches those old stones, if that's what it takes. I'm going to find out once and for all who PinkMoonLily1970 really is.

I think of Tess, a floor below me. Is she asleep, or is she lying awake too, like me? It doesn't matter, really. This is something I have to do on my own.

I get out of bed, shoving everything into my suitcase. Then I grab the little pad of hotel-branded writing paper and a pen from the bedside table.

Dear Tess,

Please forgive my rudeness in not saying a proper good-bye. I can't thank you enough for sitting with me yesterday. I wish so much that we had met under other circumstances, because getting to know you even over such a short space of time has been a true pleasure. When you see this, I'll be gone. I've realized I need to find my ending, whatever it may be, and as much as I'll regret not having your company, I feel like this is something I must do on my own.

You are a very special person, and you deserve to go on the rest of this trip free to squeeze every drop of pleasure out of it.

I really do hope we'll see each other again one day, but I'm aware that life has a habit of never really going to plan. If we don't, then please know that I'll never forget the kindness you showed me over these past few days.

I'm not sure how to sign off. All the options I'm scrolling through in my mind are too stuffy and formal. When Tess does read this, I want her to think of me fondly. Maybe she'll even take the letter home with her. I should at least end with something warm and meaningful. Isn't there an expression in New Zealand—*Kia* something—that means "your good health" or something like that? I take a stab at it, aware that time is of the essence, before going down to slip the note under Tess's door.

The receptionist seems very confused at the sight of me standing there at five in the morning, suitcase packed, asking him to order me a taxi to Stonehenge, but eventually he does so.

An hour later, as the cabbie drops me off, and I'm standing there with my suitcase in the car park, I have many questions swirling around my mind, but as a crow swoops past, cawing at me, the most pressing one just now is this: What time does Stonehenge actually open?

51.

BLISTERS

THEN

We had no idea how hard rejuvenating the County Arms was going to be. To make things even more challenging, we were still living in London while we went about refurbishing the temporarily closed pub, so we were making constant trips back and forth.

Eventually we were able to move into the room upstairs. We jettisoned so many of our belongings that it really did feel like we were starting from scratch. There wasn't a day that passed in those interim months when I didn't fear we'd made a huge mistake. The moment that curbed my anxiety, around two months into the renovation, was when Lily made good on her suggestion and persuaded the chef she'd got to know when she was at the magazine to come down to run our kitchen. I'd not seen her so excited and happy in months.

We managed to get all the renovations done in time for our grand reopening. I'll never forget how nervous we were that night. We only had a few customers at first, and despite a good deal of practicing, I still cocked up someone's Guinness when I poured it. But then gradually more people arrived—suspicious former regulars who seemed pleasantly surprised by what we'd done, first-timers who'd seen our adverts in the local paper and had come to try out the dinner menu. Lily was a natural, particularly with the regulars, who were clearly enamored with her. I would joke later that if they'd had their guitars and fiddles with them, they'd have been composing mournful Irish ballads about the redheaded Lily who broke hearts while she poured pints.

"So that went pretty well then," I said to her in bed after that long first day.

"It really did," Lily said. "It feels a bit like a dream, doesn't it? Like we'll wake up back in London tomorrow."

"I guess we just take it a day at a time, right?"

"Right."

BUT IT'S HARD to take life a day at a time when they're all blending into one. I honestly don't know how we did it, keeping the place running so well during the two years that followed. It was like a high-wire act. It didn't matter what kind of shoes I wore, I'd end up getting blisters on my feet regardless from the constant rushing around. If there weren't drinks to be served or food orders to be taken, then there were new beer arrivals to sort or guests to check in. But I absolutely savored those moments, particularly when Lily and I were both behind the bar, weaving around each other, limbs through limbs, in our own glorious ballet. It was around then when Lily and Jeff began playing their games of Consequences, Lily plucking a pencil from behind her ear to dash off a new sentence before hurrying away to the latest job that needed attending to.

There were days when we barely saw each other. There were others when we didn't spend a single moment apart. At night, one of us might collapse into bed with only a few hours to go before the other was getting up. But as tough as it was, I relished it. I'd hated it so much when we'd been in the depths of our grief—the silence of that house, the prison of it—but here, we were constantly on the go, a moving target for our residual pain.

By the time the two-year anniversary of our grand opening came about, we were fully booked most of the time—rooms as well as dinner and lunch reservations, usually weeks in advance. Perhaps it was because we'd built this thing of ours, just the two of us, but we were reluctant to hire full-time staff until it was clear we had no choice. With that cover in place, we were able to go away for a short break to belatedly celebrate our thirty-eighth birthdays.

We'd decided on Corsica. I remember sitting on the plane waiting to take off, Lily reaching across to steady my leg, which I'd been jigging up and down.

"You OK?"

"Yes, fine. Just keen to get there."

In truth, I was worried about leaving the pub. What if something went wrong? Even when we were in our resort, prone on sun loungers, I couldn't keep still. And by this point, neither could Lily.

"I don't quite know what to do with myself," she said, putting down her novel. "I've not sat so still for this long in, well, two years. It's like I've forgotten how to relax."

"I know," I said. "I sort of don't trust it. Like they're going to come out of that bar over there and say they need us to sling on a uniform and cover a double."

We rectified the situation, under Lily's instruction, by getting stuck into what turned out to be lethally strong cocktails. It was then, finally able to unwind, that we started to enjoy ourselves. I couldn't remember the last time we'd laughed so much. We found some board games in our hotel lobby, and there was so much cheating involved I'm surprised nobody called the authorities. We ate delicious local fish and drank perfectly chilled white wine, watching the sun slide into the sea.

"Do you ever wish I'd proposed to you somewhere like this?" I asked Lily, standing behind her with my hands around her waist.

"Not at all," she said, putting her hands over my arms. "But I knew you were planning on doing it in Barcelona."

"What? How?"

"Because after you booked that holiday you seemed so manic. And I bet you got the ring the next day, because every time I went even vaguely near your bottom drawer you'd tense up. So when you asked me in the rain in Wales it was a genuinely lovely surprise."

I held her for a moment, watching the sun finally dipping below the horizon, and kissed her neck.

"I love you," I said.

"I love you too."

We went back to our hotel room. Later, tangled in sheets, Lily said, "What is it about hotel sex that makes it so exciting?"

"A good question," I said. "Hang on . . ." I reached over to the phone by the bed and pretended to make a call. "Yes, hello, I'd like to see the manager please. I've got a question for him . . ."

Lily laughed and began plumping pillows. I remembered the first time I'd watched her do that in that old flat of mine—attacking them with a violence that made me think she'd do quite well in a street brawl. When she'd finished, she lay back down and, after a moment, took my hand.

"It's been a while since we talked," she said.

I rolled onto my side, facing her. "About whether to try again, you mean?"

She nodded. "Sorry," she said. "This has been so lovely. I don't want to ruin it."

"You aren't," I said. "Not at all."

"Well. What do you think?"

"I think about it a lot," I said. "I know we've been so frantic with the pub, but of course I do still wonder. What about you?"

"I do," she said. "But . . ."

"What?"

"Well, don't you think it's telling that this is the first time we've properly spoken about it in, well, you tell me? I mean, I know we've been absurdly busy, but still . . ."

The air-conditioning was blasting overtime, and Lily pulled the sheet up over us.

"That's true," I said. "But we did say we should wait. Didn't we?"

"Wait to try, maybe. Not to talk about it."

We were quiet for a moment, listening to the air con whir.

"Say if we did try," I said. "The pub . . . it's not exactly babyproof, is it? And would we be able to cope, do you think? The business is still so new."

I winced as I said this. It sounded so callous. But Lily squeezed my hand again.

"I know," she said. "I've been having all those thoughts too. But I don't think that's how we should look at it. I think maybe we just see what happens and not plan too far ahead. I'll stop taking my pill. And then if it happens it happens, and we'll find a way to cope. Love and chaos, remember?" She put her hand on my cheek, brushing her thumb against it.

"Love and chaos it is," I said.

She smiled at me, and in that moment I wanted it so much, for both of us. But I resolved not to hope, or pray, or beg. We were happy together, and if we got lucky, then that would be wonderful, but if not, our love would see us through.

52.

STONEHENGE

There is something in Stonehenge almost reassuring; and if you are disposed to feel that life is rather a superficial matter, and that we soon get to the bottom of things, the immemorial gray pillars may serve to remind you of the enormous background of time.

—HENRY JAMES, 1875

Honestly I CANNOT believe these rocks haven't been drilled down already. SUCH a boring site. The rocks have no meaning behind them, it doesn't matter how they got there. Worst trip ever.

—ONLINE REVIEW, STONEHENGE, 2020

NOW

I'm the only person in Stonehenge car park. I can just make out the sound of the taxi that brought me here as it heads back up the road, and then it's silent save for birdsong. I'm completely thrown by how quiet it is. It's very early, but the sun has risen, so where are all the druids? I'd expected to see a gaggle of Gandalfs sitting in the back of a Toyota Yaris, doling out pork pies, but the only sign of life is the dim light coming from what must be the visitor's center—an odd-looking building, like a lump of corrugated iron held up by huge toothpicks. As I approach the door, a security light comes on and I have to shield my eyes. I hear the jangle of keys and then someone slides a door open.

"Can I help you there?"

It's a man's voice, deep, with a West Country burr.

"Yes," I say, still shielding my eyes. "I was hoping to, you know, see Stonehenge?"

It's a stupid thing to say—I realize that as I'm saying it—but it's still annoying to hear the man chuckling at me. "You and a thousand other people today, matey."

"Well, yes," I say, taking a step forward, "but I thought I'd get a head start on them. Get in there early and settle in for the day, you know."

This time the man laughs even louder. "Oh right, you thought you'd just wander up there, did you?"

"I'm sorry?"

"Thought you'd just stroll on up to the stone circle at half six in the morning?"

I don't take the bait of the rhetorical question. But I'm still confused.

"Mate," the man—who's presumably a security guard—continues, "we're not open yet."

"Not open? How can it not be open? It's just—"

"I'm warning you now," the man says, all humor suddenly gone from his voice, "if you say 'big pile of stones,' you and me are gonna fall out."

I'm a grown man, but the sound of hearing someone speak like a disappointed head teacher still has me cowed, so I mumble an apology.

"It's just I thought that everyone came at sunrise," I explain.

"Yeah, your problem there is you've seen too many photos of the place on the internet. We only do that on the solstice, and that ain't for a little while. So I'm afraid you're going to have to wait until nine thirty like the rest of Joe Public today."

I must look like a broken man, because he takes pity on me, allowing me to put my suitcase in the cloakroom and saying I can rest up in one of the chairs in reception. I pull my coat up over me as a blanket and close my eyes. But every time I do, I think of Lily—in that hotel bed in Corsica, the hope in her eyes. In the bar of the pub, dressed in blue, that smile. It's all too much, and I give up on sleep, pacing around under the watchful eye of the security guard instead.

By opening time I'm manic. I watch the first cars beginning to appear, and each time a door opens I have my heart in my mouth. The security guard is baffled when I don't take him up on his offer to go and see the stones first before everyone else. In fact, I have no real intention of seeing them at all. I'm going to stay here in the lobby, watching every single person who comes through that door.

But my best-laid plans go almost instantly awry. Because of course it's not as if people are filing in politely so I can check them off one by one. There are families with kids running around, pensioners who've forgotten their thermoses. Then the huge coachloads of tourists arrive, each with their own guide carrying an umbrella or a little flag so people can follow them. It's not long before my view of the door is obscured, and I'm forced to give up and head up to the stones with everyone else.

I walk the paths, turning my head this way and that. *Come on*, I think, *please be here. Please be here, Lily.*

By lunchtime, the place is absolutely teeming with people, and I'm in danger of giving in to panic. Some of the early visitors are already beginning to make the return journey back down to the visitor's center. What if I've missed her?

I'm looking out for groups that fit the profile of the *And Breathe . . .* followers. I have a flash of inspiration when I realize there'll be some sort of booking on the computer system here—maybe even one that lists individual names. I'm about to make it down to the visitor's center to search out that security guard, desperately thinking of a way to convince him to let me look at his computer, when a man in a bulky waterproof grabs me by the arm.

"I'm sorry," he says in a tone that would suggest he's unfamiliar with the concept, "but I have reason to suspect that you might be a pickpocket."

"Sorry, what?"

"I've been watching you—and you've done nothing but look at people and follow them around."

Is he an undercover policeman or something? Either way, I really don't need this, so I attempt to push past him. But he steps in front of me. He's quite big, but if he thinks he's going to perform a citizen's arrest on me, he's mistaken.

"Get out of my way, please," I say, polite but firm.

"Don't raise your voice at me," he says. "I'm from Yorkshire," he adds, inexplicably. This has all escalated rather quickly, and I'm running out of time, but I decide on a different approach.

"Look, I'm sorry for the confusion. You're quite right to challenge me. I can assure you, though, I'm not a pickpocket."

He narrows his eyes and then, with a dismissive snort, he

walks away, and I breathe a sigh of relief. I look up, and there, for the first time, I see the stone circle. It's something I've seen so many times on television, and on the front of books, and in newspapers, that at first it feels faintly unreal—a hologram or something. I'm in danger of getting sucked into its orbit, shuffling forward like everyone else, but I clench my fists and turn on my heel, hurrying back down to the visitor's center.

There's no sign of the security guard, so I rush into the car park in case he's out there checking parking tickets. The sun is baking the tarmac, and I'm forced to cover my eyes as it glints off a reversing car's window. As I do so, I hear the Yorkshireman's voice again, in the distance, and I screw my eyes shut. If he's about to come back and have another go at me, I'm not sure I'm going to be able to stay calm. And I'm just gearing up for this confrontation, feeling my heart starting to beat a little faster, when I hear him say the words "Come on, Lily, let's get going."

53.

A TERRIBLE SOUND

THEN

We came home from holiday. Time passed. Lily didn't get pregnant. These were the brutal facts of it. But with the pub getting busier and busier, the disappointment and the pain seemed to exist in the background, like the hum of a fridge, and they only came to the fore if I deliberately tuned in. Which is why I didn't. The breeziness of us saying we'd "see what happens" only provided a surface level of comfort, a flimsy mantra.

The only way I knew how to cope was by not sitting still for a second. If I was always on my feet, if there was always something to do, then I could stop thoughts of how unfair it all was, how the universe was continuing to play a horribly cruel trick on us, from overwhelming me. More than anything, though, I didn't want Lily to see me sad. If I ever felt it all getting too much, and the temptation came to give in to my sadness, I'd find more work to do. I would keep going. I would be strong for both of us.

Perhaps it was because I was trying to stay so busy, but it took me a while to notice the change in Lily. There were afternoons when she'd stay in our room upstairs, rather than being front of house where she normally was. We had hired more staff by this point, and there were jobs that could be delegated. While I still felt the need to do as much as I could myself, if Lily wanted to enjoy the fruits of our labor by taking time off when she could, then why not?

When she began to go out on evening walks by herself, I did find it a little strange that she never told me when she was heading out. It wasn't like I kept track of her movements, but I began to get the sense that she was deliberately slipping out when she knew I was busy.

One evening, my curiosity got the better of me.

"You off out on your walk this evening?"

"Oh," she said. "No. No, not today."

But a little later, as I went to clear some glasses from the beer garden, I saw her—already down over the stile and into the field, heading toward the cliff tops. I found myself starting after her. I didn't question what I was doing until there were only fifty yards between us. She stopped. And so did I.

Why did it suddenly feel so wrong to be doing this? Maybe she'd just changed her mind about the walk. I got a bit closer. She was standing by the tree stump, looking out to sea. But something was wrong. Her fists were clenched. Her shoulders were moving up and down. She was sobbing. Automatically, I started forward, wanting to console her. But then in one swift movement she opened her arms wide and howled—a terrible, terrible sound—and I stopped still, paralyzed.

I stood there, feeling Lily's broken voice ripping through

me. All I wanted was to rush forward and take her in my arms. But I was too weak, too afraid. Because in that moment, I didn't know whether my embrace would comfort her or cause her more pain. And if she pushed me away, then I knew we could never come back from that, and everything would be over.

54.

A SINGLE WORD

NOW

At first, I can't bring myself to open my eyes. I'm as immobile as I was on that cliff top. When I do finally trace where the Yorkshireman's voice came from, I'm confronted by two buses parked in a row, passengers filing onto each of them, and I've no idea which one he got on. I start forward and I'm nearly flattened by a Mini, but I hurry on, calling Lily's name. I push past the people moving onto the bus on the left, jumping up the steps.

"Lily!" I shout. "It's me—it's Brian."

There are people standing in the aisle, putting their bags under the seats, and everyone goes quiet. But nobody says anything. Then a voice says, "*Quel est le problème, monsieur?*"

Shit.

I look through the window and see the doors of the other bus closing. I'm going to be too late if I don't move fast. Sprawling down the steps and out, I run until I'm blocking the other bus's path, jumping up and down and waving my arms to get the driver's attention. I gesture that I'm going to come around to the door. He's looking at me warily, but he reaches to push a button and the doors spring apart. As I start up the steps the driver says, "We're a full house here, mate—this isn't a taxi." I ignore him, but at the sight of me looking to make my way down the aisle he slides from his seat and puts a meaty arm across my chest.

"Whoa, whoa, whoa—where d'you think you're going?"

"I think my wife's on this bus," I say, not looking at him, scouring the seats instead. The driver begins to explain that even if she is, that's no concern of his, that he's counted everyone on and that they're running late as it is without this kind of nonsense, and the pressure of his thick, hairy arm begins to grow against my chest, pushing me back toward the stairs. I call Lily's name again, no longer a shout but a desperate moan. I feel like at any moment my legs are going to give way and I'll fall back down to the tarmac, and that's when I hear a woman's voice.

A single word.

"Yes?"

55.

LILY CLARK-SMITH

Lily Clark-Smith, born in 1970, is fifty-four years old and lives in a village just outside Halifax, Yorkshire, where she has spent most of her life. She is married to David and has three children—two girls and a boy. She and David run their own catering business. Her father, who's still going strong in his nineties, is a keen record collector. His main area of interest is folk music from the 1960s and '70s. His favorite musician is oft-overlooked singer-songwriter Nick Drake. Six months ago, Lily lost her sister, Hannah, to a sudden illness. A free spirit, Hannah had been planning to take on the journey she had been reading about in a bestselling book called *And Breathe . . .* Although it wasn't the sort of thing Lily would go in for herself, she decided to honor her sister's memory by completing the journey on her behalf. The best place to follow her adventures is via her blog, where you can also find a link to her JustGiving page raising money in Hannah's honor. Coming from the catering business, she is also a bit obsessed with reviewing things online, and in addition to her blog she's been posting reviews of the experiences themselves in a bit more depth on her Tripadvisor page. Her husband, David, has let her get on with the journey herself while he looks after the business, but he's always wanted to go to Stonehenge.

He wasn't very impressed, though, in the end.

56.

JUST GIVING

I learn some of these facts firsthand, Lily Clark-Smith remaining remarkably calm and helpful in the face of my interrogation, as if she's under the impression that this is the new way they're doing the census. The rest of the information I will glean later, from her blog, before making a small donation to her Just-Giving page in memory of her sister.

In any other scenario such as this—finding myself at the center of attention, very much on the verge of causing a scene—I would have become skittish and meek, offering profuse apologies and hoping to scuttle away to hide, avoiding everyone's eyes as I go. But here, now, I feel numb. These people staring at me don't feel like people at all. As I move slowly down the bus, I find myself looking at all of them as I pass, like I'm casting my eye along portraits on the wall of a gallery. Some people hold my gaze, looking anxious or perturbed. Others look away or begin talking to their neighbors, trying to pretend I'm not there.

None of this feels real. I climb down from the bus, but I don't know where to go. In the end I walk through the car park, ignoring people blaring their horns when I walk in front of their cars, and I end up at a raised bank of grass. I sit down, cross-legged, my back against a tree. A few feet away there's a toy teddy bear. It's missing an eye, and both its legs are torn at the seams. It could have been here months or minutes, I'm not sure.

As a car near me revs its engine, louder and louder, and I feel the vibrations, it's like the plates are shifting beneath my feet. I will the tarmac to split apart. All I want is to disappear, because I can feel the truth circling, waiting to pounce. I've been running from it for so long. But it's all over now.

I close my eyes and I see Lily's watch, the hands turning and turning and turning.

57.

LILY, DRESSED IN BLUE

THEN

I waited for the right moment to tell Lily that I had seen her that night, down by the cliff tops. Perhaps I was struggling with how I wasn't supposed to have been there and the invasion of her privacy. We were married, but that didn't mean we shouldn't be our own people, or that we couldn't have thoughts and feelings that we kept to ourselves. Time passed, and the more days and weeks and months that went by, the harder I found it to tell Lily what I'd seen, until eventually I came to the uneasy conclusion that I never would.

One morning I woke up to find Lily sitting up next to me in bed, reading. The blister pack for her pill was next to her on the pillow. She was aware that I had stirred, but she kept her eyes on her book.

"Do you want to talk about it?" I said, head propped up on my arm.

"I don't think so," she said. "What is there to say, really? I'd rather feel in control of the situation, rather than getting upset every time I get my period."

When I didn't reply, she turned to look at me. I sat up then, and moved over to put my arm around her.

"I think that's the right thing to do," I said. It was a strangely formal choice of words, but it was the best I could come up with. This was, I suppose, the time when we might have spoken of "other options." But when Lily rested her head against mine and said, "I'm just so tired," it felt like my job was to hold her, try to loosen the tension in her shoulders, and for her to know how much I loved her.

"You should take today off," I said. "Stay in bed. I'll cook you breakfast. Bacon on that thick white bread—or whatever you fancy."

"That sounds good." She held my arm then, tight, as if we were both hanging on over a steep drop. "But can you just stay here awhile? I don't want to be on my own."

And so I did.

THINGS CHANGED AFTER that. An unspoken grief pulsed between us, and there was something brittle about our happiness. It wasn't that we loved each other any less, but I found myself clinging to the feeling that we needed time to hurry up and pass, so that we could break free of the sadness that seemed to be permeating us.

That isn't to say we didn't make time for each other. When it was warm enough, we'd sit in the beer garden after closing time and have a nightcap under the stars. Lily had suggested this the first time, bringing a bottle of brandy and a candle. Moments like this, that reminded me of how happy we could be, eased my uncertainty, but when they occurred I'd celebrate them too much, which just shone a light on how novel they were. I couldn't help but watch the candle gasping for oxygen under the glass dome, besieged by moths, and think it looked as vulnerable as us. I'd tell Lily how happy she made me, how the feeling of her body curled into mine was still my favorite thing in the world. But when I said "I love you," and she said it back, the silence that followed felt like we were groping for something just out of reach.

When July arrived, and with it the prospect of us both turning forty, I don't think either of us had given much thought to celebrating it. But then, out of the blue, I had a phone call from Ed. The conversation was somewhat stilted at first, as always when we caught up after a time. But the longer we spoke, the easier it got, and I ended up inviting him and Cynthia to come and stay at the pub on our birthday weekend.

It felt like such a novelty, having friends to visit. I found I was strangely nervous on the day of their arrival, my heart beating a little more urgently every time I heard a car pulling into the car park. Lily seemed the same. She changed what she was wearing twice and couldn't sit still. When Ed and Cynthia did finally arrive, they seemed tired and a little fractious after the long drive, and I wondered if this had been a mistake. In the end, it only took a gin and tonic in the beer garden for us all to relax. My godson, Jack, now nine, already had the easy charm of his father and the inquiring mind of his mother. I felt a pang of guilt at how little I'd seen him in recent years. I tried to talk to him about the video game he was playing, but he replied monosyllabically and I was forced to accept that I was a stranger to him now.

As Ed and Cynthia told us of their London lives, it felt like they were talking about another planet. Lily seemed spellbound, even when Ed was complaining about how expensive everything seemed to have got, and when Cynthia lamented the horror of a recent work party. As the day wore on, and we'd had a bit more to drink, the conversation flowed from the silly to the serious, but it still felt a little jarring when Lily asked Cynthia and Ed if they were planning on having more kids.

"Nope," they replied in unison, then laughed.

"No, we love our little guy," Cynthia said. "But that's it for us."

Neither Lily nor I responded to this, and a silence followed. It felt like Cynthia knew she might have said something wrong but didn't know whether to apologize, and none of us knew how to move the conversation on until Jack returned from the loo and asked why we'd all gone quiet—and when we were having chips.

It was later, as we ate dinner and opened more wine, that Ed told us he'd recently bumped into Daniel.

"We chatted for about four minutes and he managed to tell me about his new promotion and his new car, naturally, but did you know he and what's-her-face—Tabitha—had divorced?"

"Shame," I said. Ed laughed, but Lily didn't, and Ed swiftly changed the subject. Lily kept returning the conversation to London, and listened rapt as Cynthia told her about a new restaurant that had become their favorite of late. I'd not seen Lily this animated in a long while. By the time we were on our third nightcap, I'd hit my limit and had to head up to bed. I lay awake, listening to the distant chatter of the others in the beer garden. Lily laughed her glorious laugh, and I realized I couldn't remember the last time I'd heard that sound. Sleep wouldn't come. I kept wondering when Lily was going to come to bed. When she eventually crawled under the covers, she didn't curl around me as usual.

"Have you been smoking?" I asked, wincing as soon as I said it.

"Yes. Sorry."

"You don't have to apologize."

"Oh. Thanks. Anything else I don't have to apologize for?"

She was clearly spoiling for a fight, and I didn't know why. But I was determined not to go down that route, and so I said nothing.

THE TENSION OF that night stayed with us long after Ed and Cynthia had gone home. Lily began to spend more and more time in the room upstairs on her own. One day we were in the middle of a mundane conversation about a beer delivery when she broke off to answer her mobile. When she picked up I heard the tiredness in her voice, but moments later it was like a completely different person was speaking.

"Oh my god, hello! It's been so long. Hang on a sec."

I heard her going upstairs, and then the door closed. She was up there for a long time, until after I'd closed up. Occasionally I could hear laughter. When she came downstairs later she poured herself a large glass of white wine and sat over by the window.

"Who was that on the phone?" I asked her.

"Earlier, you mean? Oh, that was Daniel—just calling for a catch-up."

I sensed an affected casualness to her voice. "I see. And how's he? Still very much Daniel?"

Lily rolled her neck around her shoulders, one way, then the other, her pre-bedtime ritual.

"And how's the divorce playing out? I bet he and Tabitha have one of those celebrity lawyers each, don't they?"

Lily ignored this. She took one earring out. Then the other. She seemed to do this with great deliberateness.

"He's holding up well," she said. "All things considered."

The image came to me of the night of Lily's party all those years ago. The game. Daniel slipping in at the end of the line. Lily's hands in his hair. I looked up and saw that she seemed to be studying me.

"I'm going to bed," she said.

"OK."

She left, but I heard her pause on the stairs. A moment later she was back in the bar.

"He's invited me to his birthday party," she said. "Next weekend."

"In London?"

"In London."

"Just you?"

"Well, he said 'you should come' and I didn't stop to ask him if that meant the collective or singular, mainly because I assumed you wouldn't want to come."

She looked at me and waited for me to challenge this assumption, which I didn't.

"You should go," I said. "I'll be OK here. You deserve a break."

Lily gave me another long look. Then she said good night and left. I waited to see if she'd pause on the stairs again, but this time she didn't.

During the next week I could sense how excited she was

about the party, and despite myself the whole thing had me feeling on edge. I came upstairs one evening and came into the bedroom to find Lily trying on a dress, and my reaction was to apologize and close the door, as if I'd just walked in on a stranger.

On the morning of the day itself, we were particularly busy. Lily grabbed me in a brief respite to tell me she was off to catch her train. She looked so beautiful. I wanted to tell her that, but for some reason I couldn't. As I wrestled with this, I missed the moment to say a proper good-bye. The next thing I knew, Lily had pecked me on the cheek and was making her way outside. I watched her as she waited for her taxi to the station, but then a commotion in the kitchen dragged me away from the window. By the time I'd come back, she was gone. Feeling a rush of panic, I grabbed my phone and called her.

"Have I forgotten something?" she said as she picked up.

I found my voice catching in my throat as I went to reply.

"Brian?"

"No. But, I . . . I just wanted to say I'm sorry . . . for—"

"Brian? You there? Sorry, bad signal, I only cau—bit of tha—"

The line came and went and came again, but never long enough to actually talk.

"Lily? Oh, that's better. No, wait, I've lost you."

"Sorry, the line's just really bad. What did you say?"

Finally, it cut out completely.

"I said I've lost you," I murmured.

WHEN LILY RETURNED on Sunday evening, I felt as nervous as I had when she'd arrived that night at my flat for our first proper date. We greeted each other with a tentative hi. Lily lowered her bag to the ground. I walked over and put my arms around her.

"How was it?" I asked. But she didn't reply. I could feel her heart thumping.

"It was OK," she said at last.

I didn't say anything. I just wanted to hold her. I pulled her tight and kissed her forehead. I went to pull away, but Lily stopped me. The tightness with which she held me made it feel like when we'd part it would be the end of something. The wind was picking up, starting to howl at the windows. We stayed in our embrace for a long time, in the quiet of the bar, like diligent actors on set, waiting for someone to shout *Cut*.

Later that evening, Lily was pouring drinks for the regulars. The sun was casting beautiful light across the bar, catching motes of dust in the air. Lily had changed into a blue dress, one she hadn't worn for a while. She was in her element, the regulars rapt. With a final flourish, she reached the end of a story, dust spiraling like a puff of smoke. I saw the smile on her face and felt such a flush of hope that it left me winded. When I would think back to that night, conjuring that memory, this was where it ended, as what I saw next made me feel lost, desperate, like there was sand in my lungs. Because when Lily turned back to reach for a new glass, I saw her smile vanish. Hidden from her audience, there was only sorrow and hopelessness on her face. And I knew then how much she was hurting. And that unless I did something drastic, I was going to lose her.

When we went to bed that night, I thought of all the things I was going to say to her the next day. I was going to tell her how much I loved her. I'd suggest we go away for a while, maybe even have something of a second honeymoon. I was nervous about what the morning would bring, but I was hopeful too. We had been through so much, but I knew we could get through this. We owed it to our younger selves, who'd met on Primrose Hill that summer's night. I traced my finger over my arm, remembering where she'd written her address. I could smell the jasmine in the air. Hear the soft buzzing of the streetlight overhead. *Tomorrow*, I thought as I turned to Lily and watched her breathing peacefully. Tomorrow, everything would be different. It was that thought that allowed me to sleep.

When I woke and automatically reached across to Lily, she wasn't there. That wasn't unusual, we were often up early and at different times than each other. Her side of the bed was still warm, but I knew something was wrong. I got up and went downstairs, looking for her in the bar and the cellar and the kitchen, then the beer garden. I called her phone, but it was off. I told all of this to the police, Lily's family and friends too. What I didn't tell them is what happened next.

I'd found myself in the room upstairs, looking out of the window at the white horses peaking on the distant waves. Something seemed to fall into place, and then I was hurtling down the stairs, out into the beer garden, over the stile, down the track, past the cows—the dew-drenched grass soaking my ankles—past the barns, down to the jumble of stones on the cliff tops.

The waves below me were smashing into the cliffs, the sea swelling and snarling. But just then the sun pierced the clouds, glinting off something nearby. And there, on the tree stump, lying on its side, as if curled up in sleep, was Lily's watch.

58.

WITNESSED BY STONE

NOW

I can still remember the feel of the watch in my pocket as I walked back to the pub. I went up to our room and slumped to the floor, cradling the watch in my hands. *It's not real. This isn't happening.* That's what I told myself, over and over again. By the time I was calling people, and then the police, my brain was already working overtime—shutting down what I knew had happened. If I didn't believe it . . . If I didn't tell anyone . . . and then that postcard arrived. It was like a magic trick—like I'd made the universe bend to my will.

From then on I buried the image of Lily's watch on the tree stump that morning so far down it was lost and out of reach. Maybe I had actually imagined it, I thought. I could have been half asleep. Or even sleepwalking. Hadn't I done that once when I was a child? All I knew was, I'd never doubt Lily again. She needed some time, that's what the postcard said, and then she'd be home. The closest I came to telling anyone was when I turned up drunk at the police station, waking up to find that I'd brought in Lily's watch. I hated myself for being so weak. How did I deserve Lily's return if I'd give up on her so easily? I would never, ever do that again.

I've been sitting here on this grass bank for a very long time now. The last visitors are about to leave. I wonder what they've all made of Stonehenge. Is it just something they've ticked off the list, or might they have had a moment of profound realization about themselves and their place in history? My own drama today, witnessed from a distance by those hulking stones, is merely one of thousands to have played out in their shadow. There will have been heart attacks and proposals, broken bones and shattered dreams. Did the stones see me find an ending? I still can't really tell. I don't feel any different. All I know is I'm tired, and I want to go home.

The car park is empty now, but just then a Volvo swings around the corner. A stressed-looking woman gets out of the car and starts dashing around, clearly looking for something. She hasn't noticed I'm here, so it's a bit awkward. I end up coughing just so she's aware of my presence.

"Oh, hello," she says, startled. Then she runs her hand through her hair and says, "Sorry, but I don't suppose you've seen a little toy bear anywhere? It's my daughter's."

"You're in luck," I say, pointing to the patch of grass where the bear is.

"Yes! You're a lifesaver," the woman says, dashing over to retrieve it. She goes back to the car and opens the rear passenger door. There is a brief squeal of delight as she passes the bear over. As she shuts the door and makes her way around to the driver's seat, she catches my eye again.

"It's almost worth it, isn't it? Losing something, just so you can get it back."

59.

HOME

The security guard, who I find out is called Fergus, shows me an awful lot of kindness. He doesn't even seem that thrown by the fact I'm sitting out here in the desolate car park on my own.

He isn't able to get an answer out of me when he asks me how I'm planning on getting back to . . . "well, wherever it is you're going." Eventually, hands on hips, he tells me to get in his car, and I meekly do as he says.

It's not the first time in these past few days that I've been the beneficiary of someone's kindness. As we drive away my thoughts turn to a delicate tattoo, a fleck of purple nestled in chestnut, a note in a hotel wastepaper basket.

I spend the night on Fergus's sofa. He cooks a chicken pie and it's more delicious than it has any right to be, given that it was made by a man wearing an apron with a pair of naked buttocks on it. Eventually I find the power of speech, and my manners, and tell Fergus to come down to the County Arms one day for a meal and beer on the house.

"Did I not hear something about that place on the news?" he asked.

"I wouldn't have thought so."

IT'S THE DAY after, and I'm in a taxi from Exeter station, the final leg of my journey. The days of the week have lost all meaning since I've been away, and the taxi driver is quite confused when I ask him to confirm that it is indeed Monday. As we wind our way through the country lanes, wafts of farmyard and salty sea air drifting through the window, I feel an ache growing in the pit of my stomach. I picture the beer pumps and their badges, the shabby furniture, the floorboards and the sound they make under my feet. I shift in my seat, pulling the seat belt away from my chest. But then just as suddenly I sit back.

The place I'm imagining coming home to is the shiny, magical version of the pub. The one I first clapped eyes on before I knew I'd own it. While there is a comfort in the idea of being back behind the bar, and sleeping in my own bed, I can't see the pub in the same light anymore. The dream pub, we called it. But the truth tells a different story. I was so desperate for it to be the place where Lily and I found happiness again. And it worked, for a while. But I can only keep believing that if I continue to stop the memory of Lily behind the bar at the moment before the smile falls from her face. Played in full, the memory stands as a monument to my failure to banish the past, to bring Lily the happiness she deserved. More prosaically, of course, it's a failing business. And Lily's not coming back to save it. Or me. I know that now. So I think that means I'll have to call time.

"Everything all right?" the cabbie asks.

"Fine," I say. "Long few days, that's all."

"Well," he says, "you'll get a good pint and nice company at the Arms." Here, he suppresses a smile, I assume either because of the rude name the pub's trading under, or because he knows it's very unlikely I'm going to get any company at all there, let alone the good kind.

We drive on in silence. As we round the corner that affords you the first glimpse of the sea, I spot Farmer Davis coming the other way in his tractor. I'd noticed the headline in the local paper at the station: *Police baffled by new farm break-ins.* No wonder he looks even more miserable than usual.

"Really wish I could knock off now and come in for a beer or two," the cabbie says. And I'm starting to take umbrage at this sarcasm and the private joke he's having with himself. But then we come around the corner, and I see the beer garden, and I'm starting to think he might be serious after all.

60.

BLISTERS, AGAIN

"We did try calling you," Oliver says.

"Like, *a lot*," Sophie adds.

"But you never picked up."

"And then we didn't want to worry you."

"And because you said we could handle it . . ."

". . . we thought we'd better prove you right."

One of the strange things about this conversation is that they're managing to have it while Sophie balances a towering stack of pint glasses in one hand, plates in the other, and Oliver chops up fruit and vegetables for Pimm's with the skill of a Michelin-starred chef.

I have never seen the place as busy as this. Even at the height of our popularity. It's surreal. Some of the chairs in the front bar haven't been sat on for years—now they're all occupied. The beer garden is so rammed that people are having to sprawl on the grass, like it's a festival.

When someone asks me impatiently if I'm queueing for the bar, I simply apologize and say I'm not, rather than telling them

I'm the owner. Eventually I manage to pull Oliver aside and ask him what on earth's going on.

"Go out the front," he says with a shrug.

When I get outside, it's to find that there are scores of people huddled on the tarmac. Partly this is due to the prime drinking spots having been taken in the garden, but mainly it's because they're all queuing up to have their photos taken by the sign, which remains as offensive as the day I left.

When I come back inside and try to ask Sophie more questions—all of which can essentially be summarized as "What the fuck?"—she tells me she hasn't got time to stop, and then she hands me two bowls of chips and says, "Table nine? Beer garden?" and I decide I'm just going to do exactly as she says.

IT'S A LONG while since I've felt the telltale signs of blisters forming on my toes. I've been back and forth from the kitchen—where Jacques is in full and furious flow, a kind of mania in his eyes—bringing out plates of food, and I've done a solid shift behind the bar too. I couldn't tell you how many pints I've pulled. Even the Winchester Gold is getting an outing today.

By the time Oliver finally locks the front door, I feel dead on my feet. Sophie grabs a just-opened bottle of rosé from the fridge, yanks the cork out with her teeth, and pours three glasses. We sit side by side on a sofa in the back bar, and finally I'm able to ask them to explain.

Sophie tells me that, far from wearing off, the novelty of the rude sign has only intensified, and that more and more people have started turning up every day. Walkers, holidaymakers, locals who've not been in for years. Even Farmer Davis has been in, apparently. They've not had any bookings for rooms yet, but people who were in for drinks and food made inquiries about rates, so that may not be too far behind.

"But what about the council?" I ask. "They were pretty insistent we fix the sign and that was days ago when I left."

Sophie and Oliver look at each other a little nervously.

"We sort of decided to take an executive decision on that front," Sophie says. I raise my eyebrows in response. "Because, it was just so amazing to see this place full, and we thought it would be a huge shame to miss out, so we kind of thought, you know, fuck the council, if that makes sense?"

"But," Oliver says, in a voice that, hilariously, makes it sound like he's about to be the voice of reason, "they *are* now saying that if we don't change it by next Monday, they're going to, you know . . . close us down."

"Ah."

"Yeah," Sophie and Oliver reply, and we all take a big swig of wine.

FOR THE NEXT week, I decide that we're just going to keep going. If the council have given us that deadline, then I can't see the problem with squeezing as much as we can out of the remaining six days. I start to have second thoughts when I realize just how hard it is to keep up with all these customers, which makes me realize what an extraordinary achievement it's been for Sophie and Oliver to do this on their own. At the same time, it's blissful to throw myself into work, to not have a second to let my mind wander. Because when it does, I'm back on that grass verge once again, and I really can't face thinking about all that at the moment.

In the evenings, after we'd closed up, I'd normally sit and

have a drink with Jeff. With that no longer an option, and keen not to get sucked into the pull of drinking on my own, I finally decide to get to grips with the chest of drawers in the room upstairs—all the paperwork and accounts that I've neglected for so long. But by the fourth evening spent slogging my way through it all, I'm starting to regret that too. I may only possess a layman's understanding of our finances, but it's clear to me that even if we were to be fully booked (with both rooms and meal reservations) from now into the autumn, we'd still not be out of the woods financially. And given that we also need to renovate to stop the place from falling down, it's especially unlikely that we'll make it through. Not to mention the fact that in two days' time we're going to have to get rid of the one thing that's been attracting new customers, or we'll be closed down even sooner. The weight of all of this seems to bear down on me, and I realize that the temporary peace I've found amidst the chaos of the busy pub is just that—temporary.

I let out a long, low breath and look up at the postcard attached to the noticeboard. I still haven't found an answer to that. Even if this place goes under and I move away, back to London, to a new job, a new life—am I ever going to be free of that unanswered question? Perhaps I'll never find an ending.

When I wake up the next morning, it's to find that the weather has taken a turn. Rain and wind are hammering at the windows. I try to go back to sleep, but there's something that's been nagging at me from the moment I first got back. Eventually I sit up and move over to the side of the bed. Then I open Lily's bedside drawer and reach inside.

61.

RETRACING STEPS

The watch feels cool to the touch. I turn it over in my hands, observing every part of it. I never did ask Lily how old it is, or how her grandmother came to own it. Was it a present from her husband, perhaps? Or does it go even further back in her family? I wish with every part of me that I could find her and ask her these questions. I miss her. I miss her so much.

I look out through the window at the cliff tops and the gray water beyond. The pub is quiet when I go downstairs, like the building is holding its breath.

I grab my coat and go outside. The strength of the wind and the freezing rain is shocking as I step out. I pull my hood up and cross my arms around myself and set off into the heart of the squall. When I climb over the stile, I'm expecting to see the cows in the field as usual. But they must be sheltering somewhere out of sight.

I reach into my pocket, just to double-check I've still got Lily's watch. I hope it's staying dry in there. The farm track is waterlogged and I nearly lose my footing a couple of times as I grapple with the mud. With each step, it's impossible not to think of Lily and how she was feeling as she walked down this track. Was she full of adrenaline, or was there a numb acceptance about what she was going to do? I clutch the watch tightly in my fingers as I press on against the wind. The marks on my skin will still be there this evening. Maybe even tomorrow.

Finally, I reach the cliff tops. The tree stump is slick with rain. I take out Lily's watch and put it down on the slimy wood. Its rightful place. This is where Lily left it.

I'm shivering now, the wind and rain showing no signs of letting up. I edge a couple of steps forward. I want to know what it was like to stand where Lily did. I want to know how she felt. The water seems so close, spitting and snarling at the rocks. I'm shaking. To be where she stood is unbearable.

"Brian!" someone calls from behind me. "Brian, is that you?"

62.

KIA NIRO

Tess's rain-soaked hair is plastered across her face, but when she scrapes it away and I see her properly, the knowledge that it really is her leaves me light-headed. Given my current circumstances, this isn't exactly ideal. Without waiting a second longer Tess marches forward and grabs me by the arm, pulling me back.

"That didn't look very safe," she calls over the wind. I don't really know what to say. I'm so embarrassed that she's found me like this, but I'm not sure what would have happened if she hadn't. We stand in the wind and rain, buffeted by it, clinging onto each other.

"As much as I'm enjoying yet another taste of your British weather," Tess shouts, "I vote we get you back home now, eh?" She's trying to sound lighthearted, but I can see the concern in her eyes, and it's that which makes me want to do as she says. I let her lead me back in the direction of the pub.

"How did you know where to find me?" I yell over the wind as we stumble on.

"You don't forget the name of your pub in a hurry," she shouts back. "Did you know you were briefly one of the most popular news stories on DevonOnline?"

"I didn't actually, no."

We go on, past the barns, slipping and sliding through the mud.

"Another question," I shout.

Tess looks at me, one eye closed as the wind assaults us again. "Yeah?"

"*Why* did you come and find me?"

Tess nearly slips, and grabs hold of me for support. "Let's just get back first, shall we?"

WE ARRIVE AT the pub, dripping wet, and I shut the door behind us. There are still a few hours before we open, and we're the only ones here. It's very quiet, almost churchlike. We take off our coats. Tess looks around, unsure of where to put hers. I take it from her and hang it up next to mine. I'm about to offer her something to drink when she takes me by the shoulders and looks up into my face. I glance away, unable to look her in the eye.

"What on earth were you doing out there?" she says. "That really scared me, seeing you like that."

My first instinct is to brush it off. Pretend it was nothing. But I think I've reached the point where I'm going to stop doing that.

"I'm not completely sure, to be honest," I say in a low voice. "But I'm very glad you're here."

Tess still looks concerned, but she pushes a clump of hair off my face and then drops her hand. Both of us are dripping water onto the floor.

"Hang on," I say. "Come over here."

When Jeff and I lit the fire a couple of weeks ago, I thought that would be its last outing before the autumn. But here I am again, burying a fire lighter under kindling in the grate. I try to light a match, but my fingers are shaking.

"Here, let me," Tess says gently, and she strikes the match for me. As she passes it over, our fingers touch. The wood is dry enough that there's soon a hearty fire growing in the grate. I go to the kitchen and return with two steaming mugs, and we sit by the fire, slowly drying out.

"Good tea," Tess says after a few minutes. It feels unreal that she's here.

"Have I made this up," I say, "or do Kiwis refer to putting the kettle on as 'boiling the jug'?"

Tess smiles. "That's one of our little sayings that you *have* got right."

It takes me a while to work out what she means. *The letter.*

"Oh. What did I write again? Kia niro. That's not right, is it?"

Tess shakes her head. "It's 'Kia ora,'" she says. "But I appreciated the effort."

"So what does Kia niro mean then?"

Tess sips her tea. "I wouldn't worry about it."

We're quiet once again, watching the fire. I realize I have a lot of explaining to do. About the letter. About what has happened since. About everything, really.

"I'm aware," I begin, "that I've spent far too much time in your company talking when I should have been listening, because I'd much rather hear you telling me about your life than the other way around. But if it's OK, and because I do owe you a rather big explanation, do you mind if I hog the, you know, metaphorical microphone one last time?"

I really don't know why I decided to say that, and I think with anyone else I might have died of embarrassment. But Tess mimes taking a mic out of its stand.

"Testing, testing . . . ," she says, and then she hands the mic over to me.

63.

DAISIES IN A JAR

The jug has been boiled twice more before I've finished telling Tess about what happened with Lily and me, and the full story of the morning she disappeared. Even though I know Tess must be judging me for having never told anyone this information, her expression does not show it.

"I should have said something. I know I should."

"It's OK," Tess says, taking my hand. We sit like that for a while. I'm aware of Tess's thumb slowly brushing my hand.

"I'm sorry," I say. "For running off again. I don't know how long you've got left before you go home, but . . ." But what? What am I trying to say?

"Brian," Tess says softly. And I know what's coming.

"I know. I know I need to tell the police. And Lily's family too. Even though . . . I still don't know how it fits in with the postcard."

Just then, I hear the low put-put of a moped engine outside. That'll be Jacques. Sophie and Oliver will be here soon too.

"Listen," I say. "I know I need to call people, and I will. I promise. But, and I don't know if you have any plans today . . .

but if not, you could stay here and then, maybe later, we could have dinner?"

Tess considers this carefully. *Please say yes*, I think.

THE STORM'S BLOWN over, replaced by pale blue skies and watery sunlight. We're quiet at lunchtime, but as people's faith in the new weather holds, they begin to arrive for afternoon drinks. I've no idea how many days I have left serving behind the bar. It's a strange feeling, wondering if these are the last people I'll ever pour pints for. But it's made even stranger by knowing that Tess is sitting in the corner. She's reading a novel, but I keep catching her eye. The idea that she's watching me at work makes me stand up a little straighter. It feels important for her to see I'm good at this.

The wind and rain return by the evening, and the last customers make their way out by eight. I can't imagine any new ones will arrive, so I send Jacques, Sophie, and Oliver home, but ask them to meet me at the pub the next morning at eleven, because there's something I need to talk to them about.

I push all the tables to one side, apart from one, which I set up in the middle of the front bar, Tess still watching on from the corner. After I've pulled out a chair for her, and added one final flourish to the table with a candle stuck in the neck of a wine bottle, and some rather damp daisies from the field outside plonked in a jar, I ask her what she'd like to drink.

"A pint of your mustiest English ale, please," she says.

"Coming right up."

As I pass by Jeff's plaque, I give it a little pat. I hope he's not going to be too cross with me for giving this place up. In his honor, I pour two pints of Winchester Gold, taking extra care with each pull of the pump, and carry them over to our table.

I ask Tess to tell me about the rest of her trip, the highlight (or possibly lowlight) of which apparently involved an ill-fated evening at a comedy improv night in Cambridge, after she'd decided to skip Stonehenge.

"There was this guy who kept talking over everyone, and this is very unlike me, and perhaps it's because he looked a lot like Marc, but I just snapped and told him to shut his stupid face, and apparently that was against the spirit of the whole 'yes and . . .' thing."

I am, I confess, pleased to hear that Marc with a C hasn't managed to get his foot back in the door. When Tess goes home, I really hope she stays steadfast on that front. Before I have the chance to say anything to that effect, our fish and chips arrive. (I decided on balance to get some delivered rather than attempt to mess with Jacques's kitchen setup.)

"So what's left of the trip?" I ask Tess. "I didn't have a chance to read any more of the book."

"To be honest," Tess replies, "I think I'm done. The improv thing kind of killed it. I don't really know if any of the stuff I did helped, or made me feel less shitty about my marriage. I mean, it's certainly been a pretty unforgettable trip, don't get me wrong. Just not necessarily for the reasons I was expecting." She leaves this thought hanging, then continues. "But anyway, my plan is still to head to London for a week, spoil myself with stupidly indulgent afternoon teas and whatnot. And then I've booked to go to St. Paul's on my last day."

I frown at the mention of St. Paul's.

"What?" Tess asks.

"No, nothing."

There was something Tess told me about the cathedral that I hadn't been aware of. Then I remember. The whispering gallery, where she went with her cousin.

We finish our chips, and the conversation falls into a natural lull. The candlelight is soft and low. I wonder if I should light the fire again. But then Tess carefully, deliberately, arranges her knife and fork on her plate.

"Thanks for a lovely evening," she says.

"You too," I reply.

It's time. I know it is. But I really wish it wasn't. I take out my phone and put it on the table. I suppose I've still got the local police station's number saved in there somewhere. I find it and pause, thumb pressed over the call icon. Sensing my reluctance, Tess leans forward, puts her hand on mine.

"Don't worry," she says. "I'm here."

64.

CRUMBS

There are a husband and wife, in their seventies I'd guess, standing by the ticket machine on the station concourse. They're wearing differently colored but matching windbreakers. He is in charge of their hiking poles, she the cool box for their lunch. She reaches inside and hands him a cookie, which he silently accepts. He is swiping on his mobile phone as if he's never used it before, frowning. She takes it out of his hands, evidently more adept than he, and finds what he's been looking for. In the moment when the phone is out of his hands, he pretends to freeze like a statue, only to resume swiping once she's handed the phone back. She laughs at this and nudges him. He smiles, pleased that the joke has worked. As he puts his phone in his shirt pocket, she reaches up to turn down his wayward shirt collar and takes his arm. I'm pleased that Tess is off buying herself a coffee, because I need a moment to compose myself after watching this little play. It is, I think, moments like these when you see people in love. Not posing for photographs or making grand speeches. Real love is in the little gestures, in the cookie crumbs brushed away.

My train of thought is broken by an announcement over the Tannoy. It's one of those that you only really get in Britain—somehow far too loud yet entirely unintelligible, the only certainty being that it's definitely bad news. Sure enough, a flurry of *Canceled* signs appear on the display board. When I see that Tess's train isn't one of them, I feel a pang of disappointment. She's leaving for London, and then back home to New Zealand, and I would do anything to keep her here for just a little while longer. I won't ever forget how she sat with me yesterday as I made that phone call, gently encouraging me when I faltered.

At first I was only able to speak to a rather confused desk sergeant at the police station, but he happened to be with Detective Fairbanks, one of the people who had dealt with Lily's disappearance at the time. He listened to what I had to say without interruption. I suspect he was calculating in real time whether what I was telling him made any kind of material difference. But given the postcard, and the time that had elapsed since all this started, I don't think it has. Regardless, he duly thanked me for calling and told me he'd take this new piece of information into account. Once I'd hung up, I was very glad that Tess was still there. We shared a final drink in the bar, and then she slept in one of the guest rooms that I'd made up for her upstairs.

But now here we are, all too soon, and she's all set for her departure. I've been trying to put together some semblance of a speech that will do justice to how important it's been to have had her come into my life. I hoped that the words would arrive by now, but I'm no closer to finding what I want to say to her.

"No snacks this time?" I ask instead, uselessly.

Tess shakes her head. "I thought I'd keep my powder dry

until my plane home. Twenty-four hours in that tin can requires a serious haul of Funtime Fizzy Straws, I reckon."

We're hit then with another blast of unintelligible squawking over the Tannoy.

"I think I might have heard my platform in among all that," Tess says. "So. I should probably head . . ."

She pushes the button on her suitcase handle, which shoots up. But she doesn't move.

"You sure you're going to be OK?" she asks.

"Yeah, absolutely," I say, in a voice that sounded much breezier in my head. We stand there for a moment as everyone else moves around us.

"I should—" Tess begins, and then I find myself taking her by the hand, the words finally coming to me.

"I know we've not really known each other that long," I say, "but I feel like you should know that, for the rest of my life, if things ever get too much for me, I'll think of you, and what you'd say, and then I'll feel much better. So thank you. For everything."

After a moment, Tess lets go of her suitcase and puts her arms around me.

"It's a mark of how hard I'm finding it to leave," she says, "that I would rather stay and hug you than elbow little old ladies out of the way to make sure I get a table seat. I hope you know that."

I smile.

She pulls away, giving me one final searching look. Then she lets me go.

"Take care of yourself, Brian."

And with that she heads off, and I watch her go through a

crowd of people until she's out of sight, and I'm left thinking that life really is the most maddening, complicated, baffling thing, but if you're lucky enough to have had Tess drop in, then, for the time she's there at least, it all makes a lot more sense.

I WAIT FOR a while in the train station, just in case Tess has a change of heart. But after it's clear she's on her way I've no choice but to head back to the pub. If I weren't feeling down enough already, I'm faced with the sight of Jacques, Oliver, and Sophie waiting for me outside on my return. Their faces are grim, in contrast to the two walkers who have just stopped by to have their pictures taken in front of the sign.

"We too early for a pint?" one of them asks as I approach.

"I'm afraid so," I say. *Or too late.*

After they've gone I'm faced with my apprehensive trio of staff, and I'm just feeling my way into an awkward speech about how much I value them when Jacques cuts me off and demands I "spit it out."

"Are we closing?" Sophie asks, and I nod.

"When?" Oliver asks, putting his arm around her.

I explain about the accounts I've finally dug into and the money problems we're up against. I feel dreadful telling them this, even more so when I ask them for help in fixing the sign. In the end we decide that, given the precarious state of the rest of the letters, we should just remove what's left of the second word and simply leave the name as the Arms. It's hard to stop there, to be honest. Because there's a real part of me now that wants to keep going and take down all the letters and start on the tiles, and then the rafters and the brickwork, pulling and digging with my bare hands until there's nothing left at all.

65.

REACHING OUT

It's a few days later, and already the pub is much quieter. For the first time since I've been back I've had time to stand still. When I take my laptop out, it's not to check Tripadvisor anymore. I'm looking for jobs. It's been a long while since I got out of the insurance game, but realistically it's my only transferable skill. I look up a few old colleagues who all seem to be doing very well for themselves. It's not a prospect that brings me much pleasure, but I fire off a few casual emails, asking whether someone might have heard of any opportunities. I'm pleasantly surprised when I almost instantly get a reply from someone, saying it's good to hear from me and that he'll ask around. We exchange a few more messages, and then I think of Ed, and Cynthia, and my godson, Jack. Before I can find an excuse not to, I send Ed an email too, asking if he might be free for a visit.

As I sit behind the bar in the increasingly long gaps between serving customers, I find myself picturing Tess in London—looking elegant in a hotel enjoying an afternoon tea, or at a gallery, head cocked as she appraises a painting. I've been keeping my phone nearby in the optimistic hope that she might call or send me a message. Even when I'm startled by the landline ringing, I'm hoping it's her, even though I know it'll just be someone booking a table. In the end it's neither.

"Mr. Taplowe? It's Detective Fairbanks here. I was wondering if you could come down to see me. There have been some developments."

THE POLICE STATION seems strangely deserted for a weekday afternoon. There's a desk sergeant on duty, and a few other people at their desks, but we don't pass anyone else as we go down a long corridor. I can hear Fairbanks's black brogues squeaking audibly as we walk. I wonder if his colleagues tease him about this, give him a nickname perhaps. He leads me into a dingy room with a whiteboard on the wall, scrubbed clean but still bearing the ghosts of what was written before. In the corner is a brown metal filing cabinet. Propped up on top of it is a TV with built-in VCR that looks like it should be in a museum.

"Take a seat," Fairbanks says, gesturing to a brown chair with yellow foam spilling out of its cushion. He asks me if I want something to drink and I decline, even though my mouth has gone dry.

Fairbanks clears his throat and links his fingers together in his lap. When he starts to speak, I'm struck by how quiet and deep his voice becomes. *He would be good for voice-overs*, I think. I'm trying to distract myself, because I also recognize that this tone is designed to prepare me for something upsetting.

"You're aware, Brian, of the thefts that have been going on around the area for some time now—farm machinery and so on?"

This wasn't what I thought he was going to say.

"To a certain extent, yes," I reply. "I see the headlines in the paper every now and then. Why?"

"The most recent occurred in Ansley farm, at the barns belonging to John Davis."

"OK . . ."

"We asked Davis to provide us with his security footage from the barns. And when he went back to look through his archives, he found a tape that he thought he'd wiped in order to use again. But evidently he hadn't."

A phone rings in the distance. A door slams shut.

Fairbanks glances over at the TV, and I realize why it's there. He looks at me, and I give him the slightest of nods.

He presses play and the screen flickers. The date shown is the day Lily went missing. The time is 6:25 a.m. In the foreground is the muddy track that runs in between the barns. It's clearly blowing a gale, as dust kicked up by the wind is spiraling along, and a seagull that tries to perch on the barn opposite thinks better of it, pulling out of its landing. The scene is empty for a few seconds, and then I see her, Lily, walking along the track between the barns, buffeted by the wind. I sit forward in my chair. With her fists clenched, she presses on. The further away she gets, the further I lean forward. She stops, as I knew she would, by the tree stump. It's hard to tell from this distance, but I know this is where she is reaching to her wrist, unclasping her watch, placing it on the tree stump. I'm not sure I can keep watching this. I want Fairbanks to turn it off, for the footage to cut out. Lily stands there with her head bowed. I am waiting for the awful moment where she steps forward. But then something happens. Slowly—*so* slowly—she raises her head, her posture now undeniably defiant. And then she turns, and my heart leaps as she takes a few steps toward me. But this is the moment when Fairbanks swallows, as if in warning. Because Lily hasn't got far before a sudden gust of wind catches her, and she stumbles back a couple of paces. I nearly shout. Lily pushes back against the wind. She seems to be holding her ground, but then another gust arrives. It seems to sweep down and pick her up, setting her tumbling back, and there's a moment when she nearly manages to stop the momentum, planting her legs wide, bracing herself, but it's too much for her, and then she falls backward over the edge of the cliff.

I can sense Fairbanks looking at me. But my eyes are still on the screen, watching the long grass rippling in the wind. The clock in the bottom corner ticks on. I realize that this is the moment when I will just be waking, reaching out a hand and feeling the last hint of warmth from Lily's side of the bed. Fairbanks picks up the TV remote and gently clears his throat. After a moment, he turns the TV off, and the screen goes black.

66.

CLOUDS

The next few days are like a fever dream. I barely sleep, but when I do it's so deep that waking up feels like I'm having to drag myself up through ten feet of mud. There are strange gaps in my memory. I can't remember getting home from the police station. I'll make a cup of tea and then find an undrunk one by the kettle.

When I think about Fairbanks asking me to confirm that it was Lily in the footage, it's like I'm remembering an out-of-body experience. He asked me whether I wanted to be the one to inform Lily's family. I said yes, then no. I didn't know what was best. The next thing I knew, Fairbanks had his hand on my shoulder and was looking down at me, asking if I was OK. I must have just been sitting there, unresponsive.

I told Sophie and Oliver that I was ill and asked them to look after the place, though our customer numbers had dwindled even further. I lie on my bed upstairs, the radio on—anything to fill the silence. There is rolling news coverage about a natural disaster. I listen to the same clips of eyewitnesses. It's updated every hour or so. The same horror from different perspectives.

I've forgotten to eat. When I do eventually go down to the kitchen and Jacques takes pity on me and makes me a salad, there's something so kind about the act that I'm briefly on the verge of tears. Later, I make myself go outside and get some air. I don't go on my usual walk. Instead, I head up to where Jeff used to live, finding a bench at the center of the village green.

I sit there, eyes closed, listening to birdsong and distant lawn mowers. It provides a jarring soundtrack to what I'm picturing, over and over again—the moment when Lily turns and starts to walk back in the direction of the pub, bracing herself against the wind. Would she have come back up into our room and woken me, if she'd made it? What would she have said? Was she going to tell me that it was over? Or would she have said we had to work out a way forward, because she was going to stay and fight for us? Maybe she would have simply crawled back into bed, curled her body into mine. I can't stop imagining how that would have felt. How I would have clung on and never let her go.

After a moment, I get off the bench and lie down on my back on the grass, staring up at the sky. I watch the clouds go by. None of them look like anything.

When I get home it's to find I've had a missed call from Rebecca. And then a text, asking me to come and see her.

67.

THE POSTCARD

As I walk through the Cotswold village where Rebecca and Rupert live, I'm sick with nerves, so much so that I nearly turn back. But I keep going. One foot in front of the other. The house is the old rectory, a beautiful if imposing place set back from the road, all ruddy bricks and clematis bracketing the front door. I ring the bell. When the door opens and I'm met by the sight of a lanky boy with a blond fringe waterfalling over his eyes, I think I might have got the wrong place. But then I realize who it is.

"Hello, Alexander," I say, just about managing to stop myself from adding: "I buried your poo on the beach once." I introduce myself as his uncle and reach out my hand to shake his, but he just looks at it. Eventually he realizes what I'm doing and rolls his eyes, offering his own hand in a way that's deliberately performative. Only a teenager could manage to shake someone's hand sarcastically.

He leads me through the hallway, which smells like a posh hotel lobby, and out into the garden, where Rupert is on his hands and knees, working away at the border with a trowel.

He's developed a bald patch, and there's a good deal of gray in the remaining sandy curls. He's wearing headphones—I can hear the faint strains of jazz—and so he isn't aware of our presence at first. Alexander decides to rectify this by kicking a stone in his direction. When Rupert looks up, Alexander points at me by way of an explanation. Job done, he skulks away.

"Brian!" Rupert says, taking off his headphones. He shakes my hand warmly, then apologizes and hands me an old towel to wipe off the compost.

"It's good to see you," I say, and I surprise myself with how much I mean it. It's been a long time since we were last together, and I forget that he was always kind and welcoming, in his own way.

"It's good to see you too," Rupert says. I can tell he wants to say something, offer condolences perhaps, but he's not sure if that's appropriate. Instead, he clears his throat and tells me he's going to go and put the kettle on. He appears through the French windows a few minutes later holding a tray of tea and cookies. We sit and make small talk for a while. I'm starting to wonder where Rebecca is. But then she appears, striding across the grass, and Rupert and I fall silent.

"Have you brought it?" she says, dispensing with a greeting. It was Fairbanks who called her in the end. But she wanted me to bring her the tape, so that she could watch the footage herself.

I reach into my backpack and hand her the videotape. I stand, but she motions for me to stay where I am, then she turns and goes inside. Rupert and I are left with our tea, talking haltingly about the holiday they've just been on, and how—remarkably—Edie is about to graduate from Oxford. There'll soon be another lawyer in the family. I picture her as a flower girl—how we exchanged silly faces in the church on my wedding day. That seems like a lifetime ago. My conversation with Rupert falters. We're waiting for Rebecca. When she reappears she's wearing sunglasses, despite its being overcast. She hands the tape to me, and I put it in my bag. I'm half expecting her to ask me to leave, but instead she asks Rupert to go inside and make a start on dinner.

After he does so, Rebecca pours herself some tea.

"Only Lily could think it was a good idea to go wandering along a cliff top in a gale," she says. "I mean, what on earth was she thinking?"

This is a very Rebecca thing to say, but I still find it painful to hear. I'm formulating the most neutral response I can when my eye is caught by a spot of pink in the sky above Rebecca's head. It's a hot-air balloon, looking oddly motionless, out of place—like a speck on an overhead projector slide. Like a smudge.

Rebecca sips her tea, grimaces, then pours the rest onto the grass. "I hate Earl Grey. He *knows* I hate Earl Grey."

I don't know if my hanging around any longer is going to help either of us, and I feel inclined to leave. But then I realize that this could quite possibly be the last time we ever see each other.

"I'm sorry that I failed her." The words tumble out before I can filter them. "That I failed all of you, in fact. I should have taken better care of her. And I'm sorry that I didn't tell you about finding her watch."

It's hard to tell if Rebecca is going to respond. Or if she's even listening. She seems to be watching the hot-air balloon, which is close enough that we can hear the blast of its propane. She continues to stare resolutely at it as it moves overhead, and that feels like a signal that I should leave. Thankfully there's a side gate that allows a quicker path back to the road. I'm not sure Rebecca would want me talking to Rupert and Alexander again if I went through the house. Hurriedly, I stand up and say good-bye, accidentally putting my cup down on the saucer so hard I'm surprised it doesn't crack.

I'm halfway down the street when I hear footsteps behind me, and I turn just as Rebecca calls my name. She's taken her sunglasses off. Her eyes are raw, her cheeks wet with tears.

"I need to tell you something," she says.

"OK. Do you want . . . Shall we go back to the house, or—"

"Lily came to see me. Just before she died."

I stare at her. "What do you mean? She was in London. At that party."

"She'd been there, yes," Rebecca says. "But she came here early, the next day, before she went home to you. I wasn't expecting her. Rupert was away on business. She was wired, manic almost. She told me . . . she told me that she'd done something silly and impulsive, and that she didn't know what to do."

"You mean at the party? With Daniel?"

"I assumed so. Frankly, I didn't want to pry, and I wasn't particularly sure why she'd come to see me to tell me about it. Like I said, she seemed manic. When you called me the next day and you said she was missing—I assumed she'd gone back to Daniel in London. I didn't want to be the one to break it to you. That's why I fobbed you off when you first called me. Of course, when it seemed she was actually missing, I phoned Daniel."

"And?"

Rebecca lets out a deep, sorrowful sigh. "And he said she wasn't there and, in fact, that she'd barely been at the party five minutes. She'd left and said she wasn't feeling well, and went to stay with a colleague from her old magazine instead. I called them, and they confirmed that's what had happened, but that they hadn't heard from her since. I told the police, of course. But given that she'd come home to you after seeing me, and wasn't with Daniel now, there didn't seem any point in telling you about that. Whatever 'silly and impulsive' thing she'd done wasn't anything to do with him, after all."

I have the strangest feeling that there's something just out of my grasp—something that will make all of this fall into place. And then it hits me.

"What is it?" Rebecca says.

I'm not sure how far back to go. I end up starting with what I only now realize has been staring me in the face all this time. Greece, her holiday with the girls. Stalking the postman after she'd written that letter to me about having kids—how she'd sent it before she could stop herself so that she'd have to deal with the consequences later.

"She'll have sent that postcard to me the morning she came to see you," I say. "Second-class, probably. She'd have known then that she'd have to make a decision about whether to go away for a while or not."

"Oh, Lily," Rebecca says, shaking her head. She goes to say something else, then thinks better of it. When she does speak her voice is a little softer. "So, in that footage, when she turns back . . . What do you think she'd decided to do?"

"That, I don't know."

But as I say those words, I think I do. I think she was coming back to me, to crawl into bed. That this was the moment the wind took her is not something I can bring myself to think about right now.

It's clear that Rebecca is also struggling, because without warning her knees buckle, and she crumples to the grass verge.

I hurry over, unsure of whether to try to help her up. In the end, I sit down beside her. A car drives past, blaring music. The driver gives us a bored look.

After a moment, Rebecca lifts her head and rests it on my shoulder. I think this is the first time she's ever made physical contact with me longer than the brief hugs we'd exchange in greeting. A few more cars drive past in quick succession.

"School run's started," Rebecca says, and then she clears her throat loudly and starts to get to her feet. I follow suit and stand up. Rebecca brushes herself down. There is a sense of finality to this.

"I should head off," I say. "The trains only seem to be every hour."

"Yes, it's a nightmare. We've written to the council about them."

There's a very distant blast of propane, but the hot-air balloon is out of sight behind the rooftops now.

"OK," I say. "Well, I'll see you then. Say bye to Rupert for me, will you? And Alexander."

I'm a little way down the road when I hear Rebecca calling after me. I turn around and wait until she catches up with me.

"Unless . . . you wanted to stay for dinner?"

68.

TODAY'S MEMORIES

Her terrible dancing at every wedding we ever went to.

Pasta making. The dough stretched between her hands. "The hammock of panic, we'll call this stage . . ."

Guinness foam on our noses, yet again, to make Edie laugh.

The voice she used, when she said everything was going to be OK.

Her Attenborough impression, when I woke from a nap: "The male is disoriented, and grumpy."

Primrose Hill.

A Pembrokeshire beach.

The cliff tops, turning. Coming home.

69.

A MAN IN A SUIT

In the end, I stay the night at Rebecca and Rupert's. I'm very glad I do, because it gives us the chance to talk and, finally, to share our memories of Lily. We do this over endless cups of tea (not Earl Grey) and—when the sun goes down—over wine and Rupert's excellent cooking. There are tears from all of us, of course there are, but they're needed. There is a freedom in being allowed to grieve.

There's enough time the next morning to get to know Alexander for an hour or so. I listen politely as he explains about an impossibly complicated-sounding video game he's been playing, and he listens politely as I tell him how when I was fifteen, we used to have something called Blockbuster. It's a cultural exchange for the ages. When I leave, and Rebecca hugs me—a properly warm embrace, this time—and says I should come back soon, I think she really means it. I resolve to take her up on her offer and make a note of when Alexander's birthday is. I may not have had the chance to try to be a good dad, but I can do my best to be a good uncle. When I check my phone on the train home, it's to see I've had an email from Ed inviting me to stay in London. He says I can move in until I'm sorted. Jack will be there, of course, so I'll be taking up the godfather mantle again too.

I'm feeling a very strange mix of emotions when I arrive back at the pub. It's just after lunchtime, and the place seems deserted. I think I can hear Jacques in the kitchen. There's no sign of Oliver and Sophie, although I remember that when things used to get quiet they tended to disappear off together to carry on the love affair to end all love affairs.

I can see through the window that there are a couple of pint glasses that need collecting from a table out in the beer garden. I head out and pick them up. I'm about to come back in when the sun breaks through a gap in the clouds, and I stand there for a moment with my head tilted back, basking in the warmth. It's only when someone clears their throat that I realize I'm not alone. I turn around to see there's a man sitting at a table on his own. He's wearing a suit straight out of 1983, and sports what I can only describe as a heroic comb-over. A pint of bitter, nearly finished, is on the table in front of him.

"Sorry," he says. "Didn't mean to startle you."

"Not to worry," I say. "Can I get you another?"

"I shouldn't really," he replies, looking mournful at having to reject this offer. "I'm here on business, technically, but I couldn't resist a drink in this garden." He drains his beer. "I don't suppose you know where the proprietor is?"

It's been a while since I've been referred to as formally as that.

"That'll be me," I say.

"Mr. Taplowe? Mr. Brian Taplowe?"

I nod. I really hope he's not from the council. We got the sign down, didn't we, what more do they want?

"I'm here," he says, "regarding the will of Jeff Mackintosh."

70.

BIG IN LATVIA

It's the second time in a week that I've summoned my workforce and asked them to gather, late morning. Jacques, Sophie, and Oliver are looking at me with a look that says: *Now what?!* For a moment I do actually feel quite bad about letting them think that this is more bad news. I'd been planning to draw the story out a bit, but Jacques looks murderous, so I get on with it.

What I learned from the lawyer the previous afternoon is that, in addition to every single one of Jeff's exotic stories being true—including the one about his having had a number one hit in Latvia—he had also ended up doing rather well for himself over the years. Very well, in fact. When I mention the specifics to the others, and in truth I'm slightly rounding down, there is a symphony of excitable swearing, which only grows louder when I reveal that Jeff has, in fact, left almost all of it to the pub.

"But what do you mean, 'to the pub'?" Oliver asks.

"Well," I say, "he's leaving us a fairly vast sum of money but on the strict proviso that it's used to renovate, refurnish, and 'maintain the good running of the pub.' I know," I add. "It's . . . well, it's bonkers, isn't it?"

"It's fucking brilliant, is what it is," laughs Sophie. And before I can say anything else, she and Oliver are piling down into the cellar to retrieve champagne, and dragging me and Jacques out into the beer garden.

The champagne is delicious. There is a soft breeze drifting over the fields. The next hour or so is completely blissful.

I still haven't quite worked out what this means for me and the pub. I have, to put it mildly, mixed feelings about this place. I decide that, for the next couple of hours at least, I'm simply going to live in the moment and enjoy myself.

A little later, Sophie starts asking me about my recent travels. I'd forgotten that I hadn't exactly given them the full explanation of what I was doing before I left.

I'm not the best storyteller, nor do I particularly enjoy holding court, but surprisingly—after a tentative start—I find I'm quite enjoying the attention, particularly when I can casually drop in phrases like ". . . and then I went skydiving," and "So I found myself at Stonehenge . . ."

Sophie pops another bottle of champagne open, with her teeth this time, and I see Oliver watching on misty-eyed, as if this is the most wonderful thing he's ever seen. I know I said I'd leave big decisions for another day, but I think I probably know what I'm going to do about the pub.

"Why are you looking at us like that?" Sophie asks.

"No reason."

"Well, anyway," she continues, nudging my arm, "in a lot of these stories you keep saying 'we.' You know, '*we* ended up on a river cruise, blah blah blah'—who were you actually with?"

It wasn't a conscious decision, I don't think, to leave Tess's name out of it. But maybe there was some part of me holding back. I can sense from Sophie's look that there's no chance I'm going to get away without explaining, and so I do, trying to sound as neutral as possible when I talk about who Tess is. I suspect it's probably the booze, but I find myself unexpectedly opening up about how sad I am that she's heading back home to New Zealand.

"Wait," Oliver says, "you said she's 'heading' back home. So does that mean she's still here?"

I swish some foamy dregs around in my glass, then watch them settle. I realize then that I do actually know where she'll be tomorrow, if I've remembered what she told me right.

"What is it?" Sophie says. "What are you thinking?"

I look past her, down to the sea. It's a rich, chalky blue, waves sparkling in the sun. Later, I'll go down there. And I'll speak to Lily. I'll tell her how much I miss her. And then, if I feel ready, I'll ask her if it's OK if I do what I'm planning to.

"Brian?" Sophie asks.

"Well, the thing is . . . ," I begin.

71.

LONDON

And high above this winding length of street,
This moveless and unpeopled avenue,
Pure, silent, solemn, beautiful, was seen
The huge majestic Temple of St. Paul
—WILLIAM WORDSWORTH, 1808

Pretty disappointed that you would pay to go into a cathedral. Went in the store in the basement instead. Had a bowl of soup in the cafeteria.
—ONLINE REVIEW, ST. PAUL'S CATHEDRAL, 2020

A SHORT HISTORY LESSON

St. Paul's Cathedral as we know it—domes and all—was built by the great architect Sir Christopher Wren, who declared it officially finished in 1710. He had laid the first stone in 1675. A place of worship of some sort has been on the same site since 604.

A SHORT ARCHITECTURE LESSON

The nave of the cathedral is decorated with a mural of a compass rose. There are two hundred and fifty-nine steps leading from the cathedral's nave to the base of the dome and the walkway known as the whispering gallery. To better imagine the dome and the walkway, picture a thimble on top of a wedding ring. The walkway is thirty meters above the nave, roughly the height of eight London buses.

A SHORT PHYSICS LESSON

When a person speaks, they create a sound wave. Sound waves travel varying distances. The circular walls of the dome of St. Paul's are tilted very slightly inward. Because the angles are so slight, if a person speaks close to the walls the waves will bounce off them multiple times and "creep" along the wall. The effect is so strong that it is possible for a person to stand on one side of the dome and speak into the wall and to be heard on the opposite side, over a hundred feet away. Whispering exploits this strange quirk better than raising your voice, as the sound waves that whispers create are "low intensity," meaning that they are less susceptible to background interference.

A SHORT LANGUAGE LESSON

"Kia ora" is a Māori-language expression that literally translates as "be healthy." It is also used as an informal greeting in New Zealand English.

"Kia Niro" is a small Korean car.

A SHORT BIOLOGY LESSON

When we're scared, our nervous system tells our body to produce hormones such as cortisol, adrenaline, and noradrenaline.

This is known as the fight-or-flight response. To take a case study at random: Imagine a forty-seven-year-old man who does exercise roughly as often as Halley's comet visits Earth. He has just climbed the two hundred and fifty-nine steps that lead from the nave of St. Paul's Cathedral to the whispering gallery. Having just about recovered, he sees across the other side of the gallery a woman who he has only recently met, but who has already made him feel like life is worth living again. Logic tells him that he should call out to her so that she will hear him above the hubbub, but he has just read on an information board in the lobby that whispering into the wall is a more effective way of communicating here. As he prepares to whisper, he is consumed with nerves, and his body presents him with two options: *Fight or flight?*

Well, I think, *what's it going to be?*

EPILOGUE

Jeff's Bar
(formerly The County Arms, Thrupstone, UK)
★★★★★ (1)
AgathaJohnson77 wrote a review, September 12, 2017

First class for first visitor!!

I can't believe I'm the first person to review this amazing pub, which I stumbled across on a countryside walk by the sea. It has only very recently reopened its doors after a long refurbishment. The owners have spent a long time restoring it, and what a job they've done! I was greeted on arrival by the young managers, Sophie and Oliver, who could not have been more enthusiastic and diligent.

As I was leaving, I asked them to pass on my best wishes to the owner. Apparently he's off traveling the world at the moment, with plans to settle down in New Zealand, keeping tabs on the place from afar. I do hope I'll end up bumping into him one day if he comes to visit, just to tell him how great this place is. Highly recommended!

ACKNOWLEDGMENTS

To my editor, Tara Singh Carlson, for all her brilliant notes and the hour-long editorial Zoom calls when I'd sit with my head in my hands for forty-five minutes, occasionally piping up with, "What about if he . . . No, that wouldn't work . . ." only for her to calmly suggest something that solved everything. Elsewhere at Putnam: to Aranya Jain for her invaluable editorial support, to Brennin Cummings and Katie McKee for ace marketing and publicity work, to Marie Finamore and Ryan Richardson for their production editorial work, to Hannah Dragone for her production management work, to Ashley Tucker for designing the text, and to Vi-An Nguyen for designing the cover.

Thanks to my agent, Laura Williams, who remains excellent despite her choice of football team.

To Sophie Wilson, Lucy Dauman, Fran Pathak, Ben Willis, Holly Harris, Ellen Parr, Sophie Wilson, Caroline Hulse, Joe Yule, Gill Hornby, Robert Harris, Elizabeth Masters.

To the Polhills, for rave reviews, home-cooked meals, military support/brutally effective word-of-mouth sales, et cetera.

To Mum, Dad, Libby, Jack, Katy, JJ, Will, and Eleanor—thanks for being the best.

To my readers—especially those who have been kind enough to send me messages of encouragement.

Finally, to Georgie—thank you for listening to me say "Is there a book in it?" a hundred times, and then making sure I actually sat down and wrote it when there was. And, more importantly, for being the best incentive imaginable to hit my word count.

THIS DISASTER LOVES YOU

RICHARD ROPER

A Conversation with Richard Roper

Discussion Guide

Excerpt from Something to Live For

PUTNAM
— EST. 1838 —

A CONVERSATION WITH RICHARD ROPER

What inspired you to write this story?

I was in a pub in York, my first post-Covid trip, when I heard a customer complaining to staff, going so far as to invoke "the weights and measures act of 1985." I knew without doubt that this person would follow up by writing a review online, and sure enough they did. I became weirdly obsessed with why people do this, reading lots of one-star reviews of things like the Sistine Chapel. But then it struck me that someone who owns a pub or café or shop might be having the worst day of their lives, only to read a review that completely slated them, even though they were doing their best. As I took the train home from York, the character of Brian appeared, and I feverishly wrote down what became the plot of the book. I think the person next to me must have thought I was composing an incredibly intense WhatsApp to someone . . .

Your description of owning and running a pub is so vivid. Have you ever worked in a pub or interviewed anyone who has?

I am tempted to say that yes, this was all down to some thorough research, but the truth is I just really love pubs. We don't get much right when it comes to food and drink in Britain, but a beer garden by a babbling brook or a fifteenth-century inn with a fire roaring away in winter—that's where we come into our own . . .

Do you relate to Brian at all? Or Lily? Were any of these characters based on real people?
Most of my male protagonists tend to have a little bit of me in them, so Brian's inept attempts to impress women are of course directly inspired by my own experiences. This is why if my books are ever made into films it's not going to be The Rock playing the lead.

In chapter 12, Brian imagines what a blue plaque about him would say. What would you want a blue plaque about you to say? Where would you want the plaque to be posted?
"Richard Roper, inventor of the color blue and the concept of commemorative plaques, was born here." Ideally on the side of Buckingham Palace, but if not I'd settle for 10 Downing Street.

What was your favorite scene to write, and why?
The scene where Brian and Lily first spend time together on Primrose Hill was one of those scenes where it felt like my typing fingers couldn't keep up with my brain, which was a glorious feeling. (I wish I could say the same about the rest of the book . . .)

If you were in Brian's position, seeing the PinkMoonLily1970 review, what would you have done?
I'd almost certainly have had a cup of tea and big old think.

Which of the locations featured in Brian's trip would you most like to visit or revisit next?
I have visited all the places in the book, aside from Stonehenge, unless you count seeing it from a moving car from five miles away.

What significance does the Maori phrase "Kia ora" hold for you?
I would love to say that it was something more profound than the fact I came up with a funny joke involving that phrase, but alas . . .

If you could give Brian any advice at the end of this book, without any spoilers, what would it be?
Instinctively, I think of Monica's advice to Chandler: "Be yourself. But not too much." (I also give this advice to myself quite a lot.)

If you were to cast Brian and Lily as actors in a movie, who would you choose? How about Tess?
As I say above, it's unlikely to be The Rock for Brian. And then I've got younger and older actors to think of! I'll have to get back to you on that one . . .

DISCUSSION GUIDE

1. Seven years is a long time to watch a door, hoping that someone will come through it. Is there anything unlikely you've hoped for, for such a long time? What made you keep hoping?

2. What did you think had happened to Lily, or where and why did you think she had gone, early in the novel? How did your opinion change as the novel went on?

3. Do you ever leave reviews online? What influences your decision?

4. How might Brian be different now if Lily had never left? Did he change for the better or for the worse when she disappeared?

5. How do you think Brian being dermographic acts as a metaphor for his personality? How do metaphors of cryptic signs and permanent words shift through the novel?

6. What was your favorite scene in the novel and why?

7. Early in her courtship with Brian, Lily says, "I suppose we're all pretending to be people we're not." Do you think Lily was ever pretending to be someone she wasn't?

8. The username PinkMoonLily1970 is enough to convince Brian that this is his Lily. Which brief username, which doesn't include your full name, might your loved ones most immediately recognize for you and why?

9. What do you think Tess brings out in Brian? What do you think Lily brings out in Brian? How do the two compare?

10. How might Brian's and Lily's lives have turned out differently if he had approached her by the cliff tops in chapter 53? Would anything have changed?

11. Were you surprised by the ending?

KEEP READING FOR AN EXCITING EXCERPT FROM

SOMETHING TO LIVE FOR

BY RICHARD ROPER.

CHAPTER 1

Andrew looked at the coffin and tried to remember who was inside it. It was a man—he was sure of that. But, horrifyingly, the name escaped him. He thought he'd narrowed it down to either John or James, but Jake had just made a late bid for consideration. It was inevitable, he supposed, that this had happened. He'd been to so many of these funerals it was bound to at some point, but that didn't stop him from feeling an angry stab of self-loathing.

If he could just remember the name before the vicar said it, that would be something. There was no order of service, but maybe he could check his work phone. Would that be cheating? Probably. Besides, it would have been a tricky enough maneuver to get away with in a church full of mourners, but it was nearly impossible when the only other person there apart from him was the vicar. Ordinarily, the funeral director would have been there as well, but he had e-mailed earlier to say he was too ill to make it.

Unnervingly, the vicar, who was only a few feet away from

Andrew, had barely broken eye contact since he'd started the service.

Andrew hadn't dealt with him before. He was boyish and spoke with a nervous tremor that was amplified unforgivingly by the echoey church. Andrew couldn't tell if this was down to nerves. He tried out a reassuring smile, but it didn't seem to help. Would a thumbs-up be inappropriate? He decided against it.

He looked over at the coffin again. Maybe he was a Jake, though the man had been seventy-eight when he died, and you didn't really get many septuagenarian Jakes. At least not yet. It was going to be strange in fifty years' time when all the nursing homes would be full of Jakes and Waynes, Tinkerbells and Appletisers, with faded tribal tattoos that roughly translated as "*Roadworks for next fifty yards*" faded on their lower backs.

Jesus, concentrate, he admonished himself. The whole point of his being there was to bear respectful witness to the poor soul departing on their final journey, to provide some company in lieu of any family or friends. Dignity—that was his watchword.

Unfortunately, dignity was something that had been in short supply for the John or James or Jake. According to the coroner's report, he had died on the toilet while reading a book about buzzards. To add insult to injury, Andrew later discovered firsthand that it wasn't even a very *good* book about buzzards. Admittedly he was no expert, but he wasn't sure the author—who even from the few passages Andrew had read came across as remarkably grumpy—should have dedicated a whole page to badmouthing kestrels. The deceased had folded the corner of this particular page down as a crude placeholder, so perhaps he'd been in agreement. As Andrew had peeled off his latex gloves he'd made a mental note to insult a kestrel—or indeed any member of the falcon family—the next time he saw one, as a tribute of sorts.

Other than a few more bird books, the house was devoid of anything that gave clues to the man's personality. There were no records or films to be found, nor pictures on the walls or photographs on the windowsills. The only idiosyncrasy was the bafflingly large number of Fruit'n Fibre boxes in the kitchen cupboards. So aside from the fact that he was a keen ornithologist with a top-notch digestive system, it was impossible to guess what sort of person John or James or Jake had been.

Andrew had been as diligent as ever with the property inspection. He'd searched the house (a curious mock-Tudor bungalow that sat defiantly as an incongruous interlude on the terraced street) until he was sure he'd not missed something that suggested the man had any family he was still in touch with. He'd knocked on the neighbors' doors but they'd been either indifferent to or unaware of the man's existence, or the fact it was over.

The vicar segued unsurely into a bit of Jesus-y material, and Andrew knew from experience that the service was coming to a close. He *had* to remember this person's name, as a point of principle. He really tried his best, even when there was no one else there, to be a model mourner—to be as respectful as if there were hundreds of devastated family members in attendance. He'd even started removing his watch before entering the church because it felt like the deceased's final journey should be exempt from the indifference of a ticking second hand.

The vicar was definitely on the home stretch now. Andrew was just going to have to make a decision.

John, he decided. He was definitely John. "And while we believe that John—"

Yes!

"—struggled to some extent in his final years, and sadly departed the world without family or friends by his side, we can take comfort that, with God waiting with open arms, full of love and kindness, this journey shall be the last he makes alone."

ANDREW TENDED NOT to stick around after the funerals. On the few occasions he had, he'd ended up having to make awkward conversation with funeral directors or last-minute rubberneckers. It was remarkable how many of the latter you would get, hanging around outside, farting out inane platitudes. Andrew was well practiced at slipping away so as to avoid such encounters, but today he'd briefly been distracted by a sign on the church noticeboard advertising the troublingly jaunty "Midsummer Madness Fete!" when he felt someone tapping him on the shoulder with the insistence of an impatient woodpecker. It was the vicar. He looked even younger close up, with his baby-blue eyes and blond curtains parted neatly in the middle, as if his mum might have done it for him.

"Hey, it's Andrew, isn't it? You're from the council, right?"

"That's right," Andrew said.

"No luck finding any family then?"

Andrew shook his head.

"Shame, that. Real shame."

The vicar seemed agitated, as if he were holding on to a secret that he desperately wanted to impart.

"Can I ask you something?" he said.

"Yes," Andrew said, quickly deciding on an excuse for why he couldn't attend "Midsummer Madness!"

"How did you find that?" the vicar said.

"Do you mean . . . the funeral?" Andrew said, pulling at a bit of loose thread on his coat.

"Yeah. Well, more specifically my part in it all. Because, full disclosure, it was my first. I was quite relieved to be starting with this one, to be honest, because there wasn't anybody here so it sort of felt like a bit of a practice run. Hopefully now I'm fully prepared for when there's a proper one with a church full of friends and family, not just aguy from the council. No offense," he added, putting a hand on Andrew's arm. Andrew did his best not to recoil. He hated it when people did that. He wished he had some sort of squidlike defense that meant he could shoot ink into their eyes.

"So yeah," the vicar said. "How'd you think I did?"

What do you want me to say? Andrew thought. *Well, you didn't knock the coffin over or accidentally call the deceased "Mr. Hitler," so ten out of ten I'd say.*

"You did very well," he said.

"Ah, great, thanks, mate," the vicar said, looking at him with renewed intensity. "I really appreciate that."

He held out his hand. Andrew shook it and went to let go, but the vicar carried on.

"Anyway, I better be off," Andrew said.

"Yes, yes of course," said the vicar, finally letting go.

Andrew started off down the path, breathing a sigh of relief at escaping without further interrogation.

"See you soon I hope," the vicar called after him.

CHAPTER 2

The funerals had been given various prefixes over the years—"public health," "contract," "welfare," "Section 46"—but none of the attempted rebrands would ever replace the original. When Andrew had come across the expression "pauper's funeral" he'd found it quite evocative; romantic, even, in a Dickensian sort of way. It made him think of someone a hundred and fifty years ago in a remote village—all mud and clucking chickens—succumbing to a spectacular case of syphilis, dying at the fine old age of twenty-seven and being bundled merrily into a pit to regenerate the land. In practice, what he experienced was depressingly clinical. The funerals were now a legal obligation for councils across the UK, designed for those who'd slipped through the cracks—their death perhaps only noticed because of the smell of their body decomposing, or an unpaid bill. (It had been on several occasions now where Andrew had found that the deceased had enough money in a bank account for direct debits to cover utility bills for months after their death, meaning the house was kept warm enough to speed up their body's decomposition. After the fifth harrowing instance of this, he'd considered mentioning it in the "Any other comments" section on his annual job satisfaction survey. In the end he went with asking if they could have another kettle in the shared kitchen.)

Another phrase he had become well acquainted with was "The Nine O'Clock Trot." His boss, Cameron, had explained its origin to him while violently piercing the film on a microwavable biryani. "If you die alone"—stab, stab, stab—"you're most likely buried alone too"—stab, stab, stab—"so the church can get the funeral out of the way at nine o'clock, safe in the knowledge that every train could be canceled"—stab—"every motorway gridlocked"—stab—"and it wouldn't make a difference." A final stab. "Because nobody's on their way."

In the previous year Andrew had arranged twenty-five of these funerals (his highest annual total yet). He'd attended all of them, too, though he wasn't technically required to do so. It was, he told himself, a small but meaningful gesture for someone to be there who wasn't legally obligated. But increasingly he found himself watching the simple, unvarnished coffins being lowered into the ground in a specially designated yet unmarked plot, knowing they would be uncovered three or four more times as other coffins were fitted in like a macabre game of Tetris, and think that his presence counted for nothing.

AS ANDREW SAT on the bus to the office, he inspected his tie and shoes, both of which had seen better days. There was a persistent stain on his tie, origin unknown, that wouldn't budge. His shoes were well polished but starting to look worn. Too many nicks from churchyard gravel, too many times the leather had strained where he'd curled his toes at a vicar's verbal stumble. He really should replace both, come payday.

Now that the funeral was over, he took a moment to mentally file away John (surname Sturrock, he discovered, having turned on his phone). As ever, he tried to resist the temptation to obsess over how John had ended up in such a desperate position. Was there really no niece or godson he was on Christmas-card terms with? Or an old school friend who called, even just on his birthday? But it was a slippery slope. He had to stay as objective as possible, for his own sake, if only to be mentally strong enough to deal with the next poor person who ended up like this. The bus stopped at a red light. By the time it went green Andrew had made himself say a final good-bye.

He arrived at the office and returned Cameron's enthusiastic wave with a more muted acknowledgment of his own. As he slumped into his well-weathered seat, which had molded itself to his form over the years, he let out a now sadly familiar grunt. He'd thought having only just turned forty-two he'd have a few more years before he began accompanying minor physical tasks by making odd noises, but it seemed to be the universe's gentle way of telling him that he was now officially heading toward middle age. He only imagined before too long he'd wake up and immediately begin his day bemoaning how easy school exams were these days and bulk-buying cream chinos.

He waited for his computer to boot up and watched out of the corner of his eye as his colleague Keith demolished a hunk of chocolate cake and methodically sucked smears of icing from his stubby little fingers.

"Good one, was it?" Keith said, not taking his eyes off his

screen, which Andrew knew was most likely showing a gallery of actresses who'd had the temerity to age, or something small and furry on a skateboard.

"It was okay," Andrew said.

"Any rubberneckers?" came a voice from behind him. Andrew flinched. He hadn't seen Meredith take her seat.

"No," he said, not bothering to turn around. "Just me and the vicar. It was his very first funeral, apparently."

"Bloody hell, what a way to pop your cherry," Meredith said. "Better that than a room full of weepers, to be fair," Keith said, with one final suck of his little finger. "You'd be shitting piss, wouldn't you?" The office phone rang and the three of them sat there not answering it. Andrew was about to bite but Keith's frustration got the better of him first.

"Hello, Death Administration. Yep. Sure. Yep. Right."

Andrew reached for his earphones and pulled up his Ella Fitzgerald playlist (he had only very recently discovered Spotify, much to Keith's delight, who'd spent a month afterward calling Andrew "Granddad"). He felt like starting with a classic—something reassuring. He decided on "Summertime." But he was only three bars in before he looked up to see Keith standing in front of him, belly flab poking through a gap between shirt buttons.

"Helloooo. Anybody there?" Andrew removed his earphones.

"That was the coroner. We've got a fresh one. Well, not a fresh body obviously—they reckon he'd been dead a good few weeks. No obvious next of kin and the neighbors never spoke to him. Body's been moved so they want a property inspection a-sap."

"Right."

Keith picked at a scab on his elbow. "Tomorrow all right for you?" Andrew checked his diary.

"I can do first thing."

"Blimey, you're keen," Keith said, waddling back to his desk. *And you're a slice of ham that's been left out in the sun*, Andrew thought. He went to put his earphones back in, but at that moment Cameron emerged from his office and clapped his hands together to get their attention.

"Team meeting, chaps," he announced. "And yes, yes, don't you worry—the current Mrs. Cameron has provided cake, as per. Shall we hit the break-out space?"

The three of them responded with the enthusiasm a chicken might if it were asked to wear a prosciutto bikini and run into a fox's den. The "break-out space" consisted of a knee-high table flanked by two sofas that smelled unaccountably of sulfur. Cameron had floated the idea of adding beanbags, but this had been ignored, as were his suggestions of desk-swap Tuesdays, a negativity jar ("It's a swear jar but for negativity!") and a team park run. ("I'm busy," Keith had yawned. "But I haven't told you which day it's on," Cameron said, his smile faltering like a flame in a draft.) Undeterred by their complete lack of enthusiasm, Cameron's most recent suggestion had been a suggestion box. This, too, had been ignored.

They gathered on the sofas and Cameron doled out cake and tea and tried to engage them with some banal small talk. Keith and Meredith had wedged themselves into the smaller of the two sofas. Meredith was laughing at something Keith had just whispered to her. Just as parents are able to recognize variants in the cries of their newborns, so Andrew had begun to understand what Meredith's differing laughs denoted. In this particular instance, the high-pitched giggle indicated that someone was being cruelly mocked. Given that they kept very obviously sneaking glances in his direction, it seemed it was probably him.

"Rightio, lady and gents," Cameron said. "First things first, don't forget we've got a new starter tomorrow. Peggy Green. I know we've struggled since Dan and Bethany left, so it's super-cool to have a new pair of hands."

"As long as she doesn't get 'stressed' like Bethany," Meredith said. "Or turn out to be a knob like Dan," Keith muttered.

"Anyway," Cameron said, "what I actually wanted to talk to you about today is my weekly . . . honk! Honk!"—he honked an imaginary horn—". . . fun idea! Remember, guys, this is something you can all get involved with. Doesn't matter how crazy your idea is. The only rule is that it has to be fun."

Andrew shuddered.

"So," Cameron continued. "My fun idea this week is, drumroll please . . . that every month we have a get-together at one of our houses and we do dinner. A sort of *Come Dine with Me* vibe but without any judgment. We'll have a bit of food, I daresay a bit of vino, and it'll give us a chance to do some real bonding away from the office, get to know each other a bit better, meet the family and all that. I'm mega-happy to kick things off. Whaddya say?"

Andrew hadn't heard anything past "meet the family."

"Is there not something else we can do?" he said, trying to keep his voice steady.

"Oh," Cameron said, instantly deflated. "I thought that was actually one of my better ideas."

"No, no, it is!" Andrew said, overcompensating now. "It's just . . . couldn't we just go to a restaurant instead?"

"Toooo expensive," Keith said, spraying cake crumbs everywhere.

"Well, what about something else? I don't know—Laser Quest or something. Is that still a thing?"

"I'm vetoing Laser Quest on the grounds I'm not a twelve-year-old boy," Meredith said. "I like the dinner party idea. I'm actually a bit of a secret Nigella in the kitchen." She turned to Keith. "I bet you'd go crazy for my lamb shank." Andrew felt bile stir in his stomach.

"Go on, Andrew," Cameron said, confidence renewed by Meredith's giving his idea her blessing. He attempted a matey arm punch that caused Andrew to spill tea down his leg. "It'll be a laugh! There's no pressure to cook up anything fancy. And I'd love to meet Diane and the kids, of course. So, whaddya say? You up for this, buddy?"

Andrew's mind was racing. Surely there was something else he could suggest as an alternative? Life drawing. Badger baiting. *Anything.* The others were just looking at him now. He had to say something.

"Bloody hell, Andrew. You look like you've seen a ghost," Meredith said. "Your cooking can't be that bad. Besides, I'm sure Diane's a fabulous chef, among all her other talents, so she can help you out."

"Hmmm," Andrew murmured, tapping his fingertips together. "She's a lawyer, right?" Keith said. Andrew nodded. Maybe there'd be some catastrophic world event in the next few days, a lovely old nuclear war to make them all forget about this stupid idea.

"You've got that beautiful old town house Dulwich way, haven't you?" Meredith said, practically leering. "Five-bed, isn't it?"

"Four," Andrew said. He hated it when she and Keith got like this.

A tag team of mockery.

"Still," Meredith said. "A lovely big four-bed, smart kids by all accounts, and Diane, your talented, breadwinning wife. What a dark old horse you are."

Later, as Andrew prepared to leave the office, having been too distracted to do any meaningful work, Cameron appeared by his desk and dropped down onto his haunches. It felt like the sort of move he'd been taught in a course.

"Listen," he said quietly. "I know you didn't seem to fancy the dinner party idea, but just say you'll have a think about it, okay, mate?"

Andrew needlessly shuffled some papers on his desk. "Oh, I mean . . . I don't want to spoil things, it's just . . . okay, I'll think about it. But if we don't do that I'm sure we can think of another, you know, fun idea."

"That's the spirit," Cameron said, straightening up and addressing them all. "That goes for all of us, I hope. Come on, team—let's get our bond on sooner rather than. Yeah?"

ANDREW HAD RECENTLY splashed out on some noise-canceling earphones for his commute, so while he could see the man sitting opposite's ugly sneeze and the toddler in the vestibule screaming at the utter injustice of being made to wear not one but two shoes, it simply appeared as a silent film incongruously soundtracked by Ella Fitzgerald's soothing voice. It wasn't long, however, before the conversation in the office started to repeat itself in his head, vying with Ella for his attention.

"Diane, your talented, breadwinning wife . . . smart kids . . . Beautiful old town house." Keith's smirk. Meredith's leer. The conversation dogged him all the way to the station and continued as he went to buy food for that night's dinner. That's when he found himself standing in the corner shop by multi-bags of novelty potato chips named after celebrities and trying not to scream. After ten minutes of picking up and putting down the same four ready meals, feeling incapable of choosing one, he left empty-handed, walking out into the rain and heading home, his stomach rumbling.

He stood outside his front door, shivering. Eventually, when the cold became too much to bear, he brought out his keys. There was usually one day a week like this, when he'd pause outside, key in the lock, holding his breath.

Maybe this time.

Maybe this time it *would* be the lovely old town house behind that door: Diane starting to prepare dinner. The smell of garlic and red wine. The sound of Steph and David squabbling or asking questions about their homework, then the excitable cheers when he opened the door because Dad's home, Dad's home!

When he entered the hallway the smell of damp hit him even harder than usual. And there were the familiar scuff marks on the corridor walls and the intermittent, milky yellow of the faulty strip light. He trudged up the stairs, his wet shoes squeaking with each step, and slid the second key around on his key ring. He reached up to right the wonky number 2 on the door and went inside, met, as he had been for the last twenty years, by nothing but silence.

Photograph courtesy of the author

RICHARD ROPER is an author and book editor. He lives in London and is the author of *Something to Live For* and *When We Were Young.*

VISIT RICHARD ROPER ONLINE

RichardRoperAuthor.com
RichardRoper
RichardRoper
RichardRoper